SCIENCE
FICTION
THE BEST OF THE YEAR
2006 EDITION

SCIENCE FICTION
THE BEST OF THE YEAR
2006 EDITION

EDITED BY

RICH HORTON

PRIME BOOKS

SCIENCE FICTION: THE BEST OF THE YEAR
2006 EDITION

Distributed by Diamond Book Distributors.

Prime Books is an imprint of
Wildside Press, LLC
9710 Traville Gateway Dr. #234
Rockville MD 20850
www.prime-books.com

First Prime Books printing: September 2006

10 9 8 7 6 5 4 3 2 1

Printed in Canada.

CONTENTS

THE YEAR IN SCIENCE FICTION

Rich Horton

There are two obvious ways of looking at the state of the SF field in any given year. One is to try to assess the quality and concerns of the stories produced: are there any obsessive themes? Was it a particularly special year for great stories? Did any authors spring out of nowhere to suddenly become major? Or did any seem to exert outsize influence through some combinations of quantity and quality of stories?

The other way is more practical in a sense: how is the field doing economically? Are the magazines healthy? Are book sales healthy? Is readership expanding? This latter way is less interesting to me, but it seems the short fiction scene deserves a brief look, if only to mostly mildly echo cries of "doom and gloom." The magazines are at best stable: circulation continues to drift down, and some new starts of the past couple years didn't survive long, most notably Paizo Publishing's somewhat media-oriented relaunch of *Amazing*. A bit more optimistically, Andy Cox stamped his personality more thoroughly on *Interzone*, and after a slow start in 2004 he managed six quite strong issues in 2005. The first year of *Asimov's* under Sheila Williams's editorship was a solid year, with much continuity maintained from Gardner Dozois's reign. *The Magazine of Fantasy & Science Fiction* had a good year, and *Analog* had one of its best recent years. More distressing was the loss of the best-ever online source of new science fiction: Ellen Datlow's *Sci Fiction*, which has been closed down after another strong year. Smaller 'zines often tend to publish fantasy, horror, or slipstream, but there are a few that publish lots of science fiction: in particular I would mention *Electric Velocipede*, the Australian publication *Andromeda Spaceways Inflight Magazine*, and two electronically distributed magazines, *Challenging Destiny* and *Oceans of the Mind*.

But what of the stories? I am still delighted year after year by story after story. And this year was no different: I had an agonizing time limiting my selections for this volume. I hope they successfully indicate the breadth and scope of the imagination of contemporary SF writers. A look at common characteristics of these stories reveals a very high percentage that I would call rather "hard" science fiction—something I found somewhat surprising, but refreshing. There are stories on familiar themes, including one that explicitly responds to a nearly fifty-year-old classic. Other stories are engaging current political concerns—though I find that the best of these, like those included here, are really dealing with issues that were important in a century ago, or fifty years ago, and will probably still be nagging us in 2106. They come from a wide variety of sources, too: I saw outstanding pieces from all the traditional SF magazines (though my favorites from *F&SF* this year were fantasies), from online sources like *Sci Fiction* and *Strange Horizons*, from original anthologies, from a scientific journal, and from the fine, long-running, Canadian magazine *On Spec*, and even from a science fiction convention's program book.

And of course from a wide spread of writers: veterans and newcomers, writers best known for novels and writers who have only published short fiction, some very prolific writers and some we see much less often. Let's begin with one writer who, every year it seems, publishes a plethora of potential best of the year selections: Robert Reed. This year we see "Finished," as with many of Reed's stories an examination of a familiar science fiction idea, in this case uploading into android bodies, with a fresh viewpoint.

Michael Swanwick is another writer who seems to produce multiple top stories each year (to the extent that I once proposed renaming the short story Hugo the "Swanwick Invitational"). "Triceratops Summer" is a lovely story of dinosaurs in Vermont. (And it is also significant because of its unusual publication venue: a downloadable e-story from Amazon.com.) And James Patrick Kelly is another writer (of roughly the same SF generation as Reed and Swanwick) who is a constant presence on award ballots and in Best of the Year volumes. He's also a constant presence in the June issue of *Asimov's Science Fiction*, and his June 2005 story, "The Edge of Nowhere," is a striking story about the sources—and importance—of creativity.

As long as I am mentioning writers who have, let's say, been around awhile, I'll bring up Joe Haldeman, who contributes a pointed story about love, "Heartwired," from the latest series of

short-shorts published in the venerable UK scientific journal
Nature. Also, Tom Purdom, one of my favorite writers, who began
publishing SF in the late '50s, but who has had a truly remarkable
late career surge since about 1990, contributes "Bank Run," at once
an exciting adventure story about finance, and a challenging look at
gender roles and, once again, love. I suppose Howard Waldrop qual-
ifies as a "veteran," too, though his stories are also so individual, so
sui-generis, that he seems ever a brand new writer. "The King of
Where-I-Go" is a moving look at a Texas childhood, mixing polio
and time travel curiously.

Never fear, there are standout new writers to celebrate as well.
Leah Bobet's "Bliss" is a powerful story of drug addiction, and a
potential cure with its own downside. Douglas Lain's "A Coffee
Cup/Alien Invasion Story" uses an alien invasion (perhaps) as a
means of looking at a marriage in trouble. James Van Pelt's "The Inn
at Mount Either" is a clever and sad story of multiple dimensions,
telling of a honeymoon at a hotel built around a door between parallel universes. Daniel Kaysen's "The Jenna Set" is very smart, and
very funny, about a new mathematical theory of human interactions, and an AI telephone answering service. The longest story here
is Alastair Reynolds's deep time story, "Understanding Space and
Time," in which civilization on Earth is destroyed by a weaponized
virus, marooning a Martian expedition. One man survives on Mars
with the curious help of Elton John, and eventually gets to see the
very far future indeed.

Susan Palwick's "The Fate of Mice" explicitly invokes Daniel
Keyes's classic "Flowers for Algernon" in a story about an enhanced
mouse and his relationship with his researcher and the man's
daughter. Wil McCarthy's "The Policeman's Daughter" is set in the
same "Queendom of Sol" future as his most recent series of novels. It
thoughtfully explores questions of identity as a lawyer is forced to
oppose a version of himself in court, trying a case about another
man who thinks a version of himself is trying to murder him. Stephen Leigh's "You, by Anonymous" is effectively paranoiac about
an alien invasion of a different sort. And finally Mary Rosenblum,
happily returned to the field after a number of years concentrating
on mysteries, offers "Search Engine," a powerful story of a man
working for a government which is increasingly violating citizens'
privacy by the use of chips to track all transactions.

Science Fiction remains a vital way of not only looking at possible futures, but of looking at the present through the lens of the imagined future. I don't think truly new ideas are as common as they once were, but fresh treatments of old ideas, even explicit hommages to old stories, can be just as exciting. Our present is ever changing—and the best SF changes with us, as demonstrated in many stories here. This book showcases the very best of 2005's stories.

TRICERATOPS SUMMER

Michael Swanwick

The dinosaurs looked all wobbly in the summer heat shimmering up from the pavement. There were about thirty of them, a small herd of what appeared to be *Triceratops*. They were crossing the road—don't ask me why—so I downshifted and brought the truck to a halt, and waited.

Waited and watched.

They were interesting creatures, and surprisingly graceful for all their bulk. They picked their way delicately across the road, looking neither to the right nor the left. I was pretty sure I'd correctly identified them by now—they had those three horns on their faces. I used to be a kid. I'd owned the plastic models.

My next-door neighbor, Gretta, who was sitting in the cab next to me with her eyes closed, said, "Why aren't we moving?"

"Dinosaurs in the road," I said.

She opened her eyes.

"Son of a bitch," she said.

Then, before I could stop her, she leaned over and honked the horn, three times. Loud.

As one, every *Triceratops* in the herd froze in its tracks, and swung its head around to face the truck.

I practically fell over laughing.

"What's so goddamn funny?" Gretta wanted to know. But I could only point and shake my head helplessly, tears of laughter rolling down my cheeks.

It was the frills. They were beyond garish. They were as bright as any circus poster, with red whorls and yellow slashes and electric orange diamonds—too many shapes and colors to catalog, and each one different. They looked like Chinese kites! Like butterflies with six-foot winspans! Like Las Vegas on acid! And then, under those carnival-bright displays, the most stupid faces imaginable, blinking and gaping like brain-damaged cows. Oh, they were funny, all right, but if you couldn't see that at a glance, you never were going to.

Gretta was getting fairly steamed. She climbed down out of the cab and slammed the door behind her. At the sound, a couple of the *Triceratops* pissed themselves with excitement, and the lot shied away a step or two. Then they began huddling a little closer, to see what would happen next.

Gretta hastily climbed back into the cab. "What are those bastards up to now?" she demanded irritably. She seemed to blame me for their behavior. Not that she could say so, considering she was in my truck and her BMW was still in the garage in South Burlington.

"They're curious," I said. "Just stand still. Don't move or make any noise, and after a bit they'll lose interest and wander off."

"How do you know? You ever see anything like them before?"

"No," I admitted. "But I worked on a dairy farm when I was a young fella, thirty-forty years ago, and the behavior seems similar."

In fact, the *Triceratops* were already getting bored and starting to wander off again when a battered old Hyundai pulled wildly up beside us, and a skinny young man with the worst-combed hair I'd seen in a long time jumped out. They decided to stay and watch.

The young man came running over to us, arms waving. I leaned out the window. "What's the problem, son?"

He was pretty bad upset. "There's been an accident—an *incident*, I mean. At the Institute." He was talking about the Institute for Advanced Physics, which was not all that far from here. It was government-funded and affiliated in some way I'd never been able to get straight with the University of Vermont. "The verge stabilizers failed and the meson-field inverted and vectorized. The congruence factors went to infinity and . . ." He seized control of himself. "You're not supposed to see *any* of this."

"These things are yours, then?" I said. "So you'd know. They're *Triceratops*, right?"

"*Triceratops horridus*," he said distractedly. I felt unreasonably pleased with myself. "For the most part. There might be a couple other species of *Triceratops* mixed in there as well. They're like ducks in that regard. They're not fussy about what company they keep."

Gretta shot out her wrist and glanced meaningfully at her watch. Like everything else she owned, it was expensive. She worked for a firm in Essex Junction that did systems analysis for companies that were considering downsizing. Her job was to find out exactly what everybody did and then tell the CEO who could be safely cut. "I'm losing money," she grumbled.

I ignored her.

"Listen," the kid said. "You've got to keep quiet about this. We can't afford to have it get out. It has to be kept a secret."

"A secret?" On the far side of the herd, three cars had drawn up and stopped. Their passengers were standing in the road, gawking. A Ford Taurus pulled up behind us, and its driver rolled down his window for a better look. "You're planning to keep a herd of dinosaurs secret? There must be dozens of these things."

"Hundreds," he said despairingly. "They were migrating. The herd broke up after it came through. This is only a fragment of it."

"Then I don't see how you're going to keep this a secret. I mean, just look at them. They're practically the size of tanks. People are bound to notice."

"My God, my God."

Somebody on the other side had a camera out and was taking pictures. I didn't point this out to the young man.

Gretta had been getting more and more impatient as the conversation proceeded. Now she climbed down out of the truck and said, "I can't afford to waste any more time here. I've got work to do."

"Well, so do I, Gretta."

She snorted derisively. "Ripping out toilets, and nailing up sheet rock! Already, I've lost more money than you earn in a week."

She stuck out her hand at the young man. "Give me your car keys."

Dazed, the kid obeyed. Gretta climbed down, got in the Hyundai, and wheeled it around. "I'll have somebody return this to the Institute later today."

Then she was gone, off to find another route around the herd.

She should have waited, because a minute later the beasts decided to leave, and in no time at all were nowhere to be seen. They'd be easy enough to find, though. They pretty much trampled everything flat in their wake.

The kid shook himself, as if coming out of a trance. "Hey," he said. "She took my *car.*"

"Climb into the cab," I said. "There's a bar a ways up the road. I think you need a drink."

He said his name was Everett McCoughlan, and he clutched his glass like he would fall off the face of the Earth if he were to let go. It took a couple of whiskeys to get the full story out of him. Then I sat silent for a long time. I don't mind admitting that what he'd said made me feel a little funny. "How long?" I asked at last.

"Ten weeks, maybe three months, tops. No more."

I took a long swig of my soda water. (I've never been much of a drinker. Also, it was pretty early in the morning.) Then I told Everett that I'd be right back.

I went out to the truck, and dug the cell phone out of the glove compartment.

First I called home. Delia had already left for the bridal shop, and they didn't like her getting personal calls at work, so I left a message saying that I loved her. Then I called Green Mountain Books. It wasn't open yet, but Randy likes to come in early and he picked up the phone when he heard my voice on the machine. I asked him if he had anything on *Triceratops*. He said to hold on a minute, and then said yes, he had one copy of *The Horned Dinosaurs* by Peter Dodson. I told him I'd pick it up next time I was in town.

Then I went back in the bar. Everett had just ordered a third whiskey, but I pried it out of his hand. "You've had enough of that," I said. "Go home, take a nap. Maybe putter around in the garden."

"I don't have my car," he pointed out.

"Where do you live? I'll take you home."

"Anyway, I'm supposed to be at work. I didn't log out. And technically I'm still on probation."

"What difference does that make," I asked, "now?"

Everett had an apartment in Winooski at the Woolen Mill, so I guess the Institute paid him good money. Either that or he wasn't very smart how he spent it. After I dropped him off, I called a couple contractors I knew and arranged for them to take over what jobs I was already committed to. Then I called the *Free Press* to cancel my regular ad, and all my customers to explain I was having scheduling problems and had to subcontract their jobs. Only old Mrs. Bremmer gave me any trouble over that, and even she came around after I said that in any case I wouldn't be able to get around to her Jacuzzi until sometime late July.

Finally, I went to the bank and arranged for a second mortgage on my house.

It took me a while to convince Art Letourneau I was serious. I'd been doing business with him for a long while, and he knew how I felt about debt. Also, I was pretty evasive about what I wanted the money for. He was half-suspicious I was having some kind of late onset mid-life crisis. But the deed was in my name and property values were booming locally, so in the end the deal went through.

On the way home, I stopped at a jewelry store and at the florist's.

Delia's eyes widened when she saw the flowers, and then narrowed at the size of the stone on the ring. She didn't look at all the way I'd thought she would. "This better be good," she said.

So I sat down at the kitchen table and told her the whole story. When I was done, Delia was silent for a long while, just as I'd been. Then she said, "How much time do we have?"

"Three months if we're lucky. Ten weeks in any case, Everett said."

"You believe him?"

"He seemed pretty sure of himself."

If there's one thing I am, it's a good judge of character, and Delia knew it. When Gretta moved into the rehabbed barn next door, I'd said right from the start she was going to be a difficult neighbor. And that was before she'd smothered the grass on her property under three different colors of mulch, and then complained about me keeping my pickup parked in the driveway, out in plain sight.

Delia thought seriously for a few minutes, frowning in that way she has when she's concentrating, and then she smiled. It was a wan little thing, but a smile nonetheless. "Well, I've always wished we could afford a real first-class vacation."

I was glad to hear her say so, because that was exactly the direction my own thought had been trending in. And happier than that when she flung out her arms and whooped, "I'm going to *Disney*-world!"

"Hell," I said. "We've got enough money to go to Disneyworld, Disneyland, *and* Eurodisney, one after the other. I think there's one in Japan too."

We were both laughing at this point, and then she dragged me up out of the chair, and the two of us were dancing around and round the kitchen, still a little spooked under it all, but mostly being as giddy and happy as kids.

We were going to sleep in the next morning, but old habits die hard and anyway, Delia felt she owed it to the bridal shop to give them a week's notice. So, after she'd left, I went out to see if I could find where the *Triceratops* had gone.

Only to discover Everett standing by the side of the road with his thumb out.

I pulled over. "Couldn't get somebody at the Institute to drive your car home?" I asked when we were underway again.

"It never got there," he said gloomily. "That woman who was with you the other day drove it into a ditch. Stripped the clutch and bent the frame out of shape. She said she wouldn't have had the accident if my dinosaurs hadn't gotten her upset. Then she hung up on me. I just started at this job. I don't have the savings to buy a new car."

"Lease one instead," I said. "Put it on your credit card and pay the minimum for the next two or three months."

"I hadn't thought of that."

We drove on for a while and then I asked, "How'd she manage to get in touch with you?" She'd driven off before he mentioned his name.

"She called the Institute and asked for the guy with the bad hair. They gave her my home phone number."

The parking lot for the Institute for Advanced Physics had a card system, so I let Everett off by the side of the road. "Thanks for not telling anybody," he said as he climbed out. "About . . . you know."

"It seemed wisest not to."

He started away and then turned back suddenly and asked, "Is my hair really that bad?"

"Nothing that a barber couldn't fix," I said.

I'd driven to the Institute by the main highway. Returning, I went by back ways, through farmland. When I came to where I'd seen the *Triceratops*, I thought for an instant there'd been an accident, there were so many vehicles by the side of the road. But it turned out they were mostly gawkers and television crews. So apparently the herd hadn't gone far. There were cameras up and down the road and lots of good looking young women standing in front of them with wireless microphones.

I pulled over to take a look. One *Triceratops* had come right up to the fence and was browsing on some tall weeds there. It didn't seem to have any fear of human beings, possibly because in its day mammals never got much bigger than badgers. I walked up and stroked its back, which was hard and pebbly and warm. It was the warmth that got to me. It made the experience real.

A newswoman came over with her cameraman in tow. "You certainly look happy," she said.

"Well, I always wanted to meet a real live dinosaur." I turned to face her, but I kept one hand on the critter's frill. "They're something to see, I'll tell you. Dumb as mud but lots more fun to look at."

She asked me a few questions, and I answered them as best I could. Then, after she did her wrap, she got out a notebook and took down my name and asked me what I did. I told her I was a contractor but that I used to work on a dairy farm. She seemed to like that.

I watched for a while more, and then drove over to Burlington to pick up my book. The store wasn't open yet, but Randy let me in when I knocked. "You bastard," he said after he'd locked the door behind me. "Do you have any idea how much I could have sold this for? I had a foreigner," by which I understood him to mean somebody from New York State or possibly New Hampshire, "offer me two hundred dollars for it. And I could have got more if I'd had something to dicker with!"

"I'm obliged," I said, and paid him in paper bills. He waved off the tax but kept the nickel. "Have you gone out to see 'em yet?"

"Are you nuts? There's thousands of people coming into the state to look at those things. It's going to be a madhouse out there."

"I thought the roads seemed crowded. But it wasn't as bad as all of that."

"It's early still. You just wait."

Randy was right. By evening the roads were so congested that Delia was an hour late getting home. I had a casserole in the oven and the book open on the kitchen table when she staggered in. "The males have longer, more elevated horns, where the females have shorter, more forward-directed horns," I told her. "Also, the males are bigger than the females, but the females outnumber the males by a ratio of two to one."

I leaned back in my chair with a smile. "Two to one. Imagine that."

Delia hit me. "Let me see that thing."

I handed her the book. It kind of reminded me of when we were new-married, and used to go out bird-watching. Before things got so busy. Then Delia's friend Martha called and said to turn on Channel 3 quick. We did, and there I was saying, "dumb as mud."

"So you're a cattle farmer now?" Delia said, when the spot was over.

"That's not what I told her. She got it mixed up. Hey, look what I got." I'd been to three separate travel agents that afternoon. Now I spread out the brochures: Paris, Dubai, Rome, Australia, Rio de Janeiro, Marrakech. Even Disneyworld. I'd grabbed everything that looked interesting. "Take your pick, we can be there tomorrow."

Delia looked embarrassed.

"What?" I said.

"You know that June is our busy season. All those young brides. Francesca begged me to stay on through the end of the month."

"But—"

"It's not that long," she said.

For a couple of days it was like Woodstock, the Super Bowl, and the World Series all rolled into one—the Interstates came to a standstill, and it was worth your life to actually have to go somewhere. Then the governor called in the National Guard, and they cordoned off Chittenden County so you had to show your ID to get in or out. The *Triceratops* had scattered into little groups by then. Then a dozen or two were captured and shipped out of state to zoos where they could be more easily seen. So things returned to normal, almost.

I was painting the trim on the house that next Saturday when Everett drove up in a beat-up old clunker. "I like your new haircut," I said. "Looks good. You here to see the trikes?"

"Trikes?"

"That's what they're calling your dinos. *Triceratops* is too long for common use. We got a colony of eight or nine hanging around the neighborhood." There were woods out back of the house and beyond them a little marsh. They liked to browse the margins of the wood and wallow in the mud.

"No, uh . . . I came to find out the name of that woman you were with. The one who took my car."

"Gretta Houck, you mean?"

"I guess. I've been thinking it over, and I think she really ought to pay for the repairs. I mean, right's right."

"I noticed you decided against leasing."

"It felt dishonest. This car's cheap. But it's not very good. One door is wired shut with a coat hanger."

Delia came out of the house with the picnic basket then and I introduced them. "Ev's looking for Gretta," I said.

"Well, your timing couldn't be better," Delia said. "We were just about to go out trike-watching with her. You can join us."

"Oh, I can't—"

"Don't give it a second thought. There's plenty of food." Then, to me, "I'll go fetch Gretta while you clean up."

So that's how we found ourselves following the little trail through the woods and out to the meadow on the bluff above the Tylers' farm. The trikes slept in the field there. They'd torn up the crops pretty bad. But the state was covering damages, so the Tylers didn't seem to mind. It made me wonder if the governor knew what we know. If he'd been talking with the folks at the Institute.

I spread out the blanket, and Delia got out cold cuts, deviled eggs, lemonade, all the usual stuff. I'd brought along two pairs of binoculars, which I handed out to our guests. Gretta had been pretty surly so far, which made me wonder how Delia'd browbeat her into coming along. But now she said, "Oh, look! They've got babies!"

There were three little ones, only a few feet long. Two of them were mock-fighting, head-butting and tumbling over and over each other. The third just sat in the sun, blinking. They were all as cute as the dickens, with their tiny little nubs of horns and their great big eyes.

The other trikes were wandering around, pulling up bushes and such and eating them. Except for one that stood near the babies, looking big and grumpy and protective. "Is that the mother?" Gretta asked.

"That one's male," Everett said. "You can tell by the horns." He launched into an explanation, which I didn't listen to, having read the book.

On the way back to the house, Gretta grumbled, "I suppose you want the number for my insurance company."

"I guess," Everett said.

They disappeared into her house for maybe twenty minutes and then Everett got into his clunker and drove away. Afterwards, I said to Delia, "I thought the whole point of the picnic was you and I were going to finally work out where we were going on vacation." She hadn't even brought along the travel books I'd bought her.

"I think they like each other."

"Is that what this was about? You know, you've done some damn fool things in your time—"

"Like what?" Delia said indignantly. "When have I ever done anything that was less than wisdom incarnate?"

"Well . . . you married me."

"Oh, that." She put her arms around me. "That was just the exception that proves the rule."

So, what with one thing and the other, the summer drifted by. Delia took to luring the *Triceratops* closer and closer to the house with cabbages and bunches of celery and such. Cabbages were their favorite. It got so that we were feeding the trikes off the back porch in the evenings. They'd come clomping up around sunset, hoping for cabbages but willing to settle for pretty much anything.

It ruined the yard, but so what? Delia was a little upset when they got into her garden, but I spent a day putting up a good strong fence around it, and she replanted. She made manure tea by mixing their dung with water, and its effect on the plants was bracing. The roses blossomed like never before, and in August the tomatoes came up spectacular.

I mentioned this to Dave Jenkins down at the home-and-garden and he looked thoughtful. "I believe there's a market for that," he said. "I'll buy as much of their manure as you can haul over here."

"Sorry," I told him, "I'm on vacation."

Still, I couldn't get Delia to commit to a destination. Not that I quit trying. I was telling her about the Atlantis Hotel on Paradise Island one evening when suddenly she said, "Well, look at this."

I stopped reading about swimming with dolphins and the fake undersea ruined city, and joined her at the door. There was Everett's car—the new one that Gretta's insurance had paid for—parked out front of her house. There was only one light on, in the kitchen. Then that one went out too.

We figured those two had worked through their differences.

An hour later, though, we heard doors slamming, and the screech of Everett's car pulling out too fast. Then somebody was banging on our screen door. It was Gretta. When Delia let her in, she burst out into tears. Which surprised me. I wouldn't have pegged Everett as that kind of guy.

I made some coffee while Delia guided her into a kitchen chair, and got her some tissues, and soothed her down enough that she could tell us why she'd thrown Everett out of her house. It wasn't anything he'd done apparently, but something he'd said.

"Do you know what he *told* me?" she sobbed.

"I think I do," Delia said.

"About timelike—"

"—loops. Yes, dear."

Gretta looked stricken. "You too? Why didn't you tell me? Why didn't you tell everybody?"

"I considered it," I said. "Only then I thought, what would folks do if they knew their actions no longer mattered? Most would behave decently enough. But a few would do some pretty bad things, I'd think. I didn't want to be responsible for that."

She was silent for a while.

"Explain to me again about timelike loops," she said at last. "Ev tried, but by then I was too upset to listen."

"Well, I'm not so sure myself. But the way he explained it to me, they're going to fix the problem by going back to the moment before the rupture occurred and preventing it from ever happening in the first place. When that happens, everything from the moment of rupture to the moment when they go back to apply the patch separates from the trunk timeline. It just sort of drifts away, and dissolves into nothingness—never was, never will be."

"And what becomes of us?"

"We just go back to whatever we were doing when the accident happened. None the worse for wear."

"But without memories."

"How can you remember something that never happened?"

"So Ev and I—"

"No, dear," Delia said gently.

"How much time do we have?"

"With a little luck, we have the rest of the summer," Delia said. "The question is, how do you want to spend it?"

"What does it matter," Gretta said bitterly. "If it's all going to end?"

"Everything ends eventually. But after all is said and done, it's what we do in the meantime that matters, isn't it?"

The conversation went on for a while more. But that was the gist of it.

Eventually, Gretta got out her cell and called Everett. She had him on speed dial, I noticed. In her most corporate voice, she said, "Get your ass over here," and snapped the phone shut without waiting for a response.

She didn't say another word until Everett's car pulled up in front of her place. Then she went out and confronted him. He put his hands on his hips. She grabbed him and kissed him. Then she took him by the hand and led him back into the house.

They didn't bother to turn on the lights.

I stared at the silent house for a little bit. Then I realized that Delia wasn't with me anymore, so I went looking for her.

She was out on the back porch. "Look," she whispered.

There was a full moon and by its light we could see the *Triceratops* settling down to sleep in our backyard. Delia had managed to lure them all the way in at last. Their skin was all silvery in the moonlight; you couldn't make out the patterns on their frills. The big trikes formed a kind of circle around the little ones. One by one, they closed their eyes and fell asleep.

Believe it or not, the big bull male snored.

It came to me then that we didn't have much time left. One morning soon we'd wake up and it would be the end of spring and everything would be exactly as it was before the dinosaurs came. "We ever did get to Paris or London or Rome or Marrakesh," I said sadly. "Or even Disneyworld."

Without taking her eyes off the sleeping trikes, Delia put an arm around my waist. "Why are you so fixated on going places?" she asked. "We had a nice time here, didn't we?"

"I just wanted to make you happy."

"Oh, you idiot. You did that decades ago."

So there we stood, in the late summer of our lives. Out of nowhere, we'd been given a vacation from our ordinary lives, and now it was almost over. A pessimist would have said that we were just waiting for oblivion. But Delia and I didn't see it that way. Life is strange. Sometimes it's hard, and other times it's painful enough to break your heart. But sometimes it's grotesque and beautiful. Sometimes it fills you with wonder, like a *Triceratops* sleeping in the moonlight.

BANK RUN

Tom Purdom

Sabor was sitting in the passenger shack with his concubine when his personal assistant spotted the other boat. Sabor was devoting half his attention to the concubine and half to the numbers on his information display—a form of multitasking that combined his two major interests.

Choytang rested his hand on Sabor's shoulder. He pointed toward the rear window and Sabor immediately dimmed the numbers floating in front of his eyes.

The other boat was fueled by coal and propelled by a screw. It was moving approximately three times faster than the solar-powered paddlewheel transport that was carrying Sabor and his two companions up the lake. Eight soldiers were formed up on the right side. The six soldiers in the front row were lean hardbodies. The two soldiers standing behind them were massives who looked like they could have powered their boat with their own muscles. Their tan uniforms were accented with chocolate helmets and crossbelts—a no-nonsense, low contrast style that had become the trademark of one of the more expensive costumers on the planet.

Sabor's wristband had been running his banking program, as usual. The display was presenting him with the current status of the twelve-hour loan market. Twelve-hour loans were routine transactions—accounting maneuvers that maintained reserves at an acceptable level—and he usually let his alter run his operations in the twelve-hour market. He always checked it at least twice a day, however, to make sure his competitors hadn't developed an unpleasant surprise.

Sabor's concubine had already activated her own display. "There's a fishing commune called Galawar about four kilometers from here," the concubine reported. "You financed a dam and a big breeding operation for them. Their militia setup gets its real-life practice pursuing poachers and running rescue patrols. They can probably have a small force here eight minutes after their watch master initiates assembly."

Sabor returned the twelve-hour market to his alter and replaced it with the latest figures on the current status of the Galawar loan. "I'll talk to our captain. See if you can exercise your charms on the appropriate officers of the commune."

The captain had isolated herself in her control shack fifteen minutes after her boat had left the dock. She was sprawling in a recliner with her eyes fixed on the top of a window and her attention focused on the material her personal display was imprinting on her optic nerves.

"I'm afraid I may be about to cause you some trouble," Sabor said. "I registered a counterfeit identity when I boarded your boat. My true name is Sabor Haveri. As you probably know, I'm the proprietor of the bank that furnishes your company its primary line of credit."

The captain had looked tall when she had been stretched across her recliner but she looked even taller when she stood up. She had been operating lake boats for eighteen years, but the information in the public databanks had made it clear her boating work was primarily a money job. Most of the entries Sabor had collected from the databanks had highlighted her exploits as a member of one of the top aquatic hunting clubs on the lake. She would create an awesome vision standing on the back of a riding seal, in hot pursuit of a yellow-feathered swordbeak.

"I've been having a problem with one of my less reasonable customers," Sabor said. "He requested a loan I consider unwise. He's trying to force me to make the loan and I decided it might be best if I put some space between us. Unfortunately, he appears to be pursuing me on the steam propelled boat coming up behind us."

The captain returned her attention to her display. Her uniform had been created by a designer who favored clean, uncluttered lines and she had arranged it with a flair that gave her an air of rangy competence. She jabbed her finger at the air and frowned at the response she received.

"I think I should ask you your customer's name, Honored Sabor."

"Possessor Kenzan Khan. The boat appears to have eight soldiers on it. I would appreciate it if you would help me resist if they try to board us."

"With a crew of one?"

"I have good reason to believe I'm going to be receiving a little armed assistance from the militia maintained by a fishing commune called Galawar. My personal assistant has some useful skills and I can assure you I'm not totally helpless myself. If you'll give us some help at this end, I believe we can hold off our assailants until our friends at Galawar can ride to our rescue."

The captain braced her hand on the upper part of the bulkhead and stared out the window. It was a windy morning in the last days of autumn. The surface of the lake looked dark and rippling.

"I hate to sound melodramatic," Sabor said, "but the entire financial system of our planet could be at risk. Kenzan tends to be impulsive. If his psych staff gets me under his control . . . and I make untenable loans in response to their manipulations . . ."

"Most of my ammunition stock consists of non-lethal ammunition. Will non-lethals be sufficient?"

"I'm just trying to stay out of their hands. Killing them isn't necessary."

Sabor's concubine was standing in front of the rear window watching the other boat eliminate the last two hundred meters that separated them. "So how did your chat with the commune go?" Sabor asked her. "Are they feeling amenable?"

Purvali's designers had started with a fleshy woman with a strong sex drive. Then they had stretched out the basic design, added an upper-percentile intelligence, and enhanced the aspects of her genome that influenced coordination and gracefulness. The result was a finely calculated combination of elegance and voluptuousness—a pairing that triggered all the erotic and emotional yearnings the designers had detected when they had given Sabor their standard customer profile tests.

The designers had also produced an exceptionally competent human being who could satisfy all Sabor's yearnings for good support staff. Purvali doubled as his administrative assistant, in addition to her other functions. Purvali and Choytang constituted his entire permanent staff.

"I talked to the Primary Coordinator's executive officer," Purvali said. "She's talking to the Primary Coordinator now."

"Shall I give them a call?"

"I have a feeling they may want to bargain."

Sabor stared at the oncoming steamboat. The Galawar commune had bargained down to the last hundredth of a percentage point on both the projects he had financed for them. If he called again, and let them know he was worried. . . .

"The soldiers you're looking at belong to Colonel Jina," Purvali said. "I estimate we can hold them off for approximately seven minutes minimum, nine maximum, after they come into range."

"Even if I bring you in as a surprise?"

"Yes."

"It looks like I may have to exercise my talent for stalling. Tell the Primary Coordinator I want to have a chat. See if you can put me through to our friend the Colonel."

The most prominent feature in Colonel Jina's publicity portraits was the smile that adorned his globular, well nourished face. He was sporting an especially cheerful version of his trademark when his image popped onto Sabor's optic nerves seconds after Purvali initiated the call.

"Good morning, Honored Sabor. It's a pleasure to hear from you."

"I understand I'm being pursued by soldiers who are affiliated with your enterprise, colonel."

"I've dispatched eight of my best. They have orders to board your boat and take you prisoner."

"I've examined your rate schedule. I'm prepared to offer you fifty percent more than you're being paid."

The colonel frowned. Soulful regret replaced The Smile. "I'm afraid I have to inform you I can't consider your offer. I appreciate your interest but I never entertain counter offers once I've committed my armed staff to an operation. My reputation for dependability is one of my primary business assets."

"I understand that, colonel. I should advise you, however, that the situation may not be as one sided as it appears. I have some capacity for violence, too."

Choy was bustling around the passenger shack overturning tables and chairs and lining them up in front of the windows. He and Purvali had wrapped themselves in defensive vests and planted hats with defensive units on their heads. Sabor had slipped into a vest but he had laid his hat on a windowsill.

Purvali pointed at the air in front of her eyes. Sabor nodded and his display split in half. A lean man in a recyclable work suit occupied the left section. A subtitle reminded Sabor he was looking at the Primary Coordinator of Galawar Commune.

"Good morning, Honored Sabor," the Primary Coordinator said. "My executive officer says you've asked for assistance."

"My principal advised me you would probably resist," Colonel Jina said. "I took that into account when I assigned a completely equipped squad. You can surrender now or we can take you prisoner five minutes from now."

Sabor's attention started multi-tracking the two conversations. His communication implant had automatically initiated a switching program when it bifurcated the display. The implant transmitted a real time image to the appropriate person whenever Sabor spoke and the other person received a temporary simulation. The Primary Co-ordinator and Colonel Jina were probably using similar programs.

The conversation with the Primary Coordinator was essentially a standard business bargaining session. The Coordinator recog-nized his obligation to resist anyone who attacked honest merchants as they plied their trade on the lake. He was even willing to let Sabor and his party make a short stop on the commune's territory once they eliminated their difficulties with Colonel Jina's representatives. But he also knew an opportunity when he saw one.

"We have several members who feel we should refinance our primary loan, Honored Sabor. You may have heard about the inter-esting line of crabs the Renwar Institute unveiled two tendays ago. We're bidding for the exclusive reproduction rights. The numbers indicate we could draft an unbeatable offer if we could decrease the cost of our current debt servicing."

With Colonel Jina, Sabor concentrated on more lofty matters— and the time-eating speeches that lofty matters tend to generate. "Your principal is endangering the entire financial system of our planet, colonel. Kenzan Khan is one of the most fiscally irresponsi-ble personalities I've worked with. If he gets my bank under his con-trol, he'll drain my resources until he triggers an uncontrollable financial chain reaction. You wouldn't accept a contract to poison the lake. The collapse of my bank would be just as devastating."

"I appreciate your concern," Colonel Jina said. "But it's my un-derstanding there are three other banks with assets that are as exten-sive as yours."

The steamboat had pulled abreast of the starboard windows. The soldiers were still grouped in their parade formation.

"And they're all interlinked," Sabor said. "If one of us fails, the others will all be affected. The relationships and interactions in a financial system can be just as complex as the relationships and interactions in an ecological system."

The six hardbodies on the other boat trained their weapons.

"I appreciate your willingness to help us," the Coordinator said. "Our rescue force should reach you in about seven minutes."

A crack slithered across the window directly in front of Sabor. More cracks appeared in the windows on either side. Clouds of particles replaced all three windows. Chilly autumn air flooded the passenger shack.

Sabor had thrown himself flat as soon as he had seen the first crack. He stretched out his right arm and started crawling toward the barricade Choy had assembled in front of the window.

Choy had assembled three guns. He and Purvali were lying on their backs with their weapons raised above the barricade and their eyes fixed on the aiming screen mounted on the rear of each barrel. Sabor picked up the third gun and tapped a symbol on the control screen built into the stock. The screen clicked off a ten second count. A line of boldface announced that the gun had linked with the short-range interface built into his wristband.

"They're firing at the barricade," Choy said. "They'll have it dissolved in about two minutes."

"What are you aiming at?"

"We're concentrating on the hardbody on the left of the line. I'm assuming we should try to completely eliminate one gun."

Sabor had already raised his gun above the barricade. He marked the hardbody on the left with a mental command and the barrel swiveled on its mount. The gun was an elegant piece of smoothly functioning machinery, emitting a well mannered *slap* . . . *slap* . . . *slap* as its internal computer calculated the range, checked the position of the barrel, and transmitted a fire command once every four seconds. The anti-personnel loads contained molecular devices that temporarily disrupted the central nervous system. The defensive system built into the soldier's uniforms deployed defensive molecules that could neutralize the incoming moles. A concentrated attack could overwhelm the defensive moles and remove a hardbody from the firing line for several minutes. The gun wasn't programmed to compensate for the rocking of the waves but Sabor's own brain could handle that aspect of the situation.

He rotated the gun to his right, to keep his target on the aiming screen, and realized the other boat was turning.

"They're turning onto a possible interception course," Choy said.

"I've checked the databanks for information on their jumping capacity," Purvali said. "There's nothing explicit but I estimate the hardbodies can probably hop across a two meter separation without making an extraordinary effort."

"Can you do me a favor?" Sabor said. "Can you find out what kind of cargo this floating palace is carrying? Perhaps we can find something our captain will be willing to part with. And gain a small increment in our forward progress."

Sabor's cool, chinup elan was one of his trademarks. His mother had included it in his specifications and he considered it one of her better decisions. He had even ordered a biochemical reinforcement when he had reached legal maturity. He could put several million yuris in play and cheerfully sleep, eat, and dally with a concubine while he waited for the results. There were times, however, when he suspected some hidden segment of his personality was trembling in terror while it watched the rest of him treat major calamities as if they were trivial disruptions.

A list popped onto Sabor's display—a complete catalog of the boat's cargo, assembled from the contracts that had been posted in the databanks. Public posting couldn't be enforced by law but people who ignored the custom enjoyed short business careers. There was no central government on Fernheim. The business community enforced its rules by monitoring deals and invoking the ancient human customs of shunning and ostracism.

The bulkiest item on the list was a crate containing ten ceramic microwave receptors. The last starship to orbit Fernheim had included a passenger who had brought the program for producing the most advanced model available in the solar system. The receptors would capture fifteen percent more energy than the most competitive model available on the planet—a big increase for a world on which fossil fuels were still under-exploited and only five microwave generators had been placed in orbit.

The receptors took up most of the cargo space. The rest of the cargo consisted of small orders of luxuries. Meat taken from real animals. Organically grown wine. Nine golden swans.

"We could use the swans as harassers," Choy said. "All I need is the activation codes."

Sabor pipped the captain. "I would like to buy your cargo. My figure for the total retail value is three hundred and sixty thousand. I'll add ten percent to cover delays and aggravation."

"To lighten ship?"

"Yes."

"It won't add more than a kilometer per hour to our speed. Given their current position . . ."

"We're in an every-second-counts situation."

"It's yours."

"I'll need the activation and control codes for the ornamental swans. Please transmit them to my assistant, Choytang."

The overturned table Sabor was using for cover metamorphosed into dust and fragments. Sabor rolled backward and huddled beside the hatch in the middle of the shack.

Lights turned on as soon as he dropped through the hatch. The crate containing the ceramic receptors took up almost half the floor space. The eight swans had been arranged on a pallet with a low guard rail. The rest of the cargo had been packed in neatly stacked boxes.

Choy stepped up to the swans and activated their implants with a command from his own communications implant. Their feathers were as glossy as pure gold leaf. Ripples of light ran along their bodies when they stretched their necks and rustled their wings.

The boat was a typical example of Fernheim's betwixt-and-between economy. A big loading hatch on the left side of the boat responded to a direct signal from the captain's brain and rolled upward on a wheeled track. The crate holding the receptors opened in response to another impulse from the captain's cerebral cortex. And Sabor and Purvali picked up two of the receptors and lugged them across the hold with the chemical energy stored in their own muscles.

The hatch was so close to the water line they could have dipped their hands without bending over. Three hundred meters of dark water stretched between the boat and the shore. Two houses stood beside a creek that emptied into the lake. Terrestrial oaks and sycamores spread branches that were covered with autumn leaves. The entire shoreline had been completely terrestrialized for over two decades.

The captain had given them free access to the information integrator in her command interface. They could examine the entire composite picture the integrator assembled from the sensory moles embedded in every meter of the boat's structure. They trudged back and forth across the hold with most of their attention focused on the positions of the two boats.

Choy waited until the other boat was making its last maneuvers for boarding position. The swans lumbered across the hold in two ragged lines. Their huge wings pounded at the air. Choy guided them through the hatch and they turned as soon as they gained altitude and drove toward their adversary's deck.

The coal burner had overcome their captain's best efforts. It was lying almost parallel with the right side of their boat, with a three-meter gap separating the two hulls. The hardbodies were lined up with their guns at port arms. They were obviously primed to jump as soon as their boat's sidewise drift brought them close enough. The nine swans covered their helmets and torsos with a blanket of hammering wings.

The hardbodies reacted with the remorseless calm that had been built into their personalities. Their right hands dropped off their guns and gripped the swans around their necks. The two massives reached into the storm of writhing feathers and applied their oversized muscles to the necks the hardbodies had neglected.

"Have the captain open the right loading hatch," Purvali said. "Enough for us to shoot out."

Sabor started moving toward the hatch while he was still pipping the captain. The hatch creaked open and they each took a single hardbody and poured moles into his armor. They had to shoot upward at a steep angle, through the commotion created by the swans, but a hit anywhere on the armor would wear it down.

Dead swans dropped into the water in front of Sabor. The gap between the two hulls narrowed. The side of the other boat loomed over them. On Sabor's display, the omniscient eye of the electronic system presented him with a less pessimistic picture. Three hardbodies had dropped out of the line—presumably to recharge their armor. Two swans were still defying the pitiless hands closing around their necks.

Three hardbodies jumped across the gap. Boots pounded on the deck over Sabor's head. He scurried away from his firing position and aimed his gun at the hatch he had used to enter the hold.

A hardbody suddenly started firing his gun. The display responded to the shift in Sabor's attention and presented him with two figures in skintight wetsuits. Two more figures were crowding in behind them. In the water, just a few meters from the boat, three seal riders were standing on their mounts as they poured a stream of projectiles into the hardbodies.

"I requested a son who was restless and adventurous," Sabor's mother had told him. "I suppose I shouldn't be surprised when he tells me he wants to put twenty-two light years between himself and all the pleasures he's been enjoying since his eyes first registered the light."

"As far as I can tell," Sabor had responded, "the only pleasures I'm leaving behind are the pleasures that are irrevocably associated with my family. The only difference between the ship and the home I've been honored to share with you and my sisters is the fact that the ship will be moving away from the sun instead of traveling around it. I'll have almost every luxury I have here. We'll still have fabricators when we reach Fernheim. The first thing I'm going to fabricate after we make landfall is a bottle of Talini."

Sabor had been fifty-two when he had broken the news. His mother had been reigning over their family enterprises for almost a century. Billions of neils and yuris bounced around the cities of the asteroid belt during every twenty-four hour day-period and their economists estimated that thirty percent of the total visited their databanks during its rambles.

Rali Haveri was a placid woman for all her power. She had produced him, Sabor believed, because she felt her life needed a dash of turbulence. Adventurous people stirred her. Most of her temporary consorts had been self-centered erratics.

Sabor had reached maturity in an environment that surrounded him with gentle music, decorous parties, and amiable personalities. Alajara had been one of the pleasantest cities in the asteroid belt—a mansion inhabited by ten thousand people who were all employees of his family's business. Sabor mastered three musical instruments, pursued his hobbies and enthusiasms with equipment that would have made most professionals groan with envy, and dallied with his choice of concubines when he reached the appropriate age. His mother and his older sisters took care of the details that generated the family income.

There had been a time when many visionaries thought the fabricator would make bankers obsolete. Press the right buttons and your magic box would generate a fully cooked roast on demand. Press another combination and it would extrude furniture for your dwelling place, clothes for your body, and toys for the idle hours it had bestowed on your life. Why would anyone need money?

Fortunately, it hadn't quite worked out that way. Fabricators had been universal household appliances for two centuries and Sabor's family was still engaging in its traditional business. The introduction of the fabricator had disrupted Earth's economic system for approximately two decades. It had triggered a catastrophic massive deflation. Prices and wages had tumbled by seventy percent, by most calculations. But when the turbulence had subsided, Sabor's family had still been negotiating loans and pulling profits out of microscopic variations in interest rates.

Fabricators could provide you with the basics at a ridiculously low cost but they still needed energy and raw materials. They needed programs that directed their operations and time to run the programs. And there were commodities that couldn't be manufactured by the best machines available. Fabricators couldn't manufacture social status. Fabricators couldn't engage in the genetic manipulations and the years of post-natal management that produced personalities like Purvali and Choytang. Above all, fabricators couldn't manufacture *expertise* and *imagination*. They couldn't design their own programs. They couldn't visualize the new products that would make consumers lust after the programs that would produce them.

Money, Rali Haveri liked to remind him, was essentially irrational. It had value because people agreed it had value. She had placed two million yuris in Sabor's account when he had established his residence on the *Carefree Villa* and everyone on the starship had agreed he could use it to buy goods and services and make loans. They had accepted it as money through three rests and four awakes and they had continued to accept it when he had landed on Fernheim. They even accepted the additional numbers his mother had radioed him since he had landed on the planet. The fact that every message had to travel for twenty-two years made no difference. Human societies needed some sort of monetary system and he was the son of a woman who could obviously bless him with any sum he could reasonably desire. The financial system in the solar system even recognized the numbers he transmitted when he paid his mother the interest she charged him.

"I would be avoiding my maternal responsibilities if I didn't demand interest," Rali had lectured him across the light years. "I'm only imposing the same discipline on you that I would try to impose on myself—the same discipline the solar financial system imposes on me."

Sabor reentered the boathouse and dropped into a corner two minutes after the captain returned their boat to the main channel. Purvali ran a test on the boathouse fabricator and ordered pharmaceutical drinks that would moderate their emotional stress. Colonel Jina's immobilized soldiers were being relieved of their armor and weapons and placed on the deck of the other boat. The boat itself would be turned around and sent back upstream under its own control.

The Primary Coordinator had already advised Colonel Jina he could pick up his soldiers' equipment in two days. There would be no request for ransom or damages.

"We try to maintain good business relations with Colonel Jina," the Primary Coordinator had explained. "We usually use his services when we hire guards for our more valuable shipments."

Purvali swayed toward Sabor with a drinking cup in her hand. He held up three fingers as she bent over him.

"We have three projects we have to advance simultaneously," Sabor said. "We have to organize our fellow bankers into a united front, we have to find a weakness we can exploit, and we have to prepare for a sojourn in the splendors of the unterrestrialized wilderness. I'll start work on number one. I want you to work on the others. Assume we'll embark on our wilderness holiday as soon as we're properly equipped."

Purvali checked her display. "They only have eight widemounts in the whole commune."

"Try to purchase four. I'd like to pack a *few* comforts."

The effects of the drink flowed through Sabor's muscles and nerves. His display projected his own image in front of him and he observed his delivery as he created his message to his three colleagues.

"I regret to tell you that I have just fended off an armed attack financed by Possessor Kenzan Khan. I believe we should immediately suspend all dealings with Kenzan Khan. I will be taking other actions shortly but I believe an unequivocal display of unity is absolutely essential."

He paused the recording and took another swallow of his drink. Purvali had flavored it with banana and coconut—an aroma he had treasured since he had first savored it sometime around his fifth birthday.

"Kenzan has become obsessed with his long term feud with Possessor Dobryani. He wants to mount an armed occupation of the land around the mouth of Winari Brook. Kenzan and Dobryani have both been eyeing that area and Kenzan has convinced himself Dobryani is preparing to seize it by force. He wants me to finance the purchase of one hundred soldiers. I have decided I have to refuse. I've been subsidizing his excesses since he first took control of his possession. I have reached my limit. Firm action is absolutely necessary."

The attachments included a statement by the Coordinator of Galawar, visuals of the encounter with Colonel Jina's force, and a copy of the message from Kenzan Khan that had convinced Sabor he had to evacuate his primary apartment in Tale Harbor.

There was no room in Kenzan Khan's worldview for a simple clash of desires. The heart of his message was a long flood of denunciations. Possessor Dobryani wasn't opposing him merely because she wanted the same thing he wanted. She was a malevolent spirit with a compulsion to control every patch of terrestrialized land on the planet.

"We all know what she is, Sabor," Kenzan had proclaimed. "I've been defending myself against her attacks since the year I succeeded my uncle. The days when you can wiggle and sidestep and make your little jokes are over. Give me what I need or I'll take it. And everything else you have with it. Money isn't the only form of power."

Kenzan had framed his message so his face would appear to be crowding against the person who received it—a juvenile trick, but it was Kenzan's childishness that made him dangerous. Kenzan's parents had apparently believed an imposing frame still had its advantages. Kenzan was over two heads taller than Sabor, with bone and muscle in proportion. Lately, he had been neglecting his physical maintenance. He had compensated by costuming himself in ornate belted robes that hid his paunch. A tangled black beard obscured his jowly cheeks.

The robes were a convenient wrapping for a sexual impulsive. Sabor had witnessed the advantages of Kenzan's turnout during a tediously elaborate lunch. Kenzan could simply grab the nearest concubine who appealed to him, untie his robe, and indulge himself without any bothersome need to undress.

Kenzan's uncle had been a methodical, patient man who drew his deepest satisfactions from the steady expansion of his wealth. If the uncle purchased the genome for a new type of fruit tree, he sold a hundred fruits for every bite he ate himself. He had been murdered by an heir who gorged according to his impulses, fed the leftovers to his animals and favorites, and borrowed to buy any novelty that caught his fancy. Kenzan's banquet garden was bigger than most playing fields. His stables housed two hundred of the costliest riding animals the biodesigners had managed to generate.

Kenzan's feud with Possessor Dobryani had begun when Dobryani had stolen the genome of one of his prized meat animals. Kenzan had purchased exclusive rights to the genome from an immigrant who had stored it in his auxiliary intelligence when he had left the solar system. Kenzan had been the only possessor on the planet who served the animal on his table. He retaliated by deliberately mining titanium from a low-concentration site that ruined the view from one of Dobryani's favorite villas.

There was no central bank on Fernheim but the four leading bankers all tried to abide by the rules a central bank would have enforced. Sabor maintained reserves that equaled eighteen percent of his loans—a conservative choice that was based on his family's most rigid traditions. The other three favored reserves of twelve to fifteen percent. Sabor's money management program borrowed from the others when his reserves dropped below his minimum and loaned to them when they were short. Money bounced between the four banks in a continuous, unending balancing act, at short-term interest rates their programs negotiated in thousandths of a percentage point. At the present moment, Sabor owed Heinrich Dobble approximately eight million yuris, at an average interest rate of 2.116 percent. The other two bankers owed Sabor twelve million.

His display presented him with Heinrich's standard business image twelve minutes after he had dispatched his message. As usual, Heinrich was standing rigidly erect and wearing a black, high collared outfit that gave him a reassuringly formal air.

"I'd already seen a report on the attack," Heinrich said. "I would have thought your client was just ranting if I hadn't seen that."

"I have to confess Kenzan took me by surprise, too. I vacated my quarters as a precaution—to give him some time to calm down."

"How long can he last if we institute a freeze?"

Sabor dropped his social persona and slipped into his straight business mode. He and Heinrich never wasted words. "Two to four tendays with the freeze alone. But the freeze is only a first step. I'm hoping I can neutralize him in three or four days."

"Neutralize?"

"Permanently. He's a spendthrift. He won't recover if I hit him hard enough."

"If he doesn't get you under control first."

"I'm retreating to the wilderness. First he has to locate me. Then he has to catch me."

Heinrich frowned. "How much time have you spent in the wilderness, Sabor?"

"I've been funding expeditions for twenty standard years. I probably understand the survival requirements better than some of the gadabouts I've bankrolled."

"You can't hire fifty soldiers and surround yourself with a solid defense?"

"And where would I place my temporary fortress? The Primary Coordinator has given me permission to disembark in Galawar. He hasn't told me I can stay there. We're dealing with a random force, Heinrich. Kenzan could attack me even if he knew I had him outnumbered five to one. He could turn a place like Galawar into a disaster."

"Kenzan's irrationality is one of the factors I'm weighing. I could find myself in a very serious situation if I oppose him and he gets your resources under control."

"And you'll find yourself in a worse position if I give in to his demands. He isn't going to stop with one extortion. He doesn't know how to stop."

"I intend to look after myself, Sabor. I reserve the right to reappraise my options. At any time."

They entered the wilderness five hours after they stepped onto the Galawar docks. A twelve-meter electric hedge separated the terrestrialized land from the native ecosystem. On the terrestrial side of the barrier, they were surrounded by rose bushes, vegetable gardens, and fields covered with high yield fuel vines. On the wilderness side, thick tree trunks towered over the hedge. Cold autumn sunlight spread across leaves that had become white and translucent as the season had advanced. The trees on Fernheim produced leaves that tended to be smaller and paler than the leaves of terrestrial trees—a response, presumably, to the dizzying pace of the planet's year. Every organism on Fernheim had to speed through seasons that were only half as long as the seasons on Earth.

The gate in the bottom of the hedge had been designed with a grudgingly narrow aperture. Their widemounts passed through it in single file, with their carriers scraping the leaves. Choy led the way, with Sabor in the second position.

Widemounts had been created by reducing the size of the terrestrial elephant and modifying the chemical foundations of its temperament. Sabor's widemount barely reached the top of his head but its broad back and columnar legs could support a load that included Sabor and all the equipment that would keep a civilized human reasonably content with his lot. The fourth widemount carried an extra fabricator, extra prefabricated supplies, and twelve bottles of wine that Sabor had ordered from Galawar's communal fabrication facility.

Sabor had linked his display to Purvali's. He could monitor her survey of Kenzan Khan's financial situation while he concentrated his attention on the normal complexities of his business. Half his display tracked the ebb and flow of the planetary high-yield market. The other half presented him with Purvali's attempts to untangle the web of loans and expenditures that dominated Kenzan's economic life.

"There are times when the speed of light limitation has its comforts," Sabor said. "I can imagine what my mother would say if she knew I'd been loaning real money to someone with that kind of balance sheet."

A cloud of birds had surrounded Sabor's widemount as soon as he had passed through the barrier hedge. Fluttering bodies banged against the transparent upper half of the carrier. Flocks of ground birds scurried away from the relentless plod of his animal's legs. The pale leaves created a subtly alien atmosphere that many humans found disturbing.

His auxiliary intelligence fed him data about the birds and the different species of trees—some of it information that had been collected by expeditions he had financed. Most of the settlers on the planet were primarily interested in making homes for themselves but a small minority had been captivated by the opportunity to study a new biological system. Mankind had discovered four life-bearing worlds so far. Two were examples of parallel evolution—the life forms roughly resembled the life forms on Earth. Fernheim was one of the parallel worlds but it had its share of anomalies. Earth had never passed through an age dominated by birds. Fernheim had reached that stage without generating an age of giant reptiles—a finding that had set evolutionists twittering as soon as the first glimpses of the fossil record had filtered back to the solar system.

Purvali was linking every loan Kenzan had been given with the items he had spent it on. She had started with a thorough analysis of Kenzan's accounts with Sabor. From there she would move on to the public records. Kenzan liked to brag. The public databases contained detailed information on every animal, food, woman, or grandiose display that had sucked purchasing power out of his accounts.

Sabor activated a high-level search alter and put it to work. So far he had only heard from one other member of the four. Ar Badov had responded with a brief text message—*I will give your efforts my complete support. Don't let us down.* Ar Badov had been the first banker on the planet. He and Sabor had been locked in an intense, highly personal rivalry from the moment Ar had learned that a scion of the Haveri family had set up shop on *his* planet.

The fourth power center in the financial system was controlled by a remote, almost reclusive woman named Zara Nev. It had been three hours since Sabor had advised her Heinrich and Ar had joined the fray—almost seven hours since Zara had received his first invitation.

The research alter presented him with a report twelve minutes after it started burrowing through the databanks. Zara had buried her machinations in a transaction network that included three other deals. It was a perfunctory attempt at camouflage by the standards maintained by Sabor and his colleagues.

"I would consider that an unequivocal negative response to my appeal for help," Sabor said. "She hasn't sent me an outright rejection but she's only made a token effort to hide her support for our respected opponent."

"There's nothing unequivocal about the pool of capital she's placed at Possessor Khan's disposal," Purvali said. "He can hire one hundred manunits at Colonel Jina's standard price—two full squads for over four days, with one fully loaded airship."

They were riding into a broad, heavily forested area that stretched between two major rivers. Sabor had asked his display for a random course and it had angled them fifteen degrees southward, toward the hills that bordered the Ratagava River. The widemounts plodded through the forest undergrowth at a steady eight kilometers per hour. Once every hour they stopped for fifteen minutes and foraged. The widemounts had been equipped with intestinal addons that could convert the planetary vegetation into digestible molecules but it was an inefficient process. They needed forty percent more food, by weight, than they would have consumed if they had been processing terrestrial food stocks.

The humans stayed inside their carriers while the widemounts stuffed bushes and leaves into their mouths. Eight guard cats patrolled the area that surrounded them. Choy received the transmissions from their implants and rotated part of his attention from cat to cat.

The forest had slipped into darkness by the time they made their second stop. The cats refueled on meat produced by the fabricators and Sabor took Choy's advice and let the animals rest for a full hour. He had already decided they would keep moving for another three hours.

They were assuming Colonel Jina would probably mount his pursuit force on an airship. The planetary helicopter population had slipped past the two hundred mark but an airship was almost as fast and it could creep along under solar power if it slipped beyond its normal range and exhausted its batteries. According to Purvali's analysis, every hour they traveled could add thirty minutes to the time an airship would eat up looking for them if it used an optimum search pattern.

The exploration of the databanks was almost as tedious as their step-by-step progress through the night. Purvali couldn't hop on a promising lead and pursue it through a continuous give-and-take with the public information system. Her transmissions to the communications satellites had to be bundled into blips and randomly spaced several minutes apart.

"So far," Purvali said, "Possessor Khan's military expenditures look like they offer the most promise. He's taking on two opponents at once—you and Possessor Dobryani."

Her report hopped to a map marked with data labels. Kenzan was renting fifty soldiers that belonged to Possessor Makajida—the possessor who owned a tract on Kenzan's northern border. The fifty extra soldiers had been allocated to the force he had deployed against Dobryani.

"He needs those soldiers," Purvali said. "And Heinrich Dobble is the dominant figure in Possessor Makajida's financial affairs. Possessor Makajida has five active credit arrangements and he's restructured his debt six times in the last eleven years. Heinrich Dobble funded two thirds of the direct loans in four of the credit arrangements and he was a pivotal participant in five restructurings, once you do a little digging."

"So I say a few words to Heinrich, Heinrich says a few words to Makajida, and we both let my lady Dobryani know she can ravage Kenzan's holdings as soon as he loses control of Makajida's fifty warriors."

"It had occurred to me that might be one possibility. . . ."

"I think I would prefer something a bit less obvious. I suspect my good friend Heinrich would, too. Is there any somewhat subtler method we can use to persuade Possessor Makajida he should reclaim his property?"

"Do you have any suggestions?"

"I'd like to leave it to your creative talents for the time being. I will then apply the all-important finishing touches, as usual."

The security system awoke them twice during the night. The first time a flock of nocturnal birds assumed a formation that bore a vague resemblance to a tree-skimming airship. The second time six flightless predators approached the northern perimeter and indicated they might not retreat when three of the guard cats converged on them.

Sabor had contemplated a visit to Purvali's carrier while he had been savoring the after taste of the sauces he had chosen for his evening meal. He toyed with the idea as he stared into the darkness after both disruptions. And decided, each time, that he should accept the realities of his situation and activate his sleep control program. He was fighting a war. He would remain in warrior mode until he eliminated Kenzan Khan.

They started moving as soon as the morning sun glowed through the highest leaves. Sabor indulged in quick catnaps during their first legs but he made Purvali sleep a full two hours extra. He received his reward ten minutes after she finished her morning rituals.

"Possessor Makajida has a border rival, too," Purvali said. "Possessor Avaming. They've been feuding ever since Possessor Avaming occupied a slice of the lakefront that Possessor Makajida had planned to claim. Possessor Avaming has been a good customer but he's just as spendthrift as most of his peers. I suspect he might be induced to threaten Possessor Makajida if you offered him a satisfactory incentive."

"And Makajida would then feel he had to recall his fifty soldiers. And there would be no indication Heinrich had anything to do with it."

"The effect on Kenzan Khan could be devastating. I've been looking at his relationship with Possessor Dobryani. There is nothing shallow about their enmity."

"Do you have any theories on the source of their acrimony?"

"Their attitudes toward the opposite sex appear to be mutually contradictory. They each seem to favor the total submission of their sexual partners."

Sabor nodded. "I've had similar thoughts every time I've heard him attack her. There are times when he's so rabid he sounds like he's indulging in self-satire."

"I think there's a very high probability she would seize the opportunity to destroy him if it became available."

Sabor's widemount sloshed across a pebbly stream. On his right, one of the guardcats took the obstacle in a low, stretched-out leap, with its forepaws pulled tight against its chest and its rear legs trailing behind it. Startled waterbirds surrounded the cat with an explosion of flapping wings.

"Possessor Avaming isn't going to respond to a bribe," Sabor said. "He takes great pride in his aristocratic indifference to material gain."

"Shall I consider that a rigid limitation?"

"It would probably be wise."

"I can see three possibilities. Possessor Avaming's payments to architects and landscapers during the last ten years equal sixty-two percent of his total debt. They started declining about four years ago and he started buying musical instruments and hiring musicians. In the last year, he's started spending money on water hunting."

"He's obviously a prime example of a serial enthusiast. I suspect you'll find water hunting will present the most promising opportunities at this moment."

Purvali cut the connection and Sabor turned part of his attention to the input from a camera that watched his rear. The steady fallout from the trees had degraded the transparency of Purvali's carrier, in spite of the unbroken efforts of the cleaning moles, but he could still watch her work. He had never understood why men like Kenzan Khan preferred women with limited abilities. Purvali was a delight in every situation he normally shared with her but she could seem achingly—*hauntingly*—beautiful when her face was shaped by the total concentration she focused on her work. Many people sank into slack-faced stupors when they stared at the displays their implants transmitted to their optic nerves. Purvali looked as taut as a hunting animal.

Choy was his usual loose-jointed self. Judging by the way his hands were moving, he was probably participating in a simulated unarmed combat spree while he monitored the security system. He had started chopping and blocking when they had finished the last feeding stop. He was still pummeling the air when they lumbered into the last kilometer that lay between them and the point the information system had chosen for their next stop.

"Twelve years ago," Purvali said, "Possessor Avaming was loading the databanks with descriptions of his buildings and remodelings. Six years ago he had thirty musicians on his payroll and he was bombarding his friends with invitations to concerts. Now he's started spending whole tendays racing up and down the lake pursuing the larger members of the yellow-feathered swordbeak population."

This time Purvali had assembled a concise formal report. Option One revolved around a new prey animal—a faster, sleeker version of the yellow-feathered swordbeak. The hunting fanatics had placed a few samples of the upgrade in the lake and they wanted to triple the number. Most of the other people with an interest in the lake had registered their opposition—on the very solid grounds that the increase would tip the competitive balance in favor of the enhanced swordbeaks, with the usual unpredictable consequences for the aquatic ecosystem. Avaming had joined the campaign to overcome the opposition but he was still a novice. If Sabor could help him arrange a victory, his status would take a substantial leap.

Sabor shook his head. He could offer Avaming a financial subsidy that would overwhelm the opposition. It wouldn't be the first time he had financed a little opinion engineering. But it would plunge him into a political situation that was just as unpredictable as the ecological effects.

Option Two was another play on Avaming's appetite for social status. Killing was only a part of the sport. To win the full admiration of your colleagues, you had to ride and slaughter with impeccable style. Avaming had bought the most expensive performance implants on the market, but the programs he had planted in his nervous system could only take him so far. To reach the highest levels of the sport, he needed a coach—someone who could teach him all the accepted nuances of true deportment.

"He's demonstrated he has an above average drive for social status every time he's surrendered to a new enthusiasm," Purvali argued. "His music mania included a series of private concerts that became some of the most sought-after invitations on the planet. Now he's applied to the hunting coach everybody wants. And she's treated him just like any other novice and put him on the bottom of her waiting list."

Sabor scanned Purvali's profile of the coach. He tipped back his head and stared at the light at the top of the forest.

"I believe it's time we committed to a higher risk level," Sabor said. "There are certain kinds of communication that simply can't be compressed into blips."

"It will take Colonel Jina's technicians about seventeen minutes to locate us," Purvali said. "We're now about three hours by airship from Colonel Jina's hangars. I can't find any indication they've positioned an airship in a closer location."

The coach's welcomer had been costumed in the kind of understated, scrupulously draped shirts Sabor's mother had favored. It had been shaped by one of the best known designers on the planet—a hard working stylist with several hundred thousand high earning yuris on deposit in Sabor's databanks. The coach would return Honored Sabor's call in approximately twenty minutes, the image informed him. The coach was Working with a Student.

The coach didn't list her fees in the databanks but Purvali had researched her life style and produced a reasonable estimate of her income. Sabor had decided a hundred thousand yuris would probably win him a fast acceptance. He raised his estimate by fifty thousand when he saw the designer's logo floating in the lower left of the display—and reduced it by twenty-five when the coach returned his call fifteen seconds after his system reminded him the twenty minutes had come to an end.

"I'd like to offer one of my better customers an impressive gift," Sabor said. "I'm prepared to pay a substantial fee."

He switched his display to a forty-five second recording of Avaming on seal back. "I'm no connoisseur of these things, but it seems to me Possessor Avaming may have some natural talent, in addition to his obvious enthusiasm."

The coach nodded and looked suitably thoughtful. "It's hard to make a proper evaluation from recordings, of course. I always evaluate my prospective students in person."

"I understand. I can offer you a hundred thousand yuris for your trouble. I'll be happy to transfer the whole amount in advance of your evaluation."

A familiar look flicked across the coach's face. She restored her air of cool indifference with a speed that made Sabor feel grateful he hadn't tried to offer her a few thousand less. "I should advise you Possessor Avaming has acquired several of the less obvious bad habits," the coach said. "He will have to demonstrate he is willing to relearn the basics."

An oversize text message from Purvali preempted the space next to the coach's head. *Your transmission is being examined. I can't defend it without interfering with your conversation.*

"I'm confident Possessor Avaming will welcome the opportunity to be evaluated by someone of your stature," Sabor said.

"Then you have my permission to tell him I can schedule an evaluation within the next three or four days."

Purvali replaced the coach the moment he terminated the call. "Colonel Jina seems to be making an all out effort," Purvali said. "I think we should assume he has us located."

"I wrapped that up in thirteen minutes!"

"They identified the call faster than I thought they would. They may have gotten lucky. But I'd feel better if we acted on the assumption they're making an extra effort."

"Do you have any information on Avaming's whereabouts? Is there any danger I'll be calling him while he's indulging in a sybaritic lunch?"

"Possessor Avaming is currently riding with the Benjori Hunt. He's been riding with them every fourthday since he first started hunting. The hunt left the dock about half an hour ago. I'm looking at the Recording Secretary's log. The hound seals are tracking a swordbeak that just went below for the first time."

Sabor added the secretary's log to his display. He was looking at the same view the hunters were receiving—a real-time composite created from the sensors in the hunters' water suits. A direct transmission from the hunters' optic nerves would have presented him with a useless image of murky lake water. The composite transformed the darkness into a vision of hunters and hound seals slipping through water that was so clear they could have been sailing across a cloudless sky.

"The average chase lasts about an hour," Purvali said.

"And then there's the traditional social rituals after the return to the dock. I should be able to call him in about three hours, right?"

"Yes. There's a hunt lunch followed by a ceremonial closure."

"Then I suppose I may as well tend to a few business matters."

"Can you limit your efforts to activities that don't require long transmissions?"

"I'll pull in one last download and settle for whatever distraction it can offer me."

The hunting seals sped through the waters in a portion of his display he located on the upper left quarter of his vision field. On the upper right quarter, images and numbers updated the situation on the north shore power delivery project. The trees and the incessant movement of the bird life provided an odd, clashing backdrop for both halves.

Five hundred thousand human beings now lived on Fernheim. In theory, they didn't need any kind of centralized power system. In theory, they could have fulfilled all their needs with the solar power panels that roofed most of their homes. The panels would have powered their fabricators and their fabricators would have provided them with all the essentials a rational human could possibly need.

In practice, of course, very few people were satisfied with the basics. In the average Fernheim household, the fabricators were sucking up energy five times faster than the average solar installation could supply it. The champagne Sabor had stocked in his carrier would have used up several days of the average individual's solar consumption. A proper standard of living, by most people's standards, required a proper energy infrastructure, complete with large-scale hydrogen-fusion reactors, orbiting power satellites, and all the other sources of energy human ingenuity had developed.

And, of course, a network of cables and wires that would deliver the energy to all the needy individuals who would be reduced to champagne-deprived poverty without it. In some societies the network would have been constructed by a government. On Fernheim, so far, nobody seemed to be interested in the tedious bickering—or outright violence—that normally preceded the establishment of a central government. The North Shore Energy Matrix was an exercise in long term speculation. Ninety percent of the people in the lake community—forty-five percent of the population of the planet—lived on the south shore. The entrepreneurs behind the north shore project were assuming a power network would pull new arrivals and restless current residents to the unterrestrialized wilderness on the other side of the lake. The profits would come tomorrow, the big expenditures had to be paid today. Obviously, a competent, upright scion of a famous banking family had to wave his wand and place the necessary numbers in the appropriate accounts. And watch every move the North Shore Development Association made. In exactly the same way his mother would have.

He had been nine when his mother's personal assistant had given him his first overview of the family business. We are a profit making enterprise, BanarJar had intoned. But we fill a social role. Bankers are the functionaries who allocate the capital resources of society. A progressive society must invest some of its resources in enterprises that increase its future wealth. We are the people who decide which enterprises will be cultivated. Governments can do that, too, but we operate under a socially valuable restraint: we forfeit some of our own wealth when we make bad decisions.

The hunting seals cornered the yellow-feathered swordbeak in a shallow cove near the south end of the lake. The meals-and-recreation charts on the North Shore display produced two numbers that looked like they warranted a request for more information—a request he would transmit primarily as a reminder he was performing his fiduciary duties. The monotonous tramp of the widemounts carried them from the trees and birds in one section of the forest to the almost-identical trees and birds in another section.

Sabor's information system pipped. "You have a message from Heinrich Dobble."

"Display."

Heinrich's recorded image replaced the North Shore display. "I've been advised Colonel Jina has dispatched two helicopters in your direction, Sabor. They were one hundred kilometers southwest of his hangars about ten minutes ago."

"They could be close enough to start running a search pattern in about forty minutes," Purvali said. "They'll be operating at the limits of their range."

Sabor grimaced. "We are reminded once again of the hazards of assuming you can predict your adversary's intentions. Is there any possibility the second copter is carrying fuel?"

Purvali paused just long enough to let him know he had impressed her—a reaction that always evoked a spurt of ridiculously irrational masculine pleasure.

"It could be. Kenzan Khan could have hired one squad. And spent the savings on the copters."

She paused for another ten seconds. "The second copter can carry enough fuel to keep both of them in the area for seventy-two minutes maximum. They could stay longer, of course, if the tanker could find a spot to put down."

Sabor stared at the transmission from the scene of the hunt. Possibilities flooded through his brain. The helicopters couldn't hover above their location and drop Colonel Jina's staffers directly on top of them. The anti-material loads in their guns made that a foolhardy move. The ground troops would probably land a few hundred meters away and pursue them on foot. If one of the copters was a tanker, and it found a spot to sit down, the copters could stay in the area and give the foot soldiers a mobility that could be decisive. . . .

"I'm beginning to feel my training in military tactics hasn't been as extensive as it should have been," Sabor said.

"They probably don't have our exact location," Purvali said. "They probably know where we are to within about thirty kilometers."

Sabor placed a small map on his right display area. The random movements dictated by the system had veered them closer to the Ratagava River. They were now about twenty-five kilometers from the river bank. Should they turn away from it? The widemounts could traverse the fords marked on the map but they would be crossing a river that harbored some of the less pleasant representatives of the aboriginal fish and feather community.

He gave the system an order and it generated a course that took them almost due east—directly toward the river.

"We'll obey the fates one more time," Sabor said. "Colonel Jina may assume we'll be avoiding the rivers—going where he can't corner us against the river bank."

The security system picked up the two helicopters as the copters slipped across the forest from the northeast. Both machines seemed to be steering toward the center of the logical search area.

The widemounts had just begun their hourly rest period. Choy thought they should let the animals have a good feed and Sabor concurred. "They won't be widening the search this far for another hour," Choy said. "It may be our last chance to give the animals a solid refueling."

Choy was scanning in one second bursts at random intervals spaced four to eight minutes apart. The system didn't register another blip until he made two more scans. The copter was just about where it should have been if it had been executing the search pattern Choy had predicted.

"They have to be refueling." Purvali said. "They couldn't be running that kind of pattern if they weren't refueling."

On the hunt display, the hunters were riding toward their dock with a piece of the swordbeak's flesh speared on each lance. The hunters had conducted their final, single-handed rushes at the swordbeak with a stately, ritualized formality but the kill itself had been a blood spattered fury of massed lance thrusts.

"It's going to take them another half hour to reach the dock," Purvali said. "Are you sure you can't contact Possessor Avaming now? Don't you think he may be very aware he was one of the people who didn't receive any applause when he made his final attack? Isn't it possible that might make him exceptionally receptive, Sabor?"

"It's too risky," Sabor said. "He could shut me off in a second if he decided he had to let me know I'm dealing with someone who truly understands style. I'd never get another chance."

The info from Choy's display appeared in front of Sabor. A helicopter symbol occupied the northeastern quadrant. A vector line indicated the copter was traveling in their direction.

"It's abandoned the search pattern," Choy said. "They've probably located us. Shall I keep the radar active?"

"We might as well stay informed."

They heard the rattle of the copter's engines when the display placed it about a kilometer behind them. It closed to a hundred meters and the symbol stopped advancing.

Choy had hung four cages on the side of his widemount. The

top of one of the cages flipped up and a white bird flapped toward the treetops. Choy paused the bird just above the canopy, where its color would blend with the leaves, and copied its transmissions to Sabor's display. Three of Colonel Jina's hardbodies were executing a classic rope descent from the copter. A guard cat was being lowered in its harness.

"It looks like he's opted for a quick-victory, low-personnel budget," Purvali said. "Two copters. One eight man squad and six cats. Eight cats if you limit the squad to hardbodies—which would probably be the optimum configuration for a combat unit under these conditions."

"It should take them about five minutes to lower the soldiers and their cats," Choy said. "I'm placing five of our cats between them and us. The other three will watch our front and flanks."

Purvali added her consultant's edge to her voice. "I recommend we launch a counter attack. While they're vulnerable. I can go back and try for the copter. Our cats can attack them while they're unloading."

Sabor frowned at the display. The three hardbodies had already slipped beneath the canopy. A second guard cat tumbled out of the door and he watched it start its descent.

Purvali was the logical person to try a ground to air shot. Choy was the security expert but he was operating the cats. And the rest of the security system.

"The copters have to operate together," Purvali said. "A hit on the troop hauler should drive both of them out of the area."

"Attack with the cats, Choy. All five. Try to do as much damage to their cats as you can. Don't waste effort on the humans."

"You can always negotiate for me afterward if I get unlucky," Purvali said. "You can't do anything if they capture you."

She had already picked up her weapon and raised the side of her carrier. Her feet were resting on the top step of the dismounting ladder.

"We won't get another opportunity like this, Sabor. We can't afford to waste it."

A third cat dropped out of the copter door. "If my estimate is correct," Purvali said, "they're going to deploy eight hardbodies and eight cats against eight cats and one financier with two assistants."

"Give them one burst," Sabor said. "Just one. And get back here."

Purvali dropped to the ground as if she had just been told she could run outside and play. The trees and the underbrush came between them before she had taken five steps.

Choy added an overhead map view to Sabor's display. Five blue cats were racing toward the area under the copter. There would be no feed from Purvali. They had to assume someone was sitting in the helicopter monitoring their transmissions.

Three red cat heads appeared on the display. Four red circles marked the positions occupied by the hardbodies who had reached the forest floor. Choy disregarded his instructions—quite rightly, Sabor realized—and directed two of his cats at the red circles. The cats couldn't attack the other team's cats if they were paralyzed by moles from the enemy guns.

Three of Choy's cats converged on one of the red cat heads. Slashing, snarling cartoon animals replaced the blue cat symbols.

Sabor had split the right side of his display top and bottom, with the map on the bottom and the image of the copter on top. The hardbodies on the ropes ripped their guns off their crossbelts as if they were conducting an exercise in simultaneous movement. They twisted around on their ropes and aimed their weapons one handed. The muzzles were all pointed in the same general direction.

On the map view, a grinning cartoon cat clasped its hands over its head. The basic blue cat symbols replaced the cartoon and sped away from the landing site.

"We crippled one of their cats," Choy said. "I figured that was good enough. Run in, do some damage, get out before we lose anybody."

"Quite right. My sentiments exactly."

Something glistened on the upper half of the copter. Choy zoomed in. The side of the copter filled the upper half of Sabor's display. The metal seemed to be covered with a thin film.

"I think she hit a fuel tank," Choy said.

Choy pulled back the view. Cats were rolling out the door of the copter. Two hardbodies leaned over the side and grabbed at the ropes that were already being used. The hardbodies who were already hanging on the ropes were still firing at the point they had selected.

Choy's cats formed a defensive line thirty meters behind the widemounts. Sabor twisted around on his pillows and peered into the forest. Purvali's carrier blocked a third of his view. Her wide-mount eyed him with bored indifference.

His mother had warned him. *Are you sure you should ask for a woman like that, Sabor? Remember—you are asking for someone who has all the qualities you find most attractive. You are asking for someone who will draw the maximum response from your own personality structure. You will be in control of the situation in one, very limited, sense. She will love you. She will want to please you. But can you control the emotions she will arouse?*

There had been times when his mother had contented herself with male concubines. For her, they had obviously been a respite from the masculine storm centers that normally diverted her. She would never have requisitioned a concubine who could engage her deepest hungers. Sabor's sisters seemed to feel the same way.

The side of Purvali's carrier swung up. She trotted around a tree with her gun held across her breasts and hopped onto the ladder.

"Did I do any damage? Could you see if I did any damage?"

Sabor's widemount swayed underneath him. Choy had started them moving again without waiting for instructions.

"We think you hit a fuel tank," Choy said. "They're dumping people and cats like the copter crew is very anxious to get out of here."

Sabor rose to his knees inside his carrier. "I told you one burst! You disobeyed me. You disobeyed a clear instruction."

"They couldn't see me. I had plenty of cover."

"They knew where you were. I could see it. They had every gun trained on the same position."

"They had a general idea. Just a general idea. I was surrounded by leaves."

"How many hits did your armor have to absorb?"

Purvali lowered her eyes.

"How many?"

"I quit when it told me it was approaching its limit."

"Two more hits! *Two more*. That's all it would have taken! *Two hits*. And you'd be in their power right now."

"I hit their fuel tank, Sabor. They're sending the copter back! We won't have to worry about airlifts and air attacks. I evaluated the situation and balanced the risks—the danger they might capture me versus the danger we'd be in if they kept the copters in the area. I was the one who was there. I could see I was in a good position."

Sabor returned his attention to his display. Purvali's pleading face disappeared behind the three segments of his montage. The scout bird was fluttering through the upper reaches of the trees and picking up glimpses of the force gathering behind them. Choy's map showed him the positions of their cats and the estimated positions of their adversaries.

The members of the Benjori Hunt were riding up to their home dock with their mounts pressed into a tight, two-file formation. Four servants were waiting for them behind a table crowded with glasses and champagne bottles.

"I suspect an analysis of our situation may be in order," Sabor said. "How much time do we have before Colonel Jina's bravos wear down our defenses with their unsporting superior numbers?"

Purvali focused on the images floating in front of her eyes. Concentration nullified the emotions that had been playing across her face.

"Our rest stops are our biggest problem," Purvali said. "We can stay ahead of them indefinitely. But they can catch up at our rest stops. And whittle away our defenses. The big variable is Choy's maneuvers with the cats. And the kind of luck he has."

Sabor skimmed the report she had placed on his display. The widemounts were faster but Colonel Jina's hardbodies had more endurance and the feedback from the sensors indicated they had ended up with six armed men supported by seven cats. They could stay on the trail indefinitely, close the gap at each rest stop, and concentrate their extra numbers on one or two cats at each stop. They could launch a final, irresistible onslaught as soon as they eliminated three or four of the guard cats.

"Colonel Jina tends to be a thrifty tactician," Purvali said. "I think we can be confident he won't launch a direct attack on our moving fortresses until he's thinned out our cats. We have to make sure he understands we're willing to kill his cats, Choy. He has to know he's going to lose some valuable assets if he attacks us too early."

A new set of simulations raced across the display. A diamond representing a figure with a gun entered the fray. The diamond darted through the woods with all the speed a certain very familiar woman could muster. A note at the bottom of the display reported the results. In 527 simulations, the addition of the extra combatant had added three extra march periods, on average, to the length of time they could stave off the inevitable.

"And how many times did our little diamond get captured?" Sabor asked.

"Almost none. I can break off combat any time the odds get too rough."

"But will you, my dear? Will the real life, vulnerable human being always have the good sense to retreat?"

"You're fighting for your freedom, Sabor. For your control over your own mind."

"And how free will I be if they take you hostage? You may not believe it, but if Kenzan Khan gets you in his unpleasant clutches, he'll have all the influence over my actions he could possibly desire."

The hunters of the Benjori Hunt chattered and gestured as they downed their champagne and bundled off the pier. They isolated themselves in private changing rooms and entered their dockside banquet hall in ceremonial costumes that draped them in white and red.

Colonel Jina's hunters were much more businesslike. Choy was monitoring them electronically, with supplemental glimpses from his visual scouts. On the map on Sabor's display, the hardbodies steadily fell behind but their speed never slackened. When Choy called for the first halt, the hardbodies were a little over one kilometer behind—about ten minutes marching time at their current speed. Choy deployed the cats in a defensive formation and Sabor watched the hardbody symbols move relentlessly forward.

"They're speeding up for the assault," Purvali said. "They're really driving themselves. Possessor Khan must be paying Colonel Jina something extra if the colonel's willing to inflict that kind of stress on his cadre."

The hardbodies and their cats followed the script predicted by Purvali's simulations. They concentrated three cats and four hardbodies on the cat at the extreme left of Choy's defensive line. Choy was faced with a classic dilemma. If the outnumbered cat held its position, it could be eliminated. If Choy pulled it back, the assault force could sweep around the flank and strike directly at the widemounts and their passengers. Choy responded by ordering two cats to the defense of the animal under attack. His other cats extended their line and took up defensive positions.

Sabor resisted the temptation to damp his stress reactions as he watched the tactical exhibition on his display. He knew he needed all the alertness his brain could muster. Visuals from the aerial scouts offered him flashes of the real life violence hidden under the symbols moving across the map. Cats leaped on other cats from ambush and disengaged after a flurry of bites and slashes. Hardbodies slipped through the forest with their guns searching for targets.

Sabor's widemount was demolishing a bush that was covered with thick leaves and dangling pods. The other widemounts were gorging on the local vegetation with the same concentration. Choy had thoughtfully placed a time strip on the map display, so Sabor could see how many minutes they had to wait before the rest stop ended.

Sabor decided to intervene when the countdown reached ninety seconds. "I think we should go now, Choy—if you feel you're in a position in which disengagement looks feasible."

Sabor's widemount raised its head from the bush. A huge snort jostled its frame. It turned away from its chosen collation and lumbered toward its place behind Choy's mount.

On the map display, Choy conducted a fighting disengagement that drew a flurry of claps from Sabor's hands. Colonel Jina's cats abandoned the fight and settled into their walking pace the instant it became obvious they had done all the harm they could for the moment.

"Those people know what they're doing," Choy said. "They didn't waste a calorie."

"You're doing a rather impressive job yourself, Choy."

"We've got two cats that took a mauling. I may have to sacrifice one of them at the next stop."

The hunters of the Benjori Hunt were sampling the fruits and dessert wines that had been arranged along the table. The camera drifted down the hall and Sabor saw Avaming busying himself with his food while the women on both sides of him chatted with other partners. The hunters rose from their chairs with their glasses raised and the Recording Secretary terminated the transmission with an image of a waving banner.

"So what does Avaming do now?" Sabor said. "Go home and recuperate from his endeavors?"

"I'm afraid I can't help you," Purvali said. "He doesn't seem to have a regular post-hunt schedule."

"Then it obviously might be best if we assumed he's in a receptive mood. Will you advise his welcomer I've been talking to one of the better known hunting coaches and I have some information that he may find of interest? Phrase it in your own irresistible style, of course."

Sabor's time strip clicked off the minutes while he waited for Avaming's reply to his call. The widemounts plodded through a complete, forty-five minute march segment. Purvali expressed her disgust at the "affectations" of an "outmoded class."

"He's taking about as long as I thought he would," Sabor said. "Moneylenders have to be treated with a certain condescension. We belong, after all, to a coterie that devotes most of its conscious hours to the pursuit of mere wealth."

Avaming's welcomer was an off-the-shelf female figure. She was so undistinguished Sabor was confident Avaming had spent hours searching for a design that would impress his callers with his total indifference to trivial matters such as the way his welcomer impressed his callers.

"Possessor Avaming has advised me he is now available, if you're still interested in talking to him."

"Please advise Possessor Avaming I'm still interested."

Sabor's widemount had once again settled its bulk in front of a large bush and started grinding leaves and branches between its molars. On the map display, the hardbodies were making another run at the defensive line Choy had formed with the cats. They had split into two groups. The larger group—three cats and five hardbodies—was driving toward the left flank of Choy's line. The other group was obviously supposed to harass the center and keep it occupied. It had been six minutes since Choy had called the rest stop.

Avaming had exchanged his ceremonial finery for a loosely belted lounging robe. He received Sabor's gift with a superbly aristocratic response: he recovered his control of his facial muscles seconds after he heard the news and he immediately offered to return the favor.

"That's a most generous gift," Avaming said. "I must admit you've quite taken me by surprise, Honored Sabor."

"It's our pleasure, Possessor."

"I hope there's something I can do for you. I would be embarrassed if there wasn't."

"There's no reason for you to be embarrassed. The opportunity happened to come to my attention and it seemed like the appropriate thing to do, given the fact that your deposits have made such an important contribution to the capital formation that keeps our planetary economy functioning. You and your colleagues have created a tradition that sets a high standard of courtesy."

"But there must be *some* way I can display my appreciation," Avaming said. "I realize the theorists are undoubtedly right. We large landowners will eventually be supplanted by the masters of capital, just as our counterparts were on Earth. But that day hasn't come yet. We still have some influence."

The three enemy cats had located one of Choy's mauled cats and ganged up on it. Choy inserted a transmission from the cat's optic nerve in the upper left corner of the map display. The cat rose to all fours seconds before three furies leaped across the bushy fallen tree it had been using for cover. The glistening black skin of the cat's assailants filled its visual field. Trees and sunlight rolled past its eyes as it tipped back its head in response to the wounds it was receiving.

Choy had placed another cat where it could act as a reserve. It popped out of its hiding place ten meters behind its doomed teammate and Choy switched to a direct transmission from its nervous system. Sabor peered through its eyes as it bored toward the heaving bodies in front of it. It lunged at the hindquarters of one of the enemy cats and apparently closed its jaws around part of a leg.

The display shifted to map-and-symbol mode. The symbol that represented the second cat broke contact and angled away from the fracas.

I think we should go, Choy transmitted.

Sabor's fingers danced across an imaginary keyboard. *Go.*

"As a matter of fact," Sabor said, "I have been thinking about a problem I have. I discovered your interest in the aquatic chase, in fact, when I was researching the problem."

"Feel free to tell me what you need."

"I believe you and Possessor Makajida have had some disagreements."

"You could say that. I think most impartial observers would inform you we're not on the most cordial of terms."

"As you may be aware, his military forces are somewhat smaller than normal at this moment. He has rented about fifty of them to another Possessor. It would be very helpful to me if you could place some of your military personnel on your southern border—enough that he would feel he had to bolster his own defenses."

Avaming smiled. "As I understand it, he's rented his soldiers to Kenzan Khan."

"That's my understanding, too."

"I can see how that could be of value to you, Honored Sabor. I've received two rather boastful messages from Kenzan."

The widemounts had trudged away from their feast and settled into line. The cats that had attacked the left flank were sweeping toward the widemounts unopposed. Had Choy realized the cats would move that fast when he had made his tactical calculations? Did he really think the widemounts could pull away from the cats before the cats closed in. . . .

"As a matter of fact," Avaming said, "I've been thinking about conducting an alert exercise. There's no reason why it can't take place on my border with Possessor Makajida."

Avaming smiled again. "I would have to notify Possessor Makajida I was conducting an exercise, of course. I wouldn't want him to misunderstand my intentions."

Sabor smiled back. "That would certainly be the most prudent way to go about it. I hope you'll be able to schedule it soon."

"I'll get onto it as soon as we terminate this call. I gather it would be most helpful to you if it were done promptly."

"That could make a significant difference, Possessor."

"Consider it done. I'm only sorry you didn't ask for something that required more of my resources."

The enemy cats had dropped back to marching speed. The tactician on the other side had earned another burst of applause from Choy. The cats had aborted their attack at the first sign the widemounts were pulling ahead.

"Our widemounts have now lost six minutes of refueling time," Choy said. "Four this feeding period, almost two last period. I can't keep them moving at their maximum pace if they don't get a full feeding period soon."

"We have no idea how long Possessor Avaming is going to dally," Purvali said. "I can understand why you didn't want to give him any sense of the time constraints we're working with. But he could spend the next three hours wandering around his domains admiring his building projects."

"He said he would get on it as soon he terminated the call, Purvali. I'm inclined to think he will—given his personality structure. I should also note that we aren't the only combatants who are testing their limits. Our pursuers are driving themselves, too. As you yourself have advised me."

Sabor turned his attention to the material he had downloaded from the databanks. Now that they were being pursued on the ground, he could assume their pursuers knew where they were. He could transmit and receive without worrying about security. He could turn away from all the stresses and tensions of their situation—including the tensions Purvali was creating—and lose himself in profit projections, trading opportunities, brilliant-but-unworkable ideas for new projects, gossip that might tell him something about the character of possible customers, and all the other details that made his working life so endlessly fascinating. He had never understood people who thought "getting and spending" was an empty way to fill your days. The numbers and facts in his databanks absorbed him in the same way the interactions of individuals fascinated dramatists and the intricacies of natural systems fascinated ecologists.

He could probably claim, in fact, that he had a better understanding of human relationships than most of the creative minds who had tried to depict them. A dramatist's errors might be overlooked by some segments of the audience. His cost him real purchasing power.

He kept on working after they stopped for the next fueling period. He didn't call up Choy's displays until the halt had reached the five minute point. This time Choy deliberately left one flank wide open. Choy's opposite number committed his forces to an all out attack on that side and Choy responded with a precisely timed counterattack. Three of Choy's remaining cats threw themselves into a melee in which they were hopelessly outnumbered. Choy lost one cat but he achieved his immediate objective. The widemounts placidly completed a full fifteen minute feeding.

"Quite good, Choy," Sabor said. "You had that timed to the second."

He waited for a nag from Purvali but she apparently decided to fume in silence.

Choy now had six cats left. He grouped four in a loose formation in the center the next time they stopped. The other two were positioned further out, one on each flank.

The opposition came in fast, in an attack that seemed to be spread across Choy's entire front. Then, just when Sabor thought they were committed to a straightforward linear assault, they behaved like the kind of highly trained, purpose-shaped soldiers they were. Four hardbodies and four cats coalesced into a compact mass and started a wide swing around Choy's right flank.

Choy responded by detaching two cats from his central formation. They joined forces with the cat he had placed on the right flank and the three animals raced toward an intersection with the assault party.

"I need a decision," Choy said. "I can put up a strong fight when they make contact, gain us three or four extra minutes of feeding time, and probably lose one cat. Or I can put up a weak fight, hold them off just long enough for us to get moving, and probably save all the cats."

Sabor scowled. The widemounts had accumulated about eight minutes of browsing time.

"Recommendation?" Sabor said.

"I can't make any," Choy said.

"Light resistance."

It was a random decision. He said the first thing that popped into his head and hoped he could live with it. Choy started the widemounts moving, Choy's cats engaged in a brief flurry of action—and a shot from a hardbody reduced one of the cats to a set of rigid, totally paralyzed muscles. They had sacrificed several minutes of feeding time and lost a cat, too.

"Not my most brilliant decision," Sabor said.

"I'm sorry," Choy said. "I thought I could save the cats."

"You're working with percentages, Choy. You make your bet and accept the results."

He returned his primary focus to the databanks but it had become a pointless exercise. Information flowed across his brain like water washing across a stone floor. Nothing penetrated.

They were down to five cats. The next feeding period could be the last. Choy might be able to stave off a breakthrough one more time but it was a fifty-fifty proposition—at best.

A blinking prompt advised him Purvali's carrier had come open. He ordered it closed and received an immediate *not responding*.

"You seem to have a problem with your carrier, Purvali."

"You have two options, Sabor. You can give Choy permission to integrate me into his tactical schemes or you can make me fight on my own."

"Please remove the pillow or whatever it is you're using to jam your carrier open. I've already given you my decision."

"And how are you going to stop me? I can drop off this animal and be lost in the trees before you or Choy can touch the ground."

He could give her an order, of course. But would she obey it? He asked her designers for a concubine, not a robot. He had her loyalty and her devotion. For machine-like obedience he would have to console himself with the companionship of machines.

"Don't do this to me, Purvali. Please."

"You're rolling the dice, Sabor. That isn't good enough. Not when your survival is at stake."

"I have been running simulations," Choy said. "I have a suggestion you may find worthy of consideration, Sabor."

"I would be a fool if I didn't consider your suggestions, Choy."

"The simulations indicate we could probably lethal two or three of their cats at the next rest stop if I employed Purvali as a surprise ambusher. The risk to her would be minimal. She would only have to expose herself for a few seconds—just long enough to fire at their cats when I told her to."

"Look at the simulations," Purvali said. "Just look at the simulations."

"Show me the simulations, Choy."

A summary popped onto Sabor's display. Choy's program had run five hundred simulations. They had killed one cat in twenty-seven percent of the simulations, two in fifty-four percent, three in thirteen percent, and none in six percent. There had been no simulation in which Purvali had been captured or injured.

The display zipped through a random selection of quick-play runs that included samples with all four outcomes. Choy had conscientiously included all the unknowns he and the program would have to work with during a real attack. There would be important blanks, for example, in Choy's knowledge of the terrain. He wouldn't know the location of every tree trunk and the sight lines it would interrupt.

"An impartial observer might note that you've left out one important factor," Sabor said. "You're assuming Purvali will obey your orders with scrupulous precision. If you included the possibility she might dally for a few seconds before she retreated—in the hope that she might be able to kill two of their cats instead of just one, for example—the outcomes of some of those simulations might have been less acceptable."

"You are running out of time," Purvali said. "You'd be running out of time even if Possessor Avaming called you right now and told you he's kept his word. How long will it be before Possessor Makajida reacts to the news he has a hostile force threatening his borders? It could take him hours, Sabor."

Sabor eliminated Purvali's face from his display. He scowled at a block of text that summarized the current financial status of the second largest mobile submarine restaurant on the lake.

"Whatever happens," Sabor said, "I'm obviously not going to have any peace until I let you prance around the forest. Take care of her, Choy."

He watched her as she made her preparations. She fired her gun at a passing tree. She recharged her armored coat. She slipped into a relaxed meditation state and gave herself a half hour nap.

She dropped to the ground as soon as Choy brought the widemounts to a halt. Choy positioned her on the left flank and removed her symbol from the map display. Choy would track her movements with his memory. There would be no possibility the opposition could pick up a stray transmission.

Sabor raised the side of his carrier. Cold air bit at his cheeks. He couldn't watch Purvali's movements on the display but Choy furnished an explosion graphic when she shot the cat that was leading the assault on the left side. Another graphic announced a hit on a second cat. Choy transmitted a command and the widemounts backed away from their food sources.

Purvali raced out of the woods with her eyes focused on her goal. She leaped for her mounting ladder when she was a full stride away from her widemount. She pulled a pillow into position and lowered the side of the carrier as she rolled inside.

Sabor jumped away from the tree he had been using as a cover. He grabbed the pillow and threw it at the ground. A command shot out of his brain. The lock on the carrier returned the appropriate signal.

He ran to his own widemount without waiting for Purvali's response. On the display, the hardbodies called off their attack and let the widemounts widen the gap once again.

Sabor switched to the view from his rear camera. Purvali had folded her arms across her breasts. She was staring silently at the back of her widemount's head.

Sabor's system pipped. Possessor Avaming's stock welcomer replaced Sabor's pouting paramour.

"Possessor Avaming has asked me to inform you he has deployed thirty of his security personnel on the border he shares with Possessor Makajida. He has advised Possessor Makajida of his actions."

"Please convey my thanks to Possessor Avaming," Sabor said. "Please let him know I deeply appreciate his kindness."

He gave his system another order and it immediately put him in contact with a more ostentatious image—the muscular, thickly robed flesh-and-blood human male who served as Possessor Dobryami's welcomer.

"Good afternoon, Financier Sabor. May I ask your business?"

"I have some intelligence I would like you to convey to Possessor Dobryami. Please tell her I have reason to believe Possessor Kenzan Khan is about to lose the services of the fifty soldiers he is currently renting from Possessor Makajida."

Wrinkles creased the welcomer's square, manly forehead. "Is there any way Possessor Dobryami can verify this information?"

"I could give her the names of other people she should query but I think it would be best if I didn't. I suggest that she prepare to act on this development—if she wishes to act on it—and watch for evidence it is taking place."

The welcomer frowned again. Sabor could visualize the turmoil in his mind. This was not, obviously, a routine call from a routine caller.

The welcomer decided a terse nod would be the appropriate physical response. "I will advise her at once."

"I suggest you give the message your highest priority."

"I will include your request with my transmission, Financier."

Purvali had removed a scarf from her luggage and wrapped it around her head. Her hidden face and her straight body communicated the same message kilometer after kilometer, without a single change in her position, every time Sabor popped her image onto his display.

"You have a realtime call from Colonel Jina," Sabor's system announced.

Sabor glanced at his time strip. It had been forty-one minutes since Avaming had announced he was deploying his troops. "That could be interesting. Put the good colonel on. Copy to Choy and Purvali."

Colonel Jina flashed his unforgettable smile. "Good afternoon, Sabor. We're having a busy day, aren't we?"

"It's always good to stay active, colonel. What can I do for you?"

"I've been keeping track of the time you've devoted to rest stops. We will be resolving this situation the next time you're forced to stop for a feeding session—in about twenty minutes, by my calculation. You don't have enough cats to counter another assault and your widemounts don't have enough energy to outrun us."

"My assistant Choytang is in charge of our logistics. But I believe twenty minutes is a reasonable estimate."

"Kenzan Khan is determined to take you prisoner and acquire total control of your assets. It seems to me there should be some room for compromise. If you were to forgive all his current debts, for example, he would be in a position to borrow more capital from you and maintain the forces he needs to pursue his conflict with Possessor Dobryami. I would be happy to convey such an offer to him."

"Doesn't that create some conflict with your professional ethics, colonel?"

"I have several assets at risk. I would rather not lose them in an avoidable assault."

"They are all replaceable."

"But replacement takes time. And time has a financial value. As you, of all people, should know. The proposal I am making would be in everyone's interest, Honored Sabor."

"I have to think about time, too—the long term consequences. I would still be surrendering to extortion. I would be encouraging all the other ruffians who would find such actions appealing."

"It seems to me this wouldn't be the first time you have yielded to the threat of violence. You and your colleagues have consistently bestowed large loans and special rates on the more powerful possessors."

"No possessor has ever attempted anything this blatant. If we're going to discuss our mutual interests, it seems to me it would be in your interest to advise Kenzan Khan you aren't going to fulfill his contract. Your business, colonel—like all businesses—depends on a system for an orderly transfer of payments. In most societies, that infrastructure normally rests on the rule of law. We have not established such a rule here and we are therefore dependent on other means. But that doesn't mean you can live without the infrastructure."

"You are going to be taken. You will be captured. Your concubine and your assistant will be captured. You will be taken to Possessor Khan. Your minds and all your assets will fall under his control."

Sabor's fingers tapped out a silent message to Choy. *What's the maximum time you can keep the widemounts moving?*

Thirty-three minutes.

Do it. Postpone the next stop for as long as you can.

"Kenzan Khan is endangering a key social structure, colonel. Do you really want to live on a planet in which the banking system can be corrupted by anyone who controls enough soldiers?"

"I can only interpret that statement as the plea of a desperate man, Honored Sabor. You may call me any time you wish to discuss my offer."

The colonel's image vanished. Purvali's image leaped into the center of Sabor's visual field.

"It's settled," Sabor said. "I will not give Kenzan some kind of compromise. There will be no end to his demands if I do that."

He cut Purvali out of his display and started recording a message for Possessor Dobryami. "This is a follow up to the message I left with your welcomer, Possessor Dobryami. If you launch an attack on Possessor Khan's forces within the next forty minutes, I will reimburse you for the cost of any losses you sustain. The reimbursement will be based on the cost of an accelerated replacement at the fastest possible tempo."

A blinking light on the edge of his display announced a text message from Purvali. *I presume we can at least drape our widemounts in their armored blankets?*

The armored blankets had been rolled into telescoping cylinders and attached to the carriers. The cylinders would extend fore and aft on command and the widemount would be sandwiched between two blankets that extended along its sides from head to tail. The blankets would interfere with the widemounts' side vision and general maneuverability but their smiling adversary had made it clear they had to reorder their priorities.

"We'll lower the blankets when we make our rest stop," Sabor said. "Sooner if it looks like they're attacking the widemounts."

And how about me? I'm going to have a few problems shooting at our adversaries if you keep me locked inside my boudoir.

"We'll deal with that when the time comes."

You are being irrational, Sabor. Do you really think you'd be doing me a favor if you kept me alive just so I could spend the rest of my life as one of Possessor Khan's harem bodies?

"You have a real time call from Counselor Tarakelna."

"Put her on."

Counselor Tarakelna was the member of Dobryami's staff who handled most of her financial negotiations. She greeted him with her usual controlled, carefully measured smile and Sabor responded with his best simulation of his normal business façade.

"Possessor Dobryami examined your last offer, Sabor. She feels you're offering her a minor return on a major risk. You are asking her to attack before she is certain Possessor Kenzan Khan has lost his extra forces."

"I can assure you those forces are going to be returned to their owner. It should happen at any minute. If Possessor Dobryami accepts my suggestion, she will have soldiers in position, in Kenzan Khan's territory, when it happens."

"Possessor Dobryami believes the risk/reward ratio is higher than it should be. She feels a complete cancellation of twenty percent of her debt load would be more logical."

"Possessor Dobryami has been granted a major opportunity, Counselor. We both know it would be to her advantage to seize it."

"Possessor Dobryami fully understands the value of your information. But she feels she can take full advantage of it after she is certain Possessor Khan has lost control of his extra troops."

Sabor nodded. "I've been looking at her account data while we talk. You can tell her I can offer her a nine tenday stretchout—ninety days, starting now, with no payments of interest or principal."

Counselor Tarakelna frowned. She studied Sabor's face and he looked back at her blandly.

"I will advise the Possessor of your offer," Counselor Tarakelna said.

Sabor ordered the blankets dropped as soon as they settled into their next feeding stop. Choy formed the three passenger widemounts into a defensive triangle, with the cargo widemount positioned about thirty meters outside the triangle.

This time, Colonel Jina's emissaries slipped into a dispersed formation. Three of the hardbodies and two of the cats disappeared from the display. Elongated ovals indicated their estimated positions.

A text message from Choy flickered across the map display. *I am releasing all my reconnaissance birds. I gather I should consider this our last stand.*

"Pull out all the stops," Sabor said. "Maximum effort. Do or die."

Birds whirred out of Choy's cages. Symbols lit up on the map display. The hardbodies and their cats had formed a wide arc about seventy meters from Choy's triangle.

"I am being attacked by anti-material molecular missiles," Sabor's carrier announced. "My armor is responding."

"Our carrier's shells will dissolve in about ten minutes," Choy said. "We should counter-attack sometime before then. While our personal armor is still at maximum."

"Can we attack on the widemounts?"

"For a few minutes. They still have some short-term energy reserves."

"Hold off for as long as you can. Colonel Jina is obviously taking his time. The longer he takes, the better for us."

The display monitored the effect of the invisible rain falling on the carrier shells. The widemounts munched on whatever nourishment they could scavenge from their immediate surroundings. Choy's cats formed a tight formation between the widemounts and the snipers in the trees. Sabor shifted his attention between the display and the real world and tried to spot the hardbodies when they broke cover and fired.

"We have to get very physical when we attack," Choy said. "We have to break bones. We can't possibly overwhelm their armor before they overwhelm ours."

"I understand," Sabor said. "Try to avoid killing and irreversible damage. We'll leave that possibility in reserve—as a retaliatory threat if Colonel Jina starts thinking you and our female companion are expendable."

"Get ready to move out. Our carrier shells will dissolve in about one minute."

Sabor's widemount shifted out of the triangle. The three passenger widemounts formed a rough line and lurched toward the left end of the hardbody line.

"I'm going to attack the two snipers on the far left," Choy said. "The widemounts are our primary weapon. Concentrate on keeping low."

Sabor's carrier shell disappeared. A fog of fine particles blurred his image of the forest before the remains of the shell dispersed. Dishes and pillows slid off the platform that had formed the foundation of the shell. He stretched out flat on the platform, with a pillow between his head and the hardbodies, and noted that Purvali had acted like a sane human for once and engaged in the same maneuver.

Cats charged out of the trees. The three cats they had left screamed as they received the attack. A cat leaped at the head of Choy's widemount. Claws ripped bloody gashes in the widemount's skin. Choy raised his gun and fired into the animal's mouth.

Purvali yelled. Sabor turned his head and saw another cat pulling itself onto the back of Choy's mount. His hands reacted while his consciousness was still assimilating the situation. Four shots streamed into the cat. It reared on its hind legs, with its front claws reaching for Choy's head, and slid off the platform.

A command flashed out of Sabor's brain. His information system dispatched a message to Colonel Jina.

"We are avoiding inflicting irreversible damage on your expensive assets, colonel. I would appreciate it you would render my assistants the same courtesy."

He had been bargaining and haggling all his life. The process apparently continued when you switched to non-monetary situations.

Choy's platform rose half a meter. Sabor turned his head and realized his own widemount was sinking. He checked his display and discovered the widemount's armor had been overwhelmed. The hardbodies had apparently been concentrating their fire on their ultimate objective.

"Get on my platform," Choy said. "The extra widemount is right behind us. We'll continue the attack."

Sabor scrambled onto Choy's platform. He checked his personal armor and discovered he had only absorbed two hits. He had kept his head and stayed low when he had fired at the cat attacking Choy.

"This is rather exhilarating," Sabor said. "Isn't there some saying about war being the continuation of diplomacy by other means? Should we assume the same maxim can be applied to financial activities?"

They were now about five paces from the point they had been driving toward. The two hardbodies in front of them were holding their position and pouring moles into the four-legged fortresses bearing down on their position. On the display, symbols marked the places where the other hardbodies were firing from Sabor's right.

The fourth widemount pushed into the gap created by the loss of Sabor's animal. Choy gestured at its back and Sabor slid off Choy's widemount and flattened himself on top of the bin that hung from the cargo animal's side. His right hand tightened around a braided cable.

"You have a message from Heinrich Dobble."

"Run it."

Heinrich's image rose between Sabor and the action at the front of Sabor's visual field. "Dobryami has crossed the border, Sabor. My sources advise me she has forty soldiers advancing through Kenzan's possession."

Sabor reacted without missing a breath. "Message for Financier Zara Nev. Apply simulation seven. Text: I believe it would be in your best interest to reconsider your position and join our common stand against Kenzan Khan's attempt at extortion. Kenzan is doomed. Possessor Dobryami has taken advantage of Kenzan's current weakness and invaded his possession. She is not in a negotiating frame of mind. The total destruction of Kenzan's financial position is the most likely outcome."

Simulation seven was Sabor's cheeriest, brightest communications facade. He usually used it when he distributed invitations to informal gatherings.

Choy forced the three widemounts into a trot—a move that would probably drain any spare energy they still had left in their reservoirs. The two hardbodies started to fall back but they had waited too long. Choy and Purvali edged ahead of Sabor. Their widemounts lowered their heads. Broad skulls shoved against the two hardbodies. Choy and Purvali slid to the ground and leaped like a pair of dancers. They pulled themselves back on their widemounts—they couldn't have spent more than ten seconds on the ground—and Sabor stared at the two figures writhing in the organic debris that covered the forest floor. Both hardbodies had legs that had acquired an extra joint. Their weapons had been tossed into the trees.

Sabor's widemount ripped a mass of leaves and blossoms from the lowest branch of a flowering tree. Sabor could feel its back trembling underneath him. The other widemounts had become as motionless as mounds of dirt.

Five symbols raced across the map display. Jina's human staffers had broken cover and initiated their final assault.

Purvali and Choy jumped off their widemounts. "Use everything you've got, Purvali," Sabor said. "There's little point in trying to conceal your potential now. But please abide by the rules of engagement. No permanent damage."

He crawled onto the back of his widemount and fired half a dozen moles at one of the oncoming hardbodies. Purvali and Choy had dropped into on-guard crouches below him. The hardbodies were veering around trees and sailing over obstacles with a controlled, absolute silence that was a thousand times more unnerving than a chorus of battle cries.

The hardbodies could have split their forces. Two could have gone after Sabor while the rest tried to keep Choy and Purvali occupied. Sabor could have held off his assailants for a few seconds while his dedicated staff demonstrated their ability to deal with three-to-two odds, and the three of them could then have joined forces and completed a final rout of Colonel Jina's minions. Instead, the hardbodies clumped into a line as they approached the widemount and the entire group converged on Choy and Purvali. Jina's tactician had apparently gained some respect for the abilities Sabor's assistants brought into the arena.

Purvali's upper body swayed. She stepped toward an oncoming hardbody and made a small movement to her left. The hardbody twisted to follow her, she made another small movement—and suddenly she was positioned *behind* the hardbody, with her body leaning backward and the bottom of her foot slamming into his kidney.

Sabor had seen her make moves like that during training sessions. In actual combat, the spectacle had a power that transcended the excitement evoked by the kind of speed and grace her hyped-up physiology could attain.

His awe turned into horror within seconds. Purvali hooked her foot around the stunned hardbody's ankle and pulled him to the ground. She leaped half her height straight up and came down on his back. She kicked downward as she landed and hit him with the maximum impact. It was a lethal blow—an attack that would drive splintered bones into the heart directly under her heel. The shock wave forced through the hardbody's chest would probably rupture the heart if the puncture wounds didn't do the job.

Choy was defending himself against two hardbodies. One of his attackers jumped back and disengaged. Three silent demons turned on Purvali.

Sabor didn't need a message from Colonel Jina to advise him the rules had changed. He could see it in the way the three hardbodies held their hands as they closed. Purvali was fast and she was stronger than the curves of her body and the silkiness of her skin indicated. But she couldn't survive an attack from three purpose-nurtured soldiers who had decided they could remove an obstacle without fretting about the damage they inflicted on it.

Sabor wedged his gun between a pair of cargo bins. He rose to a crouch and jumped, feet first, on the hardbody who was slipping behind Purvali's back.

It was an impulsive act but his body knew what it had to do. His boots slammed into the hardbody's helmet. His target shied away from him as the blow hit and he threw out his arms and grabbed at anything he could get his hands on.

His fingers dug into the hardbody's uniform. His left heel pounded on the hardbody's foot. It was a weak effort but it did the job. The odds against Purvali were reduced to two to one. It was only a momentary respite but it could be all Purvali needed.

Unfortunately, the hardbodies immediately realized he had placed their true objective in reach. The hardbody facing Choy abandoned his opponent and danced toward Sabor. The other two hardbodies slipped around Purvali. A hardbody twisted Sabor's arm behind his back. Three hardbodies formed a wall in front of him.

Sabor jerked his head toward Choy. "*Stop her. Don't let her attack. They'll kill her.*"

Choy stepped behind Purvali. He gripped her wrist and trapped her in the same kind of hold the hardbody was using on Sabor. Purvali tensed and then let herself relax.

"You'll just get yourself killed," Sabor said. "And I'll still be a prisoner."

"It's the only hope you have, Sabor. Why couldn't you stay out of it? We could have handled them."

The pain in Sabor's arm suddenly disappeared. The four hardbodies moved before his brain could adjust to the change in his situation. Choy tried to defend Purvali and a hardbody stepped behind him.

Colonel Jina smiled out of Sabor's display. "Good afternoon, Honored Sabor. We seem to have a change in the fortunes of war. Possessor Dobryami has occupied Possessor Khan's personal abode. It is now obvious Possessor Khan can no longer fulfill his contractual obligations."

"You've been a formidable opponent, Colonel. I'll be certain to recommend your services in the future."

"Your associate destroyed one of my most valuable capital assets. In spite of our agreement not to exceed certain limits."

"I'm afraid she has a tendency to become overzealous."

"I understand, Honored Sabor. Our relationships with the other sex can become difficult to control, in spite of our best efforts. But I think I'm entitled to some reasonable compensation."

"How much did you have in mind?"

Purvali straightened up. "Don't be a fool, Sabor! Pay him a ransom and you'll have to defend me against every hoodlum on the planet."

"We're not discussing a ransom," Sabor said. "He's asking me for compensation for the soldier you killed."

"He was trying to destroy you. They would have succeeded if I hadn't done that."

"She managed to destroy my asset because we were exercising restraint," Colonel Jina said. "We would have killed her before that if we hadn't accepted your bargain."

Data flowed across Sabor's vision. A hardbody could be replaced in approximately eleven standard years at a total cost of four hundred and sixty thousand Fernheim neils. Colonel Jina's estimated cash flow indicated each hardbody generated approximately fifty-four thousand neils per standard year. The lifetime of the hardbody was, of course, unknown, but one could estimate the cost of the maintenance required over an eleven year period and that, obviously, should be subtracted from the total cash flow. . . .

"I can offer you one million, four thousand neils," Sabor said.

"I believe you are underestimating the loss of business I may suffer. Every contract requires a carefully calculated number of personnel. If I need five hardbodies for one assignment, for example, and three for another, and I only have seven, I may be forced to refuse one of the assignments. According to my figures, I should ask you for at least one million, two hundred and fifty thousand."

Sabor studied the numbers the colonel presented him. "I really must point out that you're overlooking the interest you'll be earning each year on the unused portion. Your figure for lost employment seems a bit inflated, too, if you don't mind my saying so. But I'll offer you another hundred thousand anyway."

The colonel frowned. Sabor concentrated on the colonel's calculations and carefully avoided looking at Purvali.

"One million, one hundred and seventy-five," the colonel said.

Sabor hesitated. It was a large sum. His mother would have haggled for another hour just to keep a few more thousand.

"It's getting late," Sabor said. "If you'll agree to keep the whole sum in your account with my institution until it's paid out, I'll consider the extra hundred and seventy-thousand a small honorarium to a valued customer."

The hardbodies released Purvali and stepped back. Sabor gave his system a signal and one million, one hundred and seventy-five thousand neils jumped into Colonel Jina's account.

Colonel Jina beamed. "What other bank would I patronize?"

Sabor crossed the distance that separated him from his concubine. He put his arms around Purvali and felt her soften at his touch.

"You're a fool, Sabor."

She said the same thing again after they had struggled back to the guest quarters in the Galawar Commune and he had proved to his satisfaction (and hers, by all the signs) that he had successfully discarded his warrior mode.

"Is there any possibility," Sabor responded, "just the slightest possibility, you will ever realize you mean just as much to me as I mean to you? That you ignite—in me—exactly the same kind of feelings I provoke in you?"

"But I was designed to feel that way, Sabor. You have choices."

"Somehow, my dove, I never seem to feel I have a choice. And I am quite confident—annoyingly confident—I can offer you some assurance I never will feel I have a choice. *Never*. Not ever."

She would never fully believe him, of course. He could glance at her face and see that. But she was there. She was alive. His hand was resting on her stomach. His display was running projections of the demand/profit curve for the line of crabs the Galawar Commune was bidding on, assuming the most plausible ranges of the six most relevant variables. Sabor Haveri was focusing his attention on his two major interests.

A COFFEE CUP/ALIEN INVASION STORY

Douglas Lain

The UFOs in the sky over Portland look like hubcaps. Silver or chrome-plated saucers, all of them roughly the same size and all of them spinning, hang miraculously in midair, but most people either don't see them or pretend that they don't see.

It's a sunny day despite the patches of shadow the discs cast on the city. The sunshine finds its way through the gaps, bending along the sides of the ships and shining.

Down below, a young married couple, Alex and Shelly, share drinks underneath a cloth umbrella at the Blue Moon Pub. It's a hot day, and across the street, in a park squeezed into one quarter of a city block, there is a fountain bubbling away.

"Are we going to talk about it?" Alex asks.

Shelly knows exactly what the "it" is that Alex is referring to, but she just gives him a blank look and tips back her glass to take another suck on her last ice cube.

The UFOs have been up there for three weeks. At first the saucers were news everywhere. The same shot of a silver disc hovering over the White House dominated every television broadcast. But when nothing more happened, after administration officials appeared on the Sunday morning talk shows and denied that there had necessarily been an alien invasion, after the President called for more study, the cameras were turned back towards earth. By the end of the second week the saucers were no longer a serious topic of conversation, and now, at the end of the third week, most people barely remember that they are up there at all.

"Are we going to talk about it?" Alex asks.

"I don't know. I'm out of booze again," Shelly says.

* * *

Shelly is the name of a girl I knew in high school. I didn't know her very well, but I knew of her. I decided to use her name because I recently found out that Shelly is dead. She died several years ago, in a car accident. She was twenty-seven years old.

Shelly was a cheerleader when I knew her, and a member of the homecoming court. She was pretty and blonde and in my high school yearbook she's listed as a member of the Young Life Club, whatever that was. Shelly's Senior quote was a steal from the movie *Ferris Bueller's Day Off*: "Life moves pretty fast. If you don't stop and look around once in a while, you could miss it."

Alex is also the name of a kid I used to know. He was a friend of mine for years when I was growing up, but I lost track of him after he was institutionalized during our freshman year of high school.

Alex and his mother lived in a small apartment on Nevada Avenue, and she used to take in cats. They had about fifteen cats and kittens in their three-room home, and Alex always smelled of cat piss because of it.

In middle school Alex often spoke to me of suicide, so I wasn't really surprised to hear that he'd tried to do it. Not even when I heard that he'd reached over from the passenger seat of his mom's station wagon and tried to grab the steering wheel out of her hands. He was aiming for a telephone pole.

Alex and Shelly aren't unusual or strange. Being dead or disturbed are very ordinary things to be.

Last year, on July 4th, I spent the day at home with my wife and kids; we rented the 1978 version of *Superman*, the one starring Christopher Reeve and Gene Hackman. I watched the movie with the kids, and we all drank Coca-Cola and ate hot dogs. The only thing slightly un-American was the fact that the hot dogs were made of tofu because my wife is a vegetarian.

I tried to find the experience incongruous and ironic, but it was really just inevitable, even natural. I didn't want to celebrate the Fourth of July. I intended to let the war spoil the holiday, to ignore all the sparklers and flags. Instead, I watched Margot Kidder and Christopher Reeve fly over a beautiful New York skyline, over the Statue of Liberty.

"Why are you here?" Kidder asked.

"To fight for Truth, Justice, and the American Way."

"I don't believe this."

"Lois, I never lie," Reeve said.

"Are we going to talk about the saucers, or are we going to leave it to the people on television?"

"I'm relieved," Shelly says. She brushes her blonde hair out of her eyes, and smiles as she lies to him. "You start off with this cryptic question: 'Are we going to talk about it?' And I thought you were going to leave me or something."

"How could I do that? A love as true as ours?" Alex waves to the bartender, holds up two fingers in a victory sign and hopes that the bartender's nod indicates comprehension. Alex pushes back in his chair and lights up a cigarette as he waits for more gin. "You do see them, don't you?"

Shelly nods.

The bartender approaches their table with the drinks, but he's gazing at the sky. He looks down just long enough to avoid spilling their drinks. "What the hell are they doing up there? What do they want?" he asks.

"He sees them too," Shelly says.

"Everybody sees them."

"What are they?" the bartender asks.

"Nobody knows," Shelly says.

"Speak for yourself. I've got a damned good theory about them."

"What the hell are they?" The bartender is not listening; he's just repeating himself over and over.

"Looks like an alien invasion to me. That's my theory," Alex says.

Shelly takes a sip from her drink, and then a gulp. "Nobody knows what they are or why they're here. It's best not to speculate," she says.

"There are so many," the bartender says. "Just hanging there."

Alex and Shelly don't say anything more, but keep their heads down. They don't want to look at the saucers with the bartender. They want to keep their problems private.

Alex is plastered. He's fumbling around with his cigarettes, his neck is craned back as he stares at the flying saucers. He slumps forward to look at Shelly and takes a swig of beer. He's switched over to beer, ice-cold Pabst, and this gin and beer combination is churning a hole in his stomach. His belly lets out a low moan in nauseous protest.

Shelly is enjoying a Coca-Cola. She says she doesn't want to get drunk after all. It's not a good idea.

"Remember in *The Day the Earth Stood Still* when the aliens turned out all the lights?"

"I'm not even sure I see them. For me they're only there when I first get up, or if I wake up in the middle of the night," Shelly says. "I don't really see them when I'm awake."

Alex takes Shelly's hand. "Of course you see them. Just use your eyes. Look, see?"

Shelly shrugs, pulls her hand out of his sweaty grip, and takes another sip of her soda.

He sees them all the time, so persistently that the saucers don't surprise him anymore. This is what's really bothering him, what's really making his skin crawl. The ships are a miracle, a complete disruption of the routine, and yet, at the same time, they look exactly how he'd expect them to look. They fit, somehow.

"Did I ever tell you about my religious conversion?" he asks.

"You're an atheist."

"Yeah, but I was a Christian. Between my freshman and sophomore years in high school, when I was fourteen, I was Born Again. I was saved all summer long."

Alex takes a sip of Shelly's drink and then shrugs as he puts it back down on the table and grabs his own glass. He decides to start over.

"Is it even possible that people knew how to dream before television?" he asks.

"Before television?" Shelly asks.

"Yeah. How could it be? What did these prehistoric dreams look like? How were they edited?"

When he was a child Alex dreamt that he didn't exist, that he'd never existed. He was a blank wall, an empty space between the door of his parents' '82 VW station wagon and the car itself. He had nightmares that involved only darkness and a failed effort to speak.

"It wasn't until after I started watching TV in earnest, shows like *Zoom* and *Sesame Street* every day, that I could dream properly."

Alex is stirring his beer with the green straw from his gin and tonic; he's sweating and he pushes his hair off his brow, reveals just how far his hairline has receded. He takes a sip through the plastic straw and grimaces. He removes the straw.

"I had a conversion experience like a dream, while I was watching television," Alex says. "I changed channels from MTV to HBO, and caught the beginning of the Home Box Office promotional film. This family was gathered in their living room, and the father rose from the couch and turned on the TV. He turned on HBO and for an instant there they were again, the family on television was on television, and the father on their television turned on the TV and there they were again, and so on to infinity. Just for an instant. And then the camera pulled back, up and back, through the chimney, over the rooftop, and into space."

Alex pauses, stares blankly, remembering what he'd seen. He refocuses on Shelly, tries to read her face to see if she's getting it.

"It was just a feeling. I think the word for what I experienced is satori," Alex says. "In literature the word would be epiphany."

In the HBO promo, the camera drew nearer to the UFOs and it became clear that what was really flying through space were three metallic letters: H, B, and O. Red, blue, and green lasers shot through the logo. The introductory segment came to a conclusion as the HBO craft filled the screen completely.

"I actually got down on my knees and prayed when the promo ended. I prayed to a John Cusack film. I surrendered to *One Crazy Summer*."

"You saw God in the logo for HBO?" Shelly asks.

"I saw God in everything, but the feeling went away. I got over it."

Shelly finishes her drink, tipping her glass back and then chewing on the ice in her mouth. She puts the glass down heavily, pushes her hair back behind an ear, and stares at her husband.

"For the past few weeks I've had that same feeling, only I know it isn't God this time."

"I need another drink," Shelly says. She looks down at the table and puts her hands around her empty glass.

"There's something else. Something I can do," Alex says.

"What something?"

"I'll show you." He stands up, brings his hands up over his head, and waves them around.

Alex starts humming, a sort of deep toneless hum, and he keeps his arms flailing. And slowly he rises up, he floats, until his tennis-shoe-clad feet are even with the tabletop.

"Get down." Shelly glances furtively into the restaurant window. "Stop it, I don't want to see this."

Alex has his eyes closed, his arms are spinning in circles, and the humming is getting louder.

"Alex!"

At the sound of his name he comes back down. He lands awkwardly, and then slowly picks himself up, and inspects himself. He looks for cuts and bruises.

"Nice one," Shelly says.

"Thanks."

"Really good," Shelly says.

"You're welcome."

In 1995 I attended a writers' workshop in Seattle. One of the instructors, a very fine writer whose work has won all sorts of awards, taught us that there are many different ways to write stories. There aren't any solid rules. Sometimes you can show too much and not tell enough, for instance. And sometimes you don't really need a plot, but you can just make a story out of two people sharing a cup of coffee or a pint of beer.

These plotless stories, he called them "*New Yorker* Cup of Coffee Stories," are subtle. All that happens is that a situation is set up, explained, and then two people sit down, share a cup of coffee, and through the course of their interaction the situation is changed. There is only a little movement, maybe just a millimeter. A millimeter is apparently enough.

In August of 2001 my sister-in-law visited Disneyland. She sent my kids Mickey Mouse ears as souvenirs and they arrived about a week before 9/11. So after the attack, while I was surrounded by flags and fear, while I was worrying about anthrax and the possibility of nuclear retaliation, my kids were constantly in their ears.

They kept asking me to teach them to talk like Mickey, kept asking me to pretend to be Donald Duck.

On September 12th we went to the park across the street from a Starbucks and the Blue Moon Pub, a little park that only took up a quarter of a city block. We stood and stared at the fountain. It burbled away. Water streamed out the mouth of a cement frog.

I didn't want to talk like Mickey Mouse so I pointed out the cement amphibian.

"The Native Americans thought that frogs were good medicine," I told the kids. "Cleansing medicine."

It was a bluff. I didn't know anything about Indian religions. I'd read a few books, but I didn't really know. I should have stuck with what was familiar. I should have given in to Donald Duck and Mickey Mouse ears.

"Frogs?" my son asked. "How can an animal be medicine?"

"I thought medicine comes from a store," my daughter said.

I didn't know how to explain it to them. How could an animal be medicine? Where do you find medicine if not in a store? I didn't really understand it myself.

Shelly puts down her drink and runs her fingers through her hair. She looks down at the table and grunts. She and Alex have been together since high school, for seven years. They moved in together right after graduation. They've only been married for the past six months, but before that there were six years; how could it turn out that they haven't known each other at all?

No. He's known her, but she hasn't known him, Shelly realises.

Back then Alex was a catch—tall and broad, a junior while she was a sophomore, and even though he wasn't on any teams he was strong and athletic. He was dangerous in a way that she couldn't define. He didn't do drugs, didn't get into fights, didn't really do anything normal like that.

"I'm always unhappy and out of control in school. I don't know how to act," Alex told her after his graduation, told her as an explanation as to why he hadn't applied to college.

"It's like you're free or something," Shelly said. During her sophomore year they were in the same physics class. She used to watch Alex when she should have been taking notes. It was in physics class that Shelly chose Alex. She picked him as her lab partner.

Doing the day's experiment with her, Alex grabbed one end of the Slinky and took off down the hall with it, past the freshman lockers, while she held the other end with both hands and watched the metal loops stretch. She watched him move. She liked the way he didn't seem to care about it, liked the way he held the coil with his thumb and just kept going.

When he got to the other end of the hall, when the Slinky was pulled as far as it could be pulled, Shelly kneeled down and slipped her end of the Slinky through the shoelaces of her sneaker. Then she stood up and stretched, the metal coil twisting down to her foot. She swept her long blonde hair back and rubber-banded it into a pony-tail. She used both hands to sweep back her hair, and then she jerked on her sweater to cover her navel. She used both hands to smooth out her skirt.

She knew he was watching her adjust herself, watching her preening. Fifteen feet of hallway separated them, but they were connected by a metal strand, a taut Slinky.

"I hear voices sometimes," Alex says. "Since the saucers showed up I can hear them. At least I think it's them."

"What do they say?" Shelly asks him now. She still loves him. He's still sexy and dangerous. He's more dangerous than ever.

"They say that it's our time," Alex says. "They talk about a change, it's time for the change."

"What does that mean?" Shelly asks.

"How am I supposed to know? I don't know anything. Why doesn't anyone see them? Why does the TV keep saying they're not there?" Alex says.

"What kind of change? What's going to change?"

Alex doesn't know. He takes another swig of beer and then he hums under his breath, a long, slow hum.

"Stop that," Shelly says. "Don't do that again."

"What should we do?" Alex says.

"I don't know. I don't hear voices," she says. "I can't float."

Alex finishes his beer and then leans over to her until they're nose to nose. "You just don't want to hear voices."

"What?"

"You just don't want to fly," Alex says. "So you pretend you can't."

Shelly lights a cigarette and then waves the smoke away, flaps her hand back and forth in front of her face. "Why wouldn't I want to fly?"

"For the same reason!"

"What?"

"Why don't people see the saucers? Because they're afraid," Alex says. "You're afraid. Well, don't you think I'm afraid? Do you think I understand anything? I don't understand anything! I don't know what to believe, and don't believe in anything."

Shelly takes another puff of smoke into her lungs and stares at him. She doesn't respond.

"I'm floating, you know?" Alex leans back in his chair. "I can't even keep my feet on the ground."

Shelly is waiting to use the toilet, standing in the polluted air inside the Blue Moon Pub; she wonders which she resents more, the saucers or her husband. She glances at the skyline through the plate glass windows at the front, she sees the spinning, flashing saucers, and she resents them, but she decides that she resents him more.

It must make Alex happy, she decides. There are UFOs and he's communing with them somehow, and it's just another way for him to feel superior.

She's waiting for the restroom, thinking of all the ways she resents her husband, when she starts to sway, unconsciously at first, to the music from the jukebox. Stan Getz's "Corcovado" is on and Shelly moves back and forth to the sound of Getz's sax. Shelly is dancing with her eyes closed. She wanders out of line, and when the song comes to an end she sits down in an empty booth. She leans across the aisle to get a cigarette from a kid in a backward baseball cap.

"Thanks," she says.

"Can I buy you a drink."

"Sure," she says. "Gin and tonic."

The kid waves to the waitress as he slides in across from Shelly. He lights Shelly's cigarette and puts his hand on her knee.

He's a pudgy kid with sideburns and a goatee. He couldn't be more than twenty-one years old, half a decade younger than she is, and doesn't look too bright. In fact he looks stupid and angry, but another Stan Getz song comes on the jukebox and Shelly is distracted again.

This time it's "The Girl from Ipanema" that fills the bar with sax.

Shelly lets the kid keep his hand where he wants it. She closes her eyes again and takes a long, deep drag from her cigarette.

"Where are you from?" she asks the kid.

"Wyoming."

"Yeah?"

"Where are you from?" he asks her.

"Me? I'm from Neptune," she says. "I just got off one of those ships up there." She points, her whole body moving languidly, towards the windows.

The kid takes his hand off her knee.

"I don't know what you're talking about," he says.

Shelly blows out a cloud of smoke, and winks at the kid before tipping back her gin and tonic.

"There aren't any saucers," the kid says. "You're crazy."

Shelly takes another good look at the kid; he's almost funny sitting there in his football shirt and baseball cap. He's almost sad. She stubs out her cigarette, and then stands up to leave. She doesn't need this, and besides, she's suddenly remembered why she came inside the bar to begin with.

"Tell me that there aren't any saucers," the kid says. He stands up and blocks her exit, won't let her leave the booth.

"I've got to pee," she says. "Get out of my way or I'll get your shoes wet."

"Say it!"

"I'm warning you."

The song is over, the jukebox stops playing, and the room is suddenly quiet. The room is quiet except for this fat kid breathing on her. "Tell me that there aren't any."

"There are no saucers," Shelly says. "Now let me go to the bathroom."

Inside the stall Shelly pees and then just sits there, staring at nothing. She's obviously drunker than she'd thought. She sits on the toilet, inert for the moment, and stares at the words somebody has scratched into the green paint on the stall door.

"When will we wake up?"

Shelly stares and stares, reads and rereads. Then she wipes herself, pulls up her skirt, and leaves the question behind.

This is a story about the New Normal, about life during wartime. It would be titled "UFOs and the End of the World" if I hadn't already written enough stories with the words "the End of the World" in the title.

Last December the Washington Park Zoo had a Christmas light display. These zoo lights were shaped like crocodiles, made into leaping frogs, giant dragons, swimming otters. There were millions of tiny light bulbs clumped together, strung along the trees, and everywhere.

It was raining hard, the night we went out to see the display. The kids were excited, but I just felt wet. The zipper on my jacket was broken, I'd left my umbrella in my cubicle at work, and while my wife and kids were wearing raincoats and hats, I had only my overcoat and my unruly mop of hair to protect me.

A light-up giraffe picked up a neon heart and swung it up into place on top of a neon Christmas tree. Then the lights went out, the giraffe and the tree disappeared, and there was a moment of darkness until the giraffe lit up again and the whole process started over. The giraffe picked up a neon heart from the ground, the Christmas tree appeared, and the giraffe placed the heart at the top. And again it happened. And again. Water poured down my face.

"It's the myth of Sisyphus as a Christmas display," I said. "That giraffe is cursed."

"What's Sissypus?" my son asked.

"Look, dancing hippos," my daughter said.

Electricity. Watching the decorations through the streamlets on my glasses I saw the light-up hippos, the light-up monkeys, as just another deception. Free electricity forever, and never mind the dwindling oil supplies, the wars, the nightmare of scarcity that was just around the corner.

We finally found shelter in the monkey house. We watched real ring-tailed lemurs pace back and forth in their concrete cells.

"That one is sleeping," my daughter said. She pointed to a nest on a metal perch. She pointed to the infant lemur sleeping there and asked why the zookeeper didn't turn out the light for the monkey.

"There is no night or day in the zoo," I said.

"There is too," my son objected. "It's nighttime now, so the monkeys are inside."

I admitted my mistake.

"But there is no such thing as darkness at the zoo," I said. "It's light every day, night and day, all the time."

"I want to see the Christmas lights," my daughter said.

The kids were mesmerized as we wandered back into the rain to look at the lights. All four of us stared and stared at the lights through the rain. In the middle of it all, with "Jingle Bells" playing from the snack bar, surrounded by lights, I was overwhelmed.

I looked at the front gate of the zoo, at the huge display of lights that loomed overhead. Red and green and orange and blue lights buzzing bright. I thought about the final scene in *Close Encounters*, about the book *Childhood's End*.

The whole world seemed like a flying saucer.

Shelly and Alex don't know what to say to each other. They're both drunk, tired, disengaged. The sky above their heads is still full of saucers, but it's getting more and more difficult to make them out. The sunlight is fading, and the Blue Moon's exterior lighting, the street lamps, the headlights and neon signs are on.

"What we have to accept is that we don't know what to do."

"What's that?" Alex asks.

Shelly starts to take a sip from her last gin and tonic, but then stops and swirls the drink around in the glass; she watches the reflection of the saucers. They're lighting up now, red and yellow and green, each craft glowing and pulsing.

"They look like radioactive M&M's," Shelly says.

Alex takes her glass away from her before she has a chance to take a sip, and sets it down on his side of the table.

"What should we do?"

Shelly doesn't answer, but takes Alex's hand in her own, makes him stroke her face. She likes the feeling of his warm fingers on her cheek.

"Are we going to talk about it, or what?" Alex asks.

"We can talk about it," Shelly said. "But we can't answer it. We can't keep trying to answer."

"But we can't pretend they're not there. We can't pretend this isn't happening," Alex says.

"It's happening. We know that much. Something is definitely happening."

The saucers above their heads are blinking on and off, off and on.

"Maybe they're sending out signals in Morse code," Alex says.

"And then again, maybe they aren't."

"What do you want to do?"

"I want to go home with you. To our home."

Both Alex and Shelly gather up their belongings, try to piece themselves back together under a sky dotted by neon saucers. She grabs her handbag and he helps her with her red wool coat. Brushing herself off and trying to stand steady, Shelly slowly reaches over to Alex and takes his hand.

Alex and Shelly leave the pub, make their way down 21st to Burnside, and Shelly holds Alex's hand tight, as tight as she can. She pulls on him, hard. But despite her efforts, he is floating. She holds his hand tight, but he's lifting off.

Alex feels his wife's firm grip and squeezes back, but he isn't thinking about her. He isn't thinking at all. He's watching the sky, the saucers.

Shelly pulls on him, tries to anchor herself with a tree branch, to dig in her heels, but Alex keeps rising, and when she feels her feet leave the ground Shelly gives up. She lets go.

Alex is rising fast. She watches him drift, calls out to him, but before she can find her bearings, before she can think of what to do, he's gone.

Shelly sits down on the pavement, stunned. She lies down across the sidewalk, stares up in the air to where Alex was last visible. She pulls her wool coat around her, and hums to herself, a low, long hum, though she's not aware that she's doing it.

Shelly doesn't move for a long time, but just lies there on the concrete, watching the neon saucers.

THE EDGE OF NOWHERE

James Patrick Kelly

Lorraine Carraway scowled at the dogs through the plate glass window of the Casa de la Laughing Cookie and Very Memorial Library. The dogs squatted in a row next to the book drop, acting as if they owned the sidewalk. There were three of them, grand in their bowler hats and paisley vests and bow ties. They were like no dogs Rain had ever seen before. One of them wore a gold watch on its collar, which was pure affectation since it couldn't possibly see the dial. Bad dogs, she was certain of that, recreated out of rust and dead tires and old Coke bottles by the cognisphere and then dispatched to Nowhere to spy on the real people and cause at least three different kinds of trouble.

Will turned a page in his loose-leaf binder. "They still out there?" He glanced up at her, his No. 2 pencil poised over a blank page.

"What the hell do they think they're doing?" Rain made brushing motions just under the windowsill. "Go away. Scram!"

"Scram?" said Will. "Is scram a word?"

Will had been writing *The Great American Novel* ever since he had stopped trying to prove Fermat's Last Theorem. Before that he had been in training to run a sub four-minute mile. She'd had to explain to him that the mile was a measure of distance, like the cubit or the fathom or the meter. Rain had several books about ancient measurement in the Very Memorial Library and Will had borrowed them to lay out a course to practice on. They'd known each other since the week after Will had been revived, but they had first had sex during his running phase. It turned out that runners made wonderfully energetic lovers—especially nineteen year old runners. She had been there to time his personal best at 4:21:15. But now he was up to Chapter Eleven of *The Great American Novel.* He had taken on the project after Rain assured him that the great American novel had yet to be written. These days, not many people were going for it.

"Where do dogs like that come from, anyway?" Will said.

"Don't be asking her about dogs," called Fast Eddie from his cookie lab. "Rain hates all dogs, don't you know?"

Rain was going to deny this, but the Casa de la Laughing Cookie was Fast Eddie's shop. Since he let her keep her books in the broken meat locker and call it a library, she tried not to give him any headaches. Of course, Rain didn't *hate* dogs, it was just that she had no use for their smell, their turds hidden in lawns, or the way they tried to lick her face with their slimy tongues. Of course, this bunch weren't the same as the dim-witted dogs people kept around town. They were obviously creatures of the cognisphere; she expected that they would be better behaved.

Will came up beside her. "I'm thinking the liver-colored one with the ears is a bloodhound." He nodded at the big dog with the watch on its collar. "The others look like terriers of some sort. They've got a pointer's skull and the short powerful legs. Feisty dogs, killers actually. Fox hunters used to carry terriers in their saddlebags and when their hounds cornered the poor fox, they'd release the terriers to finish him off."

"How do you know that?" said Rain, suddenly afraid that there would be dogs in *The Great American Novel*.

"Read it somewhere." He considered. "Jane Austen? Evelyn Waugh?"

At that moment, the bloodhound raised his snout. Rain got the impression that he was sniffing the air. He stared through the front window at . . . who? Rain? Will? Some signal passed between the dogs then, because they all stood. One of the terriers reared up on its hind legs and batted the door handle. Rain ducked from Will's side and retreated to the safety of her desk.

"I'm betting they're not here to buy happy crumbs." Will scratched behind his ear with the rubber eraser on his pencil.

The terrier released the latch on the second try and the door swung open. The shop bell tinkled as the dogs entered. Fast Eddie slid out of the lab, wiping his hands on his apron. He stood behind the display case that held several dozen lead crystal trays filled with artfully broken psychotropic cookies. Rain hoped that he'd come to lend her moral support and not just to see if the dogs wanted his baked goods. The terriers deployed themselves just inside the door, as if to prevent anyone from leaving. Will stooped to shake the paw of the dog nearest him.

"Are you an Airedale or a Welsh?" he said.

"Never mind that now," said the dog.

The bloodhound padded up to Rain, who was glad to have the desk between them. She got a distinct whiff of damp fur and dried spit as he approached. She wrinkled her nose and wondered what she smelled like to him.

The bloodhound heaved his bulk onto his hind legs. He took two shaky steps toward her and then his forepaws were scrabbling against the top of her desk. The dark pads unfolded into thick, clawed fingers; instead of a dew claw, the thing had a thumb. "I'm looking for a book," said the dog. His bowler hat tipped precariously. "My name is Baskerville."

Rain frowned at the scratches the dog's claws made on her desktop. "Well, you've got *that* wrong." She leaned back in her chair to get away from its breath. "Baskerville wasn't the hound's name. Sir Charles Baskerville was Sherlock Holmes's *client*."

"You may recall that Sir Charles was frightened to death by the hound well before Dr. Mortimer called on Holmes," Baskerville said. He had a voice like a kettle drum. "The client was actually his nephew, Sir Henry."

Rain chewed at her lower lip. "Dogs don't wear hats." She didn't care to be contradicted by some clumsy artifact of the cognisphere. "Or ties. Are you even real?"

"Rather a rude question, don't you think?" Baskerville regarded her with sorrowful melted-chocolate eyes. "Are *you* real?"

The dog was right; this was the one thing the residents of Nowhere never asked. "I don't have your damn book." Rain opened the top drawer of the desk, the one where she threw all her loose junk. It was a way to keep the dog from seeing her embarrassment.

"How do you know?" he said reasonably. "I haven't told you what it is."

She sorted through the contents of the drawer as if searching for something. She moved the dental floss, destiny dice, blank catalog cards, a tape measure, her father's medals, the two dead watches and finally picked out a bottle of ink and the Waterman 1897 Eyedropper fountain pen that Will had given her to make up for the fight they'd had about the laundry. The dog waited politely. "Well?" She unscrewed the lid of the ink bottle.

"It's called *The Last President*," said Baskerville, "I'm afraid I don't know the author."

Rain felt the blood drain from her face. *The Last President* had

been Will's working title for the book, just before he had started calling it *The Great American Novel*. She dipped the nib of the fountain
pen into the ink bottle, pulled the filling lever and then wiped the nip
on a tissue. "Never heard of it," she said as she wrote *Last Prez??* in
her daybook. She glanced over at Will, and caught him squirming on
his chair. He looked as if his pockets were full of crickets. "Fiction or
non-fiction?"

"Fiction."

She wrote that down. "Short stories or a novel?"

"I'm not sure. A novel, I think."

The shop bell tinkled as Mrs. Snopes cracked the door opened.
She hesitated when she bumped one of the terriers. "Is something
wrong?" she said, not taking her hand from the handle.

"Right as nails," said Fast Eddie. "Come in, Helen, good to see
you. These folks are here for Rain. The big one is Mr. Baskerville
and—I'm sorry I didn't catch your names." He gave the terriers a wel-
coming smile. Fast Eddie had become the friendliest man in Nowhere
ever since his wife had stepped off the edge of town and disappeared.

"Spot," said one.

"Rover," said the other.

"Folks?" muttered Mrs. Snopes. "Dogs is what I call 'em." She
inhaled, twisted her torso and squeezed between the two terriers.
Mrs. Snopes was very limber; she taught swing yoga at the Town
Hall Monday, Tuesday, and Thursday nights from 6-7:30. "I've got a
taste for some crumbs of your banana oatmeal bar," she said. "That
last one laid me out for the better part of an afternoon. How are they
breaking today, Eddie?"

"Let's just see." He set a tray on the top of the display case and
pulled on a glove to sort through the broken cookies.

"You are Lorraine Carraway?" said Baskerville.

"That's her name, you bet." Will broke in impulsively. "But she
hates it." He crumpled the looseleaf page he had been writing on,
tossed it at the trashcan and missed. "Call her Rain."

Rain bristled. She didn't hate her name; she just didn't believe
in it.

"And you are?" said the bloodhound. His lips curled away from
pointed teeth and black gums in a grotesque parody of a smile.

"Willy Werther, but everyone calls me Will."

"I see you are supplied with pencil and paper, young Will. Are
you a writer?"

"Me? Oh, no. No." He feigned a yawn. "Well, sort of." For a moment, Rain was certain that he was going to blurt out that *he* was the author of *The Last President*. She wasn't sure why she thought that would be a bad idea, but she did. "I . . . uh . . ." Now that Will had Baskerville's attention, he didn't seem to know what to do with it. "I've been trying to remember jokes for Eddie to tell at church," he said. "Want to hear one?" Fast Eddie and Mrs. Snopes glanced up from their cookie deliberations. "Okay then, how do you keep your dog from digging in the garden?"

"I don't know, Will." Rain just wanted him to shut up. "How?"

"Take away his shovel." Will looked from Baskerville to Rain and then to Fast Eddie. "No?"

"No." Eddie, who had just become a deacon in the Temple of the Eternal Smile, shook his head. "God likes Her jokes to be funny."

"Funny." Will nodded. "Got it. So what's this book about anyway, Mr. B?"

"Will, I just don't know," said the bloodhound. "That's why I'd like to read it." Baskerville turned and yipped over his shoulder. Rover trotted to him and the bloodhound dropped onto all fours. Rain couldn't see what passed between them because the desk blocked her view but when Baskerville heaved himself upright again he was holding a brass dog whistle in his paw. He dropped it, clattering, on the desktop in front of Rain.

"When you find the book, Rain," said Baskerville, "give us a call."

Rain didn't like it that Baskerville just assumed that she would take on the search. "Wait a minute," she said. "Why do you need me to look for it? You're part of the cognisphere, right? You already *know* everything."

"We have access to everything," said Baskerville. "Retrieval is another matter." He growled at Spot. The shop bell tinkled as he opened the door. "I look forward to hearing from you, Rain. Will, it was a pleasure to meet you." The bloodhound nodded at Fast Eddie and Mrs. Snopes, but they paid him no attention. Their heads were bent over the tray of crumbs. Baskerville left the shop, claws clicking against the gray linoleum. The terriers followed him out.

"Nice dogs." Will affected an unconcerned saunter as he crossed the room, although he flew the last few steps. "My book, Rain!" he whispered, his voice thick. With what? Fear? Pride?

"Is it?" Rain had yet to read a word of *The Great American Novel*;

Will claimed it was too rough to show. Although she could imagine that this might be true, she couldn't help but resent being shut out. She offered him the whistle. "So call them."

"What are you saying?" He shrank back, as if mere proximity to the whistle might shrivel his soul. "They're from . . ." He pointed through the window toward the precipitous edge of the mesa on which Nowhere perched. ". . . out there."

Nobody knew where the cognisphere was located exactly, or even if it occupied physical space at all. "All right then, don't." Rain shrugged and pocketed the whistle.

Will seemed disappointed in her. He obviously had three hundred things he wanted to say—and she was supposed to listen. He had always been an excitable boy, although Rain hadn't seen him this wound up since the first time they had made love. But this was neither the time nor the place for feverish speculation. She put a finger to her lips and nodded toward the cookie counter.

Mrs. Snopes picked out a four gram, elongated piece of banana oatmeal cookie ornamented with cream and cinnamon hallucinogenic sprinkles. She paid for it with the story of how her sister Melva had run away from home when she was eleven and they had found her two days later sleeping in the neighbor's treehouse. They had heard the story before, but not the part about the hair dryer. Fast Eddie earned an audience credit on the Barrows's Memory Exchange but the cognisphere deposited an extra quarter point into Mrs. Snopes's account for the new detail, according the Laughing Cookie's MemEx register. Afterward, Fast Eddie insisted that Rain admire the banana oatmeal crumb before he wrapped it up for Mrs. Snopes. Rain had to agree it was quite striking. She said it reminded her of Emily Dickinson.

They closed the Very Memorial Library early. Usually after work, Will and Rain swept some of Eddie's cookie dust into a baggie and went looking for a spot to picnic. Their favorites were the overlook at the southwestern edge of town and the roof of the Button Factory, although on a hot day they also liked the mossy coolness of the abandoned fallout shelter.

But not this unhappy day. Almost as soon as they stepped onto Onion Street, they were fighting. *First she* suggested that Will show her his book. *Then he* said not yet and asked if she had any idea why the dogs were asking about it. *Then she* said no—perhaps a jot too emphatically—*because he* apparently understood her to be puzzled as to why dogs should care about a nobody like him. *Then he* wondered aloud if maybe she wasn't just a little jealous, *which she* said was a dumb thing to say, *which he* took exactly the wrong way.

Will informed her icily that he was going home because he needed to make changes to Chapter Four. Alarmed at how their row had escalated, Rain suggested that maybe they could meet later. He just shrugged and turned away. Stung, she watched him jog down Onion Street.

Later, maybe—being together with Will had never sounded so contingent.

Rain decided to blame the dogs. It was hard enough staying sane here in Nowhere, finding the courage each day not to step off the edge. They didn't need yet another cancerous mystery eating at their lives. And Will was just a kid, she reminded herself. Nineteen, male, impulsive, too smart for his own good, but years from being wise. Of course he was entitled to his moods. She'd always waited him out before, because even though he made her toes curl in frustration sometimes, she did love the boy.

In the meantime, there was no way around it: she'd have to ask Chance Conrad about *The Last President*. She took a right onto Abbey Road, nodding curtly at the passersby. She knew what most people thought about her: that she was impatient and bitter and that she preferred books to people. Of course, they were all wrong, but she had given up trying to explain herself. She ignored Bingo Finn slouching in the entrance to Goriot's Pachinko Palazzo and hurried past Linton's Fruit and Daily Spectator, the Prynne Building, and the drunks at the outdoor tables in front of the Sunspot. She noticed with annoyance that the Drew Barrymore version of *The Wizard of Oz* was playing for another week at the Ziegfowl Feelies. At Uncle Buddy's she took a right, then a left onto Fairview which dead ended in the grassy bulk of the Barrow.

Everything in Nowhere had come out of the Barrow: Rain's fountain pen, the books in the Very Memorial Library, Will's endless packs of blank, looseleaf paper, Fast Eddie's crystal trays and Mrs. Snopes's yoga mats. And of course, all the people.

The last thing Rain remembered about the world was falling asleep in her husband Roger's arms. It had been a warm night in May, 2009. Roger had worked late so they had ordered a sausage and green pepper pizza and had watched the last half hour of *The African*

Queen before they went to bed. It was *so* romantic, even if Nicholson and Garbo were old. She could remember Roger doing his atrocious Nicholson imitation while he brushed his teeth. They had cuddled briefly in the dark but he said he was too tired to make love. They must have kissed good night — yes, no doubt a long and tender last kiss. One of the things she hated most about Nowhere was that she couldn't remember any of Roger's kisses or his face or what he looked like naked. He was just a warm, pale, friendly blur. Some people in Nowhere said it was a mercy that nobody could remember the ones they had loved in the world. Rain was not one of those people.

Will said that the last thing he remembered was falling asleep in his *Nintendo and American Culture* class at Northern Arizona University in the fall of 2023. He could recall everything about the two sexual conquests he had managed in his brief time in the world— Talley Lotterhand and Paula Herbst—but then by his own admission he had never really been in love.

The Barrow was a warehouse buried under the mesa. Rain climbed down to the loading dock and knocked on the sectional steel door. After a few moments she heard the whine of an electric motor as the door clattered up on its tracks. Chance Conrad stood just inside, blinking in the afternoon sunlight. He was a handsome, graying man, who balanced a receding hairline with a delicate beard. Although he had a light step and an easy manner, the skin under his eyes was dark and pouchy. Some said this was because Chance didn't sleep much since he was so busy managing the Barrow. Others maintained that he didn't sleep at all, because he hadn't been revived like the rest of the residents of Nowhere. He was a construct of the cognisphere. It stood to reason, people said. How could anyone with a name like Chance Conrad be real?

"Lorraine!" he said. "And here I was about to write this day off as a total loss." He put his hand on her shoulder and urged her through the entrance. "Come, come in." Chance had no use for daylight; that was another strike against his being real. Once the Barrow was safely locked down again he relaxed. "So," he said, "here we are, just the two of us. I'm hoping this means you've finally dumped the boy genius?"

Rain had long since learned that the best way to deflect Chance's relentless flirting was just to ignore it. As far as she knew, he had never taken a lover. She took a deep breath and counted to five. *Unu, du, tri, kvar, kvin.* The air in the Barrow had the familiar damp weight she remembered from when she first woke up at Nowhere; it settled into Rain's lungs like a cold. Before her were crates and jars and barrels and boxes of goods that the people of Nowhere had asked the cognisphere to recreate. Later that night Ferdie Raskolnikov and his crew would load the lot onto trucks for delivery around town tomorrow.

"What's this?" Rain bent to examine a wide-bladed shovel cast with a solid steel handle. It was so heavy that she could barely lift it.

"Shelly Castorp thinks she's planting daffodils with this." Chance shook his head. "I told her that the handles of garden tools were always made of wood but she claims her father had a shovel just like that one." He shook his head. "The specific gravity of steel is 7.80 grams per cubic centimeter, you know."

"Oh?" When Rain let the handle go, the shovel clanged against the cement floor. "Can we grow daffodils?"

"We'll see." Chance muscled the shovel back into place on its pallet. He probably didn't appreciate her handling other people's orders. "I'm racking my brains trying to remember if I've got something here for you. But I don't, do I?"

"How about those binoculars I keep asking for?"

"I send the requests . . ." He spread his hands. "They all bounce." The corners of his mouth twitched. "So is this about us? At long last?"

"I'm just looking for a book, Chance. A novel."

"Oh," he said, crestfallen. "Better come to the office."

Normally if Rain wanted to add a book to the Very Memorial Library, she'd call Chance and put in an order. Retrieving books was usually no problem for the collective intelligence of humanity, which had uploaded itself into the cognisphere sometime in the late Twenty-third Century. All it needed was an author and title. Failing that, a plot description or even just a memorable line might suffice for the cognisphere to perform a plausible, if not completely accurate, reconstruction of some lost text. In fact, depending on the quality of the description, the cognisphere would recreate a version of pretty much anything the citizens of Nowhere could remember from the world.

Exactly how it accomplished this, and more important, why it bothered, was a mystery.

Chance's office was tucked into the rear of the Barrow, next to the crèche. On the way, they passed the Big Board of the MemEx, which tracked audience and storyteller accounts for all the residents of Nowhere and sorted and cataloged the accumulated memories. Chance stopped by the crèche to check the vitals of Rahim Aziz, who was destined to become the newest citizen of Nowhere, thus bringing the population back up to the standard 853. Rahim was to be an elderly man with a crown of snowy white hair surrounding an oval bald spot. He was replacing Lucy Panza, the pro and Town Calligrapher, who had gone missing two weeks ago and was presumed to have thrown herself over the edge without telling anyone.

"Old Aziz isn't quite as easy on the eye as you were," said Chance, who never failed to remind Rain that he had seen her naked during her revival. Rahim floated on his back in a clear tube filled with a yellow, serous fluid. He had a bit of a paunch and the skin of his legs and under his arms was wrinkled. Rain noted with distaste that he had a penis tattoo of an elephant.

"When will you decant him?"

Chance rubbed a thumb across a readout shells built into the wall of the crèche. "Tomorrow, maybe." The shells meant nothing to Rain. "Tuesday at the latest."

Chance Conrad's office was not so much decorated as overstuffed. Dolls and crystal and tools and fossils and clocks jostled across shelves and the tops of cabinets and chests. The walls were covered with pix from feelies made after Rain's time in the world, although she had seen some of them at the Ziegfowl. She recognized Oud's *Birthdeath*, Fay Wray in full fetish from *Time StRanger* and the wedding cake scene from *Two of Neala*. Will claimed the feelies had triggered the cancerous growth of history; when all the dead actors and sports stars and politicians started having second careers, the past had consumed the present.

"So this is about a novel then?" Chance moved behind his desk but did not sit down. "Called?" He waved a hand over his desktop and its eye winked at him.

"*The Last President*." Rain sat in the chair opposite him.

"Precedent as in a time-honored custom, or President as in Marie Louka?"

"The latter."

He chuckled. "You know, you're the only person in this town who would say *the latter*. I love that. Would you have my baby?"

"No."

"Marry me?"

"Uh-uh."

"Sleep with me?"

"*Chance.*"

He sighed. "Who's the author?"

"I don't know."

"You don't know?" Chance rubbed under his eyes with the heels of his hands. "You're sure about that? You wouldn't care to take a wild guess? Last name begins with the letter . . . what? A through K? L through Z?"

"Sorry."

He stepped from behind the desk and his desktop shut its eye. "Well, the damn doggie didn't know either, which is why I couldn't help him."

Rain groaned. "He's been here already?"

"Him and a couple of his pooch pals." Chance opened the igloo which stood humming beside the door. "Cooler?" He pulled out a frosty pitcher filled with something thick and glaucous. "It's just broccoli nectar and a little ethanol-style vodka."

Rain shook her head. "But that doesn't make sense." She could hear the whine in her voice. "They're agents of the cognisphere, right? And you access the cognisphere. Why would it ask you to ask itself?"

"Exactly." Chance closed the door and locked it. This struck Rain as odd; maybe he was afraid that Ferdi Raskolnikov would barge in on them. "Things have been loopy here lately," he said. "You should see some of the mistakes we've had to send back." He poured broccoli cocktail for himself. It oozed from the pitcher and landed in his coffee mug with a thick *plop*. "I've spent all afternoon trying to convince myself that the dogs are some kind of a workaround, maybe to jog some lost data loose from the MemEx." He replaced the pitcher in the igloo and settled onto the chair behind his desk. "But now you show up and I'm wondering: Why is Rain asking me for this book?"

She frowned. "I ask you for all my books."

He considered for a moment, tapping the finger against his forehead and then pointed at her. "Let me tell you a story." Rain started to object that she had neither goods nor services to offer him in return and she had just drained her MemEx account to dry spit, but he silenced her with a wave. "No, this one is free." He took a sip of liquid broccoli. "An audience credit unencumbered, offered to the woman of my dreams."

She stuck out her tongue.

"Why does this place exist?" he asked.

"The Barrow?"

"Nowhere."

"Ah, eschatology." She laughed bitterly. "Well, Father Samsa claims this is the afterlife, although I'll be damned if I know whether it's heaven or hell."

"I know you don't believe *that*," said Chance. "So then this is some game that the cognisphere is playing? We're virtual chesspersons?"

Rain shrugged.

"What happens when we step off the edge?"

"Nobody knows." Just then a cacophony of clocks yawped, pinged, buzzed in six o'clock. "This isn't much of a story Chance."

"Patience, love. So you think the cognisphere recreated us for a reason?"

"Maybe. Okay, sure." A huge spider with eight paintbrush legs shook itself and stretched on a teak cabinet. "We're in a zoo. A museum."

"Or maybe some kind of primitive backup. The cognisphere keeps us around because there's a chance that it might fail, go crazy—I don't know. If that happened, we could start over."

"Except we'd all die without the cognisphere." The spider stepped onto the wall and picked its way toward the nearest corner. "And nobody's made any babies that I know of. We're not exactly Adam and Eve material, Chance."

"But that's damn scary, no? Makes the case that none of us is real."

Rain liked him better when he was trying to coax her into bed. "Enough." She pushed her chair back and started to get up.

"Okay, okay." He held up his hands in surrender. "Story time. When I was a kid, I used to collect meanies."

"Meanies?" She settled back down.

"Probably after your time. They were bots, about so big." He held forefinger and thumb a couple of centimeters apart. "Little fighting toys. There were gorilla meanies and ghoul meanies and nazi meanies and demon meanies and dino meanies. Fifty-two in all, one for every week of the year. You set them loose in the meanie arena and they would try to kill one another. If they died, they'd shut down for twenty-four hours. Now if meanies fought one on one, they would always draw. But when you formed them into teams, their powers combined in different ways. For instance, a ghoul and nazi team could defeat any other team of two—except the dino and yeti. For the better part of a year, I rushed home from school every day to play with the things. I kept trying combinations until I could pretty much predict the outcome of every battle. Then I lost interest."

"Speaking of losing interest," said Rain, who was distracted by the spider decorating the corner of Chance's office in traceries of blue and green.

"I'm getting there." He shifted uncomfortably in his chair, and took another sip from the mug. "So a couple of years go by and I'm twelve now. One night I'm in my room and I hear this squeaking coming from under my bed. I pull out the old meanie arena, which has been gathering dust all this time and I see that a mouse has blundered into it and is being attacked by a squad of meanies. And just like that I'm fascinated with them all over again. For weeks I drop crickets and frogs and garter snakes into the arena and watch them try to survive."

"That's sick."

"No question. But then boys can't help themselves when it comes to mindless cruelty. Anyway, it didn't last. The wildlife was too hard on the poor little bots." He drained the last of the broccoli. "But the point is that I got bored playing with a closed set of meanies. Even though I hadn't actually tried all possible combinations, after a while I could see that nothing much new was ever going to happen. But then the mouse changed everything." He leaned forward across the desk. "So let me propose a thought experiment to you, my lovely Lorraine. This mysterious novel that everyone is so eager to find? What if the last name of the author began with the letter . . ." He paused and then seemed to pluck something out of the air. "Oh, let's say 'W'."

Rain started.

"And just for the sake of argument, let's suppose that the first name also begins with 'W' . . . Ah, I see from your expression that this thought has also occurred to you."

"It's not him," said Rain. "He was revived at nineteen; he's just a kid. Why would the cognisphere care anything about him?"

"Because he's the mouse in our sad, little arena. He isn't simply recycling memories of the world like the rest of us. The novel your doggies are looking for doesn't exist in the cognisphere, never did. Because it's being written right here, right now. Maybe imagination is in short supply wherever the doggies come from. Lord knows there isn't a hell of a lot of it in Nowhere."

Rain would have liked to deny it, but she could feel the insult sticking to her. "How do you know he's writing a novel?"

"I supply the paper, Rain. Reams and reams of it. Besides, this may be hell, as Father Samsa insists, but it's also a small town. We meddle in each other's business, what else is there to do?" His voice softened; Rain thought that if Chance ever did take a lover, this would be how he might speak to her. "Is the book any good? Because if it is, I'd like to read it."

"I don't know." At that moment, Rain felt a drop of something cold hit the back of her hand. There was a dot the color of sky on her knuckle. She looked up at the spider hanging from the ceiling on an azure thread. "He doesn't show it to me. Your toy is dripping."

"Really?" Chance came around the desk. "A woman of your considerable charms is taking no for an answer?" He reached up and cradled the spider into his arms. "Go get him, Rain, You don't want to keep your mouse waiting." He carried it to the teak cabinet.

Rain rubbed at the blue spot on her hand but the stain had penetrated her skin. She couldn't even smudge it.

But Will wasn't waiting, at least not for Rain. She stopped by their apartment but he wasn't there and he hadn't left a note. Neither was he at the Button Factory nor Queequeg's Kava Cave. She looked in at the Laughing Cookie just as Fast Eddie was locking up. No Will. She finally tracked Will down at the overlook, by the blue picnic table under the chestnut trees.

Normally they came here for the view, which was spectacular. A field of wildflowers, tidy-tips and mullein and tickseed and bindweed, sloped steeply down to the edge of the mesa. But Will was paying no attention to the scenery. He had scattered a stack of five looseleaf binders across the table; the whole of *The Great American Novel* or *The Last President* or whatever the hell it was called. Three of the binders were open. He was reading—but apparently not writing in—a fourth. A No. 2 pencil was tucked behind his ear. Something about Will's body language disturbed Rain. He usually sprawled awkwardly wherever he came to rest, a giraffe trying to settle on a hammock. Now he was gathered into himself, hunched over the binder like an old man. Rain came up behind him and kneaded his shoulders for a moment.

He leaned back and sighed.

"Sorry about this afternoon." She bent to nibble his ear. "Have you eaten?"

"No." He kissed the air in front of him but did not look at her.

She peeked at the looseleaf page in front of him and tried to decipher the handwriting, which was not quite as legible as an EEG chart. . . . *knelt before the coffin, her eyes wide in the dim holy light of the cathedral. His face was wavy* . . . *No,* thought Rain straightening up before he suspected that she was reading. *Not wavy. Waxy.* "Beautiful evening," she said.

Will shut the binder he had been reading and gazed distractedly toward the horizon.

Rain had not been completely honest with Chance. It was true that Will hadn't shown her the novel, but she *had* read some of it. She had stolen glimpses over his shoulder or read upside down when she was sitting across from him. Then there was the one guilty afternoon when she had come back to their apartment and gobbled up pages 34–52 before her conscience mastered her curiosity. The long passage had taken place in a bunker during one of the Resource Wars. The President of Great America, Lawrence Goodman, had been reminiscing with his former mistress and current National Security Advisor, Rebecca Santorino, about Akron, where they had first fallen in love years ago and which had just been obliterated in retaliation for an American strike on Zhengzhou. Two pages later they were thrashing on the president's bed and ripping each other's clothes off. Rain had begun this part with great interest, hoping to gain new insight into Will's sexual tastes, but had closed the binder uneasily just as the President was tying his lover to the Louis XVI armoire with silk Atura neckties.

Will closed the other open binders and stacked all five into a pile. Then he pulled the pencil from behind his ear, snapped it in two, and let the pieces roll out of his hand under the picnic table. He gave her an odd, lopsided smile.

"Will, what's the matter?" Rain stared. "Are you okay?"

In response, he pulled a baggie of cookie dust from his shirt pocket and jiggled it.

"Here?" she said, coloring. "In plain sight?" Usually they hid out when they were eating dust, at least until they weathered the first rush. The Cocoa Peanut Butter Chunk made them giggly and not a little stupid. Macaroon Sandies often hit Rain like powdered lust.

"There's no one to see." Will licked his forefinger and stuck it into the bag. "Besides, what if there was?" He extended the finger toward her, the tip and nail coated with the parti-colored powder. "Does anyone here care what we do?"

She considered telling him then what Chance Conrad had said about small towns but she could see that Will was having a mood. So she just opened her mouth and obediently stuck her tongue out. As he rotated the finger across the middle of her tongue, she tasted the sweet, spicy grit. She closed her mouth on the finger and he pulled it slowly through her lips.

"Now you," she said, reaching for the baggie. They always fed each other cookie dust.

Rain and Will sat on the tabletop with their feet on the seat, facing the slope that led down to the edge of Nowhere. The world beneath the impossibly high cliff was impossibly flat, but this was still Rain's favorite lookout, even if it was probably an illusion. The land stretched out in a kind of grid with rectangles in every color of green: the brooding green of forests, the dreaming green of fields under cultivation and the confused gray-green of scrub land. Dividing the rectangles were ribbons the color of wet sand. Rain liked to think they were roads, although she had never spotted any traffic on them. She reached for Will's hand and he closed it around hers. He was right: she didn't care if anyone saw them together like this. His skin was warm and rough. As she rubbed her finger over the back of his hand, she thought she could make out a faded blue spot. But maybe it was a trick of the twilight, or a cookie hallucination.

The rectangles and the ribbons of the land to the southwest had always reminded her of something, but she had never quite been able to figure out what. Now as Eddie's magic cookie dust sparked through her bloodstream, and she felt Will's warm hand in hers, she thought of a trip she had taken with her father when she was a just a kid to a museum in an old city called Manhilton, that got blown up afterward. In the museum were very old pix that just hung on the wall and mostly didn't do anything, and she remembered taking a cab to get there and the cab had asked what her name was but she wouldn't tell it so it called her *little girl* which she didn't like because she was seven already, and the museum had escalators that whispered music, and there was one really, really big room filled with pix of all blurry water lilies, and outside in a sculpture garden there were statues made of metal and rocks but there were no flowers because it was cold so she and Dad didn't stay out there very long and inside again were lots of pix of women with three eyes and too many corners and then some wide blue men blocked her view of the Mona Lisa so she never really saw that one, which everyone said later was supposed to be so special but one she did see and remembered now was a pix of a grid that had colored rectangles and with ribbons of red and yellow separating them, and she asked her Dad if it was a map of the museum and he laughed down at her because her Dad was so tall, tall as any statue and he said the pix wasn't a map, it was a *mondrian* and she asked him what a *mondrian* was and then he laughed again and she laughed and it was so easy to laugh in those days and Will was laughing too.

"I want to go down there." He laughed as he pointed down at the mondrian which stretched into the rosy distance.

"There?" Rain didn't understand; the best part of her was still in the museum with her father. "Why?"

"Because there are people living there. Must be why Chance won't give out binoculars or telescopes." He let go of her hand. "Because it's not here."

"You're going to step over the edge?" Her voice rose in alarm.

"No, silly." He leapt up, stood on the tabletop and raised his arms to the sky. "I'm going to climb down."

"But that's the same thing."

"No, it isn't. I'll show you." He slid off the picnic table and started toward the thicket of scruffy evergreens and brambles that had overgrown the edge of Nowhere. He walked along this tangle until he came to a bit of blue rag tied to a branch, glanced over his shoulder to see if she was still with him and then wriggled into the scrub. Rain followed.

They emerged into a tiny clearing She sidled beside him and he slipped an arm around her waist to brace her. The cliff was steep here but not sheer. She could make out a narrow dirt track that switched back through scree and stunted fir. Maybe a mountain goat could negotiate it, if there were any mountain goats. But a single misstep would send Will plunging headlong. And then there was the Drop. Everyone knew about the Drop. They traded stories about it all the time. Scary stories. She was about to ask him why, if there were people down there, they hadn't climbed up for a visit, when he kicked a stone over the edge. They watched it bounce straight down and disappear over a ledge.

"Lucy Panza showed me this," said Will, his face flushed with excitement.

Rain wondered when he'd had time to go exploring the edge with Lucy Panza. "But she stepped over the edge."

"No," he said. "She didn't."

She considered the awful slope for a moment and shuddered. "I'm not going down there, Will."

He continued peering down the dirt track. "I know," he said.

The calm with which he said it was like a slap in the face. She stared at him, speechless, until he finally met her gaze. "I'll come back for you." He gave her the goofy, apologetic grin he always summoned up when he upset her. "I'll make sure the path is safe and I'll make all kinds of friends down at the bottom and when the time is right, I'll be back."

"But what about your book?"

He blew a dismissive breath between his lips. "I'm all set with that."

"It's finished?"

"It's crap, Rain." His voice was flat. "I'm not wasting any more time writing about some stupid made-up president. There are no more presidents. And how can anyone write the Great American novel when there is no more America?" He caught his breath. "Sorry," he said. "I know that's what you wanted me to do." He gave her a sour smile. "You're welcome to read it if you want. Or hand it over to the dogs. That should be good for a laugh." Then he pulled her into his arms and kissed her.

Of course Rain kissed him back. She wanted to drag him down on top of her and rip his clothes off, although there really wasn't enough room here to make love. She would even have let him take her on the picnic table, *tie her* to the damn table, if that's what he had wanted. But his wasn't the kind of kiss that started anything.

"So I'm coming back, I promise," he murmured into her ear. "Just tell everyone that you're waiting for me."

"Wait a minute." She twisted away from him. "You're going now? It's almost dark. We just ate cookie dust." She couldn't believe he was serious. This was such a typical boneheaded-Will-stunt he was pulling. "Come home, honey," she said. "Get some sleep. Things might look different in the morning."

He stroked her hair. "I've got at least another hour of light," he said. "Believe me, I've thought about this a long time, Rain." Then he brushed his finger against her lips. "I love you."

He took a step over the edge and another. He had gone about a dozen meters before his feet went out from beneath him and he fell backwards, skidding on his rear end and clutching at the scrub. But he caught himself almost immediately and looked up at her, his face pale as the moon. "Oops!" he called cheerfully.

Rain stood at the edge of the cliff long after she could no longer see him. She was hoping that he'd come to a dead end and have to turn back. The sun was painting the horizon with fire by the time she fetched Will's binders to the edge of Nowhere. She opened one after another and shook the pages free. They fluttered into the twilight like an exaltation of larks. A few landed briefly on the path before launching themselves again into the breeze and following their creator out of her life. When all the pages had disappeared, Rain took the whistle that the dogs had given her and hurled it as far into the mondrian as she could.

Only then did she let herself cry. She thought she deserved it.

Rain found her way through the gathering darkness back to the apartment over Vronsky's Laundromat and Monkeyfilter Bowladrome. She put some Szechwan lasagna into the microwave and pushed it around her plate for a while, but she was too numb to be hungry. She would have gone to the eight o'clock show at the Ziegfowl just to get out, but she was mortally tired of *The Wizard of Oz*, no matter whom the cognisphere recast in it. The apartment depressed her. The problem, she decided, was that she was surrounded by Will's stuff; she'd have to move it somewhere out of sight.

She placed a short stack of college-lined, loose-leaf paper and four unopened reams in a box next to *The Awakening, The Big Snooze*, and *Drinking the Snow*. Will had borrowed the novels from the Very Memorial Library but had made way too many marginal notes in them for her to return them to the stacks. Rain would have to order new ones from Chance in the Barrow. She threw his Buffalo *Soldiers* warmup jacket on top of several dusty pairs of Adidas Kloud Nine running shoes. Will's dresser drawers produced eight pairs of white socks, two black, a half dozen gray jockey shorts, three pairs of jeans, and a stack of tee shirts sporting pix of Panafrican shoutcast bands. At the bottom of the sock drawer, Rain discovered flash editions of *Superheterodyne Adventure Stories 2020-26* and *The Complete Idiot's Guide to Fetish*. She pulled his mustard collection and climkies and homebrew off the kitchen shelves.

And that was all it took to put Will out of her life. She shouldn't have been surprised. After all, they had only lived together for just over a year.

She was trying to talk herself into throwing the lot of it out the next morning when the doorglass blinked. She glanced at the clock. Who did she know that would come visiting at 10:30 at night? When she opened the door, Baskerville, Rover and Spot looked up at her.

"You found the book?" The bloodhound's bowtie was crooked.

Beneath her, Rain could hear the rumble and clatter of the bowling lanes. "There is no book."

"May we come in?"

"No."

"You threw the whistle off the edge," said Baskerville.

As if on signal, the two terriers sat. They looked to Rain as if they were settling in for a stay. "Where's Will?" said Rover.

She wanted to kick the door shut hard enough to knock their bowler hats off, but the terrier's question took her breath away. If the cognisphere had lost track of Will, then maybe he wasn't . . . maybe he was . . . "I hate dogs," she said. "Maybe I forgot to mention that?"

Baskerville regarded her with his solemn chocolate eyes and said nothing.

The terrier's hind leg scratched at his flank. "Has something happened to him?" he asked.

"Stop it!" Rain stomped her foot on the doorsill and all three dogs jumped. "You want a story and I want information. Deal?"

The dogs thought it over, then Rover got up and licked her hand.

"Okay, story." But at that moment, Rain's throat seemed to close, as if she had tried to swallow the page of a book. *Will was gone.* If she said it aloud, it would become just another story on the MemEx. But she had to know. "M-My boyfriend climbed over the edge a couple of hours ago trying to find a way down the cliff. I pitched the goddamn novel he was writing after him. The end."

"But what does this have to do with *The Last President*?"

"That was the name of his book. Used to be. Once." She was out of breath. "Okay, you got story. Now you owe me some god-damn truth. He's dead, right? You've absorbed him already."

Rover started to say, "I'm afraid that we have no knowledge of ..." But she didn't give the dog a chance to finish; she slammed the door.

She decided then not to throw Will's things out. She dragged them all into the bedroom closet and covered the pile with the electric blanket. She made one more pass around the apartment to make sure she had everything. Then she decided to make a grocery list so she could stop at Cereno's on the way home from work tomorrow. That's when she discovered that she had nothing to write on. She gave herself permission to retrieve a couple of pages of Will's paper from the closet—just this once. As long as she was writing the list, she didn't have to think about Will on the cliff or the dogs in the hall. She cracked the apartment door just enough to see that all three of them were still there, heads on paws, asleep. Spot's ear twitched but he didn't wake up. She sat on the couch with the silence ringing in her ears until she got up and muscled the dresser over to block the closet where she had put Will's stuff. She thought about brushing her teeth and trying for sleep but she knew that would be a waste of time. She was browsing the books on her bookshelf, all of which she had long since read to tatters, when the phone squawked.

Rain was sure it was the dogs calling, but decided to pick up just in case.

"Lorraine Carraway?"

Rain recognized Sheriff Renfield's drawl and was immediately annoyed. He was one of her best customers—an avid Georgette Heyer fan—and knew better than to call her by her proper name.

"Speaking, Beej. What's up?"

"There's been some trouble down to the Laughing Cookie." He was slurring words. He pronounced *There is* as *Thersh*.

"Trouble?"

"Fast Eddie said you had dogs in the store today. Dogs with hats."

"What kind of trouble, Beej? Is Eddie all right?"

"He's fine, we're all just fine." Everybody knew that Beej Renfield was a drinker and nobody blamed him for it. Being sheriff was possibly the most boring job in Nowhere. "But there's been what you might call vandalism. Books all over the place, Rain, some of them ripped up good. Teeth marks. And the place stinks of piss.

Must've happened, an hour, maybe two ago. Fast Eddie is ripping mad. I need you to come down here and lay some calm on him. Will you do that for me, Rain?"

"I'll do you one better, Beej. You're looking for these dogs?"

His breath rasped in the receiver so loud she could almost smell it.

"Because I've got them here if you're interested. Right outside my door."

"I'm on my way."

"Oh, and Beej? You might want to bring some help."

She sat at the kitchen table to wait. In front of her were the shopping list and the No. 2 pencil. They reminded her of Will. He was such a strong boy, everybody in town always said so. He *had* run that 4:21 mile, after all. And she was almost certain that Baskerville had looked surprised when she'd told him that Will was climbing down the cliff. What did surprise look like on a dog? She'd see for sure when Beej Renfield arrived.

For the very first time Rain allowed herself to consider the possibility that Will wasn't dead or absorbed. Maybe the cognisphere ended at the edge of Nowhere. In which case, he might actually come back for her.

But why would he bother? What had she ever done to deserve him? Her shopping list lay in front of her like an accusation. Was this all her life was about? Toilet paper and Seventy-Up and duck sausage? Will had climbed over the edge of Nowhere. What chance had she ever taken? She needed to do *something*, something no one had ever done before. She'd had enough of books and all the old stories about the world that the cognisphere was sorting on the MemEx. That world was gone, forever and ever, amen.

She picked up the pencil again.

I scowled at the dogs through the plate glass window of the Very Memorial Library. They squatted in a row next to my book drop. There were three of them, haughty in their bowler hats and silk vests. They acted like they owned the air. Bad dogs, I knew that for sure, created out of spit and tears and heartbreak by the spirits of all the uncountable dead and sent to spy on the survivors and cause at least three different kinds of trouble.

I wasn't worried. We'd seen their kind before.

HEARTWIRED

Joe Haldeman

Margaret Stevenson walked up the two flights of stairs and came to a plain wooden door with the nameplate 'Relationships, Ltd.' She hesitated, then knocked. Someone buzzed her in.

She didn't know what to expect, but the simplicity surprised her: no receptionist, no outer office, no sign of a laboratory. Just a middle-aged man, conservative business suit, head fashionably shaved, sitting behind an uncluttered desk. He stood and offered his hand. "Mrs. Stevenson? I'm Dr. Damien."

She sat on the edge of the chair he offered.

"Our service is guaranteed," he said without preamble, "but it is neither inexpensive nor permanent."

"You wouldn't want it to be permanent," she said.

"No." He smiled. "Life would be pleasant, but neither of you would accomplish much."

He reached into a drawer and pulled out a single sheet of paper and a pen. "Nevertheless, I must ask you to sign this waiver, which relieves our corporation of responsibility for anything you or he may do or say for the duration of the effect."

She picked up the waiver and scanned it.

"When we talked on the phone, you said that there would be no physical danger and no lasting physical effect."

"That's part of the guarantee."

She put the paper down and picked up the pen, but hesitated. "How, exactly, does it work?"

He leaned back, lacing his fingers together over his abdomen, and looked directly at her. After a moment, he said: "The varieties of love are nearly infinite. Every person alive is theoretically able to love every other person alive, and in a variety of ways."

"Theoretically," she said.

"In our culture, love between a man and a woman normally goes through three stages: sexual attraction, romantic fascination and then long-term bonding. Each of them is mediated by a distinct condition of brain chemistry.

"A person may have all three at once, with only one being dominant at any given time. Thus a man might be in love with his wife, and at the same time be infatuated with his mistress, and yet be instantly attracted to any stranger with appropriate physical characteristics."

"That's exactly—"

He held up a hand. "I don't need to know any more than you've told me. You've been married twenty-five years, you have an anniversary coming up . . . and you want it to be romantic."

"Yes." She didn't smile. "I know he's capable of romance."

"As are we all." He leaned forward and took two vials from the drawer, a blue one and a pink one. He looked at the blue one.

"This is Formula One. It induces the first condition, sort of a Viagra for the mind."

She closed her eyes and shook her head, almost a shudder. "No. I want the second one."

"Formula Two." He slid the pink vial towards her. "You each take approximately half of this, while in each other's company, and for several days you will be in a state of mutual infatuation. You'll be like kids again."

She did smile at that. "Whether he knows he's taken it or not?"

"That's right. No placebo effect."

"And there is no Formula Three?"

"No. That takes time, and understanding, and a measure of luck." He shook his head ruefully and put the blue vial away. "But I think you have that already."

"We do. The old-married-couple kind."

"Now, the most effective way of administering the drug is through food or drink. You can put it in a favorite dish, one you're sure he'll finish, but only after it's been cooked. Above a hundred degrees centigrade, the compound will decompose."

"I don't often cook. Could it be a bottle of wine?"

"If you each drink half, yes."

"I can force myself." She took up the pen and signed the waiver, then opened her clutch purse and counted out ten £100 notes. "Half now, you said, and half upon satisfaction?"

"That's correct." He stood and offered his hand again. "Good luck, Mrs Stevenson."

*   *   *

The reader may now imagine any one of nine permutations for this story's end.

In the one the author prefers, they go to a romantic French restaurant, the lights low, the food wonderful, a bottle of good Bordeaux between them.

She excuses herself to go to the ladies' loo, the vial palmed, and drops her purse. When he leans over to pick it up, she empties the vial into the bottle ofwine.

When she returns, she is careful to consume half of the remaining wine, which is not difficult. They are both in an expansive, loving mood, comrades these twenty-five years.

As they finish the bottle, she feels the emotion building in her, doubling and redoubling. She can see the effect on him, as well: his eyes wide and dilated, his face flushed. He loosens his tie as she pats perspiration from her forehead.

It's all but unbearable! She has to confess, so that he will know there's nothing physically wrong with him. She takes the empty pink vial from her purse and opens her mouth to explain—

He opens his hand and the empty blue vial drops to the table. He grabs the tablecloth . . .

They are released on their own recognizance once the magistrate understands the situation.

But they'll never be served in that restaurant again.

THE FATE OF MICE

Susan Palwick

I remember galloping, the wind in my mane and the road hard against my hooves. Dr. Krantor says this is a false memory, that there is no possible genetic linkage between mice and horses, and I tell him that if scientists are going to equip IQ-enhanced mice with electronic vocal cords and teach them to talk, they should at least pay attention to what the mice tell them. "Mice," Dr. Krantor tells me acidly, "did not evolve from horses," and I ask him if he believes in reincarnation, and he glares at me and tells me that he's a behavioral psychologist, not a theologian, and I point out that it's pretty much the same thing. "You've got too much free time," he snaps at me. "Keep this up and I'll make you run the maze again today." I tell him that I don't mind the maze. The maze is fine. At least I know what I'm doing there: finding cheese as quickly as possible, which is what I'd do anyhow, anytime anyone gave me the chance. But what am I doing galloping?

"You aren't doing anything galloping," he tells me. "You've never galloped in your life. You're a mouse." I ask him how a mouse can remember being a horse, and he says, "It's not a memory. Maybe it's a dream. Maybe you got the idea from something you heard or saw somewhere. On TV." There's a small TV in the lab, so Dr. Krantor can watch the news, but it's not even positioned so that I can see it easily. And I ask him how watching something on TV would make me know what it *felt* like to be a horse, and he says I *don't* know what it feels like to be a horse, I have no idea what a horse feels like, I'm just making it up.

But I remember that road, winding ahead in moonlight, the harness pulling against my chest, the sound of wheels behind me. I remember the three other horses in harness with me, our warm breath steaming in the frosty air. And then I remember standing in a courtyard somewhere, and someone bringing water and hay. We stood there for a long time, the four of us, in our harness. I remember that, but that's all I remember. What happened next?

*   *   *

Dr. Krantor came grumbling into the lab this morning, Pippa in tow. "You have to behave yourself," he says sternly, and deposits her in a corner.

"Mommy was going to take me to the *zoo*," she says. When I stand on my hind legs to peer through the side of the cage, I can see her pigtails flouncing. "It's *Saturday*."

"Yes, I know that, but your mother decided she had other plans, and I have to work today."

"She did *not* have other plans. She and Michael were going to take me to the *zoo*. You just hate Michael, Daddy!"

"Here," he says, handing her a piece of graph paper and some colored pens. "You can draw a picture. You can draw a picture of the zoo."

"You could have gotten a *babysitter*," Pippa yells at him, her chubby little fists clenched against her polka-dot dress. "You're *cheap*. A babysitter'd take me to the zoo!"

"I'll take you myself, Pippa." Dr. Krantor is whining now. "In a few hours. I just have a few hours of work to do, okay?"

"*Huh*," she says. "And I bet you won't let me watch TV, either! Well, *I'm* gonna talk to Rodney!"

Pippa calls me Rodney because she says it's prettier than rodent, which is what Dr. Krantor calls me: The Rodent, as if in my one small body I contain the entire order of small gnawing mammals having a single pair of upper incisors with a chisel-shaped edge. Perhaps he intends this as an honor, although to me it feels more like a burden. I am only a small white mouse, unworthy to represent all the other rodents in the world, all the rats and rabbits and squirrels, and now I have this added weight, the mystery Dr. Krantor will not acknowledge, the burden of hooves and mane.

"Rodney," Pippa says, "Daddy's scared I'll like Michael better than him. If you had a baby girl mouse and you got a divorce and your daughter's Mommy had a boyfriend, would *you* be jealous?"

"Mice neither marry nor are given in marriage," I tell her. In point of fact, mice are non-monogamous, and in stressful situations have been known to eat their young, but this may be more than Pippa needs to know.

Pippa scowls. "If your daughter's Mommy had a boyfriend, would you keep her from seeing your daughter *at all*?"

"Sweetheart," Dr. Krantor says, striding over to our corner of the lab and bending down, "Michael's not a nice person."

"Yes he *is*."

"No, he's not."

"Yes he is! You're just saying that because he has a picture of a naked lady on his arm! But I see naked ladies in the shower after I go swimming with Mommy! And Michael doesn't always ride his motorcycle, Daddy! He promised to take me to the zoo in his *truck*!"

"Oh, Pippa," he says, and bends down and hugs her. "I'm just trying to protect you. I know you don't understand now. You will someday, I promise."

"I don't *want* to be protected," Pippa says, stabbing the paper with Dr. Krantor's red pen. "I want to go to the zoo with Mommy and Michael!"

"I know you do, sweetheart. I know. Draw a picture and talk to the rodent, okay? I'll take you to the zoo just as soon as I finish here."

Pippa, pouting, mumbles her assent and begins to draw. Dr. Krantor, who frequently vents his frustrations when he is alone in the lab, has told me about Pippa's mother, who used to be addicted to cocaine. Supposedly she is drug-free now. Supposedly she is now fit to have joint custody of her daughter. But Michael, with his motorcycle and his naked lady, looks too much like a drug dealer to Dr. Krantor. "If anything happened to Pippa while she was with them," he has told me, "I'd never forgive myself."

Pippa shows me her picture: a stick-figure, wearing pigtails and a polka-dot dress, sitting in a cage. "Here's my picture of the zoo," she says. "Rodney, do you ever wish you could go wherever you wanted?"

"Yes," I say. Dr. Krantor has warned me that the world is full of owls and snakes and cats and mousetraps, innumerable kinds of death. Dr. Krantor says that I should be happy to live in a cage, with food and water always available; Dr. Krantor says I should be proud of my contribution to science. I've told him that I'd be delighted to trade places with him—far be it from me to deny Dr. Krantor his share of luxury and prestige—but he always declines. He has responsibilities in his own world, he tells me. He has to take care of his daughter. Pippa seems to think that he takes care of her in much the same way he takes care of me.

"I'm *bored*," she says now, pouting. "Rodney, tell me a story."

"Sweetheart," says Dr. Krantor, "the rodent doesn't know any stories. He's just a mouse. Only people tell stories."

"But Rodney can *talk*. Rodney, do you know any stories? Tell me a story, Rodney."

"Once upon a time," I tell her—now where did that odd phrase come from?—"there was a mouse who remembered being a horse."

"Oh, *goody*!" Pippa claps her hands. "Cinderella! I love that one!"

My whiskers quiver in triumph. "You do? There's a story about a mouse who was a horse? Really?"

"Of course! Everybody knows Cinderella."

I don't. "How does it end, Pippa?"

"Oh, it's a happy ending. The poor girl marries the prince."

I remember nothing about poor girls, or about princes, either, and I can't say I care. "But what about the horse who was a mouse, Pippa?"

She frowns, wrinkling her nose. She looks a lot like her father when she frowns. "I don't know. It turns back into a mouse, I think. It's not important."

"It's important to me, Pippa."

"Okay," she says, and dutifully trudges across the lab to Dr. Krantor. "Daddy, in Cinderella, what happens to the mouse that turned into a horse when it turns back into a mouse?"

I hear breaking glassware, followed by Dr. Krantor's footsteps, and then he is standing above my cage and looking down at me. His face is oddly pale. "I don't know, Pippa. I don't think anyone knows. It probably got eaten by an owl or a cat or a snake. Or caught in a trap."

"Or equipped with IQ boosters and a vocal synthesizer and stuck in a lab," I tell him.

"It's just a story," Dr. Krantor says, but he's frowning. "It's an impossible story. It's a story about magic, mot about science. Pippa, sweetheart, are you ready to go to the zoo now?"

"Now look," he tells me the next day, "It didn't happen. It *never* happened. Stories are about things that haven't happened. Somebody must have told you the story of Cinderella—"

"Who?" I demand. "Who would have told me? The only people I've ever talked to are you and Pippa—"

"You saw it on TV or something, I don't know. It's a common

story. You could have heard it anywhere. Now look, rodent, you're a very suggestible little animal and you're suffering from false memory syndrome. That's very common too, believe me."

I feel my fur bristling. Very suggestible little animal, indeed!

But I don't know how I can remember a story I've never heard, a story that people knew before I remembered it. And soon I start to have other memories. I remember gnawing the ropes holding a lion to a stone table; I remember frightening an elephant; I remember being blind, and running with two blind companions. I remember wearing human clothing and being in love with a bird named Margalo. Each memory is as vivid and particular as the one about being a horse. Each memory feels utterly real.

I quickly learn that Dr. Krantor doesn't want to hear about any of this. The only thing he's interested in is how quickly I can master successively more complicated mazes. So I talk to Pippa instead, when she comes to visit the lab. Pippa knows some of the stories: the poem about the three blind mice, the belief that elephants are afraid of mice. She doesn't know the others, but she finds out. She asks her mother and her friends, her teachers, the school librarian, and then she reports back to me while Dr. Krantor is on the other side of the lab, tinkering with his computers and mazes.

All of my memories are from human stories. There are also a witch and a wardrobe in the story about the lion; the mouse who is love with the bird is named Stuart. Pippa asks her mother to read her these stories, and reports that she likes them very much, although the story with the bird in it is the only one where the mouse is really important. And while that story, according to Pippa, ends with Stuart looking for his friend Margalo, the story never says whether or not he ever finds her. The fate of mice seems to be of little importance in human stories, even when the mouse is the hero.

I begin to develop a theory. Dr. Krantor believes that language makes me very good at running mazes, that with language comes the ability to remember the past and anticipate the future, to plan and strategize. To humor him, I talk to myself while I run the mazes; I pause at intersections and ask myself theatrical questions, soliloquizing about the delicious cheese to be found at the end of the ordeal, recounting fond anecdotes of cheeses past. Dr. Krantor loves this. He is writing a paper about how much better I am at the mazes than previous mice, who had IQ boosting but no vocal synthesizers, who were not able to turn their quests for cheese into narrative. Dr. Krantor's theory is that language brings a quantum leap in the ability to solve problems.

But my theory, which I do not share with Dr. Krantor, is that human language has dragged me into the human world, into human tales about mice. I am trapped in a maze of story, and I do not know how to reach the end of it, nor what is waiting for me there. I do not know if there is cheese at the end of the maze, or an elephant, or a lion on a stone table. And I do not know how to find out.

And then I have another memory. It comes to me one day as I am running the maze.

In this memory I am a mouse named Algernon. I am an extremely smart mouse, a genius mouse; I am even smarter than I am now. I love this memory, and I run even faster than usual, my whiskers quivering. Someone has told a story about a mouse like me! There is a story about a very smart mouse, a story where a very smart mouse is important!

Pippa comes to the lab after school that day, scowling and dragging a backpack of homework with her, and when Dr. Krantor is working on his computer across the room, I tell her about Algernon. She has never heard of Algernon, but she promises to question her sources and report back to me.

The next day, when she comes to the lab, she tells me that the school librarian has heard of the Algernon story, but says that Pippa isn't old enough to read it yet. "She wouldn't tell me why," Pippa says. "Maybe the mouse in the story is naked?"

"Mice are always naked," I tell her. "Or else we're never naked, because we always have our fur, or maybe we're only naked when we're born, because we're furless then. Anyway, we don't wear clothing, so that can't be the reason."

"Stuart wears clothing."

"But the three blind mice don't." My personal opinion is that Stuart's a sell-out who capitulated to human demands to wear clothing only so that he could be the hero in the story. It didn't work, of course; the humans couldn't be bothered to give him a happy ending, or any ending at all, whether he wore clothing or not. His bowing and scraping did him no good.

I suspect that Algernon is non-monogamous, or perhaps that he eats his young, and that this is why the librarian considers the story unsuitable for Pippa. But of course I don't tell her this, because then her father might forbid her to speak to me altogether. I must maintain my appearance of harmlessness.

Am I a sell-out too? I don't allow myself to examine that question too closely.

Instead I tell Pippa, "Why don't you ask your mother to find the story and read it to you?" Since Pippa's mother doesn't mind letting her see naked women in the shower, she may not share the librarian's qualms about whatever misconduct Algernon commits in the story. It makes perfect sense to me that a very smart mouse would do things of which humans would not entirely approve.

"Okay," Pippa says. "The story's called 'Flowers for Algernon,' so it must have a happy ending. Mommy gets flowers from Michael on her birthday."

"Oh, that's lovely!" I tell Pippa. I've never seen humans eating flowers—Pippa favors chocolate and once gave me a piece, which I considered an entirely inadequate substitute for seeds and stems—but my opinion of people rises slightly when I learn this. I'm very optimistic about this story.

The next day, Pippa tells me cheerfully that her mother found a copy of the story, but is reading it herself before she reads it to Pippa, just in case the librarian had a good reason for saying that Pippa shouldn't read it. This frustrates me, but I have no choice but to accept it. "I told her that you'd had a good dream about it," Pippa says happily. "She was glad."

The next day, Pippa does not come, and Dr. Krantor makes me run the maze until my whiskers are limp with exhaustion. The day after that, Pippa returns. She tells me, frowning, that her mother has finished reading the story, but agrees with the school librarian that Pippa shouldn't read it. "But I told her she had to: I told her it wasn't fair not to let me know what happens to Algernon." Her voice drops to a whisper now. "I told her she was being like Daddy, trying to keep me from knowing stuff. And that made her face go all funny, and she said, okay, she'll start reading it to me tonight."

"Thank you," I tell Pippa. I'm truly touched by her persistence on my behalf, but also a little alarmed: what in the world can have shocked both a staid school librarian and Pippa's unconventional mother?

It takes me a while to find out. Pippa doesn't come back to the lab for a week. Dr. Krantor is frantic, and as usual when he's worried, he talks to me. He paces back and forth in front of my cage. He

SUSAN PALWICK | 119

rants. "She says it's because she has too much homework, but she
can do her homework here! She says it's because her mother's taking
her to the zoo after school, but how can that be true if she has all that
homework? She says it's because she and her mother and Michael
have to plan a trip. A trip! Her mother's brainwashing her, I know it!
Michael's brainwashing both of them! I'm going to lose Pippa!
They'll flee the country and take her with them! He's probably a Co-
lombian druglord!"

"Just calm down," I tell Dr. Krantor, although I'm worried too.
The string of excuses is clearly fake. I wonder if Pippa's absence has
anything to do with Algernon, but of course I can't talk about that,
because Dr. Krantor doesn't approve of my interest in human stories.

"Don't tell me to calm down, rodent! What would you know
about it? You don't have children!"

And whose fault is that? I think sourly. Often have I asked for a
companion, a female mouse, but Dr. Krantor believes that a mate
would distract me from his mazes, from the quest for cheese.

He storms back to his computer, muttering, and I pace inside
my cage the same way Dr. Krantor paced in front of it. What in the
world is wrong with Pippa? What in the world happened to Algernon? Was he eaten by a cat, or caught in a trap? Right now I would
welcome even the mazes, since they would be a distraction, but Dr.
Krantor is working on something else. At last, sick of pacing, I run
on my exercise wheel until I am too exhausted to think.

Finally Pippa returns. She is quieter than she was. She avoids
me. She sits at the table next to Dr. Krantor's computer, all the way
across the lab, and does her homework. When I stand up on my hind
legs, I can see her, clutching her pencil, the tip of her tongue sticking
out in concentration. And I see Dr. Krantor frowning at her. He
knows she is acting oddly, too. He stands up and looks down at her
workbook. "Pippa, sweetheart, why are you working so hard on
that? That's easy. You already know it. Why don't you go say hello to
the rodent? He missed you. We both missed you, you know."

"I have to finish my homework," she says sullenly.

"Pippa," Dr. Krantor says, frowning even more now, "your
homework is done. That page is all filled out. Pippa, darling, what's
the matter?"

"Nothing! Leave me alone! I don't want to be here! I want to go
home!"

I'm afraid that she's going to start crying, but instead, Dr. Krantor does. He stands behind her, bawling, his fists clenched. "It's Michael, isn't it! You love Michael more than you love me! Your mother's brainwashed you! Where are they taking you, Pippa? Where are you going on this trip? Whatever your mother's said about me is a lie!"

I stare. Dr. Krantor has never had an outburst like this. Pippa, twisted around in her chair, stares too. "Daddy," she says, "it has nothing to do with you. It's not about *you*!"

He snuffles furiously and swipes at his face with a paper towel. "Well then," he says, "why don't you tell me what it's about?"

"It's about Algernon!" she says, and now she's crying, too.

I'm very afraid. Something even worse than a trap or a cat must have happened to Algernon.

It's Dr. Krantor's turn to stare. "Algernon? Who's Algernon? Your mother has a new boyfriend named Algernon? What happened to Michael? Or she has *two* boyfriends now, Michael *and* Algernon? Pippa, this is terrible! I have to get you out of there!"

"Algernon the *mouse*, Daddy!"

Dr. Krantor squints at her. "What?"

And the whole story comes out. Pippa breaks down and tells him everything, hiccupping, as I cower in my cage. Pippa's upset, and it's my fault. Dr. Krantor's going to be furious at me. He won't let me have any more cheese. He'll take away my exercise wheel. "That's why I've been staying away," Pippa says. "Because of Algernon. Because of what happens to Algernon. Daddy—"

"It's just a story," Dr. Krantor says. It's what I expect him to say. But then he says something I don't expect. "Pippa, you have to tell the rodent—"

"His name's Rodney, Daddy!"

"You have to tell Rodney what happened, all right? Because he's been waiting to find out, and he can hear us talking, and not knowing will make him worry more. It's just a story, Pippa. Nothing like that has happened to my mice, the ones here in the lab. I promise. Come on. I'll help you."

Astonished, I watch Dr. Krantor carry Pippa across the lab to my cage. "Pippa," he says when he gets here, "Rodney's missed you. Say hello to Rodney. Do you want to hold him?"

She snuffles and nods, shyly, and Dr. Krantor says, "Rodney, if Pippa holds you, you won't run away, right?"

"No," I say, even more astonished than I was before. Pippa's never been allowed to hold me before, because Dr. Krantor's afraid that she might drop me, and I represent a huge investment of research dollars. But now Dr. Krantor opens the top of the cage and lifts me out by my tail, the way he does when he's going to put me in the maze; but instead he puts me in Pippa's cupped palms, which are very warm. She peers down at me. Her breath is warm too, against my fur, and I see tears still shining in the corners of her eyes. "See?" Dr. Krantor tells her. "Rodney's a very healthy mouse. He's fine, Pippa. There's nothing wrong with him, even though he's smart."

I don't understand this, and nobody's answering the main question. "What happens to Algernon?" I ask.

"He dies," Pippa says in a tiny voice.

"Oh," I say. Well, I'd deduced as much. "A cat gets him, or a mousetrap?" And Pippa's face starts to crumple as she strokes my back, and I hear Dr. Krantor sigh.

"Rodney," he says, "In the story 'Flowers for Algernon,' the mouse Algernon has been IQ-boosted, the way you are. Only the story was written before that was really possible. Anyway, in the story, the mouse dies as a result of the experiment."

"He dies because he's smart," Pippa says mournfully. "Except he gets stupid first. The experiment wears off, and he gets stupid again, and then he dies! The flowers are for his grave!"

"Right," Dr. Krantor says. "Now listen to me, you two. It's *just a story*. None of my mice have died prematurely as a result of the IQ boosting, and the IQ boosting hasn't worn off on any of them. All my mice stay smart, and they don't die any sooner than they would anyway. If anything, they live longer than non-enhanced mice. Okay? Does everybody feel better now?"

"But how did they die?" I ask, alarmed. "How could they die if they were here in their cages, where there aren't any owls or cats or snakes or mousetraps?"

Dr. Krantor shakes his head. "They just died, Rodney. They died of old age. All mice die, sometime. But they had good lives. I take care of my animals."

"What?" I say stupidly. All mice die? "I'm going to die? Even if there aren't any cats?"

"Not anytime soon," Dr. Krantor says. "Everything dies. Didn't you know that?" A drop of water splashes on me, and Dr. Krantor says, "Pippa, sweetheart, you don't have to cry. Rodney's fine. He's a healthy little mouse. Pippa, dear, if you're going to drown him, you'd better put him back in his cage."

And he helps her put me back in my cage, and he says he's going to take her out for ice cream, and he'll bring back some special cheese for me, and I won't even have to run a maze to get it, and they'll be back in a little while. All of these words buzz over me in a blur, as I huddle in my cage trying to make sense of what I've just learned.

I'm going to die.

I'm going to die. All mice die. That's why the stories about mice never say what happened to them, because everyone knows. The mice died. The mouse who became a horse died, and the mice who freed the lion died, and Stuart Little died. I curl into a ball in a corner of my cage and think about this, and then I uncurl and run very hard on my exercise wheel, so I won't have to think about it.

You have taught me language, and my profit on it is, I know how to fear.

Where did that line come from? I don't know, and it's not even really true. I feared things before I knew that I must die; I feared cats and snakes and mousetraps. But fear was always a reason to avoid things, and now I fear something I cannot avoid. I run on the exercise wheel, trying to flee the thing I have learned I cannot escape.

Dr. Krantor and Pippa come back. He has brought me a lovely piece of cheese, an aged cheddar far richer than what I usually find at the end of the maze. He and Pippa sit and watch me nibble at it, and then he says, "Are you all right, Rodney? Do you feel better now?"

"No," I tell him. "You aren't really protecting me by keeping me in this cage, are you? You can't protect me. I'm going to die anyway. You aren't keeping me safe from death; you're denying me life." I think of my memories, the joy of galloping down the road, of chewing through rope, of loving a bird. "You're depriving me of experience. Dr. Krantor, please let me go."

"Let you go?" he says. "Rodney, don't be ridiculous! There are still cats and snakes and mousetraps out there. You'll live much longer this way. And you represent a huge investment of research dollars. I can't let you go."

"I'm not an investment," I snap at him. "I'm a creature! Let me go!"

Dr. Krantor shakes his head. "Rodney, I can't do that. I really can't. I'm sorry. I'll buy you a new exercise wheel, okay? And a bigger cage? There are all kinds of fancy cages with tunnels and things. We can make you a cage ten times bigger than this one. Pippa, you can help design Rodney's new cage. We'll go to the pet store and buy all the parts. It will be fun."

"I don't want a new exercise wheel," I tell him. "I don't want a new cage. I want to be free! Pippa, he says he can't let me go, but remember when he said you couldn't go to the zoo? It's the same thing."

"It's not the same thing at all," Dr. Krantor says. His voice isn't friendly anymore. "Rodney, I'm getting very annoyed with you. Pippa, don't you have more homework to do?"

"No," she says. "I already did my homework. The page is all filled out."

"Well then," Dr. Krantor says. "We'll go to the pet store—"

"I don't want you to go to the pet store! I want you to let me go! Pippa—"

"Stop trying to brainwash her!" Dr. Krantor bellows at me.

I can feel my tail flicking in fury. "You're the one brainwashing her!"

"Stop it," Pippa says. She's put her thumb in her mouth, muffling her words, and she looks like she's going to cry again. "Stop it! I hate it when you fight!"

We stop. I feel miserable. I wonder how Dr. Krantor feels. Pippa goes back to the table where her homework is, and Dr. Krantor goes back to his computer, and I nibble disconsolately on the excellent cheddar. No one says anything. After a while, Dr. Krantor comes back over to my cage and asks wearily, "All right, Rodney. Ready for the maze?"

"Are you out of your mind? I'm not going to run any more mazes! Why should I? What's in it for me?"

"Cheese!"

"I've had enough cheese today." I'm being ungracious, I know. I should thank him for the excellent cheddar. But I'm too angry to mind my manners.

"It's for my research, Rodney!"

"I don't *care* about your research, you imbecile!"

Dr. Krantor curses; Pippa, at her table, has covered her ears. Dr. Krantor reaches into my cage. He lifts me by the tail, none too gently, and plunks me down at the beginning of the maze. "Go," he says.

"Go groom yourself!"

He stomps away. I sit in the maze and clean my whiskers, fastidiously, and then I curl into a ball and take a nap.

I wake to feel myself being lifted into the air again. Dr. Krantor puts me back in my cage, even more roughly than he took me out, and says, "All right, Rodney. Look, this has all been a terrible mess, and I'm very sorry, but if you aren't willing to work tomorrow, we're going to have a problem."

"Going to?" I say.

Dr. Krantor rubs his eyes. "Rodney. Don't do this. You're expendable."

"I am? Even though I represent a tremendous investment of research dollars? Well then, you should have no problem letting me go."

He glares down at me. "Don't do this. Please don't do this. There are things I can do to make you compliant. Drugs. Electric shocks. I don't want to do any of that, and I know you don't want me to either. I want to keep a good working relationship here, all right, Rodney? Please?"

"You're threatening to torture me?" Outrage makes my voice even squeakier than usual. "Great working relationship! Hey, Pippa, did you hear that? Did you hear what your father just said?"

"Pippa isn't here, Rodney. Her mother came to pick her up while you were asleep. They were going to a birthday party. Rodney: will you run the maze tomorrow, or will I have to resort to other methods?"

I'm frightened now. Dr. Krantor's voice is calm, reasonable. He's very matter-of-fact about the prospect of torturing me, and Pippa isn't here as a witness. He's probably bluffing. Coercion would probably compromise his data. But I don't know that for sure.

"Rodney?" he says.

"I'll think about it," I tell him. I have to buy myself time. Now I know why Stuart bowed and scraped. People are so much bigger than we are.

"Good enough," he says, his voice gentler, and reaches into the cage to give me another piece of the excellent cheddar. "Have a good night, Rodney." And then he leaves.

I stay awake all night, fretting. I try to find some way to escape from my cage, but I can't. I wonder if I could escape from the maze;

I've never tried, but surely Dr. Krantor has made the mazes secure also. I don't know what to do.

I dread the morning.

But in the morning, when Dr. Krantor usually arrives, I hear three sets of footsteps in the hallway outside, and two voices: Dr. Krantor's and a woman's.

"Why do you have to take her on this trip in the middle of the school year?" Dr. Krantor says. "And why do you have to talk to me about it now?"

"I already told you, Jack! Michael's family reunion in Ireland is in a month, so if we go we have to go then, and I need you to sign this letter saying that you know I'm not kidnapping her. I don't want any trouble."

Dr. Krantor grumbles something, and the lab door opens. Dr. Krantor and the woman—Pippa's mother!—come inside, still arguing. Pippa comes inside too. Pippa's mother walks to the computer; Pippa races to my cage.

"How *do* I know you aren't kidnapping her?" Dr. Krantor says. "Pippa, there's more of the new cheese over here, if you want to give Rodney a nice breakfast."

"Pippa," I whisper, "he threatened to torture me! Pippa—"

"Shhhhh," she whispers back, and opens my cage, and reaches into one of her pockets. "Don't make any noise, Rodney."

She's holding a mouse. A white mouse, just like me. Pippa puts the new mouse in the cage and we stare at each other in surprise, nose to nose, whiskers twitching, but then I feel Pippa grasp the base of my tail. She lifts me, and I watch the new mouse receding, and then she puts me in her pocket. I hear the cage close, and then we're walking across the room.

"All right, Jack, here's the itinerary, see? Here on this map? Jack, look at the map, would you? I'll tell you every single place we're going; it's not like we're spiriting her away without telling you."

"But how do I know you'll really go there? You could take her to, to, Spain or the South Pole or—"

"Michael doesn't have a family reunion in Spain or the South Pole. Jack, be reasonable."

"I'm bored," Pippa says loudly. "I'm going outside."

"Stay right by the front door, sweetheart!" That's Dr. Krantor, of course.

"I will," she says, and then I hear the lab door open and we're out, we're in the hallway, and then we go through another door and I smell fresh air and Pippa lifts me out of her pocket. She sits down on a step and holds me up to her face. "Mommy and I went to the pet store last night, Rodney, and we got another mouse who looks just like you. He was in the cage of mice people buy to feed to their snakes. Being here is better for him. Daddy won't feed him to a snake."

"But your father will torture the other mouse," I say, "or worse. When he realizes it's just an ordinary mouse he'll be very angry. Pippa, he'll punish you."

"No, he won't," she says cheerfully, "or Mommy and Michael will say he isn't taking good care of me." She puts me down on the warm cement step. I feel wind and smell flowers and grass. "You're free, Rodney. You can have your very own adventures. You don't have to go back to that stupid maze."

"How will I find you?" I tell her. As much as I yearned for freedom before, I'm terrified. There really are cats and snakes and mousetraps out here, and I've never had to face them. How will I know what to do? "Pippa, you have to meet me so I can tell you my stories, or no one will know what happens to me. I'll be just like all those other mice, the ones whose stories just stop when they stop being useful to the main characters. Pippa—"

But there are footsteps now from inside, forceful footsteps coming closer, and Dr. Krantor's voice. His voice sounds dangerous. "Pippa? Pippa, what did you do to the rodent? It won't talk to me! I don't even think it's the same mouse! Pippa, did you put another mouse in that cage?"

I find myself trembling as badly as I would if a cat were coming. Pippa stands up. The sole of her sneaker is the only thing I can see now. From very far above me I hear her saying, "Run, Rodney."

And I do.

THE KING OF WHERE-I-GO

Howard Waldrop

When I was eight, in 1954, my sister caught polio.

It wasn't my fault, although it took twenty years before I talked myself out of believing it was. See, we had this fight . . .

We were at my paternal grandparents' house in Alabama, where we were always taken in the summer, either being driven from Texas to there on Memorial Day and picked up on the Fourth of July, or taken the Fourth and retrieved Labor Day weekend, just before school started again in Texas.

This was the first of the two times when we spent the whole summer in Alabama. Our parents were taking a break from us for three entire months. We essentially ran wild all that time. This was a whole new experience. Ten years later, when it happened the second time, we would return to find our parents separated—me and my sister living with my mother in a garage apartment that backed up on the railroad tracks and my father living in what was a former motel that had been turned into day-laborer apartments a half mile away.

Our father worked as an assembler in a radio factory that would go out of business in the early 1960s, when the Japanese started making them better, smaller, and cheaper. Our mother worked in the Ben Franklin 5¢-10¢-25¢ store downtown. Our father had to carpool every day into a Dallas suburb, so he would come and get the car one day a week. We would be going to junior high by then, and it was two blocks away.

But that was in the future. This was the summer of 1954.

Every two weeks we would get in our aunt's purple Kaiser and she would drive us the forty-five miles to our maternal grandparents' farm in the next county, and we would spend the next two weeks there. Then they'd come and get us after two weeks and bring us back. Like the movie title says, two weeks in another town.

We were back for the second time at the paternal grandparents' place. It was after the Fourth of July because there were burned patches on my grandfather's lower field where they'd had to go beat out the fires started by errant Roman candles and skyrockets.

There was a concrete walk up to the porch of our grandparents' house that divided the lawn in two. The house was three miles out of town; some time in the 1980s the city limits would move past the place when a highway bypass was built to rejoin the highway that went through town and the town made a landgrab.

On the left side of the lawn we'd set up a croquet game (the croquet set would cost a small fortune now, I realize, though neither my grandparents or aunt was what people called well-off).

My sister and I were playing. My grandfather had gone off to his job somewhere in the county. My grandmother was lying down, with what was probably a migraine, or maybe the start of the cancer that would kill her in a few years. (For those not raised in the South; in older homes the bedroom was also the front parlor—there was a stove, chairs for entertaining, and the beds in the main room of the house.) The bed my grandmother lay on was next to the front window.

My sister Ethel did something wrong in the game. Usually I would have been out fishing from before sunup until after dark with a few breaks during the day when I'd have to come back to the house. Breakfast was always made by my grandfather—who had a field holler that carried a mile, which he would let out from the back porch when breakfast was ready, and I'd come reluctantly back from the Big Pond. My grandfather used a third of a pound of coffee a day, and he percolated it for at least fifteen minutes—you could stand a spoon up in it. Then lunch, which in the South is called dinner, when my aunt would come out from her job in town and eat with me and my sister, my grandmother, and any cousins, uncles, or kin who dropped by (always arranged ahead of time, I'm sure), then supper, the evening meal, after my grandfather got home. Usually I went fishing after that, too, until it got too dark to see and the water moccasins came out.

But this morning we were playing croquet and it was still cool so I must have come back from fishing for some reason and been snookered into playing croquet.

"Hey! You can't do that!" I yelled at my sister.

"Do what?" she yelled back.

"Whatever you just did!" I said.

"I didn't do anything!" she yelled.

"You children please be quiet," yelled my grandmother from her bed by the window.

"You cheated!" I yelled at my sister.

"I did not!" she hollered back.

One thing led to another and my sister hit me between the eyes with the green-striped croquet mallet about as hard as a six-year-old can hit. I went down in a heap near a wicket. I sat up, grabbed the blue croquet ball, and threw it as hard as I could into my sister's right kneecap. She went down screaming.

My grandmother was now standing outside the screen door on the porch (which rich people called a verandah) in her housecoat.

"I asked you children to be quiet, please," she said.

"You shut up!" said my sister, holding her knee and crying.

My forehead had swelled up to the size of an apple.

My grandmother moved like the wind then, like Roger Bannister who had just broken the four-minute mile, Suddenly there was a willow switch in her hand and she had my sister's right arm and she was tanning her hide with the switch.

So here was my sister, screaming in two kinds of pain and regretting the invention of language and my grandmother was saying with every movement of her arm, "Don't-you-ever-tell-me-to-shut-up-young-lady!"

She left her in a screaming pile and went back into the house and lay down to start dying some more.

I was well-pleased, with the casual cruelty of childhood, that I would never-ever-in-my-wildest-dreams ever tell my grandmother to shut up.

I got up, picked up my rod and tackle box, and went back over the hill to the Big Pond, which is what I would rather have been doing than playing croquet anyway.

That night my sister got what we thought was a cold, in the middle of July.

Next day, she was in the hospital with polio.

My aunt Noni had had a best friend who got poliomyelitis when they were nine, just after WWI, about the time Franklin Delano Roosevelt had gotten his. (Roosevelt had been president longer than anybody, through the Depression the grown-ups were always talking about, and WWII, which was the exciting part of the history books you never got to in school. He'd died at the end of the war, more than a year before I was born. Then the president had been Truman, and now it was Ike.) My aunt knew what to do and had Ethel in the hospital quick. It probably saved my sister's life, and at least saved her from an iron lung, if it were going to be that kind of polio.

You can't imagine how much those pictures in newsreels scared us all—rows of kids, only their heads sticking out of what looked like long tubular industrial washing machines. Polio attacked many things; it could make it so you couldn't breathe on your own—the iron lung was alternately a hypo- and hyperbaric chamber—it did the work of your diaphragm. This still being in vacuum-tube radio times, miniaturization hadn't set in, so the things weighed a ton. They made noises like breathing, too, which made them even creepier.

If you were in one, there was a little mirror over your head (you were lying down) where you could look at yourself; you couldn't look anywhere else.

Normally that summer we would have gone, every three days or so, with our aunt back to town after dinner and gone to the swimming pool in town. But it was closed because of the polio scare, and so was the theater. (They didn't want young people congregating in one place so the disease could quickly spread.) So what you ended up with was a town full of bored schoolkids and teenagers out of school for the summer with nothing to do. Not what a Baptist town really cares for.

Of course you could swim in a lake or something. But the nearest lake was miles out of town. If you couldn't hitch a ride or find someone to drive you there, you were S.O.L. You could go to the drive-ins for movies. The nearest one was at the edge of the next county—again you needed someone with wheels, although once there you could sit on top of the car and watch the movie, leaving the car itself to the grownups or older teenage brothers and sisters. (They'd even taken away the seats in front of the snack bar where once you could sit like in a regular theater, only with a cloud of mosquitoes eating you all up, again because of polio.)

Me, I had fishing and I didn't care. Let the town wimps stew in their own juices.

But that was all before my sister made polio up close and personal in the family and brought back memories to my aunt.

But Aunt Noni became a ball of fire.

I couldn't go into the hospital to see my sister, of course—even though I had been right there when she started getting sick. Kids could absolutely not come down to the polio ward. This was just a small county hospital with about forty beds, but it also had a polio ward with two iron lungs ready to go, such was the fear in those days.

My aunt took me to the hospital one day, anyway. She had had a big picture-frame mirror with her, from her house.

"She's propped up on pillows and can't move much," my aunt said. "But I think we can get her to see you."

"Stay out here in the parking lot and watch that window," she said. She pointed to one of the half-windows in the basement. I stayed out there until I saw my aunt waving in the window. I waved back.

Then my aunt came out and asked, "Did you see her?"

"I saw you."

"She saw you," she said. "It made her happy." Yeah, I thought, the guy who kneecapped her with the croquet ball.

"I don't know why," I said.

Then Aunt Noni gave me some of my weekly allowance that my parents mailed to her in installments.

I took off to the drugstore like a bullet. I bought a cherry-lime-chocolate coke at the fountain, and a Monster of Frankenstein, a Plastic Man, and an Uncle Scrooge comic book. That took care of forty of my fifty cents. A whole dime, and nowhere to spend it. If it would have been open, and this had been a Saturday, when we usually got our allowance, I would have used the dime to go to the movies and seen eight cartoons, a Three Stooges short, a newsreel, a chapter of a serial, some previews, and a double feature: some SF flick and a Guy Madison movie if I was lucky, a couple of Westerns if I wasn't.

But it was a weekday, and I went back to the office where my aunt Noni was the Jill-of-all-trades plus secretary for a one-man business for forty-seven years (it turned out). It was upstairs next to the bank. Her boss, Mr. Jacks, lived in the biggest new house in town (until, much later, the new doctor in town built a house out on the highway modeled on Elvis' Graceland). Mr. Jacks' house, as fate would have it, was situated on a lot touching my aunt's, only set one house over and facing the other street back.

He wasn't in; he usually wasn't in the office when I was there. Aunt Noni was typing like a bunny, a real blur from the wrists down.

She was the only one in the family who'd been to college. (Much later I would futz around in one for five years without graduating.) She could read, write, and speak Latin, like I later could. She read books. She had the librarian at the Carnegie Library in town send off to Montgomery for books on polio; they'd arrived while I was having the Coca-Cola comic book orgy and she'd gone to get them when the librarian had called her. There was a pile on the third chair in the office.

I was sitting in the second one.

"I want to know," she said as she typed without looking at her shorthand pad or the typewriter, "enough so that I'll know if someone is steering me wrong on something. I don't want to know enough to become pedantic—"

"Huh?" I asked.

She nodded toward the big dictionary on the stand by the door.

I dutifully got up and went to it.

"P—?"

"P-E-D-A," said my aunt, still typing.

I looked it up.

"Hmmm," I said. "Okay." Then I sat back down.

"They're talking like she won't walk again without braces or crutches. That's what they told my friend Frances in nineteen and twenty-one," she said. "You see her motorboatin' all around town now. She only limps a little when she gets really tired and worn out."

Frances worked down at the dress shop. She looked fine except her right leg was a little thinner than her left.

"My aim is to have your sister walking again by herself by next summer."

"Will it happen?"

"If I have anything to do with it, it will," said Aunt Noni.

I never felt so glum about the future as I did sitting there in my aunt's sunny office that July afternoon. What if she were wrong? What if my sister Ethel never walked again? What would her life be like? Who the hell would I play croquet with, in Alabama in the summer, if not her, when I wasn't fishing?

Of course, a year later, the Salk vaccine was developed and tried out and started the end of polio. And a couple of years after that came the Sabin oral vaccine, which they gave to you on sugar cubes and which tasted like your grandfather's old hunting socks smelled, which really ended the disease.

We didn't know any of that then. And the future didn't help my sister any right then.

My parents had of course taken off work and driven from Texas at the end of the first week; there were many family conferences to which the me part of the family was not privy. My parents went to see her and stayed at the hospital.

What was decided was that my sister was to remain in Alabama with my grandparents for the next year and that I was to return to my dead hometown in Texas with my parents and somegoddamnhow survive the rest of the summer there.

My sister Ethel would be enrolled in school in Alabama, provided she was strong enough to do the schoolwork. So I fished the Big Pond and the Little Pond one last time, til it was too dark to see and the bass lost interest in anything in the tackle box, and I went over the low hill to my grandparents' house, robbed of a summer.

Next morning we got the car packed, ready to return to Texas, a fourteen-hour drive in a flathead 6 1952 Ford. Then we stopped by the hospital. Aunt Noni was already there, her purple Kaiser parked by the front door. My parents went in; after a while Aunt Noni waved at the window, then I saw a blur in the mirror and a shape and I waved and waved and jumped up and down with an enthusiasm I did not feel. Then I got in the car and we went back to Texas.

Somehow, I did live through that summer.

One of the things that got me through it was the letters my aunt took down from my sister and typed up. The first couple were about the hospital, til they let her go, and then about what she could see from the back room of my grandparents' house.

We'd usually only gone to Alabama for the summer, and sometimes rushed trips at Christmas, where we were in the car fourteen hours (those days the Interstate Highway System was just a gleam in Ike's eye—so he could fight a two-front war and not be caught short moving stuff from one coast to the other like they had in the Korean War when he was running Columbia University in NYC). We stayed at our grandparents' places Christmas Eve and on Christmas morning and then drove fourteen hours back home just in time for my parents to go to work the day after Christmas.

So I'd never seen Alabama in the fall or the spring. My sister described the slow change from summer to fall there after school started (in Texas it was summer til early October, and you had the leaves finish falling off the trees the third week of December and new buds coming out the second week of January.) She wrote of the geese she heard going over on the Mississippi flyway.

She complained about the schoolwork; in letters back to her I complained about school itself: the same dorks were the same dorks, the same jerks the same jerks, the same bullies still bullies. And that was third grade. Then, you always think it's going to change the next year, until you realize: these jerks are going to be the same ones I'm stuck with the rest of their lives. (As "Scoop" Jackson the senator would later say—it's hard to turn fifty-five and realize the world is being run by people you used to beat up in the fourth grade.)

Third grade was the biggest grind of my life. My sister was finding Alabama second grade tough too; there was no Alamo, no Texas-under-six-flags. In Alabama there was stealing land from the Choctaws and Cherokees, there was the cotton gin and slavery, there was the War for Southern Independence, and then there was the boll weevil. That was about it. No Deaf Smith, no Ben Milam, no line drawn in the dirt with the sword, no last battle of the Civil War fought by two detachments who didn't know the war was over, six weeks after Appomattox; no Spindletop, no oil boom, no great comic-book textbook called Texas History Movies which told you everything in a casually racist way but which you remembered better than any textbook the rest of your life.

I told her what I was doing (reading comics, watching TV) and what I caught in the city park pond or the creek coming out of it. It was the fifties in Texas. There was a drought; the town well had gone dry, and they were digging a lake west of town which, at the current seven inches of rain a year, would take twenty-two years to fill up, by which time we'd all be dead.

I told her about the movies I'd seen once the town's lone theater had opened back up. (There were three drive-ins: one in the next town west, with a great neon cowboy round-up scene on the back of the screen, facing the highway—one guy strummed a green neon guitar, a red neon fire burned at the chuck wagon, a vacquero twirled a pink neon lasso; one at the west edge of our town; and one near the next town to the east.)

Anyway, I got and wrote at least one letter a week to and from my sister; my aunt wrote separate letters to me and my parents; they called each other at least once a week.

Somehow, Christmas dragged its ass toward the school year; my parents decided we'd go to Alabama during the break and see my sister and try to have a happy holiday.

My sister was thinner and her eyes were shinier. She looked pretty much the same except her left leg was skinny. She was propped up in bed. Everybody made a big fuss over her all the time. There was a pile of Christmas presents for her out under the tree in the screened-in hall that would choke a mastodon.

I was finally in her room with no one else there.

"Bored, huh?" I asked.

"There's too many people playing the damned fool around here for me to get bored," she said.

"I mean, outside of Christmas?"

"Well, yeah. The physical therapist lady comes twice a day usually and we go through that rigmarole."

"I hope people got you lots of books," I said.

"I've read so many books I can't see straight, Bubba."

"Have you read All About Dinosaurs?" I asked.

"No."

"I've got my copy with me. You can read it but I gotta have it back before we leave. I stood in a Sears and Roebuck store in Ft. Worth for six hours once while they shipped one over from the Dallas warehouse. The last truck came in and the book wasn't there. They were out and didn't know it. I'd saved up my allowance for four weeks! Without movies or comic books! I told anybody who would listen about it. A week later one came in the mail. Aunt Noni heard the story and ordered it for me."

"Bless her heart."

"I'm real sorry all this happened, Sis," I said, before I knew I was saying it. "I wish we hadn't fought the day before you got sick."

"What? What fight?"

"The croquet game. You hit me."

"You hit me!" she said.

"No. You backsassed Mamaw. She hit you."

"Yes she did," said my sister Ethel.

"Anyway, I'm sorry."

"It wasn't your fault," she said.

I really was going to talk to her more but some damnfool uncle came in wearing his hat upside down to make her laugh.

*   *   *

My sister grew up and. walked again, and except for a slight limp and a sometime windmilling foot (like my aunt's friend Frances when she was very tired), she got around pretty well, even though she lost most of a year of her life in that bed in Alabama.

I remember walking with her the first day of school when she had come back to Texas and was starting third grade.

"Doing okay?" I asked. We lived three whole blocks from school then, but I wanted her to take it slow and not get too tired.

"Yeah. Sure," she said.

I remember the day they handed out the permission forms for the Salk polio vaccine, which was a big shot with a square needle in the meat of your arm.

My sister laughed and laughed. "Oh, bitter irony!" she said "Oh, ashes and dust!"

"Yeah," I said, "well . . ."

"Have Mom and Pop sign yours twice," she said. "At least it'll do you some good."

"Once again, Sis, I'm sorry."

"Tell that to the school nurse," she said.

At some point, when we were in our late teens, we were having one of those long philosophical discussions brothers and sisters have when neither has a date and you're too damned tired from the school week to get up off your butt and go out and do something on your own, and the public library closed early. Besides, your folks are yelling at each other in their bedroom.

The Time Machine was one of my favorite movies (they all are). I had the movie tie-in paperback with the photo of Rod Taylor on the back; the Dell Movie Classic comic book with art by Alex Toth, and the Classics Illustrated edition with art by Lou Cameron—it had been my favorite for years before the movie had come out in 1960.

"What would I do," I repeated Ethel's question, "if I could travel in time? Like go see dinosaurs, or go visit the spaceport they're going to build just outside this popsicle burg?

"Most people would do just what I'd do: first I'd go to the coin shop, buy ten early 1930s Mercury dimes, then go back to 1938 and buy ten copies of Action Comics #1 with Superman's first story, and then I'd go write mash notes to Eve Arden."

I'd just finished watching reruns of Our Miss Brooks on TV.

"No," she said. "I mean, really?"

"No," I said. "I mean, really."

"Wouldn't you try to stop Oswald?" she asked. "Go strangle Hitler in his cradle?"

"You didn't ask 'What would you do if you could travel in time to make the world a better place?' You asked 'What would you do if you could travel in time?'"

"Be that way," she said.

"I am that way."

And then she went off to work at some Rhine-like lab in North Carolina. That's not what she set out to do—what she set out to do was be a carhop, get out of the house and our live local version of the Bickersons. (Bickering=Pow! Sock! Crash!)

She first worked as a carhop in town, from the time she was fourteen, and then she got the real glamour job over in Dallas at the biggest drive-in cafe there, twenty-five carhops, half of them on skates (not her). She moved in with two other carhops there. A few months later, King and Bobby Kennedy got killed and half the US burned down.

Something happened at the cafe—I never found out exactly what. But a week later she called home and said this research lab was flying her to North Carolina for a few days (she'd never flown before). And then she left.

I started getting letters from her. By then our parents had gotten a divorce; I was living in the house with my father (who would die in a few months of heart failure—and a broken heart). My mom had run off with the guy she'd been sneaking around with the last couple of years and we weren't talking much. I was in college and seeing the girl I would eventually marry, have a kid with, and divorce.

My sister told me they were really interested in her; that other institutes were trying to get her to come over to them and that she wasn't the only polio survivor there. My first thought was—what's going on? Is this like Himmler's interest in twins and gypsies, or was this just statistically average? This was the late '60s; lots of people our age had polio before 1955, so maybe that was it?

Her letters were a nice break in the college routine—classes, theater, part-time thirty-six-hour-a-week job. Of course I got an ulcer before I turned twenty-two. (Later it didn't keep me from being drafted; it had gotten better after I quit working thirty hours a week in theater plus the job plus only sleeping between three and six A.M. seven days a week.)

"The people here are nice," she said. "The tests are fun, except for the concentration. I get headaches like Mamaw used to get, every other day." She sent me a set of the cards—Rhine cards. Circle, triangle, star, square, plus sign, wavy horizontal lines. They had her across the table from a guy who turned the cards, fifty of them, randomly shuffled. She was supposed to intuit (or receive telepathically) which cards he'd turned over. She marked the symbol she thought it was. There was a big high partition across the middle of the table—she could barely see the top of the guy's head. Sometimes she was the one turning the cards and tried to send messages to him. There were other, more esoteric ones—the tests were supposed to be scientific and repeatable.

From one of her letters:

> I don't mind the work here, and if they prove something by it, more's the better. What I do mind is that all the magazines I read here think that if there is something to extrasensory perception, then there also has to be mental contact with UFOs (what UFOs?) and the Atlanteans (what Atlantis?) and mental death rays and contact with the spirit-world (what spirit-world?).
>
> I don't understand that; proving extrasensory perception only proves that exists, and they haven't even proved that yet. Next week they're moving me over to the PK unit—PsychoKinesis. Moving stuff at a distance without, as Morbius said, "instrumentality." That's more like what happened at the drive-in anyway. They wanted to test me for this stuff first. Evidently I'm not very good at this. Or, I'm the same as everybody else, except the ones they catch cheating, by what they call reading the other person—physical stuff like in poker, where somebody always lifts an eyebrow when the star comes up—stuff like that.
>
> Will write to you when I get a handle on this PK stuff.
> Your sis,
> Ethel

"You would have thought I set off an atom bomb here," her next letter began. She then described what happened and the shady-looking new people who showed up to watch her tests.

Later, they showed her some film smuggled out of the USSR of ladies shaped like potatoes doing hand-schtick and making candles move toward them.

My sister told them her brother could do the same thing with 2-lb test nylon fishing line.

"If I want that candle there to move over here, I'll do it without using my hands," she'd said.

And then, the candle didn't move.

"They told me then my abilities may lie in some other area; that the cafe incident was an anomaly, or perhaps someone else, a cook or another carhop had the ability; it had just happened to her because she was the one with the trays and dishes.

"Perhaps," she had told them, "you were wrong about me entirely and are wasting your motel and cafeteria money and should send me back to Texas Real Soon. Or maybe I have the ability to move something besides candles, something no one else ever had. Or maybe we are just all pulling our puds." Or words to that effect.

A couple of days later she called me on the phone. The operator told her to deposit $1.15. I heard the ching and chime of coins in the pay phone.

"Franklin," said Ethel.

She never called me by my right name; I was Bubba to everyone in the family.

"Yes, Sis, what is it?"

"I think we had a little breakthrough here. We won't know til tomorrow. I want you to know I love you."

"What the hell you talkin' about?"

"I'll let you know," she said.

Then she hung up.

The next day was my usual Wednesday, which meant I wouldn't get any sleep. I'd gotten to bed the night before at 2 A.M. I was in class by 7 A.M. and had three classes and lab scattered across the day. At 6 P.M. I drove to the regional newspaper plant that printed all the suburban dailies. I was a linotype operator at minimum wage. The real newspaper that owned all the suburban ones was a union shop and the guys there made $3.25 an hour in 1968 dollars. I worked a twelve-hour shift (or a little less if we got all the type set early) three nights a week, Mon.-Wed.-Fri. That way, not only did you work for $1.25 an hour, they didn't owe you for overtime unless you pulled more than a sixteen-hour shift one night—and nobody ever did.

Linotypes were mechanical marvels—so much so that Mergen-thaler, who finally perfected it, went slap-dab crazy before he died. It's like being in a room of mechanical monsters who spit out hot pieces of lead (and sometimes hot lead itself all over you—before they do that, they make a distinctive noise and you've got a second and a half to get ten feet away; it's called a backspill).

Once all linotype was set by hand, by the operators. By the time I came along, they had typists set copy on a tape machine. What came out there was perforated tape, brought into the linotype room in big, curling strands. The operator—me—put the front end of the tape into a reader-box built onto the keyboard, and the linotype clicked away like magic. The keys depressed, lines of type-mold keys fell into place from a big magazine above the keyboard; they were lifted up and moved over to the molder against the pot of hot lead; the line was cast, an arm came down, lifted the letter matrices up, another rod pushed them over onto an endless spiraled rod, and they fell back into the typecase when the side of the matrix equaled the space on the typecase, and the process started all over. If the tape code was wrong and a line went too long, you got either type matrices flying everywhere as the line was lifted to the molder, or it went over and you got a backspill and hot lead flew across the room.

Then you had to turn off the reader, take off the galley where the slugs of hot type came off to cool, open up the front of the machine, clean all the lead off with a wire brush, put it back together, and start the tape reader back up. When the whole galley was set and cool, you pulled a proof on a small rotary press and sent it back to the typists, where corrections would come back on shorter and shorter pieces of paper tape. You kept setting and inserting the corrections and throwing away the bad slugs until the galley was okayed; then you pulled a copy of the galley and sent it up to the composing room where they laid out the page of corrected galley, shot a page on a plate camera, and made a steel plate from that; that was put on the web press and the paper was run off and sent out to newsboys all over three counties.

It was a noisy, nasty twelve-hour hell with the possibility of being hit in the face with molten lead or asphyxiating when, in your copious free time, you took old dead galleys and incorrect slugs back to the lead smelter to melt down and then ladled out molten lead into pig-iron molds which, when cooled down, you took and hung by the hole in one end to the chain above the pot on each linotype—

besides doing everything else it did, the machine lowered the lead pigs into the pots by a ratchet gear each time it set a line. No wonder Mergenthaler went mad.

I did all that twelve hours a night three nights a week for five years, besides college. There were five linotypes in the place, including one that Mergenthaler himself must have made around 1880, and usually three of them were down at a time with backspills or other problems.

Besides that, there were the practical jokers. Your first day on the job you were always sent for the type-stretcher, all over the printing plant. "Hell, I don't know who had that last!" they'd say. "Check the composing room." Then some night the phone would ring in the linotype room; you'd go to answer it and get an earful of printers' ink, about the consistency of axle grease. Someone had slathered a big gob on the earpiece and called you from somewhere else in the plant. Nyuk nyuk nyuk.

If you'd really pissed someone off (it never happened to me), they'd wait for a hot day and go out and fill all four of your hubcaps with fresh shrimp. It would take two or three days before they'd really stink; you'd check everywhere in the car but the hubcaps; finally something brown would start running from them and you'd figure it out. Nyuk nyuk nyuk.

That night I started to feel jumpy. Usually I was philosophical: Why, this is hell, nor am I out of it. Nothing was going on but the usual hot, repetitious drudgery. Something felt wrong. My head didn't exactly hurt, but I knew it was there. Things took on a distancing effect—I would recognize that from dope, later on. But there was no goofer dust in my life then. Then I noticed everybody else was moving and talking faster than normal. I looked at the clock with the big sweep second-hand outside the linotype room. It had slowed to a crawl.

I grabbed onto the bed of the cold iron proof-press and held on to it. Later, when I turned fifty or so, I was in a couple of earthquakes on the West Coast, but they were nothing compared to what I was feeling at that moment.

One of the tape compositor ladies, a blur, stopped in front of me and chirped out "Doyoufeelallright, Frank?"

"Justa headacheI'llbeokay," I twittered back.

I looked at the clock again.

The sweep-hand stopped. I looked back into the linotype room.

People moved around like John Paul Stapp on the Sonic Wind rocket sled.

I looked at the clock again. The second hand moved backward.

And then the world blurred all out of focus and part of me left the clanging clattering linotypes behind.

I looked around the part of town I could see. (What was I doing downtown? Wasn't I at work?) The place looked like it did around 1962. The carpet shop was still in business—it had failed a few months before JFK was shot. Hamburgers were still four for a dollar on the menus outside the cafes. The theater was showing Horror Chamber of Dr. Faustus and The Manster, which was a 1962 double feature. Hosey the usher was leaving in his '58 Chevy; he quit working at the theater in 1964, I knew. I had a feeling that if I walked one block north and four blocks west I could look in the window of a house and see myself reading a book or doing homework. I sure didn't want to do that.

Then the plant manager was in front of me. "Hey! You've got a backspill on #5, that crappy old bastard, and #3's quit reading tape."

"Sorry," I said. "I just got a splitting headache for a minute. Got any aspirin?" I asked, taking the galley off #5.

"Go ask one of the women who's having her period," he said. "I just took all the aspirin in the place. The publisher's all over my ass this week. Why, I don't know. I robbed the first-aid kit: don't go there."

"That would have been my next stop," I said. I brushed a cooled line of lead off the keyboard and from the seat and up the back of the caster chair in front of the linotype. I closed the machine back up and started it up and went over and pounded on the reader box of #3. It chattered away.

For a while I was too busy to think about what had happened.

"Feeling a little weird?" asked my sister, this time on a regular phone.

"What the hell happened?"

"Talk to this man," she said.

She put on some professor whose name I didn't catch.

He asked me some questions. I told him the answers. He said he was sending a questionnaire. My sister came back on.

"I think they think I gave you a bad dream two thousand miles away," she said. "That would be a big-cheese deal to them."

"What do you think?" I asked. "I saw Hosey."

"Either way, you would have done that," she said.

"What do you mean, either way? Why are you involving me? Is this fun?"

"Because," she said, "you're my brother and I love you."

"Yeah, well . . ." I said. "Why don't you mess with someone you don't like? Who's that guy who left you in Grand Prairie to walk home at 5 A.M.?"

"I killed him with a mental lightning bolt yesterday," she said. Then, "Just kidding.

"Well, I'm glad you're just kidding, because I just shit my pants. I don't want to ever feel like I did last night, again, ever. It was creepy."

"Of course it was creepy," she said. "We're working at the frontiers of science here."

"Are you on the frontiers of science there," I asked, "or . . ."

She finished the sentence with me: ". . . are we just pulling our puds?" She laughed. "I don't have a clue. They're trying to figure out how to do this scientifically. They may have to fly you in."

"No, thanks!" I said. "I've got a life to live. I'm actually dating a real-live girl. I'm also working myself to death. I don't have time for hot dates with Ouija boards, or whatever you're doing there. Include me out."

She laughed again. "We'll see."

"No you won't! Don't do this to me. I'm . . ."

There was a dial tone.

So the second time I knew what was happening. I was at home. I felt the distancing effect; the speeding up of everything around, except the kitchen clock. It was the kind where parts of numbers flipped down, an analog readout. It slowed to a crawl. The thin metal strips the numbers were painted on took a real long time before they flipped down.

A bird rocketed through the yard. The neighbor's dog was a beige blur. I could barely move. My stomach churned like when I was on the Mad Octopus at the Texas State Fair. The clock hung between 10:29 and 10:30 A.M. Then it was 10:29. 10:28. 10:27. Then the readout turned into a high whining flutter.

*   *   *

This time everything was bigger. Don't ask me why. I was at my favorite drugstore, the one next to the theater. The drugstore was at the corner of Division and Center Street. I glanced at a newspaper. June 17, 1956. If memory serves, I would have been over in Alabama at the time, so I wouldn't be running into myself. I reached in my pocket and looked at my change. Half of it hadn't been minted yet. (How was that possible?) The guy at the register ignored me—he'd seen me a million times, and I wasn't one of the kids he had to give the Hairy Eyeball to. When I came in, I came to buy.

I looked at the funny book rack. Everything except the Dell Comics had the Comics Code Seal on them, which meant they'd go to Nice Heaven. No zombies, no monsters, no blood, no Blackhawks fighting the Commies, who used stuff that melts tanks, people—everything but wood. No vampires "saaaaking your blaaad." Dullsville. I picked up a Mad magazine, which was no longer a comic book, so it wouldn't be under the Comics Code, but had turned into a 25¢—What, me cheap?—magazine. It had a Kelly Freas cover of Alfred E. Neuman.

I fished out a 1952 quarter and put it down by the register. There wasn't any sales tax in Texas yet. Fifty years later, we would be paying more than New York City.

I looked at the theater marquee when I stepped outside. Bottom of the Bottle and Bandido—one with Joseph Cotten and Richard Egan, the other with Glenn Ford and Gilbert Roland. I'd seen them later, bored by the first except for a storm scene, and liked the second because there were lots of explosions and Browning .50 caliber machine guns. Nothing for me there.

I walked down toward Main Street.

There was a swooping sensation and a flutter of light and I was back home.

The analog readout on the clock clicked to 10:30 A.M.

I went to the coin shop. I went to my doctor's office. I went to a couple of other places. I actually had to lie a couple of times, and I used one friendship badly, only they didn't know, but I did.

Then I found the second letter my sister had sent me from North Carolina and got the phone number of the lab. I called it the next morning. It took awhile, but they finally got Ethel to the phone.

"Feeling okay?" she asked.

"Hell no," I said. "I'm not having any fun. At least let me have fun. Two days from now give me an hallucination about Alabama. In the summer. I want to at least see if the fishing is as good as I remember it."

"So it is written," she said, imitating Yul Brynner in The Ten Commandments, "so it shall be done."

I knew it really didn't matter, but I kept my old fiberglass spinning rod, with its Johnson Century spinning reel, and my old My Buddy tackle box as near me as I could the next two days. Inside the tackle box with all the other crap were three new double-hook rigged rubber eels, cheap as piss in 1969, but they cost $1.00 each in 1950s money when they'd first come out.

This time I was almost ready for it and didn't panic when the thing came on. I rode it out like the log flume ride out at Six Flags Over Texas, and when the clock outside the college classroom started jumping backward, I didn't even get woozy. I closed my eyes and made the jump myself.

I was at the Big Pond and had made a cast. A two-pound bass had taken the rubber eel. The Big Pond was even bigger than I remembered (although I knew it was only four acres). I got the bass in and put it on a stringer with its eleven big clamps and swivels between each clamp on the chain. I put the bass out about two feet in the water and put the clamp on the end of the stringer around a willow root.

Then I cast again, and the biggest bass I had ever had took it. There was a swirl in the water the size of a #2 washtub and I set the hook.

I had him on for maybe thirty seconds. He jumped in the shallow water as I reeled. He must have weighed ten pounds. When he came down there was a splash like a cow had fallen into the pond.

Then the rubber eel came sailing lazily out of the middle of the commotion, and the line went slack in a backflowing arc. It (probably she) had thrown the hook.

There was a big V-wake heading for deeper water when the bass realized it was free.

I was pissed off at myself. I picked up the stringer with the two-pound bass (which now didn't look as large as it had five minutes ago) and my tackle box and started off over the hill back toward my grandparents' house.

I walked through the back gate, with its plowshare counterweight on the chain that kept it closed. I took the fish off the stringer and eased it into the seventy-five gallon rainbarrel, where it started to swim along with a catfish my uncle had caught at the Little Pond yesterday. In the summer, there was usually a fish fry every Friday. We got serious about fishing on Thursdays. By Friday there would be fifteen or twenty fish in the barrel, from small bluegills to a few crappie to a bunch of bass and catfish. On Fridays my uncle would get off early, start cleaning fish, heating up a cast-iron pot full of lard over a charcoal fire and making up batter for the fish and hush puppies. Then, after my grandfather came in, ten or eleven of us would eat until we fell over.

Later the cooled fish grease would be used to make dogbread for my grandfather's hounds. You didn't waste much in Alabama in those days.

I washed my hands off at the outside faucet and went through the long hall from the back door, being quiet, as the only sound in the house was of SuZan, the black lady who cooked for my grandmother, starting to make lunch. I looked into the front room and saw my grandmother sleeping on the main bed.

I went out onto the verandah. I'd taken stuff out of the tackle box in the back hall, when I'd leaned my fishing rod up against a bureau, where I kept it ready to go all summer.

I was eating from a box of Domino® sugar cubes when I came out. My sister was in one of the Adirondack-type wooden chairs, reading a Katy Keene comic book; the kind where the girl readers sent in drawings of dresses and sunsuits they'd designed for Katy. The artist redrew them when they chose yours for a story, and they ran your name and address printed beside it so other Katy Keene fans could write you. (Few people know it, but that's how the internet started.)

She must have been five or six—before she got sick. She was like a sparkle of light in a dark world.

"Back already?" she asked. "Quitter."

"I lost the biggest fish of my life," I said. "I tried to horse it in. I should have let it horse me but kept control, as the great A.J. McClane says in Field and Stream," I said. "I am truly disappointed in my fishing abilities for the first time in a long time."

"Papaw'll whip your ass if he finds out you lost that big fish he's been trying to catch," she said. "He would have gone in after it, if he ever had it on." He would have, too.

"Yeah, he's a cane-pole fisherman, the best there ever was, but it was too shallow there for him to get his minnow in there with a pole. It was by that old stump in the shallow end." Then I held up the sugar-cube box.

"Look what I found," I said.

"Where'd you get those?"

"In the old chiffarobe."

"SuZan'll beat your butt if she finds you filchin' sugar from her kitchen."

"Probably some of Aunt Noni's for her tea. She probably bought it during the Coolidge Administration and forgot about it." Aunt Noni was the only person I knew in Alabama who drank only one cup of coffee in the morning, and then drank only tea, iced or hot, the rest of the day.

"Gimme some," said Ethel.

"What's the magic word?"

"Please and thank you."

I moved the box so she took the ones I wanted her to. She made a face. "God, that stuff is old," she said.

"I told you they was," I said.

"Gimme more. Please," she said. "Those are better." Then: "I've read this Katy Keene about to death. Wanna play croquet til you get up your nerve to go back and try to catch that fish before Papaw gets home?"

"Sure," I said. "But that fish will have a sore jaw til tomorrow. He'll be real careful what he bites the rest of the day. I won't be able to tempt him again until tomorrow."

We started playing croquet. I had quite the little run there, making it to the middle wicket from the first tap. Then my sister came out of the starting double wicket and I could tell she was intent on hitting my ball, then getting to send me off down the hill. We had a rule that if you were knocked out of bounds, you could put the ball back in a mallet-head length from where it went out. But if you hit it hard enough, the ball went out of bounds, over the gravel parking area, down the long driveway, all the way down the hill and out onto Alabama Highway 12. You had to haul your ass all the way down the dirt drive, dodge the traffic, retrieve the ball from your cousin's front yard, and climb all the way back up to the croquet grounds to put your ball back into play.

My sister tapped my ball at the end of a long shot. She placed her ball against it, and put her foot on top of her croquet ball. She lined up her shot. She took a practice tap to make sure she had the right murderous swing.

"Hey!" I said "My ball moved! That counts as your shot!"

"Does not!" she yelled.

"Yes it does!" I yelled.

"Take your next shot! That counted!" I added.

"It did not!" she screamed.

"You children be quiet!" my grandmother yelled from her bed of pain.

About that time was when Ethel hit me between the eyes with the green-striped croquet mallet; I kneecapped her with the blue croquet ball, and, with a smile on my swelling face as I heard the screen door open and close, I went away from there.

This time I felt like I had been beaten with more than a mallet wielded by a six-year-old. I felt like I'd been stoned by a crowd and left for dead. I was dehydrated. My right foot hurt like a bastard, and mucus was dripping from my nose. I'm pretty sure the crowds in the hall as classes let out noticed—they gave me a wide berth, like I was a big ugly rock in the path of migrating salmon.

I got home as quickly as I could, cutting History of the Totalitarian State 405, which was usually one of my favorites.

I called the lab long distance. Nobody knew about my sister. Maybe it was her day off. I called the Motel 6. Nobody was registered by her name. The manager said, "Thank you for calling Motel 6." Then he hung up.

Maybe she'd come back to Dallas. I called her number there.

"Hello," said somebody nice.

"Is Ethel there?"

"Ethel?"

"Yeah, Ethel."

"Oh. That must have been Joanie's old roommate."

I'd met Joanie once. "Put Joanie on, please?" I asked.

She was in, and took the phone.

"Joanie? Hi. This is Franklin—Bubba—Ethel's brother."

"Yeah?"

"I can't get ahold of her in North Carolina."

"Why would you be calling her there, honey?"

"'Cause that's where she was the last two weeks."

"I don't know about that. But she moved out of here four months ago. I got a number for her, but she's never there. The phone just rings and rings. If you happen to catch her, tell her she still owes me four dollars and thirty-one cents on that last electric bill. I'm workin' mostly days now, and I ain't waitin' around two hours to see her. She can leave it with Steve; he'll see I get it."

"Steve. Work. Four dollars," I mumbled.

She gave me the number. The prefix meant south Oak Cliff, a suburb that had been eaten by Dallas.

I dialed it.

"Ethel?"

"Who is this? What the hell you want? I just worked a double shift."

"It's Bubba," I said.

"Brother? I haven't heard from you in a month of Sundays."

"No wonder. You're in North Carolina; you come back without telling me; you didn't tell me you'd moved out from Joanie's . . ."

"What the hell you mean, North Carolina?! I been pullin' double shifts for three solid weeks—I ain't had a day off since September 26th. I ain't never been to North Carolina in my life."

"Okay. First, Joanie says you owe her $4.31 on the electric bill . . ."

"Four thirty-one," she said, like she was writing it down. "I'll be so glad when I pay her so she'll shut up."

"Okay. Let's start over. How's your leg?"

"Which leg?"

"Your left leg. The polio leg. Just the one that's given you trouble for fifteen years. That's which leg."

"Polio. Polio? The only person I know with polio is Noni's friend Frances, in Alabama."

"Does the year 1954 ring a bell?" I asked.

"Yeah. That was the first time we spent the whole summer in Alabama. Mom and Dad sure fooled us the second time, didn't they? Hi. Welcome back from vacation, kids. Welcome to your new broken homes."

"They should have divorced long before they did. They would have made themselves and a lot of people happier."

"No," she said. "They just never should have left backwoods Alabama and come to the Big City. All those glittering objects. All that excitement."

"Are we talking about the same town here?" I asked.

"Towns are as big as your capacity for wonder, as Fitzgerald said," said Ethel.

"Okay. Back to weird. Are you sure you never had polio when you were a kid? That you haven't been in North Carolina the last month at some weird science place? That you weren't causing me to hallucinate being a time-traveler?"

"Franklin," she said. "I have never seen it, but I do believe you are drunk. Why don't you hang up now and call me back when you are sober. I still love you, but I will not tolerate a drunken brother calling me while I am trying to sleep.

"Good-bye now—"

"Wait! Wait! I want to know, are my travels through? Can I get back to my real life now?"

"How would I know?" asked Ethel. "I'm not the King Of Where-You-Go."

"Maybe. Maybe not."

"Go sober up now. Next time call me at work. Nights."

She hung up.

And then I thought: what would it be like to watch everyone slow down; the clock start whirling clockwise around the dial til it turned gray like it was full of dishwater, and then suddenly be out at the spaceport they're going to build out at the edge of town and watch the Mars rocket take off every Tuesday?

And: I would never know the thrill of standing, with a satchel full of comics under my arm, waiting at the end of Eve Arden's driveway for her to get home from the studio . . .

> *Dedicated to Ms. Mary Ethel (Waldrop)*
> *Burton Falco Bray Hodnett, my little sister . . .*

THE POLICEMAN'S DAUGHTER

Wil McCarthy

1.
Bourbon, Interrupted

The courier didn't come bearing packages, or letters marked *Carmine Strange Douglas, esq., Adjudicant, Juris Doctor and Attorney at Law.* He didn't need to. Instead, he came barreling down the hallway like a team of horses, shouting "Door!" at the wall of my office. When a rectangle of frosted glass appeared and swung inward, he jumped inside.

"Carmine. I have something for you," he panted.

"Did you run all the way over here?" I asked him. "There are quicker ways—"

But the courier didn't answer. Instead, he approached the fax machine—a vertical plate of gray material, vaguely shimmery in the wellstone light of my office—and said, "Reconverge." Then he threw himself at the plate and vanished with a faint blue sizzle.

Reconverge, hell. I'd sent two couriers out to question potential witnesses in the Szymanski divorce, and one had self-destructed rather than share his waste of time with me. The other, apparently, had come back with something both critical and hard to explain. Go figure.

Myself, I'd just finished researching the details on the case, poring over written documents and public records, mental notes and fax traces in an effort to figure out who, if anyone, had promised Albert the cabana boy permanent residence on that tiny estate. Certainly he'd made the claim in public several times, within the hearing of one or both Szymanskis, and neither had corrected him.

This by itself carried a certain legal weight, even if the original claim was baseless, so if the Szymanskis sold the property—and it looked like they were going to have to—Albert's claim might have to be bought out at his own named price, or sold along with the property as an easement in perpetuity. And in a world without death, perpetuity could be a long damned time! Oh, what a jolly old mess.

It was four-thirty in the afternoon, late enough to kill brain cells with a clear conscience, and I'd just cracked the seal on an open-source bourbon of excellent pedigree. Damn. Sitting open to the atmosphere would not improve it. Still, the courier's news sounded important in a pay-the-mortgage kind of way, and like most decent bourbons this cost almost nothing to print. And when you're immorbid, baby, there's always tomorrow.

Sighing, I got up from my desk, from my too-comfortable chair, and strode over to the fax's print plate. "Confirming reconvergence, all parameters normal." Then I followed the courier through.

Stepping into a fax machine is like falling face-first into a swimming pool. The sensation isn't cold, or liquid, or electric, but it's just as distinct. There is, of course, no sensation of being *inside* the fax machine, since the part of you that passes through the print plate is immediately whisked apart into component atoms. Technically speaking, there should be no consciousness at all as the head disappears, as the body is destroyed and rebuilt, sometimes in combination with other stored images. But consciousness is a funny thing, an illusion that struggles to preserve itself against any insult. The courier and I stepped out of the plate only a moment after I'd stepped into it. Facing *into* the room, now, not out of it.

The courier was, of course, myself. We were one and the same, briefly split and now rejoined in that seamless ball of wonderfulness that was Carmine Strange Douglas. Like any good investigative counsel, I did this five or six times a day. Hell, if not for plurality laws—three thousand copy-hours per month, rigidly enforced by the fax network itself—I'd do it more than that.

Anyway, now that I was one person again I knew details of my—of the courier's—meeting with Lillia Blair, *and* I knew all the details of my morning and afternoon research. Reconvergence: the collapsing of two waveforms into one. Like any scattered thoughts the pieces took a few seconds to come together in my mind, but when they did, the legal strategy was clear.

"Call Juniper," I said to the wall.

The wall considered this for a moment before answering, "I assume you mean Juniper Tall Szymanski."

I glared at the wall without answering, irritated because I'd already called June Szymanski twice this week, and the only other Juniper I knew—Juniper Pong—I hadn't spoken to in months. Taking the hint, the wall patched the message through, and created a hollie window beside the open doorway.

For two seconds it displayed nothing but gray; that deep, foggy, *three-dimensional* gray that some people—myself included—use for a null screen. But then, presently, June Szymanski's face appeared in the hollie, and behind it her living room. She might as well be standing right outside my office. She might as well be solid, physical, *here*. I've had some practice in distinguishing real windows from hollies, but it takes a microscope and some patience.

"Hi," June said, looking both anxious and pleased to hear from me. "What've you got?"

People are always glad to hear from Carmine while their case is unresolved, and especially when the strategy hadn't been figured out yet. At times like these, I'm everybody's best friend. If the issue came to trial, I figured June and I would be friends for another week, week and a half. But in light of what I'd just figured out, a trial seemed rather unlikely.

"According to Lillia," I said, "Albert's exact words were 'I can stay until I decide to leave.'"

"So?" she asked, absorbing that without really getting it.

"So, that's a very different thing from 'I can stay forever,' or even 'I can stay as long as I want.' Because 'decide to leave' is a distinct event in time and space. It can be measured, logged, and read into the court records. And we can make a case—a strong one—that simply setting foot outside that cabana will bring the implied contract to an end."

"Huh. Meaning what? I can evict him?"

Can anyone evict anyone these days? "No," I told her. "Not now, and not without a lot of work. But you can inform him that leaving the poolhouse is *grounds* for eviction."

Juniper's face relaxed. "Oh, my God. Thank you so much. I do want to be civil about this, but I can't have that . . . I can't face this . . . well, this makes everything a lot easier. You're a genius, Carmine."

And that was true. I *was* a genius, I am, but so are all the other lawyers in town. These days it's impossible practice law—to practice much of anything—if you aren't unimaginably good at it. Because if you're not, someone who *is* will simply print an extra copy of him- or herself, and take over another chunk of your market.

False modesty is bad for business; I'm not ashamed to say I aced my bar exam, went to the best schools and did well in them. I reckon I'd make a good generalist, not only in the practice of law but in a range of other fields. I was one hundred years old, immorbid, and absorbed knowledge voraciously.

But even that wasn't enough to hold a job in Denver anymore. You had to be generalist an*d a* specialist. You had to be broad and brilliant, but lensed down to a unique pinpoint. You had to get your name associated with some particular little quirk or gimmick of the business so that people, when they ran afoul of it, would know whom to call. Even 'interpersonal disputes' cut too broad a swath for a viable legal practice. And anyway it was boring: the same disputes over and over again, with only the names and faces changing. And anymore the faces—sculpted by faxware to beauty and perfection— weren't so different either.

But I've always had a flair for the dramatic and a nose for the bizarre. My directory ad said it all: "If you've been wronged, call a lawyer. If you've been *stranged*, call Carmine Strange Douglas."

"This could still turn ugly," I warned June. "That's a wellstone cabana, right? Fully programmable, no restrictions? And he's got his own fax machine in there. Creme brulee and ostritch bisque, anytime he likes. If he decides to make a siege of it, he could hold out for a long time."

"Can't we just shut off the electricity?"

"Ahem! No. And even if you could, he's got the right to generate his own. Wind, sun, and rain—the Free Three, as they say. Albert has taken sides, Mrs. Szymanski. Specifically he's taken your husband's, and he's not going to vacate just because you ask him nicely. He wants this to be difficult.

"I'll write a threatening letter if you want, give him something to think about, but my advice to you as a friend is to talk things over with your husband. It's all right to get bored with each other—if we're going to live forever, it's almost inevitable. But somebody's got make a gesture, here. This is no way for two people to behave, who ever loved each other."

At this, Juniper Szymanski's face closed down. "You don't know anything about it, Carmine. Beyond the bare facts. I'm guessing it's a long time since you've been hurt."

And then she cut the connection, and her hollie window winked out.

What a small-minded thing for her to say! I'd been hurt plenty, and bad. In the broken-heart shuffle that began the moment people stopped dying, everyone got hurt. Or maybe they always had, and always would. This was just one of those facts of life, which you could put out of mind if you didn't happen to be an inter-personal lawyer. Divorces were far and away the worst part of the job, and if I didn't get the strange ones—the ones snarled hopelessly in unique legal challenges—I don't know what I would've done. Soldiered on, probably; an eternity of less-than-happy labors.

"Close door," I said to the wall, and it obliged me by swinging shut that rectangle of white frosted glass and, with a slight crackle of programmable matter, merging it back with my yellow marble decor again.

Too late, I realized there was someone out there in the corridor. There came a polite rapping on the wall outside, and a muffled voice murmuring, "Door. Door."

With a whispered command, I could make the wall perfectly soundproof. I even did it sometimes, but only when I was really busy and wanted the world to go away. Generally, I liked to feel I was part of the world.

Anyway the office would, of course, not obey the commands of a stranger, so I said, "Door." And like some crayon rubbing on a bas relief, the door magically reappeared, then clicked and swung open with a phony creak of phony hinges. A man stood on the other side with his hat pulled down and his shoulders hunched, glancing fur-tively to his left and then his right. He stepped inside, then quite rudely pushed the door until it swung closed again, engaging with a click of imaginary latches. "Carmine Douglas," the stranger said, "I hear you solve people problems."

"I help people *with* problems," I answered guardedly.

"That's fine," the man said. "That's close enough. It's good to see you, Carmine. You're looking well."

The lighting in my office—yellow spotlights and venetian-blinded daylight—created pools of atmospheric shadow, and the man had gravitated into one of these, denying me a clear view. But suddenly there was something very familiar about his face, his voice, the way he moved. "Double apparent brightness," I told the room, though I hated it the way that washed things out. "And whiten it up a bit. Kill these shadows."

The windows and ceiling did as I commanded, and there, plain as day, like a ghost from the past, was the face of Theodore Great Kaffner, my old roommate from my last three years at North Am U. He hadn't aged a bit, which shouldn't surprise me at all, since I'd never known anyone who did. But still, the sight of my old friend was a shock, a discontinuity. How many decades did that image leap across?

"Theddy?"

"Hey, Carbo. It's been a long time."

"You look terrible," I said, because that was true as well. "What sort of problem are you having?"

Theddy seemed to cringe at the question. He pointed to the windows on the office's other wall. "Can we darken those? D'you have some sort of privacy mode, here? A really strong one?"

I did, though I rarely used it. Speaking the commands, I watched my prized yellow marble and peach plaster melt away, turn cold. Within moments the whole room—floor and walls and ceiling alike—was seamless, featureless gray steel, and would obey only my commands, and only from within.

"All right?" I asked, waving my hands at the new decor.

"No," Theddy said. "Conductive surfaces block EMI, but lend themselves to transmissive tampering. We need an insulating layer on top."

Did we, now? How interesting. "Glass?"

"Glass will do."

I gave the appropriate commands, then gave my old friend an annoyed "Well?" sort of look.

And when Theddy shrugged his shoulders noncommittally, I advised him, "Nothing you say will leave this office, or be recorded in anything but my own brain, and yours. But be advised, with a proper warrant the court can search those. They can also take this room apart electron by electron, recording the quantum traces. Nothing is ever truly secret."

"It isn't secrecy I'm concern about," Theddy said, eyeing the walls warily, "it's security. Someone very clever is trying to kill me."

Naturally this statement brought me up short, because it was virtually impossible to kill a person in the Queendom of Sol. Oh sure, you could kill their body, could destroy whatever memory they'd built up since the last time they stepped through a fax machine, or stored their atomically perfect image in an archive somewhere. But the archives themselves were unassailable. People had died in the chaos of the Fall, eighty years before, and since that time a lot of precautions had been put in place. A *lot* of precautions.

Fearing some sort of transient mental illness in Theddy—a delusional paranoia?—I chose my next words carefully. "Thed, that sounds like a matter for the police. If what you say is true, they can have a team on it before you draw your next breath. We can make the call from here."

But Theddy was shaking his head. "I'm not an idiot, Carbo. This isn't a criminal matter. It's civil, or maybe administrative, or something which if I knew what it was, I wouldn't need *you.*"

"Slow down, Theddy," I tried. "You're stringing words together, but you're not making sense. Administrative murder? What's that? Who exactly is trying to kill you?"

And here, Theddy fixed his old roommate with a level, half panicked gaze. "I am. And I'm doing a good job of it, too."

2.
Xerography, Complicated

Generally speaking, keeping old copies of yourself was like keeping anything else. Found objects, hobby collections, treasured letters or artifacts from childhood—whatever. You could only fit so many in a shelf or cabinet, so at some point you boxed them up and stuck them in the attic, or fed them into the fax to be stored as data. And once that happened, chances were you wouldn't see those things again, nor ever miss them.

Archive copies were exactly the same way: there were people who kept only one, the latest and greatest incarnation of their perfect selves. There were even those who, for financial or aesthetic reasons, stored only the differences between themselves and some idealized manikin of human perfection.

But with either strategy it was possible to make a mistake, to internalize and record some experience which weakened or cheapened or traumatized the soul. And you couldn't always know that this had happened, and if you'd overwritten your earlier backups then you were pretty much stuck with the results for eternity. You could also, in the same way, lose track of what you were supposed to look like, lose track of your God-given body which had been really good at baseball or algebra, which had just *felt right* somehow. Most people had a bit of this disconnection in their lives—it was pain of an ordinary sort—and admittedly the real horror stories were rare.

But they happened, and in fact I'd encountered enough victims in my practice—their circumstances ranging from tragic to absurd—that for more than half my life I'd been following the costlier and more restrictive change control regimen favored by the various mental health councils. This involved archiving my entire self every five to ten years, and storing each copy, with annotations, alongside the previous ones in a facility that was guaranteed to remain uncorrupted by natural forces for a minimum of ten million years. Effective infinity, in other words, because even if I somehow lived that long, I reasoned that I'd be unlikely to care what I'd thought or felt or looked like as a mere centenarian.

Theddy had apparently followed a similar practice, though in some dangerous and backward-looking way. "Being unhappy with your life doesn't mean you necessarily want to scrap the whole decade and start over. We all have our troubles. I *like* the wisdom I've accumulated, but along the way I seem to have lost the spirit I had as a younger man. Some of it, enough of it. And shouldn't we, as immorbid beings, have both? I guess I was mixing and matching."

"You guess?"

"Listen, I *was* attending a matter programming conference on Mars. The rest of me were all back home, taking care of personal and professional minutia. Or so I presume. So I infer from the circumstances, as an outsider. As for what I was thinking, what exactly I was doing, I can only speculate."

I thought that over. People had different viewpoints on plurality; some even claimed that every copy of them had its own unique soul. Fortunately, the law rarely ruled in their favor with a legal twinning, or the world would quickly overpopulate with nearly identical people. Xeripollution: the arrogant assumption that the world needed more and more and more of your precious, perfect self. And *that* question had been settled—with fire and blood—in the Dallas of the Late Modern era, and I doubted very much whether society wanted to repeat the experiment.

I personally liked to keep my copies close together in both time and space. I didn't send myself on vacation while the rest of me worked. I didn't cover multiple long-term assignments in parallel, and then reconverge afterward. It just gets confusing, when the experiences of your copies have diverged that much. My sense of self was, I suppose, a small thing: capable of encompassing only a handful of very similar instantiations. But while Theddy Kaffner had his fair share of faults, timidity was not among them.

Nor, tellingly, was malice. The Theddy of old was an irate fellow, but never a hurtful one. If he pushed someone down the stairs every now and then, he did it in the spirit of horseplay, knowing that no permanent harm could possibly result. Broken bones were just a fax plate away from their old glory, right? And Theddy, the programmer, was far more likely to just hack your shirt's wellcloth with a smear of ink or something, or throw *himself* down the stairs for a laugh. He'd been full of rages and frustrations, but he'd channeled them into useful hobbies, which included running and acting and the building of wooden models. The idea of his committing a *murder*, or even threatening one was . . . strange.

"What do you mean by mixing and matching?"

Theddy's stressed-up expression relaxed for a moment, into a smile as wistful as I had lately seen. "You're the food freak, Carbo. You know how it is: a pinch of this, a dash of that . . . a soupcon of my angry young self, to spice up my flavor a bit. I suppose I overdid it. Angry Young Theddy was a force to be reckoned with; did even I, myself, underestimate him? Did ten percent of him overwhelm ninety percent of the canonical me? Or maybe it just felt good. Maybe I kept turning the knob, adding more and more of him until it was too late."

I spread my hands, unsure what to say. "More than anything, Thed, this sounds like a communication problem. Have you tried talking to yourself?"

"Yeah, briefly," Theddy said, the stress snapping back down over his features like a new matter program. "Until I kidnapped myself, with a force of three Theddies. These guys, who said they were me, they lifted me right off the floor. They were going to throw me through the print plate of my own goddamn fax machine in my own goddamn living room. Can you imagine? 'You're the last one,' they said, 'and it's one too many.' The way they were laughing, the way they were—I don't know, *handling* me. It went beyond contempt, Carbo. This was hatred. 'How could I turn into a fuck like you?' That was what Angry Young Theddy said to me.

"But *he* underestimated the power of fear. They meant to kill me, erase me—there was no question about that. They weren't fighting for their lives, and I was, so in the end they couldn't hold me. I felt their bones breaking. I felt an eyeball pop. As long as I live, I never want to feel a thing like that."

Okay, yeah, this was complicated. If there was a right place for Theddy to come to with this problem, my office was probably it. But where to begin?

"I'll need a full power of attorney," I said for starters, "and since you appear to have valid concerns for your physical safety, it may be best to store you here, in my office fax, under a seal of attorney-client privilege. The state can open that—the state can open anything—but *you* can't. The pattern that comprises you right now, right here, will be preserved no matter what Angry Young Theddy thinks or does."

"He's cleverer than you suppose," Theddy warned.

But I just laughed. "Nobody's cleverer than I suppose."

There was a bit more to it than that, but Theddy wanted help, and wasn't in a mood to argue. His agreement was not difficult to secure, and neither, as a result, was his physical person. It didn't take three guys to push him through the plate, and truthfully, I wasn't sure three guys could have stopped him if they'd been here to try. It was a safer place, and he wanted in.

3.
A Pedestrian Encounter

When you traveled by fax machine—and who didn't?—no place in the solar system was more than a few hours away, and if you were the one being transmitted, not the one waiting around at the other end, then from your point of view the journey was instantaneous. With a handful of steps, I could have found myself on the landing outside any home or apartment, anywhere. It was a funny thing, though: Theddy had lived less than a mile from my office for almost twenty years. How strange, that we should live so close for so long without realizing it! But living forever can be like that: it's easy to put things off, to assign them to the infinite and amorphous future. Even important things; even close friends.

Anyway, Denver was a historical preservation zone where walking was actively encouraged. In the eight square kilometers of the downtown district, faxing was actually illegal for anything but official business or the direst emergencies, and the city was adorned for tens of kilometers all around with roads and sidewalks, trails and quaint little bridges arching across the streams and rivers. This classic look was a large part of the city's appeal, and I wasn't about to abuse it by teleporting six blocks. The walk might take me twenty minutes, and might represent more exercise than most people got in a year, but my body, rendered eternally youthful by the fax filters, was surely up to the job. Whose wasn't? People who don't like walking, who don't like mountain views and fresh air and strangers on the street, well . . . they should live someplace else. Denver was not made for indoor souls.

Still, once outside I felt a twinge of regret for my decision, as the November afternoon rolled over me with shocking, unseasonable heat. "Mild winter" didn't begin to describe the weather we were having that year, but I kept forgetting. I kept dressing for wind and fog and the possibility of snow. My jacket did its best to fight off the heat (blasting it behind me in a stream of warm air), but in the shade of downtown's towers it had no ready power source, so there wasn't a lot it could actually do.

There's an irony for you: on a hot day it's cooler in the sun than the shade! But the shirt underneath was having a hard time as well, and I couldn't remove the jacket without revealing the sweat stains it was failing to disperse from under my arms. Life can be so unfair.

Anyway, Theddy's case was heavy on my mind, and June Szymanski's still hadn't left it, and the two were filling up very different pieces of my brain. So I was deeper than usual in thought, and found the bustle and jangle of the crowds annoying. Some street wisdom I heard that day:

"Hollywood is a *plant*, Gabriel. The city, they were calling it that way before they started making hollies there."

"There's nothing noble about boredom, aye? Are there people you could be helping? Societies you could enrich? Don't you give me that look, you vegetable."

"Oh, of course you have the right to design a new life form. Everyone does. But for criminy's sake, John, that doesn't mean you have the right to instantiate it in the real world."

Yeah. Real pearls, those. The streets of this city had always been crowded, or nearly always, but even I, a mere centenarian, could remember a time when the crowds had all had someplace to go, some purpose in their steps. As often as not it was someplace they were *forced* to go, to stave off economic ruin in a scarcity-based economy, but still. The city's loitering laws had never been repealed, and ought at least occasionally to be enforced.

With its bright colors and piled-high fashions, its buskers and mimes, its living sculptures 'dancing to the din of a dozen decades', the city resembled a carnival that day as much as a center of business or residence or learning. And for some reason I found this deeply irritating.

On the other hand, it wasn't like anyone was holding a sword to my neck, forcing me to interact, to be here at all. I was a champion of strangeness, and these, for better or worse, were my people. And anyway it *was* a short walk before I found myself in front of Theddy's apartment building, a retro-opensource brownstone in the 22nd century style.

"How may I help you, sir?" The building asked, in what was surely its politest voice.

"I'm here to see Theddy Kaffner."

"I'm afraid Mr. Kaffner isn't in at the moment," the building clucked, with quite a good semblance of regret.

"It's a serious matter," I told the building. "A *legal* matter, I'm afraid. If you have a buffer copy of Mr. Kaffner on hand, and I imagine you do, then I must request you print him and allow me to speak with him at once."

The building's intelligence didn't like that one bit, and sounded cross. "On what grounds? You're not a police officer." (And this was true, although I knew a lot of police, and had once loved a policeman's daughter.) "Nor do you bear the carrier signal of a government official. By studying your face I can make a guess as to your identity, but I would prefer that you simply explain yourself."

Fair enough. "My name is Carmine Strange Douglas. Mr. Kaffner's attorney. The rest I'll say to him, if you don't mind."

"I have no record of this association," the house said skeptically, "although your face and pheromone signature match that name, and the social network archives indicate you have fraternized with Mr. Kaffner in the past. Do you have any proof that this arrangement exists?"

I held up a bonded, self-notarizing copy of the power of attorney, and the building opened instantly, curling aside a broad doorway of gold and pearl and other substances I couldn't identify. "Please come in, sir, and excuse my rudeness in detaining you. One can't be too careful these days, and in any case my security settings are at legal maximum."

"No offense taken," I assured it, since the thing was only doing its job, following its program, and had no actual feelings. Or so the law declared. Inside, among furnishings assembled from white puffy pillow-cubes, I found Theddy in deep conference with the wall.

Presumably, he was receiving a briefing on this turn of events— my arrival and such—since from his own perspective he had just moments before stepped through the fax machine on his way to somewhere quite different. This was a buffer copy, probably not more than a few hours old, and he had no way of knowing why I was here.

When Theddy saw me, he looked up with an expression of wonder. "Carbo? My God, man, what're you doing here? It's great to see you! But when exactly did you become my lawyer?"

"About half an hour ago," I said, extending a warm handshake. "There's a copy of you in my office who claims he was assaulted. By *you*, or rather, by several instances of you. I was hoping you could shed some light on the subject."

Theddy's hand withdrew from mine, and his face grew cautious, and right away I could see there was something different about him. He was less like the Theddy in my office, and more like the one I'd remember if I really thought back. The angry prankster. A composite sketch of New Theddy would be all broad lines and shallow curves, but while Young Theddy looked the same, he wore it differently. Here was a fellow of edges and points and sharp, stacatto movements.

"There was an altercation," Theddy admitted, "but he started it. All I did was defend myself."

"Against what?"

Theddy's answering look was not quite a sneer. "That copy must have got some bad poison along the way, Carbo. He was irrational, and slow. It would have taken a lot of patience to get any sense out of him, and who's got the time?"

Well, *that* sounded believable enough.

"Did you try to push him into the fax?"

"It was the only way I could think of to, you know, figure out what his problem was. Merge a little bit of him with a lot of myself, and see what was on his mind."

I'd never been one to beat around the bush, so I came right out with it: "Theddy, have you been mingling your image with archive copies of yourself? Would a personality scan reveal sudden, dramatic changes in your character?"

"Yes," Theddy said, as if it were the most normal thing the world.

"Hmm. Well, listen, this allegedly deviant copy of yourself is the contemporary version. It's who all his friends and neighbors and colleagues are used to seeing. If he were in fact stored in your personal fax machine, per your plans, would you ever print him out again?"

"Hell no," Theddy answered, with that same matter-of-fact, self-righteous conviction. As if people did that sort of thing every day. Oh boy. Oh boy, oh boy. Some dangerous cocktail of thoughts and experiences had come together in this copy's brain. Theddy—the *real* Theddy—was right to be afraid: this man was not only capable of self-murder, but felt it was, in some way, his legal right. And I wondered: where was the case law to prove otherwise?

And to think I'd thought the Szymanski divorce was a mess! "What we have here," I said cautiously, "is a case of disputed identity. Two divergent copies of the same individual, laying claim to editorial rights over each other. That being the case, I personally have a conflict of interest, and must make no further contact with you, except if necessary in court. If you intend to prosecute your rights in this matter—and I find it difficult to imagine otherwise—you'll need to retain your own counsel. I cannot advise you in this."

Theddy scowled. "Oh you can't, can't you? Maybe the years have eroded your memory, dear friend, but you and I have an agreement which predates any contract you may have with . . . that other bloke. That failed experiment. That shriveled old creature who does not deserve to wear Theddy Kaffner's skin."

Though it might be a breach of ethics, I took the bait. "What agreement is that?"

"I'll find it."

Theddy stepped to the wall and began whispering to it. A hollie window appeared there, displaying lists of text with little thumbnail images beside them. Theddy poked at the display several times, muttering, and finally said, "Ha! Found it."

A beer-stained cocktail napkin tumbled out of the fax machine, into Theddy's waiting hands. He scanned it briefly, nodding, then handed it to me. It said, in appallingly familiar handwriting:

I, Carmine Douglas, through the power vested in me by the state of inebriation, do solemnly swear that I will never lose my faith or spirit, and that I will look out for my friend Theddy come what may, for all eternity and throughout the universe.

It was signed and even—though the hologram was hard to make out—notarized.

"You can't be serious," I said, waving the thing as if to dry it. "This isn't legally binding." But even as the words were out of my mouth, I realized it might not be so. There were times in the historical past when what was legal and what was right were two different things, when valid arguments could be crafted to excuse almost anything, but the Queendom of Sol took a dim view indeed of broken promises. Theddy saw it in my face, too; he was a hard man to hide things from. I sighed and asked, "What do you want? What does it take to make this thing go away?"

Theddy sneered in youthful triumph. "If you want to go legal on me, old friend, I can only respond in kind. I *do* want my own counsel, as promised to me in this old contract. I want *you*. Not this stuffy alien creature you've become, but the young, angry, lovesick Carbo I went to school with. Well, I suppose you'd have to add a couple of years to that, or he wouldn't be a lawyer yet, but you see what I mean. I want my old roommate to defend me."

With a sinking feeling I realized that might just stick. Theddy might just have a point which the law, in its finite wisdom and limited experience, had never yet addressed. The right of archive copies to be revived? To seek the company of their peers? To repudiate their future lives?

"Call my office," I said, sighing uneasily. "I'll authorize it to set something up. Not because I have to—and certainly not because I want to—but because you've raised an interesting point, and it needs to be properly explored. Even a younger me, a green me fresh out of school, is better qualified than most attorneys to wrestle this particular alligator. In fact, if I didn't buy into it voluntarily, the court might well assign it. In which case they'd offer you a disposable copy of me, which would self-destruct once the dispute was resolved. And that, my friend, is an involuntary servitude I would not wish on my younger self, who was an innocent and charming lad."

All of which was true, insofar as it went. Unlike Theddy, and with a single and quite excusable exception, my own younger self could be *trusted*. So why, in my heart just then, did the prospect of unleashing him bring nothing but dread?

4.
Passions, Revived

Rummaging through the archives took a lot longer than I expected. The storage companies are happy to take your money to capture the backup, but when it comes time for the free restore they're a lot less helpful. Wading through the layers of bureaucracy and "technical assistance" proved so difficult and involved that in the end I had to print out a dedicated copy of my recent self, who spent several days working on the problem exclusively.

Of the fifteen images I'd stored at one point or another in my life, the best fit for young Theddy seemed to be a Carmine two years out of law school, working at a big firm in Milan and flush, for the first time in his short life, with the income and respectability of gainful employment.

Memories washed over me. Those had been good years, but turbulent ones, too. Money and power and youth were a potent combination, and bred the sort of arrogance that led to personal troubles. And if there was a god of Love—and Strife, for they were bound together as a single entity in Queendom mythology—then poor Eros had spent some busy seasons that year, looking after the torrid romance between myself and Pamela Red. Even now, more than seventy years after the fact, the memory brought a poignant flutter of excitement and pain. I'd had a number of lovers before her, and quite a bit more after—I'd even been married twice—but when I looked back over the conquests and treaties, surrenders and defeats of my immorbid love life, Pamela's shadow seemed to loom over all of it. She was the standard against which all others were measured.

This was of course no great novelty in the Queendom, where the phenomenon was common enough to have its own name: the guidepost affair. And rumor had it that if you lived long enough, if you loved well enough, your guidepost would fade, would be replaced, or even—strange thought—subsumed entirely by the one true love of your life, who would stay with you forever. A guidepost affair was, by definition, buried deep in your past—something that didn't or couldn't or wouldn't work out. Something painful. But ah, we still believed in a higher sort of love than that, else how could we face eternity?

Not that there wasn't other strife in that era, as well. Like any human being, the Carmine of that day had had a sackload of mundane troubles which to him seemed very serious and immediate, though today I could scarcely remember them. But I did my best to align myself with that mental space, in the hours and minutes—and finally the seconds—before Angry Young Carmine stepped out of the fax.

"Welcome," I said to myself, for I remembered this young man with great fondness and admiration. Angry Young Carmine, looking me up and down, recognized me at once, but the first thing he said was, "Hello, Carmine. You look . . . different. Considering the fact that I've *just this second* archived myself, for the benefit of my future self, I can only assume that some years have passed."

"Correct," I said, beaming at this lad's quick mind.

"Something has gone wrong, then. Ah, Carmine, have you been poisoned? Traumatized? Worn down or worn out with the passage of years?"

"There is a problem," I agreed with gentle amusement, "but not with me. It's Theddy."

"Theddy needs an archived copy of *me*? That sounds damned peculiar, and complicated. Brief me on the specifics, if you would."

And here I felt the first tingle of irritation, for I was clearly the senior partner in this endeavor, and this young man had no right to give me orders. But without noticing or without caring, Young Carmine pressed on: "I also need to orient myself. I'll need news highlights for each of the intervening years, and if you don't mind, a sampling of the clothing and music fashions as well. And the *food*."

"Ahem. Young man, you might find it helpful to let others get a word in now and then. The time capsules you describe are in the fax's buffer memory right now, awaiting your attention."

"Ah. What year is it, anyway?"

I told him, and watched his expression tense briefly and then relax.

"That's a long time, old man. I assume it's a short-term assignment you've woken me for?"

"It is."

Young Carmine's smile was pained. "Reconverging our experiences could be problematic when this is finished. You should probably check with a doctor, or maybe a quantum physicist, but I'm not sure consciousness can bridge a gap that large."

I adopted what I hoped was a look of patience. "My plan is to filter you in as a percentage, to reintegrate a tincture of you with my current self. Carefully, of course, but everything admirable about you will be preserved and magnified, and with luck our flaws will mask one another."

"Oh really. I see." Young Carmine's tone was skeptical, poised on the cusp of anger. "And what percentage, exactly, did you plan on granting me? Twenty-five percent?"

At this, I was afraid to answer truthfully, because the actual figure I had in mind was .25%, or possibly .5%. But to this living, breathing young man, that would sound like murder. I had the legal right to do exactly that, to print disposable copies of myself and then, you know, dispose of them. But I'd never done it when there were major life experiences at stake. Why would I? I wouldn't want to *be* the disposable copy whose memories died, and I wouldn't want to be the one who lived on without those memories, either. A no-win scenario.

But this was different, right? Everything important about Young Carmine was preserved in me. I was a superset of him, and in that sense his erasure would mean nothing, cost nothing, hurt nothing. Except from his point of view. And to enforce the right of erasure against his will . . . To enforce the right, I might have to print extra copies of my current self, and overpower Young Carmine, and hurl him forcibly into the fax. Or contact a lawyer of my own, and let the courts decide. And didn't *that* put Theddy's case in an interesting light?

Afterward, I was never sure what my younger self read in my face at that moment, but whatever it was, he answered with an obscene gesture and a barked command at the office wall, which, recognizing the voice of its owner, opened a door and let him out.

"Ah, hell," I said, following behind, trying to put a hand on his shoulder to reassure him. To reassure myself. But Young Carmine was having none of that, and in fact took the gesture as a hostile one. Which might not be too far from the truth. Young Me jerked his shoulder away, then ducked and ran down the hallway.

I said, "You're going to want—you'll need—hey!" But the lines of communication had broken down entirely, and the next comments I received from Young Carmine would, I realized, have a letterhead at the top. Damn. My body hadn't aged a day in all this time, and I supposed I could simply run after myself, tackle myself, fight it out physically and force myself to listen. But I'd be hard pressed to win against so equal an opponent, and if the concept of "youth" meant anything at all in this day and age, would it really be so equal?

What I actually did, like a useless old man, was race down the hallway and scream down the stairwell at myself: "You stay away from Pamela Red, do you hear me! You caused her enough trouble when you were . . . back when you were . . ." Real.

5.
The Daughter's Policeman

The next morning found me on the far side of the moon, in a scenic dome at the pit of Jules Verne crater, with the sharp-toothed hills of the crater lip rising up all around. Here it wasn't morning at all, but early evening by the Greenwich Mean shift clock and somewhere close to midnight by the actual position of the sun. Given the full moon in Denver last night—always a peak time for strangeness—it made sense that the moon's sulking farside, faced always away from Earth, should be bathed in darkness.

Any school child of the early Queendom knew that on that big, pre-terraformed moon, the sun rose and set every 28 days. But unless you'd spent time on Luna yourself, it was hard to appreciate just how irrelevant the daylight really was. Aside from the anachronism of gravity tourism, Luna didn't really offer anything the rest of the Queendom particularly needed, and as a result the great dome cities at Tranquility and Grimaldi were money pits, gone to seed in a state of not-quite completion. The moon's million permanent residents were mostly scattered in small, economically depressed communities, and the great bulk of its housing was underground. You lived there because you loved it, basically. Because you'd bought into the romance of it: a wild frontier on Earth's very doorstep.

And on that frontier, for some historical reason I'd never bothered to learn, the clocks were set, planetwide and regardless of longitude, to British time. Not that it really mattered to me—the hour or the darkness. Such transitions—day to night, winter to summer to hard vacuum—were common to the point of dullness in a faxwise society. That's just the way things were.

In any case, Verne was a small town inhabited mainly by astronomers and small-time trelium prospectors, who had taste enough to keep the dome lights low and green. Night lights, so that the stars could shine down in all their glory through the near-invisible well-glass of the dome. I'd seen this place in the daytime once—on a sadly similar errand—and the dome had been frosted a translucent blue-white which didn't mimic an Earthly sky so much as pay homage to it. Good for the soul, I reckoned at the time. Better for the plants and animals than the searing unfiltered light of Sol herself.

Also tasteful was the way Verne's visitors were encouraged, through transit fee structures and heirarchical addressing, to enter through the fax ports in the park level immediately beneath the dome. It wasn't a big park as such things go, but its colored brick pathways folded back on themselves many times, with the view of grassy meadows blocked here and there by stands of dwarf bamboo and twisty, lunar-tall apple trees. So it felt bigger than it really was, and the walk from fax to elevator took a good three minutes. An actual elevator, yes; to get to any particular home, office or storefront in Verne you had to find the right color-coded shaft, and ride the elevator down to the appropriate subsurface level.

As a longtime resident of Denver—a city similarly trapped in the romantic past—I could only approve. Beauty was so much finer a thing than convenience! Even (or perhaps especially) when you were in a hurry.

Too bad it was guilt, not beauty, that brought me there that day. But hey, even that guilt, that shame and worry, could ultimately be blamed on beauty. On one particular beauty, in fact, which I had sought above all others. Nearly to my ruin, yes, and I might spend the rest of eternity shaking off the consequences, but in this sense I regretted nothing, and would do it all again if I could.

By blue starlight and the green glow of the dome's perimeter, I trod a path of yellow bricks in platinum-white mortar. My bootheels clopped and rang. I'd come here expecting to ask directions, from a wellstone pillar if not a live human, but I found to my surprise that my feet still knew the way. Through the gloom of an orchard and back out into starlight again, I came to a low pink cottage with the words GOVERNMENT AND UTILITIES carved into its lintel and glowing that same soft green, with modestly animated crests on either side to emphasize the point.

I entered the building, and found myself in a traditional lobby complete not only with elevators but with a human security guard seated behind a desk. This might seem laughable in an age where superweapons had nearly obliterated the sun, but the man's gray uniform—bearing the five-pointed star of the Verne Crater Sherrif's Office—was thicker than ordinary wellcloth, and lent him a formidable air. In time of trouble, the suit would no doubt extend to cover his face, his head, his hairy-knuckled hands, and the thing's capacitors and hypercomputers would be prepared to amplify his strength, to shoot all manner of energy beams from his fists, from his eyes, from the edges of any wound an attacker might somehow manage to inflict.

This, too, was nothing special—most cops dressed this way most of the time—and anyway a pair of gleaming, hulking Law Enforcers lurked robotically in the corners behind him, just in case anyone still had any thoughts about getting cute.

"Carmine Douglas, Attorney at Law," I said, although by now the guard must already know this. Like all professionals everywhere, he'd be unemployed if he weren't uncannily competent. "I'm here to see Waldo Red."

"Yeah?" The cop looked me over with a bored expression. "What for?"

"Personal business."

The guard thought that one over. "I don't have you on my visitors list. Is he expecting you?"

"No. Well, possibly." Depending on what Angry Young Carmine had or hadn't done, Waldo might well be drafting a warrant for my arrest. Or tying a hangman's noose. "But he knows me."

"So he does," the cop said, glancing down at some social network display on his desktop. He tapped the surface several times in quick succession, like a harp player working the strings. "He . . . will see you. But—whoa. According to my stats, there's a ninety percent chance of verbal confrontation and an 8% chance of violence. On *his* part; *you're* down in the noise, an innocent victim of potential attack. My goodness. Do . . . you want an armed escort?"

"No," I said. "Thank you. I'm here to make peace."

"Huh. Well, go on ahead. Level nineteen, end of the hallway and turn right."

"Thanks."

The guard shuffled uncomfortably in his chair. "Hey, buddy? Uh, you don't have to answer this or anything, but, I mean . . . Deputy Waldo isn't exactly a thug. What does a guy have to do to burn him off like that?"

"Sleep with his daughter," I said, and turned for the elevator.

6.
The Law

The first thing Waldo said to me when I walked into his office was, "Hmmph. So now you're stalking *me*."

And there was a lot of evidence coded in this statement: it meant that Young Carmine had gone to see Pamela, and that the visit had been less than welcome. It meant that she'd called her father afterward, and that he considered the incident, at least in his heart, to be a criminal offense. Which was silly, because that old restraining order had expired forty years ago, and I had no history, either before or since, of criminally rude behavior. But then again, there was no telling what Young Carmine might've said. Or done. Truthfully, I had forgotten how forceful and intense I'd really been as a young man. And pointlessly so, for it had only gotten me in trouble.

I held up my hands in mock surrender. "Hi, Waldo. I'm sure you're angry—and not without reason!—but it's not what you think. There's an old, old copy of me running around."

Waldo studied me, thinking that one over. Whatever he'd expected me to say, that wasn't it. Waldo was seated on his desk, which had gone soft beneath him in response. His arms were crossed, and his single, heavy eyebrow was pulled down in an almost comical frown. In his harrumphy way he said, "Rogue or authorized?"

"A little of both," I answered, unsure what else to say about it.

Waldo digested that, and finally nodded. "Hmm. Humph. Yeah. One of those."

A bit of the tension went out of the room. The details must surely be unique, but Waldo had been a cop for a hundred years longer than I'd even been alive. He'd seen his share of weirdness, and understood that the law was gray. What cop didn't know that? The law was designed for assaults and robberies, angry neighbors fighting over the pruning of a tree or the disposition of its fruits. By definition, you couldn't legislate the unanticipated, and existing laws—sensible laws—sometimes yielded perverse or even contradictory results. *Do we divide the child in two?*

And in this age of plenty there just wasn't all that much thuggery. The sorts of things that had value anymore were not sorts of things you could steal a gunpoint, and anyway such obvious crimes were always solved, always punished. With enough decades behind them, even the most hardened criminals eventually got the message.

So what did that leave? Juvenile mischief, and the weirdness at the margins of the grown-up world. The need for cops and court-rooms would never go away.

"Why are you here?" Waldo asked with less hostility.

I tried on a half smile. "It seemed . . . more polite than going di-rectly to Pamela. I figured he'd go and see her. I knew he would. He's an archive copy from when that . . . issue was relatively fresh."

"So why'd you print him?"

"Contractual obligation, I guess you'd say. I'll spare you the in-sipid details."

"Hmmph. Thanks. Are you going to get rid of him?"

I could only shrug. "I'm not sure I can, Waldo. He's defending another person's archive copy against exactly that procedure. Re-moving him would be a form of pre-trial tampering, and if his case prevails—which it very well might—then it's anyone's guess what *my* legal rights are. Pray for a wise judge."

Waldo didn't like that answer. "Really. How convenient. There's a little Carmine running around from the period of the restraining order—and believe me, you where nitwit back then—and he's got all the rights of being you and none of the responsi-bilities of being himself. He can bug my daughter all he likes, unless I file an updated order against *you*. Which I guess I'll just have to do."

And that made me angry, because the revival of a seventy-year old restraining order would look bad on my record. It would hurt my image, hurt my business, hurt my *pride*. And for what? "You know, Waldo, your darling Pamela wasn't exactly an innocent in all this. If there were courts of law for faithless lovers . . ."

"You were a nitwit, and your friends were nitwits, and you made her sad. The only surprise is that it took her two years to realize the fact. And like a shit, you refused to crawl back under your block. You just couldn't leave it alone. You wanted to own her. You tried buy her like a doll."

At that, in a wildly uncharacteristic gesture, I slammed the wall sideways with my fist, hard. "I wanted nothing of the kind, *Deputy*. Even now, you refuse to acknowledge my point. It was simple enough for a small town cop and his daughter to understand, if they put their minds to it. For years I licked the wounds she inflicted so

casually. For *years*. Like an old tree, I got whole again only by growing around the scar. Burying it inside me, surrounded it with strong,
healthy tissue. But the defect itself is permanent."

"Love always is," Waldo lectured, as if to a child. "We all
have our little scars. It doesn't give you any special rights. And
just for your education, punk, you fix a tree by printing an un-
damaged copy. If that 'wound' of yours is so terrible, why do you
keep it?"

"You've been in love, Waldo. You know why."

The old cop sighed and harrumphed. "I don't know where you
crawled out from, pal, and I don't care, but understand: we keep the
peace here in Jules Verne. You know how many arrests I've made
this year? Six, and three of them were the same guy. You know how
many times I've called the Constabulary in the past decade, to solve
some capital crime of Queendom-wide importance? Zero."

"Congratulations."

Waldo answered with a mocking expression, and then a more
seriously threatening one. "I may not have jurisdiction outside this
crater, Mr. Douglas, but you've got five minutes to get your ass out of
here before I throw it in jail. Don't let me catch you here again, ever."

And this was a strong statement indeed, because Waldo Red
would never die, never grow old and retire. Never forgive a young
man's trespasses.

Well, I had my own rights to worry about, and said so: "If you do
that, or file an injunction of any kind, I'll sue for defamation. I'll
make it stick, too."

And with that I stomped out, feeling in spite of everything that
the visit had gone better than expected.

7.
Pamela, Read

Pamela herself, whom I visited next, surprised me by being a lot
more understanding.

"Daddy called," she said by way of introduction. "I heard about
your little . . . technical difficulties."

Her house was one of nine at the summit of Mt. Terror, on
Antarctica's Ross Island overlooking both the volcano's active cal-
dera and the Ross Sea coast, aglow in the lights of McMurdo City
and, across the water, of Glacia and Victoria Land. It was nighttime

here as well, in a place where night was winter, or in this case early spring. And Pamela's foyer, like many in cold climates, was poorly insulated on purpose, to discourage surprise visitors.

My wellcloth suit did the best it could, but it had been out of the sun for hours now, and its power reserves were getting low. It settled for swathing me in black velvet, lined with some crinkly, unbreathable superreflector that left my skin feeling hot and suffocated, even as my body heat bled away through my uncovered hands and head.

"You look cold," Pamela said, ushering me in through her open doorway. "You want some coffee? Soup?"

"Spiced almond chowder," I answered gratefully, following her inside. There was no such thing as a poorly furnished home in the Queendom of Sol, but there were copyrighted patterns available only to those with money, and there were expert decorators and geomancers who could customize a space to its owners with striking—and strikingly expensive—skill. And everyone had access to a fax machine, if not in their own houses and apartments then, by law, within forty paces of their door. But to *fill* a house with fax machines—I counted five in my first quick look around, including the one in the foyer—took resources. And the view, also not free, was spectacular.

"Looks like you're doing all right, here," I said, while she stepped up to her dining room fax to fetch my soup. "I hope you don't mind my saying so."

"Not a bit," she laughed. "But I'll be the first to admit, I got lucky. Matter programming is funny that way: sometimes you hit the right combination, and this substance you've just invented is gorgeous, and it's waterproof, and it's diamagnetic, and some construction outfit on Pluto is offering you cash up front and a ten percent share of their leasing profits."

"Sounds nice," I told her, fighting to keep any deeper feelings at bay. For the moment, I was succeeding; it *had* been a long time, and seeing her now was more nostalgic than painful. "Theddy became a programmer, too, you know, but he doesn't live like this."

She smiled. "Theddy. My goodness, how is he?"

"In trouble," I said.

"Well, that figures. I suppose you're representing him?"

"Yeah."

"That figures, too. As for my alleged wealth, don't be too jealous. It won't last. Unless I get lucky again, I'll have to sell this place in a few centuries. Maybe move back to farside, although they're still talking about evacuating the entire moon, and crushing it to boost the surface gravity. You can't go home again, isn't that what they say?"

Thinking about that, I looked her over, studying my feelings as they unfolded. Things weren't the same as they had been long ago, that much was definite. Her mere presence no longer panicked me, made me stupid or impulsive. Which was probably just as well, although there was a part of me that would always miss feeling that way. You can't go home, indeed.

"That would be a shame," I said, "destroying the moon like that. Where would all the shady people go?"

She could easily have taken that the wrong way, but she chose not to, and chuckled instead as she pulled my mug of steaming soup from the fax. "The shady people always find a place, Carbo. Isn't that what keeps you in business?"

"Well," I admitted, "sort of. It's the *rich* shady people that can afford my services. The poor ones get their legal help from software, which is worth every penny of the nothing they pay for it."

"Their matter programming, too," she said. And suddenly we were laughing together, just like old times. It felt good. Cleansing. If all our times had been like this . . .

"Look," I told her, "I want to apologize for inflicting Young Me on you like that. I hope he didn't scare you."

"Not in the least. Actually, he was quite charming." She handed me the soup, and I tasted it. It was *good*, and here too I sensed some vague tincture of money, some subtle designer flavor to which I myself had never been privy. And I was not exactly a poor man, nor a gustatorial simpleton.

"What did he do? What did he want?"

"The usual," she laughed. "A bit of me for his collection."

Suddenly I found myself fighting down anger again, for the second time in a single morning. Because it wasn't funny, damn it. Not to me it wasn't. The request had seemed simple enough at the time. Pamela and I had archived ourselves at the height of our passion, wanting—literally—to preserve that glorious feeling for all eternity. Later, when things had soured, when we started fighting and she finally turned me out, I had asked her to revive that feeling. Not even in her own skin, necessarily. Couldn't she print out an alternate copy, an older, younger version who was still in love with Carmine Douglas? Wasn't that the whole point of the backup?

But apparently it wasn't, at least in her mind, and apparently I had pressed the point too firmly. Well, no "apparently" about it; love could make a man do stupid things, and no force in heaven or Earth could make him regret them afterward. In love especially, we behave as we must.

In any case, my defense had taken me all way to the Solar Court itself, where my stalking and harassment convictions were narrowly upheld. I was clever enough not to lose my license over it, but the court forbade me to have any contact with Pamela Red, or her friends and family, for three long decades. The mark would be on my record forever: Carmine Douglas, sexual deviant. What was funny about that?

"Look," she said, catching my expression, "We were young. We applied our passion to each other, and when it didn't work out we applied our passion against each other. It's the oldest story in the world. I'm assuming we both got over this a long time ago, like good little grown-ups, so let's not start fighting now. Okay? I'm genuinely sorry, about all of it."

That stung too, its own way. "About *all* of it? You're sorry it even happened?"

And to my surprise, her face melted in a strange mix of amusement and dismay. "*Sorry it happened?* What . . . What are you even talking about? We were fresh, we were new, we were *burning* with passion for the first time in our tiny little lives. What's the point of living forever if you only get to feel that way once? Carmine, Carbo, baby doll, it was the hottest fling of my life."

What came next made perfect sense, because if I'd ever had any willpower in the Pamela Red department, we wouldn't be standing there talking about it. And if she hadn't loved me—truly loved me with all her heart, at least for a while—I wouldn't have had anything to press her about, to get in trouble about. An explosion could not occur without heat. But it was one more bit of strangeness, and I honestly didn't know if there were any law or rule or ethical guideline being broken. Would society prevent me from hurling myself on this additional complication?

It hardly mattered. Yes, I tumbled into bed with her, and she with me. Heedless of the consequences, we remained there for three days, refusing all calls. And it was worth any price.

8.

Orders

When I finally got home, my head was clearer somehow. It was one thing to stir up ghosts from the past, but quite another to have them walking around spouting threats. But making peace with Pamela—making more than that!—put a different face on things. Anyway, I did what I should've done in the first place, which was to file a motion for Division of Self for Theodore Kaffner, and another for Carmine Douglas.

Divisions of Self—so-called twinnings—had a sparse but readily traceable case history, and seemed the most appropriate vehicle for dealing with this mess. True, no one had ever and attempted an *involuntary* twinning before. Generally, they were granted to individuals who had lost a genuine twin somewhere along the way, or who could, for whatever reason, prove some tangible need to divide themselves into two legally distinct individuals. Because they'd grown in different ways, and no longer believed they were compatible.

Angry Young Theddy's argument was quite different: that he should have the right to delete his later self and try his whole adult life over again. But if the older and younger Theddies were two different people, then this desire would be nonsense from a legal standpoint, and acting on it would be murder. Which, to my thinking, sounded about right.

And Young Carmine's position was different still: having been granted the flesh and breath of life, he simply wanted to continue. He didn't want to be erased, and truthfully neither would I, if our circumstances were reversed. And the law was supposed to mean what was *right*, right?

The next step was to file a temporary restraining order—actually four restraining orders—prohibiting the various Theddies and Carmines from harming one another, or having any sort of contact all outside a courtroom setting. We could send legal communiques to one another through the proper channels, and that was all. Sadly, this would be another mark on my own record, another opportunity for me to look like some sort of mad stalker, but since my name was on the order as both plaintiff and defendant, it would seem more strange than incriminating. And anyone researching my background that deeply would know, *should* know, that Strange is my middle name.

Then I did another thing I should've done right away, which was to call my parents and let them know what was happening. "Aren't you a bit old for shenanigans like this?" my father wanted to know.

"I'm beginning to think so," I answered.

For good measure, I called Theddy's parents as well, and found to my mild surprise that Angry Young Theddy was actually staying there with them, having vacated his apartments in Denver. This of course forced me to cut the conversation short, but that was all right. The Kaffners were drunks and dreamers, with never all that much to say to me, nor I to them.

And since these orders were of the sort that could easily be handled by hypercomputer, the so-called Telejudges—I had a stack of bonded approvals in hand within a few minutes. The Telejudges of course demanded a flesh hearing, ten days hence, so a human judge could review the facts of the case and decide the long-term disposition of the orders, and of the humans tied up in them.

And that wasn't so hard, really. Strangeness is nothing more than the shock of the new: a thing never seen before, never felt or tasted or lived through. But strangeness by itself it didn't make this thing intractable, nor guarantee in any way that the future—the Theddies and Carmines and Pamelas of centuries hence, indeed all of society—would find them unusual. Indeed, to the extent that society took any notice of this case at all, it would be as one more precedent in the legal definition of identity. No big deal of all. Or so I reasoned at the time.

And so, somewhat anticlimactically, I found that my job was complete. With those orders posted, there wasn't a fax machine in the Queendom that would reconverge the older and younger Theddies, or a door that would open for them, if the opening might place the two in the same room. My client was safe, and so was I. And I found, also to my surprise, that I was shaking with relief. How about that! This was another thing my job had going for it: no matter how long I did it, there was still this aura of excitement and danger and fresh discovery. Most especially when it was about me.

After that there was only one thing left to do: call my office fax machine and retrieve Theddy—the real, contemporary Theddy—from storage.

9.

Wine, Interrupted

My apartment at the time was a pseudopenthouse—its large balcony was roofed over but otherwise genuine, and the rooms themselves were on the 13th floor of a hundred story building. But the balcony's overhang was programmed to look like sky—an illusion so good that I myself sometimes forgot—while the apartment ceiling was a fiction of dormer vaults and skylights looking up at the other tall buildings as though the higher stories of my own did not exist. This was not an extravagance; the patterns had to be customized by experts and hypercomputers, but it only took an afternoon. A team from Sears-Roebuck had done it for less money than I made in a week. Why, hundreds of people in Denver alone had the exact same decor, probably an even dozen in that very building. But low-cost and cheapness were not the same thing, and most visitors found the effect both striking and laudable.

In this, Theddy Kaffner was no exception. He leaped from the fax all stiff with anxiety, but once I'd explained the situation to him, and handed him a glass of wine, the first thing he did was look around and say, "Jesus Christ. Nice place."

The fireplace was also an illusion—you couldn't jab it with the ornamental poker or wave your hand through the flames—but it looked perfect, and crackled *just so*, and gave off exactly the right amount of heat for a November evening that was suddenly, finally beginning to feel like fall. I faxed up some throw pillows, and the two of us sprawled in the firelight, chugging our drinks and laughing like we had in the good old days.

The purveyors of copyright bourbon tended to regard their products as perfect, and thus subsisted mainly on royalties, reinvesting little or none of it back into research and development. Which was a losing strategy in the long run, because the opensource and public domain recipes got a little bit better every year. Not the same as the copyright brews, obviously, but just as good in their own way. This meant that spending real money on bourbon didn't make sense, except as a way of flaunting one's wealth. Since I rarely had enough to flaunt, I tended to stick with the cheap stuff.

But the wine industry, long accustomed to change and adaptation, had seen the writing on the early Queendom's walls, and rolled with the times. They still grew their grapes the old-fashioned way, with robot labor and nano-optimized soil conditioners, and while they copyrighted every vintage, they actually copied and sold only the best of the best. But except in rare cases, they revoked the old recipes at the end of every market year, replacing them with new ones from the latest crop. If you really liked a particular vintage, you were obliged to buy as many bottles as your cellar would hold, because its like would never come again. So you either had to fill a cellar with the stuff, or pay the aftermarket prices on the collectors' market. Ouch.

I, however, belonged to the Wine Resistance movement. If you knew a bit, and were a good researcher of long-dormant archives, you could dig up the pattern of some ancient vintage whose creators had died heirless and alone. The public domain wines were mostly swill, but I had personally discovered two of these grayware vintages, which could be freely duplicated to my heart's content, and I'd bartered them for a dozen more on the semisecret Resistance exchange.

They were always the same, alas, but so were the "perfect" bourbons. This particular bottle was an atomically exact Delle Venezie Pinot Grigio, from 2203 at the tail end of Late Modernity. Possibly the oldest surviving Pinot Grigio, as delicate and fruity as the day it was archived. And it was *excellent*, even when chugged.

"You'll never guess who I saw this week," I said to Theddy as I uncorked our second bottle.

"Pamela Red," Theddy answered immediately. Was I that transparent? A lawyer really did need a better poker face than this, because Theddy read even more from my expression. "Oh, you *saw* her, did you? In the biblical sense? Did you *run into* her as well? Come across her, so to speak? Good for you, old boy."

I suffered some more teasing of an even less gentlemanly sort, until Theddy finally asked, "How's she doing, anyway?"

"Well. Very well. She's got a gorgeous house down in AntiLand, on the top of Mount Terror. You should see it sometime."

"She got that on a programmer's salary?"

"Well, she calls it a fluke, and I believe her. But yes, she's a programmer. Specializing in materials design."

"Mmm," Theddy said around a heavy swallow of dirt-cheap Pinot. "That would explain it. That's where all the glory is, where all the money is these days. If you ask me, my job is harder: making sure the materials actually work. However wonderful your brick may be, if it's wellstone you've still got to run power and data from point A to point B. You've got to manage waste heat, and if there's gas and fluid transport involved, the plumbing has to go somewhere. Also, a lot of materials aren't structural without an impervium mesh woven through them, and if you ever want the brick to be anything else, to be *programmable* like the rest of the world, then you'd better have some computing elements listening for commands. These things don't happen by themselves."

"I thought hypercomputers did all that."

"Everybody thinks that. That's why the job doesn't pay well. But hypercomputers don't *feel*, Carmine, not like we do. You can load them with algorithms for aesthetics and common sense, but it doesn't make them human. It's a human world we want, right? Computers are always seeking pathological solutions—you know, kill the cockroaches by roasting the whole apartment and then faxing fresh people. That actually happened! And if nothing else it takes a human to add those boo boos to the common-sense database. No do, you stupid machine.

"But we do a lot more than just that. There are copyright issues, security and permissions issues. Hypercomputers will follow the letter of the law every time—they have to—and they're practically paralyzed as a result. To no one's benefit. And there are always profiteers exploiting loopholes, sneaking adware materials onto private property and then wrapping themselves up in the law. Sanctimonious jerks. Half my house calls are to defeat some security system or other, because the wellwood stopped working or the window glass is suddenly demanding back royalties."

"So it's an art," I said, "like everything else that matters."

"Yeah."

"Speaking of which, are you still involved with the theater?"

"Indeed I am," Theddy said. "In fact, that's where my troubles began. I was going to so many plays, and posting so many opinions about what I saw, that one of the news services finally signed me on as part of their appreciators pool."

I knew about of those, yeah: appended to the remarks of professional reviewers were the Aficionados' and People's Choice scores, along with occasional snippets of commentary from their discussion boards. I'd even considered, at one point, quitting law to become a poverty-stricken food appreciator. But I didn't see a connection to Theddy's case, and said so.

Theddy's glass was empty again, and he waved it for a refill, which I provided. "See, the other appreciators were getting really burned off with me. 'You've already got a job,' they said. 'Why're you hogging an aficionado slot as well? You're taking a livelihood away from someone on Basic Assistance. Someone who loves the theater as much as you do."

"Now that's pathetic," I said.

But Theddy's take on it was more forgiving: "There are a lot of people who have nothing else to contribute, Carbo. They make good spectators, and where would the arts be without good spectators? But they can be really pushy about it. Really defensive. Some of these people, it means a lot more to them than it should. They started getting ugly, making threats."

"Ah. And you thought Angry Young Theddy could help."

"Well, yeah. A bit of him, anyway. The fire of youth to temper the iron of wisdom. But fire is tricky."

Those were Theddy's last words, and for the record, when the Constabulary had reconstructed the events that followed, I was fully exonerated of any negligence or inaction. The tampering with my home and office records had occurred during the moments while Theddy's image was in transit, and had triggered no firewall alerts or quantum decoherence flags. The camera that appeared in my ceiling was a mesh of microscopic sensors which my eyes could not possibly have discerned, even if I'd known where to look.

And although I was in fact looking right at Theddy—pouring the last of the Pinot Grigio into his glass, in fact—when the wellcloth of the pillows beneath him crackled and turned to metal, when the floor became a grid of high-voltage lines . . . I'll feel terrible about it for the rest of my life—forever, in other words—but I didn't know what was happening, or why, and even if I did there was really nothing I could have done about it.

When the corners of Theddy's lips drew backward and upward, exposing his teeth, I thought at first that he was smiling. But then his body began to jerk, and smoke, and his eyes grew milky, and I hope to God that the brain damage happened early, because if it didn't, then Theddy, paralyzed and twitching, felt his own hair catch fire, his own skin blacken and peel away. Was the general alarm the last thing he heard?

These were not only my speculations, but those of an entire Queendom of voyeurs, for there hadn't been a lurid murder in twenty years, nor an electrocution in over a hundred. And such events—even before they'd become rare—had always been strange.

10.
Judgments, Final

The trial was only two hours long, and very nearly a formality. Theodore Great Kaffner, Sr.'s only physical body had been murdered, and the only recent copies of him—in the fax buffers of my home and office—had been expertly deleted. Angry Young Theddy did not deny his involvement in these acts, and even if he'd tried, he wouldn't have gotten very far in light of the Constabulary's overwhelming evidence.

On the face of it, he was guilty as sin, but Young Carmine, true to his beer-soaked promises, had mounted a spirited defense. Theddy was guilty, yes, but of what, exactly? Young Carmine consistently used the term "voluntary file maintenance" to describe the incident, and insisted that at the time of said maintenance, Young Theddy had had no way of knowing he'd been legally partitioned into a pair of twins. Thus, he was incapable of criminal intent in the commission of these acts, and if any loss or suffering resulted, it was—to Theddy's mind—of a self-inflicted sort which the law could frown on but not actually forbid.

It was, I thought, quite a savvy maneuver for a counselor so young. It made sense, and if justice were a purely logical affair, or an attempt to move forward with the minimum social damage, it might possibly have prevailed. But the other function of law is to frighten, to make examples, to discourage further thoughts of wrongdoing in the hearts of human beings. And the facts of the case remained incontrovertible: one legal individual was killed through the deliberate and premeditated actions of another. In the end, Young Carmine did about as well for Theddy as anyone could expect: malicious negligence resulting in death.

Tragically, of the durable archives Theddy had stored over the course of his life, the most recent was nearly twenty years out of date, and when it was printed and briefed and placed on the stand to provide commentary for the sentencing, all it could do was hang its head and weep. There was just too much missing from its life. It couldn't make sense of the actions of older *or* younger Theddy, nor of the circumstances it found itself awakened to. When the court asked if it wished to be marked disposable, and thus erased, the copy nodded slowly and was led away by the bailiffs.

As for Young Theddy, he was sentenced to one hundred years' hard labor, without the possibility of parole, and since he was barely twenty-five years in subjective age, this was about as close to a death sentence as a person could get, without murdering thousands or attempting to destroy the sun. A century of subjugation, of cheek-to-jowl contact with humanity's hardest customers. When that was over, nothing would remain of the Theddy I went to college with. Theodore Great Kaffner had managed to destroy himself, and this date was one I would always remember as the true time and place of his death.

There have always been tragedies, and perhaps there always will be: sad events with a momentum of their own, which benefit no one and which make the world a poorer place. And yet, in a way, this was a fitting end for a prankster like Theddy. Hoist on his own petard, indeed. What a lark! I sobbed off and on throughout the trial, dabbing at my tears with a wellcloth handkerchief, but even so I could not avoid the occasional giggle or snort. Even Theddy's younger self, doomed to ruin, seemed on some level to appreciate the irony. He smiled and waved as they led him away, and would no doubt make friends in prison by throwing himself down the stairs.

Ever mindful of the convenience of its patrons, the court had scheduled my own case next on the docket. And this one really *was* a formality, for I had sent an offer to myself the night before, and accepted it gratefully. I, the older Carmine, would cede that portion of my wealth which the younger Carmine had rightfully earned, and Young Carmine would cede the name, changing his own to Ralph Faxborn Douglas. He would also move to a different city, seek new acquaintances, and change his face and hairstyle in minor but telling ways. As for Ralph's ongoing maintenance, I offered a generous five-year stipend, to give him a chance to get on his feet, to find a job or found a business somewhere. But Ralph, awash in notoriety, had no shortage of job offers, and had already licensed his story—*our* story—for a tidy sum which I agreed not to dispute or attach in any way. No further settlement was needed.

On the stand I was asked by the judge to confirm that yes, these were the terms I had agreed to. And I felt a momentary pang before answering, for letting go of my youth was a hard thing to do. But I spoke clearly for the record: "Yes, Your Honor. Ralph Douglas and I are in full agreement."

It was a sad affair all the way around, made all the more stressful and surreal for me by the presence of Pamela Red in the audience. What was *she* doing here? The question plagued me throughout both trials, only to be answered at the end, when I watched her fall happily into the arms of Ralph Faxborn. This was not *my* Pamela at all, the Antarctican matter programmer, but rather the archived student, still burning with passion, over whom I had pined for a decade and more, risking nearly everything. I watched the two of them, warm and happy together, and wondered if I'd ever feel a thing like that again. Was youth a necessary component?

Against my better judgment, I went over to talk to them. "You two look . . . happy together."

"Thank you for everything," Ralph said. "For life itself. I apologize for not trusting you."

And I answered him sternly: "Never apologize for being cautious. The world is full of nasty surprises, and lawyers, at least, must stand prepared. Until I'd thought about it, I *was* going to erase you." I paused a moment and then added, "Look, I've learned a lot over the years, about being you. We should sit down. Have a chat."

"And turn me into yourself?" Ralph laughed at that. "Another generous offer, sir, but I'll have to decline. Is my own future not bright? If you survived our trials and tribulations, I reckon I won't do any worse. And time will tell, sir, but I reckon I have a certain advantage as well, coming to this world as a traveler from its past. It gives a certain outsider's perspective which ought, I think, to be useful. So if it's all the same to you, I will ignore you as I would my own father. Fair enough?"

"You're a clever boy," I said, and it wasn't entirely a compliment.

All the while, young Pamela had been looking me over with great curiosity. And if this was painful, why, returning her gaze was like leaping into a furnace. "And you, young lady," I said as evenly as I could manage. "I'm quite flabbergasted to see you here."

"I imagine you are," she said, with a sympathy that was agonizingly genuine, and equally condescending. "I don't know your history, and I don't care to. But it upsets me to think I've caused you pain."

And *that* one really knocked the stuffing out of me. Young

Pamela had always had a knack for that, for hitting me where I was weakest while trying, in some vague way, to be nice. And suddenly I was able to forgive her for that, for all of it. Because she was just some kid, and didn't know any better. How could she?

I nodded slowly. "Yes. Well. The intent behind your words is appreciated. Have you spoken with . . . yourself?"

"I have," she said, "and it's her you should be talking to, not me. I felt her letting go of a lot of anger. If you want to . . . you know, pounce in a moment of weakness . . . well, now would be time."

"Thanks for the tip," I said, laughing in spite of myself. And then, more thoughtfully: "She and I fought such battles over you. It's ironic, and rather sad, that she didn't surrender you sooner."

Pamela just looked at me then, with a wise sort of weariness, and said, "Love isn't a surrender, but a gift. Sometimes we return it unopened, but we never fail to appreciate it. If you're going to talk about me like a thing, at least have the right sort of thing in mind, all right? The real question to ask yourself is why she suddenly feels like giving."

God, she sounded so good. So lovely, so perfect. And Ralph, too, was everything a mutant, sexually deviant father could hope for. Surely *here* was a young man who could do no wrong, no matter what the provocation.

"I wish you both the very best of luck," I said with conviction.

And the two of them smiled at me as they might a distant relative, and then turned, arm-in-arm, and walked away. The perfect couple, yes. This was no longer the world they'd been copied from, and they were not those people. Not quite. Maybe things would be different this time.

The smart thing for me to do then would have been to go back home and get to work. There was plenty of work for me, always. But life was too short for that, yes? Even if it lasted forever. I had a flair for the dramatic and a nose for the strange; it was time to take a risk.

Still, it took all my strength to keep from shouting after them, "Fool! She's *five months* from dumping you!"

BLISS

Leah Bobet

Sam dragged his sister Elizabeth out of the tenement on a bright December day, her face swelling from bruises and puffed-red with tears. She didn't speak when the cops cuffed the shouting, swearing stereotype of a beater she'd called a boyfriend: Sam had given him a right hook to the face for symmetry's sake and now the jerk was none too happy. With that same hand wrapped so firmly around his sister's thin arm, he felt almost ashamed. His wrist hurt, and there had been something about those neighbour kids who'd been staring with wide, knowing eyes, like it was something they saw every day . . .

I shouldn't have hit him. I'm better than that.

Elizabeth didn't speak as Sam piled her into his car. She shivered and stared blankly at the house that had been hers, no evidence that anything was sinking in but the tear-tracks on her face. Neither did Sam; it was enough to concentrate on the road and hold the wheel with that sore wrist, one stoplight at a time until they reached his condo. Last time it had just turned into a fight, another flight back into God-knew-where, and now another call from the cops, another lie he'd have to tell his mother about knowing where Elizabeth was. He wasn't going to ask why this time, and he wasn't going to judge. It was her life.

He gripped the wheel tight and kept driving.

When he helped her out of the sedan in the parking garage, arm wrapped firmly around her waist to hold up that too-frail body, she started to sniffle again.

He could have sighed, or slapped her, or cried. "Why didn't you call me? If something was wrong, you know I wouldn't tell Mom, or . . . why didn't you call?"

"He made me so happy," she whimpered.

Fuck, thought Sam.

She was back on the Bliss.

*   *   *

Sam called his boss when they got upstairs. He had a family situation, he knew they were riding a deadline, could he please have a few days to deal with it and he'd work overtime later? Madison hemmed and hawed, finally agreed, and Sam thumbed the off button before he could change his mind.

Elizabeth was shivering on the black leather couch, poking wide-eyed at the remote control for Sam's entertainment centre. She looked just like those kids had when Sam's fist connected with that bastard's face—curious, uncaring, totally detached.

"Liz, d'you want something to drink?"

She didn't even look up.

He went into the kitchen—black countertops and black-on-white tile, shiny white fridge and stove—and poured some water into a sleek, heat-saving mug. His hands trembled as he replaced the pitcher in the neatly ordered fridge. He should call his mother, find a rehab program; he was the younger one, and shouldn't have to take care of her again; she was a junkie and a runaway, what Madison called a gutter-grubber. She chose the gutter. It was her own fault she had that shiner on her face.

I am not my sister's keeper.

When he got back into the living room she'd managed to turn on the digital stereo, and music started to sprinkle out of the speakers. It was an old band, some two-guitars and a drummer thing, not the incomprehensible anarchy of sound that passed for music these days. Elizabeth stared like a newborn child at the speakers, then clapped her hands and burst into tears.

Sam rushed over, abandoning the mug of water on his coffee table and enfolded her in his arms. She was trembling, crying, snot running down her face and onto her cracked, chapped lips.

It took him a moment to realize: they were tears of joy.

"Why did you start again, Liz? You promised me," he whispered, and it was all he could do to not cry himself.

She pulled back, shook her head, still dreamy-looking and empty and not at all herself inside. "You wouldn't understand," she said, but there was no malice in it, just simple, clear, stoned-out-of-your-skull fact.

The words punched him in the stomach and left a hole clean through to the other side. So he stood and picked up his briefcase from where he'd dropped it that morning, and worked out the bugs in five pages of code until he felt soothed once again.

*   *   *

For the rest of the day she stared at everything as if it were a jewel beyond price.

On Tuesday she shivered and furrowed her brow, wandered the condo aimlessly touching white walls, black lamps, white shelves and the black TV, a hound scenting that something was not quite right. Sam watched her from the desk and wrote one sentence of a report over and over again. The evening news was full of the Pharmaceutical Question and tired-eyed policemen; it featured a documentary on the use of Bliss as a date-rape drug. He turned it off halfway through. These problems had no numbers, too many variables, no controls: they made his head hurt and set an ache moving in his chest.

On Wednesday she curled up in the crisp white sheets of his bed and stared at the ceiling, blank-eyed with despair. She spoke only in a monotone, and Sam had to feed her himself, one spoonful of runny soup at a time from the heavy chrome spoon in his hand. She turned her face away after only a few bites, even though her stomach still rumbled and fussed; he talked in a soft, patient voice to her and massaged the food down her throat.

By Thursday the worst of the withdrawal was over, and Sam went back to work.

There was a memo on his desk when he got into the office, tired and wondering if he shouldn't have spent another day at home. *Report to the lab for seasonal testing,* it said. It was two days old.

Mac Bearns clucked his tongue and straightened a wrinkled lab coat when Sam knocked on the door. "Here for the test? You're late, man."

Sam wrinkled his nose as the chemical smell of the lab tingled and burned in his nostrils. "I wasn't in the office this week. Had a family thing."

Mac nodded. "Everyone's okay?"

"They will be."

He grabbed a clipboard, clapped it down on the sterile cloud-blue counter. "Well, full battery of tests for you this time. Gonna need a urine sample after this."

Sam sighed and rolled up his sleeve. Mac wrapped the length of rubber around his arm with one hand, snagged a small container full of vials with the other: both with a rough, almost graceful expertise. "How many years have I been working here? This some kind of punishment for the time off?"

"Sorry man; it's the holidays, so we're doing everyone. Gotta be extra careful around this time of year." Mac shrugged. "This'll sting."

The needle went into Sam's arm hard and he hissed, even though he'd felt it a million times before. He watched as Mac carefully attached vial after vial to the nozzle on the needle's other end, as they filled up with the thick red of his blood one by one. "Like nobody would notice if one of us was on the sauce."

Mac shrugged again. "Hey, nobody noticed at MilleniTech or we wouldn't have had to reconstruct our servers last month."

Sam turned just too fast, and the needle dug further into his arm. "Ow. Shit. That was drug-related?"

"Yup. One of the QA guys was on Bliss. He decided the security on the upgrade was 'good enough'; almost offed himself when they fired him because he'd been so proud of the work and they'd taken away his stash. Madison's talking about monthly tests instead of quarterly now."

"Shit," Sam said again. Bruises from Mac's bedside manner every month, just to prove he was clean enough to do his own job: soon it would be him and not Liz the cops were questioning about abuse. The idea rankled—the company didn't trust his judgement that far?—but it was in his contract. It was in all their contracts. Probably even Mac's. And these days he wasn't going to find a job that paid anything without a lab clause in the contract.

The needle slipped out of his arm with a little jerk. Mac undid the rubber tubing and deftly applied a band-aid where the needle had been. "So drop a urine sample off at the nurse's station and you're free to go."

Sam picked up the little clear cup from a stack on the counter and slid it in his pocket. "Thanks."

"No problem." Mac gathered up the full vials and started to label them in his messy doctor's hand: *Gordon, Sam; 12/17*. "Wanna grab something at the pub tonight? Kim's working late."

Sam shook his head. "Like I said, family thing. Still need to keep an eye on it."

"Oh, yeah. You'll gimme a call if you need anything, right?" He said it so flatly Sam was almost surprised. *The best nonchalant bastard of a friend I've ever had. Maybe I should have said yes.* "And if I don't see you before then, Merry Christmas."

"Merry Christmas," Sam said, and headed for the washroom.

*   *   *

Liz was asleep when he got home, curled up in his bed looking just like she had as a kid. The stress lines were smoothed out of her face, and it wasn't artificially happy, just . . . peaceful. Sam sat down next to her, closed his eyes, tried to reproduce the look on her face.

He smoothed his face to calmness, leaned back on the bit of mattress that wasn't covered with her sleep-heavy body. His thoughts slowed down, quieted; the warmth of the bed and the warmth of his own body melded into one. Maybe this was how she felt with the Bliss: sleepy and secure, totally unaware of anything outside her own body, slow. Content. Hibernatory. Consciousness bleeding into everything around—

He jolted. *No. Wake up. Live.*

Sam sat up and his hands were shaking. Liz was still fast asleep, her breathing even and steady. He almost reached out to pull the blankets over her.

Instead, he stood up and went to put on the kettle.

Monday, Christmas coming, family around for the first time in years. Sam came home with a turkey and trimmings, a bottle of wine and a store-bought chocolate cake, just in time to see Elizabeth stuff something in her mouth.

He kept his hands steady, put down the groceries and composed his face before turning to look at her. "Hi, Liz. What do you have there?"

She shifted on the couch, curling her knees up against her chest, inclining her too-thin face away. "I had a headache."

She hadn't answered the question. He took a few steps towards her, slowly. "Okay. What do you have there?"

She swallowed. "Nothing."

He dove for the couch, grabbed for her wrist and wrested the Nothing out of her hand. She yelped, screamed, but he pulled away and unfolded it in his hand. It was a packet of paper, and inside it were three little pink pills. He stared for a moment and then crumpled it in his fist. "Liz. Where did you get this?"

Tears started to seep into her eyes. "I *need* it!"

"No, you don't." His voice was so patient, more than he felt. Daddy-voice, reasonable and rational. Maybe Dad could have dealt with Liz like this. She'd always been his baby. "You can live without it."

She made another snatch at the packet. "But I don't want to! It's . . . how can you be so unhappy? I can't *do* it, Sam!"

"You're going to have to make your own happiness," he said. So prosaic. But he'd made his own: good job. Nice home. Nobody else had given it to him, that was for sure.

"I can't," she almost wailed. Sam felt a momentary surge of guilt. It was true; she probably couldn't. She'd wait forever for her handsome prince or protector or—*keeper? Don't think that*—to make everything okay. And when nobody did, she just went back to it, time after time after time.

He knew why he still hadn't called Mom. She and Liz hadn't spoken in ten years, and seeing Liz like this would break his mother's heart.

But why hadn't he taken her to the doctor?

Her eyes strayed to the crumpled packet in his hand, one more time. Would his own big sister jump him to get at her stash? Sam hesitated for one long moment; then he strode to the window, slid it open, and flung the packet of paper fifty-three stories down into the alley below.

Elizabeth's mouth dropped open. "You . . . you *asshole.*"

Sam slid the window shut. "It's for your own good," he said, and managed to keep his voice even.

"You hate me. You've always hated me. You think you're better than I am."

"I'm not the addict here, okay?" *Shit. Shouldn't have said that.*

"Addict," she hissed. "You're addicted to your own fucking holier-than-thou *pain*. And you want me on it too." Elizabeth uncurled like a snake, eyes glittering. "Well, excuse-fucking-me if I don't want to hurt all the time! I just want to be happy, okay? That's all I want, no condo, no money, no goddamned leather jacket and—"

Sam got to his feet. "Elizabeth—"

"No, you listen to me. How dare you say I don't have a right to be happy?"

Sam felt his own eyes narrowing. "Who said you did? Happiness isn't a *right*, Liz! It's a privilege. You earn it. It's not something people just get on a silver platter. You work for it, okay?"

"Right," she snorted. "Work and be good and don't talk in school and thou shalt be rewarded from on high. It doesn't work like that, baby brother."

194 | BLISS

"You don't know shit about life, Liz—"

"You're the one who's full of . . ." she hesitated, frowned. "I . . ." One by one, her muscles relaxed. A serene smile spread across her face, then started to intensify. She tightened her hands and looked down at the vase in her hand, ran her hand over its painted pattern.

She set the vase down on the floor and started to examine it from every angle, touching, smelling, drinking it in. Her eyes were wide with delight. "Look," she breathed.

Sam drew a ragged breath and let it out. He needed to put the groceries away before they got too warm, or they wouldn't have a Christmas dinner. And he needed a dinner for tonight, and to call his mother, and someone to watch Elizabeth when he went to work tomorrow in case—

He needed a doctor. He was in over his head, and he didn't dare take her to the hospital; social services would step in and he'd never see her again. Mom would find out and she'd never forgive him. He hadn't given up on her yet; he wasn't going to now.

Sam picked up the phone and punched a few numbers. "Mac? Sam Gordon. No, it's just . . . you know how you said I could call if—? I need a favour."

Mac arrived with a sharp knock on the door and his usual air of wrinkled competence, even though the lab coat had been replaced with a huge grey trenchcoat. "You rang?"

"I've got a problem," Sam said. "It's my sister. I can't take her to a hospital."

Mac's face went serious and sharp. "Lemme see." He shouldered past Sam into the apartment and regarded Elizabeth where she sat on the floor, still staring at the painted vase. "What're the symptoms?"

Sam shut and locked the door behind him, trying not to fidget. "I . . . it's . . ." He swallowed. "Bliss."

Mac frowned; not anger, but concentration. "Here, let me see." He opened his bag and pulled out instruments, gauze, a bottle of liquid that smelled sterile and sharp.

Elizabeth giggled when the needle went into her arm, and she watched the blood spurt into the vials with focused fascination. "What's your name?"

"Mackenzie," he said with a parent's indulgent smile, and changed the vial. "I work with your brother."

She clapped her hands in delight.

Sam shook his head. "If I can just keep her away from it—"

"Not that simple, man. How much do you know about Bliss?"

"It makes you a spineless vegetable," he muttered.

Mac gave him a measuring look and eased the second vial from the needle, replaced it with a third. "Bliss isn't like some of the other stuff. It's neurological: chemical stimulation of the parts of your brain that regulate sleep and processing speed and such. That regulate feelings. It suppresses the negative-emotion parts of the brain and some of the logic centres, and a dependency forms. It's like the daredevil theories about adrenaline addiction. The brain needs the chemical after a while." Mac carefully labelled the vial: *Jane Doe, 12/21.* "Emotion is chemical," he said. "It's genuine happiness they're feeling. So far as we know."

Fake happiness. Pill happiness. Bullshit. "Mac," he said. "What the hell am I going to do?"

Mac shrugged and started to pack his bag. "Look, let me get to the lab. I have an idea about fixing this. I don't know if I'll have to do a spinal tap, but this should be a start." Mac rubbed the bridge of his nose beneath the glasses and sighed. "It's been a long time since I did research," he said, but there was excitement in his voice.

He zipped up his bag and looked Elizabeth up and down one more time, how she rubbed at the bandage on her arm, how she fidgeted and plucked at her hair, her clothes, everything with a kind of satisfied glee. "It's not even supposed to be a street drug. It's an anti-depressant. Guess it just proves people will abuse anything."

"Hey," Sam said. "She's not a junkie. It was hard for her, okay?"

"Yeah." Mac replied. "It's hard for everyone."

All the words in Sam's mouth jumped back down his throat.

Mac went to the door and unlocked it. "Look, I'll let you know by Wednesday if there's anything I can do." He turned with a lopsided smile, punched Sam in the arm. "Get some sleep, huh?"

Sam managed to push out one word before his throat closed again. "Goodnight."

"G'night," Mac said, and then he was gone.

Elizabeth stared at him, doll-eyes wide and smile fixed upon her face. "Let's play a game. Wanna play?"

On Wednesday morning there was a memo on his desk: *Report to the lab.* Sam tucked his briefcase under the desk and stuffed the paper in his pocket, heart accelerating to a mile a minute. He went down the stairs, dodging the herds of co-workers dragging themselves up to their own cubicles to the sound of canned holiday cheer.

Mac's head snapped up when he pushed the door open. "Took you long enough."

"What've you got?" Sam panted. He sank into the chair where Mac usually took blood, grateful for its presence for the first time in his life.

Mac didn't shrug; in fact his stare was almost as focused as Elizabeth's. "Before I go into this, I want you to know these aren't tested or approved by any kind of authority. I mixed them in my basement, and I'll deny whatever the hell I have to. I don't know what might go wrong, but they should work in theory. Are you sure you want to do this?"

This was irresponsible. This was wildly irresponsible.

It was better than social services. It was better than this going on again and again, the tears, the withdrawal, the inevitable broken lock and stolen cash and slide back into unknowing stupor. It was better than not knowing.

Sam nodded.

Mac dug into his pocket and pulled out a dark-tinted pill bottle. The prescription label was blank. He opened it with a loud pop! and there were five little pink pills inside. "Here's your silver bullet. Well, pink."

Sam raised an eyebrow. "Mac, that's just the drug."

"Ah," he said. "Looks like, huh? Consider that a perk. It's for . . . patient cooperation, let's say. If my guess is right these little suckers will stimulate the parts of the brain the Bliss is turning off and we can get some balance going again. If I'm right."

"I'll trust you," Sam said. "My head's spinning already. I mean . . . how do you know all this shit?"

"Think I wanted to be a lab monkey my whole life?" Mac snorted. "Your piss is fascinating, but some of us trained as scientists so we could, you know, *do science*."

Sam swallowed. There was a moment of silence in which he thought about apologizing and discarded that, because it would embarrass Mac; wondered why he'd never figured Mac was that smart; wondered how many industries the Pharmaceutical Question really had affected. Figured maybe he was lucky to have wanted to go into software and not music or art or science or social work.

Mac pressed the bottle into Sam's palm. The five little pink pills inside rattled quietly against the tinted plastic. "Here's your prescription. Use it wisely, and use it well, and don't say I never did anything for you."

He blinked. "So if it's that easy to get people unhooked, why didn't—"

Mac shook his head and he looked almost pitying. "You really are naïve, man. Get back to your desk before Madison starts wondering. And let me know how it goes."

"Yeah," Sam said. "Thanks so much." He slipped the pill bottle into his pocket. It shook and danced with every step he took back to the office.

When Sam got home, he could tell Liz had been out.

They ate dinner in sullen silence, and once she fell asleep, he went hunting for her stash. Six pink pills went out of the folded napkin in the stereo speaker, and five pink pills went back into it.

For a day, there was relative peace.

Sam managed to make his excuses to Mom and cooked them Christmas dinner, the old-fashioned kind where he fumbled through an ancient recipe book and left the turkey in the oven too long and bought egg nog. It was hard to take his eyes off Liz even to cook. Of course it was too soon for any changes to show, if there were to be any changes. But the way she held her glass at dinner looked just different enough, and the way he remembered her doing it before was just fuzzy enough . . .

He shook his head. She might get off the drug, but he was going to drive himself crazy.

She was quiet throughout dinner, not the angry-quiet of the last week, but . . . almost pensive. Content. It was vaguely unnerving.

She offered to do the dishes, and she offered to warm up the eggnog, and he let her, just to get a break from staring at her face for a few minutes. He sat down on the black leather couch and stared at the black and silent television instead, stark against the white walls, reflecting across-the-street's Christmas lights through the window in a weird blur of green and red.

"Sam?"

Something was wrong. She'd found out. She was going to run

off again and he'd never find her in time. He stumbled over his own feet and practically jumped into the kitchen.

She was sitting at the table, and there was a mug before the empty black wood chair across from him. "Eggnog's ready." She was looking into her mug, and there were faint worry lines creasing her forehead.

Had she figured it out? What would he say if she did?

He took a long swallow of the eggnog, another.

Something small and solid went down his throat.

Sam almost gagged, but it was gone; he could almost feel it wending its way down into his stomach. "Liz . . . what the hell—"

"Oh, c'mon," she frowned softly. "You need to loosen up. Baby brother, always so serious. It's not good to be so serious this young. That's how you end up all perfect and empty and you don't know where it all went."

The warmth going down through his body started to burn. He coughed, then harder, as if he could force it up. But it was gone, it was in him and she'd put it—"You put something in my drink! Liz, how could you—"

She shrugged. "You're always so sad. I don't want you to be sad. I'm the big sister. I'm supposed to take care of you, right?"

She'd given him Bliss. He was going to fail his next drug test. He was going to turn into an addict. It would fry his brain.

But it wasn't Bliss, of course.

Mac's medication.

Sam's eyes went wide as his mug crashed to the floor, his knees buckled, his body hit the black-and-white tile with a *thud*.

All those thoughts went through his head at once, and then that one did too, and he realized he could see spectra in the fluorescent track lighting, he could see minute flaws in the floor tiles, he could feel the humming of the fridge in his back and calculate its frequency, and through that calculate just how cold of a temperature it was maintaining: two degrees higher than it should, and of course that was why the milk had spoiled last week.

It was incredible.

He thought he heard Liz scream.

He couldn't sleep.

Thoughts burned through his mind one after the other, hissing like racecars he could only perceive a second after they had already passed. Liz had carried—no, dragged—him to bed: he could feel *soft pillow pressure texture springs*. He could calculate his weight from how hard the mattress pushed back into his spine and a few equations he'd forgotten from first-year Physics. The zipper of his suitcase, the rustle of his phone book's pages, and then Mac was there; Sam could hear his voice somewhere above, blurring with speed, refracted into frequencies. He could pinpoint how far away it was from the acoustics alone.

The thoughts crowded his head like they never had, every bad night of worried insomnia in the world compacted into one little pill. He remembered things long forgotten or pushed by the wayside: flavours, feelings, all fuzzy and half-there, almost as if they were a dream.

I've been sleeping my whole life. I've only come awake just now.

He couldn't sleep now. He was *alive*.

Phone ring; Liz's voice, worried and with a strain of snappish stress he hadn't heard in forever; time, in which he viewed the entirety of a Picasso exhibit he'd seen at fourteen all over again, listened to symphonies, calculated his annual budget, realized what he needed to get promoted and planned it all out; then more voices, his mom's voice, hysterical, *this is all your fault you stupid—*

Shit.

His brain started planning damage control.

If Mom was here then Liz must have called, so they must have been talking, but it didn't sound good, it sounded really bad, and there it was again—*I should have known you should have been responsible you were older and your father would never have put up with he would have dealt with you*—and they were going to fight, and that couldn't happen because he had to keep the peace one way or another until he could understand her and maybe make Mom understand her so there would be peace in the house and it was Christmas, for God's sake even if statistically that was the worst time for families didn't Mac say something the other day about that? and ohyeah Mac was here, pushing something into his mouth, he could tell because Mac always smelled like those damned cleaners they used in the lab, stingy and sharp, and had to swallow or he'd choke and throw up and people died like that—

And then—

Joy.

It rocketed through his veins for just an instant before the centrifuge of his brain slowed, before his eyes could open, before his heart stopped pounding hard enough to break his ribs.

Liz's face hovered above him, tight with strain. "Sam?"

His mouth worked, experimentally. "Ummm."

"Oh God." Tears sprung from her eyes and spattered his chest. "Oh God you're okay. I'm so sorry, I'm sorry. I'll never touch the shit again. I swear. I swear."

"You're goddamned right you'll never touch—"

"Ummm." He said to his mother.

His eyes closed and the darkness took him.

When he woke up again Mac was sitting beside the bed. His eyes were far away again, the scientist eyes. Observing, calm, not at all like he'd probably been pulled away from a Christmas dinner of his own—was Mac even Christian?—and dumped into the middle of a family fight.

They were fighting. He could hear Liz screaming through the solid bedroom door. He could hear his mother's angry low cold tone sneaking beneath it.

His eyes fluttered. His thoughts were so damned *slow*. Why couldn't he think?

"Sam?" Mac stood up. Fingers pressed against his forehead, and they were freezing. "Shit, you're running a temperature. You need liquids."

". . . sorry . . ." he squeezed out, but Mac was already out the door.

He came back after what felt like an eternity with a mug and blankets, propped Sam's limp body upwards, and held the mug up to his lips. Sam sipped: hot chocolate, just warm enough to feel good, just cool enough so it didn't burn his tongue. *Chocolate releases endorphins into the bloodstream,* his mind whispered. *We like it because it's chemical.* After a few more sips he could hold it himself in steadying hands.

"Are they . . . ?"

Mac shrugged, but his eyes were dark. "I don't know what's normal around your house. They're fighting. Your sister's pretty torn up. She's a smart woman: addicts don't usually have short-term memory retention that good, especially for names." He paused. "You're lucky, man."

"She said she wasn't going to take it anymore."

"Yah. I told them about the meds."

"It works. The pills. It felt . . ." he shook his head. "Fast."

Mac's impassive Doctor Face twitched just a little. "That's something." He stood before Sam could get a good look at his face. "I'll go get your sister. I have to get home; it's almost two in the morning. Kim's probably worried sick."

"How'd you come up with that so fast? I mean—" Sam paused as the Doctor Face slipped; there was a wistfulness, a hunger in Mac's eyes that he'd never seen before.

"It's been a long time since I did research," Mac said quietly. "But I always keep my notes."

He opened the door and then shut it again behind him. A few quiet words—Sam caught *don't fuss, fragile, untested* before Liz came in and carefully sat herself down.

Sam huddled under the blankets and cupped his fingers around the mug of hot chocolate. They were freezing cold, and they moved so slowly, almost as slow as the thoughts in his head. It made him want to whimper or cry or scream; he'd been moving so fast.

And now it was gone, and he was empty, and everything was still the same. Slow and sticky and living in a dream. A nightmare of illusion and stupidity and not understanding a damn thing.

"What?" Liz said sharply.

He realized he'd been speaking out loud, that he was still muttering under his breath. Sam shook himself and took another sip from his mug. It was shiny black, and his sheets were crisp white, and both were hurting his eyes. The whole apartment was hurting his eyes.

"Sam?" her voice was anxious, raw-edged.

"Nothing," he said. "Nothing."

Hours passed, he drank, he stood up, he lay down. Liz took his temperature; his mother fussed and wept and scowled despite whatever Mac had said to them.

Finally, he was alone in bed, with the night greying into winter dawn. Christmas Day. He couldn't sleep.

Liz was going to take the meds and get off the Bliss. She and Mom were talking again. Talking loudly, yeah, but talking. He didn't need to keep her secret from Mom anymore. He could go back to his job and his life and it was going to be okay.

There was something missing.

He should have been happy.

Instead there was just this slow, dull, thickness swirling through his brain. He couldn't live like this; it was like having his legs cut off. He had had such capacity, such ability. He'd been so *himself.*

It was a drug, Sam. It wasn't real. You know it wasn't real.

"Then why do I feel so . . . ?" he asked the walls.

Curled up on the floor of his bedroom in a sleeping bag, Liz stirred and rolled over in her sleep.

He wasn't going to be an addict. Maybe he did think he was better than Liz, because he could function without fake happiness just fine, so he could function without fake knowledge too. He would go back to work and back to his life and forget this had happened, bury it away. He would never touch anything so strong as a martini ever again, and it didn't matter if he forgot things, or if there were things he never figured out or didn't know, or if there ended up being limits to his own intelligence—

It felt like being alive. I could remember how Dad's aftershave smelled.

He shoved that thought away.

He knew exactly where Liz's stash was. Three little pills wrapped in a napkin, stuffed into the back of his stereo speaker. He slid out of bed, opened the white door on silent white hinges, and padded across the living room, past his sleeping mother on the black couch, to the black wall unit with the black stereo. One hand dug in, removed one little pink pill from the folded napkin, replaced it in its warren.

Maybe he'd need it someday. Maybe there'd be a problem he couldn't solve. It was wise, he reasoned, to save something like this for contingencies, for emergencies. For a rainy day.

Sam ghosted back into his bedroom, eased himself shakily into bed with a careful glance at Liz. She didn't even twitch. There was no peace on her face this time, just sheer blank exhaustion. With or without the Bliss, she was never really going to be happy. People made their own happiness. It didn't get handed to them on a silver platter, or in a little pink pill. He'd made his own happiness.

He tucked his pill into a tissue, wedged it in the back of his nightstand drawer where the particle-board pieces met. It would be safe there, if he needed it.

He rolled over and fell asleep just as the sun started to rise.

*   *   *

After the holidays, Liz moved back in with Mom. The pills had worked. She didn't need the Bliss anymore, or at least her body didn't. Their mother still called him every few days, worried, tense, frustrated with the idea of a teenager she hadn't seen for ten years and hadn't been able to handle even then. She cried at night, Mom said. She went to work, and she went out with guys every so often—always checked out for drugs and home by eleven—but there wasn't that light in her eyes anymore, Sammy. She just isn't how she was as a little girl.

Sam would listen, and nod, and uh-huh, I understand, we have to understand. She's not going to be the same. She'll never be the same, Mom. We just have to love her how she is.

But she was such a perfect little girl, his mother would say, and trail off confused.

Sam went back to work. He remembered enough of his plan to write it down and get promoted. Mac changed jobs too, but into a new department: Chemical Research and Development, a department funded by some uncanny new developments R&D had reached; by rights it should have taken years to write a programming language like that. Sam didn't see him in the lab anymore, and the lab tests stayed quarterly. Every so often someone had an unexpected few days off after Lab Day, and nobody could quite understand it, because they seemed normal, right?

Days like that, Sam went home and his thoughts felt slow as mud. He stared at lines of code and couldn't *think*. Something cold and empty started gnawing at his guts, and the black-and-white tiles, the white sheets, the black electronics hurt his eyes and head and heart and it was just too damned much for one person to take.

Days like that, Sam went into his bedroom and dug a ratty tissue out of the back of his nightstand drawer, unwrapped it until the little pink pill rested in his hand, and stared at it for hours.

So long as he had that little pink pill, it would be okay.

He could use it if he needed it, and be fast again, be happy and sharp and powerful again, and then everything would be all right.

He had it right there.

Just in case of an emergency.

Then he would wrap it up and put it back, and make some hot chocolate.

FINISHED

Robert Reed

What did I plan? Very little, in truth. An evening walk accompanied by the scent of flowers and dampened earth, the lingering heat of the day taken as a reassurance, ancient and holy. I was genuinely happy, as usual. Like a hundred other contented walkers, I wandered through the linear woods, past lovers' groves and pocket- sized sanctuaries and ornamental ponds jammed full of golden orfes and platinum lungfish. When I felt as if I should be tired, I sat on a hard steel bench to rest. People smiled as they passed, or they didn't smile. But I showed everyone a wide grin, and sometimes I offered a pleasant word, and one or two of the strangers paused long enough to begin a brief conversation.

One man—a rather old man, and I remember little else—asked, "And how are you today?"

Ignoring the implication, I said, "Fine."

I observed, "It's a very pleasant evening."

"Very pleasant," he agreed.

My bench was near a busy avenue, and sometimes I would study one of the sleek little cars rushing past.

"The end of a wonderful day," he continued.

I looked again at his soft face, committing none of it to memory. But I kept smiling, and with a tone that was nothing but polite, I remarked, "The sun's setting earlier now. Isn't it?"

The banal recognition of a season's progression—that was my only intent. But the face colored, and then with a stiff, easy anger, the man said, "What does it matter to you? It's always the same day, after all."

Hardly. Yet I said nothing.

He eventually grew tired of my silence and wandered off. With a memory as selective as it is graceful, I tried to forget him. But since I'm talking about him now, I plainly didn't succeed. And looking back on the incident, I have to admit that the stranger perhaps had some little role in what happened next.

I planned nothing.

But a keen little anger grabbed me, and I rose up from the bench, and like every pedestrian before me, I followed the path to the edge of the avenue. Later, I was told that I looked like someone lost in deep thoughts, and I suppose I was. Yet I have no memory of the moment. According to witnesses, I took a long look up the road before stepping forwards with my right foot. The traffic AI stabbed my eyes with its brightest beam, shouting, "Go back!" But I stepped forwards again, without hesitation, plunging directly into the on-coming traffic.

A little pink Cheetah slammed on its brakes. But it was an old car with worn pads—a little detail that couldn't have found its way into my calculations—and despite the heroic efforts of its AI pilot, the car was still moving at better than eighty kilometers an hour when it shattered my hip and threw my limp body across the hood, my chest and then my astonished face slamming into the wind-shield's flexing glass.

Again, I tumbled.

Then I found myself sprawled in a heap on the hot pavement.

For a thousand years, I lay alone. Then a single face appeared, scared and sorry and pale and beautiful. Gazing down through the mayhem, she said, "Oh, God. Oh, shit!"

With my battered mouth, I said, "Hello."

Leaking a sloppy laugh, I told her, "No, really, I'll be fine."

Then I asked, "What's your name?"

"Careless," she said. "Stupid," she said. And then she said, "Or Bonnie. Take your pick."

I picked Bonnie.

A beautiful young woman, she had short dark hair arranged in a fetching fish-scale pattern and a sweet face made with bright brown eyes and skin that looked too smooth and clear to be skin. On most occasions, her smile came easily, but it could be a crooked smile laced with weariness and a gentle sadness. There was a girlish light-ness to her voice, but in difficult circumstances, that voice and the pretty face were capable of surprising strength. "What should I do?" she asked the crumbled figure at her feet. "What do you need?"

"Help," I muttered, answering both questions.

Others had gathered on the curb, observing the two of us. Yet she noticed nothing but me, kneeling beside me, grasping a hand without a second thought. "Do you need a hospital? Should I call somebody—?"

"There's a clinic up the road," I mentioned.

"An ambulance," one of our spectators recommended.

"Just help me to your car and take me there," I suggested. Then I made a joke, promising, "I won't bleed on your seat."

Bless her, she recognized my humor and flashed a little smile. Realizing that my shattered legs couldn't hold themselves upright, much less carry the wreckage on top of them, Bonnie grabbed me under the arms and pulled. But I was too heavy, and after a few hard tugs, she carefully set me down again, asking our audience, "Could somebody lend a hand?"

A pair of finished people stood among the others. But it was a teenage boy, big and raw, who leaped forwards. He seemed thrilled by the chance to drag me across the pavement, practically throwing me into the waiting vehicle. Then with a cleansing brush of the hands, he asked, "Anything hurt?"

"Everything hurts," I admitted.

He didn't believe me. He laughed and stared at the beautiful woman, relishing this chance to be part of this little drama. I was nothing now. I was a sack of dislocated parts and bottled memories, and he thoroughly ignored me, asking the only one who mattered, "Do you need me to ride along?"

But Bonnie had already climbed inside, telling her car, "Now. Hurry."

The ride took just long enough for me to thank her once more and absorb a few more apologies. Then as we pulled up in front of the nondescript clinic, I offered my name. She repeated, "Justin," and dabbed at a tear. Once again, I told her, "Thank you." Then I said, "Bonnie," for the first time, and she seemed to notice the emotions wrapped inside my sloppy voice.

Her AI must have called ahead; an attendant had already rolled out into the parking lot to wait for us.

"I'll pay for everything," Bonnie told the machine.

She couldn't afford the first two minutes. Her old car proved she was a person of modest means.

"This was my fault entirely," I confessed. Then I lied, claiming, "Besides, my insurance covers everything imaginable."

"Are you sure?" she asked.

"Dinner," I said. "If you want, buy me a little dinner."

The attendant was carrying me through the clinic door, an army of fingers already assessing the damage.

Bonnie repeated, "Dinner," before asking, "When?"

"Tonight," I suggested.

Then I asked, "Have you eaten?"

She shook her head. "No."

To the machines gathering around me, I asked, "How long will this take?"

The damage was severe but ordinary. Nothing too exceptional had to be fabricated. Thirty-five minutes was the verdict, and with an intentionally pitiful voice, I asked, "Will you wait for me?"

As the door closed, Bonnie rubbed her hands together, tilted her head to one side and smiled in her sad, sweet fashion. "I guess I am waiting," she muttered. "Yes."

Men instantly took notice of Bonnie. Perhaps her body was too meaty to belong to a model, but that was no failure. She was taller than most females, and she had an inviting walk that any man younger than ninety would notice from the Moon. Twice I saw wives or girlfriends chastising their men for gawking, and a pair of women sitting in the front of the restaurant mouthed the word, "Sweet," as my date innocently passed by their table.

I was feeling happy and sick, and very wicked, and I felt a little awful for what I had done, and a little thrilled by what I dreamed of doing.

"I've never been here," she confessed, watching the robot staff skitter from table to table, serving people like myself. "This seems like a nice place."

"It is nice," I promised. "And thank you for joining me."

Of course I'd given her no choice. But during that thirty-five minute wait, Bonnie had driven home and changed clothes, returning to the clinic smelling of perfume and youth. She let me pat the top of a hand, just for a moment, and then before either one of us could gauge her response, I pulled the hand back again. And smiled. And with a quiet but thoroughly fascinated voice, I invited her to tell me about herself.

Some details were memorable. Others slipped from my grasp before I could decide whether or not to keep them. But who doesn't experience the world in such a sloppily selective way? Even with a precious someone, not every facet can be embraced inside a single evening.

What I learned was that Bonnie worked at the university as a technician, in a DNA paleontologist's lab. She had been married once, briefly. Then she lived with the wrong man for several years, that relationship mercifully ending just this last winter. She was raised Christian, but I don't remember which species. Plainly, she wasn't swayed by the recent reactionary noise against people like me. Watching my eyes, she touched my hand, admitting, "I'm going to be thirty in another three months."

"Thirty," I repeated.

"That can be an ominous age," I said.

Her hand withdrew as she nodded in agreement.

Our meals came and were consumed, and the bill arrived along with a pair of sweet mints. The final tally took her by surprise. But one of us had left the table a few minutes ago, and of course I had purged myself, putting my food back into the restaurant's common pot, the lamb and buttery potatoes destined to be knitted back together again, the next shepherd's pie indistinguishable from the last.

Bonnie paid for her meal and for renting my food and then graciously allowed me to tip the restaurant's owner. A finished woman, as it happened.

"Good night, you two kittens," the woman told us as we left.

Bonnie drove me to my house.

I knew she didn't want to come inside. For a multitude of fine reasons—old heartaches, her Christian upbringing, and my own odd nature—Bonnie pulled away while we sat on my long driveway.

There were several ways to attack the moment.

What I decided to do, and what worked better than I hoped: I turned to my new friend, mentioning, "You haven't asked about me."

She seemed embarrassed.

"Anything," I said. "Ask anything."

Bonnie was wearing the sort of clinging blouse and slacks that a modern woman wears on a first date. Everything was revealed, yet nothing was. While a hand nervously played with an old-fashioned button, she asked, "How long ago . . . did you do it . . . ?"

"Ten years and two months, approximately."

The early days of this business, in other words.

"Okay," she whispered. Then, "How old were you—?"

"Forty-nine years, eleven months."

She couldn't decide what bothered her more, my being finished or my apparent age. "So you're twenty years old than me," she muttered, speaking mostly to herself. "Or thirty, including the last ten. I don't think I've ever gone out with anyone quite that—"

"Why," I said, interrupting her.

She fell silent, nervous for every reason.

Looking into the wide brown eyes, I said, "That's what you want to know. Why did I do it? So find the breath and ask me."

"Why did you?"

I intended to tell the story, but the intuition of a middle-aged man took hold. The better course was to take her hand and lift it to my mouth, kissing a warm knuckle and then the knuckle beside it, and with my tongue, tasting the salty heat between those two trembling fingers.

"Not tonight," I told her.

I said, "Another time, perhaps."

Then I climbed out of her old pink Cheetah, smiling with all the warmth I could manage, asking, "Do you believe in Fate, Bonnie?"

We taste food. Our bodies feel heat and fatigue. Urges older than our species still rule us, and every finished person is grateful for that continuity. Yet even the intelligent unfinished person, informed and utterly modern, has to be reminded of essentials that everyone should know: We are not machines, and we are not dead. Today, for the first time in human history, there happens to be a third state of existence: Alive, dead, and finished. And like the living, we have the capacity to learn and gradually improve our nature, and should circumstances shift, we possess a substantial, almost human capacity for change.

Another evening found us enjoying an intimate embrace. Bonnie's salty sweat mingled with my sweet, lightly scented sweat, and her nervousness collapsed into a girlish joy. What we had just done was wicked, and fun. What we would do next was something she never imagined possible. "Not in my life," she admitted. And then in the next instant, with a laughing apology, she exclaimed, "That was a sloppy choice of words. Sorry."

But I laughed too. Louder than her, in fact.

After the next pause, she asked, "Is it the same?"

"Is what the same?"

"The feel of it," she said. Her pretty face floated above me, hands digging beneath the moistened sheets. "When you climax—"

"Better."

"Really?"

"But that's because of you," I told her. "Otherwise, no. It's pretty much the same old bliss."

She was suspicious, but what soul wouldn't wish such a compliment? Against her better instincts, Bonnie smiled, and then after some more digging beneath the sheets, she remarked, "You don't act like a middle-aged man."

"Hydraulics are an old science," I replied.

She considered my body and my face. I have a handsome face, I'd like to believe. Not old but proud of its maturity, enough gray in the illusionary hair to let the casual eye pin down my finishing age. With her free hand, she swept the hair out of my eyes, and then with a quiet, almost embarrassed tone, she asked, "Is it like they say?"

"Is what like what?"

But she realized that she was mangling the question. "People claim it feels like living the same day, without end. If you're finished. You don't have the same sense of time—"

"In one sense," I agreed.

But after my next mock-breath, I explained, "Time announces itself in many ways. I have biorhythms. My mind still demands sleep on a regular schedule. And I can still read a clock. For instance, I know it's half past midnight, which means that according to an utterly arbitrary system, a new day has begun. Dawn would be the more natural beginning point, I've always thought. But I'm not going to be the one to tear down everybody else's conventions."

She nodded. Sighed.

I pulled her up on top of me, hips rubbing. "Something else," I said. "Ask."

"Why?" she whispered.

"Why did I allow myself to be finished?"

"Were you—?"

"Sick? No."

Another nod was followed by a deeper, almost tattered sigh.

"I was almost fifty years old," I explained. "Which is a good age to be a man, I think. Experience. A measure of wisdom. But the body has already failed noticeably, and the sharpest mind at sixty—if you are a man—is never as keen as it was ten years before."

She said nothing, moving her body, trying to match my rhythm.

"Women are different," I allowed. "They seem to have two popular ages for finishing. Older, post-menopausal women can enjoy it greatly. And vibrant youngsters still in their twenties or thirties. But there aren't many in their forties. Studies show. Even if the woman picks a good day to be finished . . . a moment when her mood is even, her hormones in check . . . well, not as many of you seem to love that age, I've noticed . . ."

She nodded, seemingly agreeing with me. Then she shuddered, sobbing and pressing her body flush against my mine. And with a low, throaty voice, she asked, "Were you talking? I wasn't listening."

I gave a low grunt.

"Sorry," she muttered.

Then she touched my face, and with a genuinely mystified voice asked, "Why are you crying . . . ?"

Bonnie's closest friend was the same age but less pretty—a proper woman, well dressed and infinitely suspicious. The three of us shared an uncomfortable dinner in Bonnie's little apartment, and then some mysterious errand sent my girlfriend out the door. The two women had come up with this glaringly obvious plan. Suddenly alone with me, the friend used a cutting stare, announcing, "My father is finished."

I nodded, trying to appear attentive.

"In fact, he was one of the first. Four years before you did it, about."

"Interesting," I offered.

She shrugged, unimpressed by interest. Her expression hardened to just short of a glare. "Dad was dying. Pancreatic cancer."

"Awful stuff," I said.

"I got out of school for the day. I went with him and Mom to the clinic." Suspicious eyes looked past me. "He was weak and dying, and I was thankful this new technology could save him . . . and I was very hopeful . . ."

I gave a nod. Nothing more.

"The machines rolled him away," she reported. Then with a barely contained anger, she asked, "How long does the process take?"

"Minutes," I offered.

"Boiling him down to nothing."

To be replicated, the brain had to be dismantled. A sophisticated holo of the original was implanted inside a nearly indestructible crystal. Experience and new technologies have accelerated the process somewhat, but there is no means, proven or theoretical, that allows a person to be finished without the total eradication of the original body and its resident mind.

"He was a sick old man," she reported. "Then he was this crystal lump as big as a walnut, and he had this entirely different body. It was supposed to look like him, and feel pretty much the same . . . but they still haven't learned how to make a realistic chassis . . ."

"It's a nagging problem," I agreed. "Unless you embrace your new existence, of course. Then it isn't a problem, but a kind of blessing. An emblem, and a treasured part of your finished identity—"

"It costs," she complained.

There were some stiff maintenance fees, true.

"Between the finishing and all the troubles with his new body—"

"Death would have been cheaper," I interrupted. "That's what you realized, isn't it?"

The woman shuddered, a cold and familiar pain working its way down her back. But as awful as that sounded, she couldn't argue with me. "It ate up most of their savings," she complained.

What could I say?

"Of course, Dad eventually wanted my mother to get finished, too."

"I see."

"But their finances were a mess."

"Loans are available," I mentioned. "Because the finished person can live for another thousand years, or longer, the clinics offer some very charitable terms."

"Except Mom didn't want any part of that." She was her mother's child, and she still agreed with the scared old woman. "If you're finished, you're finished. You stop learning."

"Not true."

"Yes it is!"

"No," I snapped back. "The new mind's design doesn't let fresh synapses form. But that's why it's so durable. Instead, you use subsidiary memory sinks and plenty of them, and as you learn all of the tricks—"

"He stopped changing."

I fell silent.

"My father went into the clinic as a sick man," she reported. "And the machine that came out . . . it was a sick machine, exhausted and feeling all these phantom pains running through it . . ."

"The doctors take precautions now," I told her. "They can limit certain sensations beforehand—"

"He's always going to be dying . . . forever . . ."

The apartment door began to open.

"I don't approve of you," the friend blurted. "I just wanted to tell you, and tell you why not."

I nodded as if I had learned something. As if I respected her honesty. Then as Bonnie stepped into the room—a wary attitude on her face and in her body—I said to no one in particular, "That's why if you're going to be finished, it's best to do it before you get sick. On a good day, if you can manage it."

I sighed.

To the floor, I said, "On your very best day, hopefully."

My best day was a sunny, gloriously warm Thursday. High-pressure centers have this way of causing rushes at the clinics, but I'd set up my appointment well in advance. The weather was nothing but good fortune. Arriving fifteen minutes early, I wore casual clothes and an easy smile. I was rested and well fed, and since I had sworn off sex for last few days, I felt pleasantly horny—a good quality to lock into your soul. If any doubt had whispered to me, I would have postponed the event until the doubt died. If a cloud had drifted across the sun, I would have waited in the parking lot for the shadow to pass. But the sky was a steely blue, glorious and eternal, and my only little doubt was in entering the clinic alone.

"But alone is best," somebody had warned me. "Anyone else would be a distraction for you. An imposition. Trust me about this."

I did trust her, and of course, she was entirely correct.

"Justin Gable," I told the man at the counter. "I'm at—"

"Two fifteen. Yes, sir. Right this way, Mr. Gable."

An honored guest, I felt like. I felt as if I was walking towards an elaborate celebration, or at the very least, a tidy but significant ceremony. Every stereotypic image of looming gallows or tunnels leading to bright lights was left at the front door. I felt thrilled, even giddy. For the first time in years, I whistled as I walked. Without a gram of shame, I flirted with my female nurse, and then my female doctor—finished souls, both of them. With a haste born of practice and experience, they quickly placed me inside a warm bath of benign fluids, and before my mood could dip, even slightly, they slipped a cocktail of neurotoxins into my happy red blood.

During the next furious minutes, microchines invaded and mapped my brain, consuming my neurons as they moved.

Inside a second room, a standard crystal was configured along lines defined by my delicate wiring, and inside a third room, entirely different machines fashioned a body worthy of any paying customer. Then I found myself sitting on a soft coach, inside a fourth room, wearing my original clothes and barely fifty minutes lost. And exactly as they had promised, I needed just another few moments to adapt to my very new circumstances.

The smiling staff congratulated me.

Alone, I walked outside. A little patch of clouds had covered the sun, but it didn't matter. In some deep way, I could still feel the sun's bright glare, just as I feel it today, warming me to my ceramic bones.

She was waiting where I had left her, sitting inside my car.

I drove us to my house—a smaller, more modest abode in those days—and she made a convincing show of treating me exactly as she had before. Not once did she ask if I felt different. Never did she comment on my new body. Our sex was scrupulously ordinary, pleasant but nothing more. Then I woke that next morning, and because I couldn't help myself, I said, "I know the time. And I can see it raining. But you know, I feel pretty much the same as I did yesterday afternoon."

Pretty much isn't the same as perfect. Even a mind composed of hard frozen synapses contains a certain play of mood, of emotions and alertness. The soul remains flexible enough that when your lover smiles in a grim fashion, you worry. When she says, "I'm leaving you, Justin," it hurts. It hurts badly, and even after the surprise fades, you continue to ache. For months, and for years, even. Forever, if you would allow it.

But I won't allow it.

"What about all your promises?" I blurted.

"Oh, those were lies," she admitted calmly.

"And what about helping with my medical bills?"

"I'm not giving you any money, darling."

"But I can't afford this body," I complained, "and I still owe hundreds of thousands for this brain. And you told me . . . you claimed you'd help me—"

"And I will help," she said, glancing down at her twice-eaten eggs. "But you're a bright enough man, and if you think about this problem, just for a moment or two, you'll see for yourself what I was going to suggest."

"Do you remember?" Bonnie would ask. "What happened ten weeks ago? Ten days ago? Or how about ten minutes ago? I'm just curious, Justin. What do you remember?"

At first, she was simply curious. The questions were offered in passing, and I was entirely responsible for my answers. But as her interest sharpened, her ear became more critical, and she tested me, pressing for salient details. Mentioning a specific date, she asked, "What was I wearing? Where did we eat? And what did the man in the green suit say to me?"

"You were wearing a wonderful little holo-dress, flowers changing to seeds and then back to flowers again." I dipped into an assortment of memory sinks, my eyes staring off into the foggy distance. "We ate in that Sudanese restaurant, and you had the eland, and you had shoes. Yes. Black leather with brass buckles."

"Go on."

"But the man wasn't wearing green," I reported. "It was more gold, his suit was. I don't remember his shoes, sorry. But he had this square face and a gold ring through his cheek, and he stared at you. I remember that very well. We walked into the place, and he watched you constantly. I made a joke, or you did—"

"Playing with himself—"

"Under the table, yes. I said, 'You're making that poor gentleman crazy, darling.' And then all at once he stood up and came over to us . . . in his gold-green suit . . . and he told you, 'When you get tired of that dildo, why don't you try a real man?'"

"You remember," she said happily.

"And I remember what you asked him. 'Why? Do you know a real man?'"

She was embarrassed, and pleased, laughing at the shared memory.

Like anyone in her position, Bonnie wanted to know what I could do, and what I could not do. Yes, I explained, I had limits in personal growth. For better or worse, my nature was essentially changeless. In another hundred years, if someone gave me a personality inventory, I would test out as a man still just shy of fifty: A middle-aged outlook; neatness at home; a mature man's patience, and hopefully, a measure of wisdom. Plus my present level of smoldering passion, freed from the vagaries of hormones, would hold rock solid.

"I'll be better in bed than most hundred and fifty year-old men," I joked.

A smile widened, but there was no laughter. Then with a serious voice—a thoughtful and worried but distinctly determined voice—Bonnie announced, "I want to have children."

"I've got half a dozen vials filled up with my frozen sperm," I promised. "For when the time comes."

But she hadn't mentioned my participation, and she didn't mention it now. Instead, she took a deep breath before saying, "They can harvest a woman's eggs too. After the brain's gone, I mean."

"And they're making spectacular progress with artificial wombs," I added. "In a year or two, or ten at the most—"

"What about work?" she interrupted. "Learning new jobs and the like . . . you didn't know much about cybernetics before this, but now you're some kind of consultant—"

"I lobby for the rights of the finished," I said, not for the first time. "My work earns me a small stipend."

True enough.

"If we're going to live for another century," she said, "and for a thousand centuries after that . . . can these little memory sinks keep adapting us to all the coming changes . . . ?"

With an open, patient face, I reminded her, "Technologies only grow stronger."

"Yet if we want . . . draining whatever's inside those sinks . . . we can forget what we want to forget, too. Right?"

"Which is a great gift, if you think about it."

She heard something ominous in the words. But she was a brave soul looking hard at things she wouldn't have considered just a few months ago. "Well, even if I was thinking about it," she finally admitted. "I can barely pay my rent, much less make the down payment."

We were spending the night at my substantial house—a telling detail. Bonnie was sitting in my bed, her young body illuminated by a waning moon. Not quite looking at me, she said, "I don't know what I'm thinking. Because I could never afford it."

I waited, letting the silence frighten her.

And then with a calm, warm tone, I asked, "But imagine, darling. What if some good heart was able to help you?"

More weeks passed, but I remember little about them. Bonnie had a spectacular fight with her best friend, centering on issues she wouldn't discuss with me, and two attempts at reconciliation went for naught. Which left me as her closest friend as well as her lover, and with that new power, I did very little. Just the occasional word of advice; a slight coaxing masked as praise. In glowing terms, I spoke about her body and beauty, and when we were in public, I practically reveled at the lustful stares of strangers. But the telling event was elsewhere, and inevitable. Bonnie was twenty-nine years and eleven months old, and with that birthday looming, she said, "Okay, my mind's made up."

I smiled, just enough.

Then I set out to prepare her, legally and emotionally.

My attorney was only too happy to help. A jolly fat man in life, he remained that way today—a comfortable bulk wrapped around an immortal smile. "You've picked a great moment," he promised. A wide hand offered itself to my lover. "This is the new-generation skin. Study it. Isn't it natural? Touch it now. Prick it. If you want, lick it. No? Well, believe me. You're going to look like an angel beside this clunky old automaton."

"Hey," I complained. "I'm counting my pennies for an upgrade."

Everyone laughed, although Bonnie felt ill at ease. Yet she never lost her will, never needed so much as a soft word of encouragement. Then later, once the appropriate forms and declarations had been signed and witnessed, my jolly attorney said, "A word with you, Justin?"

Bonnie waited for me in the lobby.

Straight away, my attorney asked, "Do you know how beautiful that woman is?"

"No," I kidded.

He laughed, winked knowingly, and then said, "Seriously. This is not like the others that you've introduced me to. No elegant silver in the hair. No false teeth or bothersome grandkids. And that face isn't another bag of good and botched plastic surgeries, either."

"But she is rather poor—" I began.

"Fuck money. So long as it's just her money." He laughed until he looked red-faced and breathless. "Poor is perfect, in fact. Like it was with you. It helps the soul come to terms with the world's realities."

Pride flickering, I asked, "We'll she be as successful as I am?"

"And then some!" His laughter filled the room. "I mean it, Justin. She's going to have a great time. I've seen this new skin stretched over a woman's frame, and I've felt it, and I think she's going to be pleased. You're going to be very pleased. Frankly, she's going to be fighting off the potential suitors. And for each one that she doesn't fight off—"

"Yeah."

"Of course, you'll earn just the standard commission for bringing her in," he admitted. "Until Bonnie can work off her own debts—"

"I realize."

"But for every CEO-type that she captures," he continued, "I'll make sure that you get your five percent out of her windfall."

I still owed a tidy fortune to my makers. But I was immortal, and they could afford to be patient. All of their clients were immortal, and they could take an extraordinarily long view when it came to their business.

"More pennies for the saving," he sang out.

"Sure," I said, nodding amiably. "I'll never forget that."

An appointment was made at my clinic, but Bonnie woke the day before with a smile. "Look at it out there," she said. It was a cold but utterly bright morning, three days shy of her thirtieth birthday. "Do you think we could get in? If we went down there this minute—?"

"Now?"

"I really feel in the mood," she promised.

Somehow, I wasn't ready. But I took Bonnie at her word and carefully hid my own nervousness. Accompanying her to the clinic, I repeated the old advice. "You should go in alone. Really, I'd be a—"

"Distraction. I agree."

Why did that hurt? And why, even after I used every reliable trick, did those three words continue to gnaw at me?

"No, this is best," she assured me. "Going in early like this, I mean. I think some of my colleagues and friends are planning an intervention, which has to come tonight, of course . . ." She laughed softly, asking, "Wouldn't that be something if we let them . . . ? If I get a good enough body, and if we kept the lights in the room down low enough so they couldn't tell—?"

"Are you happy?"

"Completely."

"You're certain?"

Bonnie didn't quite look at me. Then she wasn't speaking just to me, explaining, "Until a few weeks ago, I wasn't happy. Not like I thought I should be in my life. But I kept telling myself that if I just kept plugging along, eventually, maybe I'd run into somebody . . ."

Neither of us laughed.

Pulling into half-filled parking lot, she said, "Maybe they won't have a slot for me now."

For her, they would make a slot.

"Kiss me. For luck."

I did what she wanted. I kissed her on the lips and told her, "I'll see you soon," with a voice that sounded perfectly genuine. I even managed to smile, and Bonnie gave me a distracted smile and wink in return, and then she walked alone up to the front door and stepped out of sight.

I waited.

For maybe twenty seconds, I managed to do nothing.

But I have this ungraceful habit. This inclination—a reflex—that remains fixed in my nature. Preyed by doubts, I always try to follow. And afterwards, I always make myself forget that I followed. What was different this time was that my reflex struck earlier than normal. I took the clinic by surprise, which makes me feel a little better. Stepping out of the Cheetah, I started to chase after Bonnie, a quick walk becoming a near-sprint, and because another patron had stopped inside the open door, thanking one of the doctors or one of the machines, I managed to slip into the lobby before any locks could be secured.

A nurse was leading Bonnie into the back rooms.

"Wait!" I cried out.

A young man, finished and fit, vaulted over the counter. I was tackled and rudely shoved to the floor, but I managed to say, "You don't need to! I seduced you to do this! They pay me—!"

A hand covered my mouth, choking off my voice.

Bonnie's hand, I realized.

Just like that first time, the pretty face hovered above me. But on this cold morning, she smiled with a certain fetching melancholy, and a calm hard and almost disappointed voice said, "I'm not an idiot, Justin. I figured it out for myself, almost from the first day."

Her hand lifted, and she rose to her feet.

"Don't go back there," I called out. "Not now, darling. Not while your angry like this, because you'll always be—!"

"Except I'm not angry," she replied. And with a hard, wise smile, she added, "In fact, darling, this is better. I'm happy enough, but I also feel suspicious right now. Toward you, and everybody. And really, if you try and think about it, isn't that the best way to travel through the next hundred thousand years . . . ?"

THE INN AT MOUNT EITHER

James Van Pelt

After a minute spent weighing a fear of appearing foolish against his anxiety, Dorian approached the concierge. Behind the glassy mahogany of the concierge's booth, through the floor to ceiling windows, the afternoon clouds swept toward them across the neighboring peaks. As always, the view was spectacular. The sun cast long shadows through the valleys while the racing clouds caressed the mountain tops before swallowing them in grey, whale-like immensity, and when the clouds parted, the mountains would be the same but different, just a little, changed by their time in the clouds. That's why people always looked. Are the mountains the same, they seemed to say, or have they changed?

If Dorian stood at the window, he could peer down the mountain at the long, railed walkways that connected one section of the inn to the next. Curved glass covered some of the walkways so the guests could pass in comfort from the casinos to the restaurants, or from the workout facilities to the spas, or from the tennis courts to the pools, but others were open and guests could walk in the unencumbered mountain air, their hands sliding along guard rails with nothing but the thought of distance between them and the rocks in the sightless haze below.

Dorian cleared his throat. "I can't find my wife, Stephanie Wallace." His fingers rested on the polished wood.

Without raising his head from his the clipboard he'd been studying, the concierge looked at him. "It's a big inn, sir. When did you see her last?" The man's eyebrows had a distinctively rakish look to them, turning up at the ends like a handlebar moustache, and his hair was silvery-grey.

"We were supposed to meet for lunch, but she didn't show up." Dorian glanced into the lobby, hoping that she might appear. Behind him, the room towered fifty feet to skylights. Opposite the window, the mountain's rocky side made another wall. Exotic plants that would never grow outside of the inn's protection filled every nook, spilling vegetation over the deep-toned stone.

The concierge put the clipboard on the booth. "Perhaps her plans changed, sir. There's much to do here at Mount Either."

Dorian gritted his teeth. "Yesterday's lunch! I've been looking for her since last night. Stephanie's not *late*. She's *gone*."

"It won't help for you to be short with me, sir. What is your room number?"

"4128."

The concierge tapped at a personal digital assistant that nestled in his palm. "This is your wife, sir?" A picture of a smiling blonde woman, glasses slid part way down her nose peered back at Dorian from the screen.

"Yes." She'd worn her glasses on the airplane. Once they checked in, she switched to contacts.

"I show that she's still a guest."

Resisting an urge to throttle the man, Dorian said, "I know that. What I want is some help in finding her. Can't you ask the other employees to keep an eye out?"

"Of course, sir. But, as I said before, this is a big inn. Maybe she wants some privacy. Perhaps she's admiring one of our many gardens. She wouldn't be the first guest to spend a few uncounted hours sitting on a meditation vista. In fact, getting lost at the inn is a selling point. We advertise it. 'Lose yourself in the experience.'"

"It's not supposed to be literal!" snapped Dorian.

The concierge picked up the clipboard again. "I will alert the staff. You don't suppose she went through a transitionway unaccompanied, do you?"

Dorian felt himself blanching. "No, of course not." But he remembered how she'd lingered yesterday morning in the Polynesian hallway.

"Guests are to be escorted through the shift zones."

"I'm sure she wouldn't do that."

The concierge sniffed. "We're very specific in our agreement when you signed in. The management will respond strongly to guests who ignore the rules."

Dorian turned away from the concierge. A new tram-load of tourists had arrived, pulling their suitcases behind them. Most were couples. Newlyweds, by the look, or retired folk. A pack of bellboys scurried to meet them, while a mellow-voiced recording intoned,

"Welcome to the Inn at Mount Either. You are standing in the new lobby, two-hundred and fifty feet above the historical first lobby built on the site of where Mount Either's special properties were discovered. If you are interested in a guided visit to the old lobby, dial 19 on your room phone."

"If she did go . . ." said Dorian. A hand seemed to be grasping his throat. It was all he could do to croak out, ". . . unescorted?"

The concierge said, "It's a *big* inn, sir. We will do all we can to help, but we don't really count a guest as missing until forty-eight hours have passed."

Dorian didn't know what to say. He drummed his fingers on the counter. Some of the new arrivals were at the window, looking down. The glass leaned away from the mountain, and the lobby itself protruded like a shelf, so they had an unimpeded view of the two-thousand foot drop and the rest of the inn on this side of the peak, clinging to the sheer face.

"I can't wait that long. I'm going to look for her myself."

"That is your privilege, sir," said the concierge. "I'm sure she's just around the corner. Nothing stays lost here forever."

The elevator to the Polynesian transition they had visited yesterday was out of order. Dorian looked both ways down the long, curving hall, but there wasn't another elevator. The inn's maps were almost impossible to read since the inn itself was aggressively three-dimensional, riddled with elevators, stairs, ramps, sloping halls, ladders, bridges and multi-level rooms. They'd followed a guide to the Polynesian transition, but none were in sight now. Dorian went left, around the curved hall.

Finally, he reached a stairwell that spiraled down for fifty steps. He didn't recognize the hall it emptied into, but a distinctive arrow in blue and yellow pointed toward a transition. Yesterday, as they approached the zone, the wallpaper had changed from the art deco they'd grown used to, to a palm and beach motif. Following the guide, he'd held Stephanie's hand until they stepped through the transition's door and into a Polynesian mountainscape.

"You're lucky, today, folks," said the guide. "I don't think I've ever seen it looking this good."

The sun pouring through the open veranda spread heat like a warm flush on their skin. Stephanie's hand drifted from his own, and she walked to the platform's edge as if in a dream.

"Oh, Dorian," she'd said. Instead of the snow-capped mountains of the Inn at Mount Either, a series of rounded hills rose in front of them, covered with forest so thick that it was hard to imagine ground beneath it. A flock of long-necked birds wheeled below, skimming the treetops and crying out to one another. She'd stared into the distance, entranced, her blonde hair just brushing her shoulders, and for a moment he saw the young woman he'd married twenty years earlier, the jaunty athleticism in her posture, the grace in her wrists and hands.

A waiter in a flowered shirt offered them drinks off a platter.

"Can you smell it?" Stephanie said, delighted. "It's the ocean."

And Dorian could smell salt and sand under the rich vegetable forest. Stephanie loved the ocean and all that was associated with it, the seals and birds and spiny creatures crawling in tidal pools, and the way the waves slid underneath her bare toes. Her passions were intense. She'd spend hours studying art or collecting children's literature or working with other people's kids. Once she'd gotten hypothermia in a mountain stream while sorting through rocks on her hands and knees. "I thought there might be quartz crystals," she'd said through the shivers. She laughed often.

Stephanie hadn't wanted to leave the overlook. The hotel guide finally had to insist. "My shift ended twenty minutes ago, ma'am. Perhaps you can come back another day if it's still here." Then he took them back through the hallway and into the inn they had left. "This was one of the original shift zones," he'd said as they walked back to the main lobby. "They found it third."

"How marvelous it must have been," Stephanie said. "I can imagine them climbing the mountain. Squeezing through a crevice, and there they were." She looked behind them.

Dorian rushed down the corridor. He remembered fewer doors in the hallway yesterday, and the carpet had been a different color. Closing his eyes for a second, he tried to picture the inn's structure. The elevator had only gone down a couple of floors, which was about the same distance the spiral stairs had taken him, but nothing looked the same. Maybe he was in a parallel passage. He passed another blue and yellow arrow. The decor changed from dark-polished woods and brass fixtures to natural pine siding. A long mural of a desert canyon rimmed with cactus covered one wall. Then the hall ended at a door, a rough-hewn, heavy-planked structure marked by a solid iron handle to open it instead of a doorknob.

It was a transition way, but not the one from yesterday. Still, it was close. Maybe Stephanie had come down this path. The elevator might have been out of order for her too. Dorian took a deep breath and opened the door.

On the other side, a wooden bridge reached an open platform. Drooping ropes hung from thick posts that lined the bridge's side, serving as protection from the drop into the depths below. Dorian leaned on the rope at the platform's edge. The general shape of the mountains was the same, but no snow covered the peaks. The sun glared, radiating off slick-rock, dark with streaks of desert varnish. He shaded his eyes to look up the mountain. Wood structures covered most of the slope, all light-colored pine. For a moment nothing looked familiar, then he spotted the main lobby buttressed by tree-thick pylons jutting from the mountain.

A man wearing a cowboy hat and a leather fringed shirt joined him at the edge. "First time to Mount Either?" he said.

"Yes," said Dorian, confused. "How could you tell?"

"Your duds. Not quite in the motif, pard." He smiled, a gold tooth flashing in the sun, then glanced at his watch, a large-faced instrument ringed with turquoise. "You going to the barbeque? I'm going to find my wife and head that way. Gosh, I love the grub you get here." His leather boots clacked against the wood flooring as he headed to the stairs.

Dorian was alone on the platform again. "I'm looking for my wife too," he said. Overhead a lone bird circled. He thought, is that a buzzard?

A tram like a large ore cart glided past the platform, heading down. Cowboy-hatted tourists sat at one end, while a pile of saddles and bridles filled the other. At the bottom of the ravine where the tram's cable ended at a tiny building, a dozen horses no larger than grains of rice milled about in a corral.

The set of stairs that gold-tooth had ascended looked like they led to the main lobby. Dorian took the steps two at a time. If Stephanie had come this way, she hadn't returned. Would she have realized right away that she was lost? Would she have gone to the lobby for directions? She could be there even now, maybe sipping a cool drink at one of the many, nearby cafes.

But at the top of the stairs were three passages, and none of them looked like they headed up. Dorian paused. If he chose the wrong way, he could become lost himself. A bellboy in flannel shirt tucked into jeans, carrying a tray of dirty dishes on one hand above his shoulder came out of one hallway.

"How do I get to the lobby?" said Dorian.

The bellboy transferred the heavy tray with practiced ease. His suntanned face crinkled into a weathered smile. "Right hallway until you come to the elevator. The button is marked."

Dorian nodded, then started forward.

"My right," said the bellboy as he descended the stairs.

In the lobby, Dorian took a moment to orient himself. It wasn't that this sage-scented lobby was completely different; it was the similarities that threw him off. The same tall window gazing out on the deserty-looking mountains, the same exposed rock making one wall, a familiar reception desk dominating the room's center, but all the materials were different: hand-hewed timbers replaced the slick chrome support beams, big-looped throw rugs covered the plank floor where before he'd walked on expensive carpet, but what was most disorienting was the concierge, whose distinctive upward-flaring eyebrows and silver-grey hair waited for him at the reception desk as Dorian crossed the room.

"Thank goodness," said Dorian. "I wanted to find the Polynesian transition, but I ended up here instead."

"Excuse me, sir?" said the concierge. His expression was completely bland. No recognition at all.

"It's me, Dorian Wallace. I told you ten minutes ago that I was looking for my wife, Stephanie."

"I'm sorry, sir. You have me at a disadvantage."

"We talked. You said nothing stays lost forever."

The concierge shook his head. "Maybe I was thinking about something else when we chatted. What room did you say you were in?"

The situation was ludicrous. In the window behind the concierge, the sun blasted the peaks. No snow. No smoothly curved walkways stretching from wing to wing. Just heavy rope and solid wood and thick iron cable strapping the structures to the mountain. It was like an 1860 version of Dodge City turned vertical. "I'm from the *real* Inn at Mount Either. I'm in one of its rooms."

The concierge's forehead wrinkled. "*This* is the real Inn at Mount Either, sir."

Dorian stepped back. The man looked similar, but the business suit Dorian remembered had been replaced with a leather jacket, and where the silk tie had hung before, a silver clasp held a black bolo. Something about his face was different too. More wrinkles maybe? More silver in the hair? Suddenly Dorian was sure that they would have no record of his registration, and he realized he'd gone through a transition without a guide. What had the first concierge told him about management "responding strongly" to guests who ignored the rules?

Keeping the panic out of his voice, Dorian said, "My fault. I mistook you for someone else." He forced a smile. "There's so many employees here."

Nodding, the concierge turned his attention to a stack of papers on the desk. "This is a big inn, sir. Perfectly understandable."

On the way out of the lobby, Dorian paused. Had he come up a short flight of stairs to enter, or had the hallway been on the same level? At the foot of the stairs a mineral gift shop offered its wares on wooden trays inside its door. He vaguely remembered passing something like that, but he'd been in a hurry. Had he?

On an impulse, he entered the shop. Rocks and crystals of all kinds filled the shelves. "I'm looking for my wife," he said to the man behind the counter. "She might have been in here yesterday." Dorian showed him a photo from his wallet.

The man hooked his thumbs in the top of his overalls and leaned to look at the picture. "Yep, Stephanie, I know her. She liked the amethyst. I figure she spent an hour hunting for a good specimen."

Dorian caught the edge of the counter to keep from falling. His legs had no strength. He looked at the crate overflowing with purple crystals.

"Didn't buy anything, though. I offered her iron pyrite, fool's gold. She said if she couldn't have the real thing, she couldn't be happy." The man smiled. "Besides, she said her husband sometimes buys her gifts, and she didn't want to spoil his fun."

"Which way did she go?"

"Didn't really notice. Down the hallway, I reckon."

Dorian dashed to the door, then looked the way the man had indicated, as if there might be a chance to see her still. But the hall was empty. He glanced up the stairs into the lobby. The concierge was talking to a couple of men wearing six-shooters and badges. Security? The concierge pointed toward Dorian.

"Thanks," he called to the mineral shop man.

"Nice lady. I hope you find her."

The elevator at the end of the hall was not the same one he'd ridden up, but he didn't want to talk to security, so he rode it down to the transition level he'd come from. When he stepped out, the doors closed, and the elevator returned to the lobby.

We're they really after him?

After a couple confusing turns down hallways that didn't look the least bit familiar, Dorian stepped onto an open-air bridge that ended at a platform overlooking the canyon. He breathed easier. A quick dash down the transitionway, and he'd be home, but the long cables that carried the tram he'd seen earlier to the ravine's bottom were next to a platform a hundred yards farther away. An updraft ruffled his hair and dried the sweat on his face instantly. Wrong platform. The problem was how could he get from the platform he was on to the one that he'd come from without retracing his steps?

He crossed the bridge back to the mountain where three choices waited: the hallway he'd exited from, a short ramp to another hallway and a set of stairs that at least headed toward the other platform. At the top of the stairs, a blue and yellow arrow pointed in the right direction.

But the hallway's transition theme was heavy stone work, like castle fortifications, and on the door's other side, towering spires and crenelated restraining walls lined the paths. He'd missed the transition back to where he'd started. A dozen flights of stairs, two ramps and an elevator ride took him to another transition, clearly not the right one, but he needed to get back to The Inn at Mount Either he'd come from. Passing through transitions without a guide, he thought ruefully. I'm probably racking up room charges of astronomical proportions.

The next transition felt vaguely Arabic. He ran into a fellow in a rush going through the door in the opposite direction.

"Sorry, my fault," said Dorian at the same time the other man said the same thing. He only had a moment to notice the fellow was wearing the same kind of pants and shirt he wore before they dashed their separate ways.

The next had a rainforest look, but he recognized none of the birds that flew past the walkways. A blue and yellow arrow pointed down a hallway lined with jungle plants and short vines that dangled from the ceiling. He hurried past the closed doors until the hallway curved and the decor on the wall changed from matted vegetation to slick aluminum and recessed light fixtures. He pulled the door at the end of the transition zone open with relief.

The door closed behind him.

The lights were out.

He took a few steps into the darkness, then waited for his eyes to adjust. Slowly, the scene became clear. He choked back a gasp. Nothing separated him from the two-thousand foot drop to the bottom of the canyon. For a heart-stopping moment, he felt suspended, as if at any second he would drop to the rocks in an unstoppable plunge, but he didn't fall. His hands out, he shuffled forward. The floor wasn't perfectly invisible. He could see now that a walkway leapt to an opaque platform before him, and to each side, no more than an arm reach away, nearly transparent walls and ceiling enclosed him. It reminded him of an aquarium he'd visited once, where the visitors could walk in a glass tunnel right through the water. Sharks and rays swam above and below, and the illusion of being underwater was nearly perfect. Except the illusion here was that he floated in space. Dorian looked up. Stars glinted back at him with unblinking brilliance. He'd never seen a night sky so clean-edged. On the horizon, a quarter moon cast a clear, cold light on the mountain peaks in the distance, and its silver hue glinted off the Inn at Mount Either's structures that wrapped tight around the mountain above him, but it wasn't the Mount Either he'd left. Glass and metal flowed smoothly around the contours, seamlessly leading from wall to window to walkway to elevator, and the dim light of the glass told him of the inn's life behind.

Afraid for his balance, Dorian moved back to the door like a man on ice. He tugged, but the handle didn't stir. A lighted sign in red appeared above: SORRY, TEMPORARILY OUT OF SERVICE.

After tight-roping his way across the glass walkway, Dorian found himself in a vista room. A line of comfortably padded couches faced the window and the star-studded night outside. Illuminated by the partial moon, people sat in most of the couches, staring silently at the view. He looked out. Moonlight bathed the nearest mountain in greys and blues. Shadows, like black swaths of velvet, outlined ridges and rocks and filled crevices. Dorian took an empty couch, and settled in its deep embrace. Yesterday, when Stephanie missed lunch, he'd sat in the restaurant for an extra hour, and he knew something was wrong. He told himself that she must have forgotten, but that wasn't like her. Using the inn's maps as best he could—the inn's structure was complicated—he'd searched the gyms and shops, the salons and museums, hour by hour, panic building.

He realized that this was the first time he'd rested in the last twenty-four hours. Dorian closed his eyes, just for a minute, he thought.

He dreamed of Stephanie. They were in a boat crossing a broad lake. Behind them he could make out a line of trees and a distant dock, but the other shore was lost in mist. Water slapped at the bow, and the air smelled of fish and wet wood. "You're so far away," she said. Dorian wanted to weep. "I know," he said. "I know, but I'm trying to find you." He was dreaming, and he could feel the couch he was sitting in, and he could imagine the people sitting around him, staring at the night-lit mountain, but he also felt the hard wooden bench and the boat's gentle motion. "Where are you, Stephanie?" In the dream, she laughed the way she always laughed, an honest burst of humor that animated her face and eyes. She said, "No, I mean you're so far away in the boat." Dorian braced himself, lifted his feet over the seat in between them, then slid forward. Their knees touched. Stephanie placed her hands palms up on her knees. Leaning, Dorian covered them with his own.

"Your hands are so warm," she said.

Dorian kept still, his fingers resting on her wrists, her pulse beating beneath them.

Stephanie looked upon the water, the long line of ripples moving past them, breathing quietly. She said, "I could float here forever. I don't have to be going anywhere." The boat rocked, and it was like the lake stroking them. She met his gaze. "If you are with me."

A voice said, "It's beginning."

Dorian opened his eyes, and Stephanie disappeared. For a moment, he imagined the couch moved, as if the floor was the surface of a black lake, but that feeling faded, leaving him with the memory so vivid of her pulse in his fingertips and the way her lips parted when she laughed that he wondered for a second if she'd actually been there before him.

"It's beginning," an elderly woman in the couch next to him said again. Her arms looked frail, but her voice was firm.

"What?" said Dorian.

"Shhh!" she said, and hunched forward, all her attention directed out the window.

At first Dorian thought the mountain was catching fire. A flicker of red glinted from the middle of a cliff. Then it spread over the length of the rock, a brilliant, deep red like an electric ruby.

"My god," someone said. Someone else sighed.

The red spread to neighboring cliffs, but now the center glimmered with yellow, and a few seconds later almost all the red had been replaced by the yellow glow.

Leaning toward woman next to him, Dorian said, "What is that?"

"Just spectacular," she said.

"No, what is it?"

She didn't look at him. "Refracted moonlight on the crystals. It's only this good a couple times a year, and only from this spot. No other mountain in the world does this, and if this room were any other place, we wouldn't see it. The moon has to be in the right phase."

Now the yellow light enveloped the entire mountain, except at the bottom which had acquired a purple tint that crawled up the cliffs until the yellow vanished. Purple was Stephanie's color, the color of amethyst.

"There were clouds in the spring. We missed it," the old woman said, then she started crying.

Dorian sat with his hands in his lap, unsure of what to do.

"My husband was with me then. We'd never been here before." She wiped her tears before looking at him for the first time. Her eyes reflected the purple from the mountain. "It's just a superstition, I know, but they say if you see the lights with someone you love, they will be with you forever."

Gradually the purple vanished. The edges of a few of the larger rock faces glinted green for a moment. Finally, the mountain looked like it had when he entered the room. People rose from the couches and headed for the exits. Many were couples holding hands. The old woman didn't move. She'd wrapped her arms across her chest, as if she were hugging herself. Her knuckles were large and arthritic. She said, "I hope you come back when it isn't cloudy. I hope you come back with someone you love."

A chill swept the back of Dorian's head. "I'm looking for her."

She shrank a little deeper into her chair. "Not me. I'm waiting."

At the other end of the room, a bellboy bent to talk to a young couple still sitting. They smiled back at him, then each showed him a small piece of plastic. In the room, lit only by reflected moonlight, Dorian couldn't tell what the plastic was. The bellboy moved to the next lodger, who also showed him a plastic card. There were only a few people between Dorian and the bellboy when Dorian recognized that they were displaying their room keys. His own key didn't look like the ones they showed.

"What's the problem?" said a woman as she put her key back in her pocket.

"Nothing of concern, ma'am. A security issue, misplaced guest."

Dorian slipped out of the room and into a passageway. Half of the wall was transparent, like the entrance bridge near the transition, except the ceiling glowed to provide dim light. He followed the gentle curve and had walked for several minutes when an acetylene-bright brilliance flushed the hall into overexposed surfaces and shadows. He blinked against the glare before shading his eyes. From the mountain's base, the light grew more intense, until, soundlessly, a rocket, balanced on a flaming pillar rose past him and streaked into the night.

He heard the people in the hall before he saw them, but short of turning back the way he came, there was no way to avoid them. They laughed and joked loudly. At first Dorian thought they must be going to a masquerade. All wore bulky suits and carried helmets under their arms.

"I've never been outside," said a young man with glasses and a moustache.

"Just don't sit on something sharp," said his motherly-looking companion. "And be sure to listen to the safety procedures. Depressurization is nothing to fool around with."

They were too preoccupied to acknowledge Dorian as they clumped past.

When they vanished around the curve, Dorian stopped, put his hand on the glass wall, and looked out again. The stars never had seemed so sharp and unblinking, and, he noticed, there was no vegetation he could see. None at all. The landscape was as desolate and bare as the—he paused as he made the comparison—as the moon, but there was the moon, nearly resting on the horizon. He shivered. Every transition at Mount Either took the guests to an exotic location, but it had never occurred to him to wonder *how* exotic. This is Earth, he thought, isn't it? Clearly Earth! But what happened to it?

The mountains weren't just dead. They were swept clean and bare, like a planet's skeleton, solid, smooth, dry and with no ability to shrug themselves into life. He pressed his forehead against the glass and shut his eyes. Where was Stephanie? She'd be taking pictures. She'd be stopping at every new view, her head cocked a little to the side, as if she were measuring the world for a painting. She'd tell him about what she'd found, and if he was quiet for too long, she'd say, "What are you thinking?" and genuinely want to know.

Dorian pushed away from the glass and continued walking, slowly at first, but soon with a purposeful stride. At a junction he chose the hallway whose stairs led toward the lobby. An elevator took him up, and when the doors opened, a bellboy stood on the other side. The bellboy, wearing a silk vest that sported a shiny name tag that read, NED, CAN I HELP?, held a personal digital assistant in one hand with Dorian's face on the screen.

"I'm Dorian Wallace."

The bellboy checked the image in his hand. "Heavens, you *are* Dorian Wallace! Thank goodness, sir. Your wife has been worried sick. Everyone has been looking for you."

Dorian's hand flew to his heart, and he clenched his shirt in a fist. "You know where Stephanie is?"

Two short hallways later, they were in the lobby, the same long window that seemed so familiar looked out on the moon-lit mountains. Dorian's pulse pounded and his face felt hot. The same cliff face covered with plants made the back wall, and, Dorian thought, the same concierge, his handlebar eyebrows pointing upwards, waited at the reception desk. But he wasn't the same. Similar, but not the same. Shorter, perhaps? A little broader in the shoulders?

Stephanie stepped out from behind the concierge.

Wordlessly they embraced. Dorian held her tightly, his cheek pressing against the side of her head. She trembled in his arms. For a moment, all centered on her, on the feel of her breathing against him, of her fingers on his back. The smell of her skin. The texture of her blouse.

For a moment, all was perfect.

But she stiffened—he could feel it in her muscles—and she pushed away.

Stephanie looked at him, her hands still holding his. Dorian studied her. Where Stephanie's hair had been curled, it now hung straight. Where her eyes had been blue with tiny white spokes, they were now blue with tinges of green.

"Who are you?" the woman asked.

"I'm Dorian. Who are you?" He released her hands, and they hung in place where he'd left them. She took a single step back.

"Oh, no," said the concierge. "This is distressing."

"Where's my husband?" the woman said. "Where's my Dorian?"

The concierge took a position between them. "The inn is not at fault here. It doesn't happen this way. If you'll come with me, sir." He took Dorian by the elbow and walked away from the reception desk. "How many transitions did you go through?" he whispered harshly.

"I . . . maybe . . ."

"You went through at least two, didn't you?"

Dorian stopped, pulled his arm away from the concierge. "The damn inn is so confusing that anybody can get lost. Give me a guide, and I'll be happy to go back to where I belong."

"It's a *big* inn. How many?" The concierge wasn't smiling, and he didn't look friendly in the least.

"What does it matter? Five or six, I think."

The concierge blanched. "You don't understand, sir. There are nine transition zones."

"So?"

"When you go through one, you come out at a different Inns at Mount Either. Each inn has nine transition zones too. Nine different ones. When you go through two transitions, there are eighty-one different inns you might have come from. If you went through five. . ." He paused, closing his eyes for a second. They popped open, "You could have come from any one of 59,049 realities. If you went through six, we'd have over a half million possibilities." He grabbed Dorian's elbow again with urgency. "Where did you come from to get here?"

Dorian winced and found himself half walking and half trotting. "A jungle, I think. Ouch! What's the hurry?"

They reached an elevator. The concierge punched the button. Then he punched it again. "Zone drift. When you go through a zone, the door you came from is the way back for two or three hours, but if you wait too long, the place you came from isn't there anymore. It'll be another version of the inn. It might even be a really,

really close version of the one you came from, but it won't be the same one. If you didn't dawdle in any of the zones, though, you should be okay."

Dorian glanced at his watch. When had he gone through the first transition?

The elevator door opened. "Jungle?" asked the concierge.

Dorian nodded. "Another version? Like a parallel world?"

The concierge grunted as the elevator started down. "Um, sort of. We prefer to call them non-convergent. There's a lot of variation."

"But the door to the jungle is out of order. I would have gone back through it on my own."

"We locked all the doors when we realized a guest was making unguided transitions."

Dorian followed the concierge who made turns down hallways and chose stairwells with practiced confidence. They crossed the transparent bridge, but now the door was lit and they passed into the rainforest transition Dorian remembered.

"Okay, how did you get here?" The concierge reached behind a curtain of vines hanging next to the wall, and pulled a phone from a hatch behind.

"From a kind of a desert world, I think."

The concierge's forehead furrowed in frustration.

"I'm sure it was desert, like the Arabian Nights."

He said something into the phone, then listened to the reply.

They hurried around a hallway's long curve. Dorian hadn't looked at the scenery the first time through, but now he noticed solid vegetable weaves that made the walls, and the sweaty smell of wet wood and dripping leaves.

"How come you are here? I mean, you're just like the concierge from the inn that I came from."

They trotted up a flight of stairs, crossed a dizzying walkway over a ravine and entered a small court circled with open booths. Guests sat on stools drinking from tall bamboo cups or coconuts with straws stuck in them. An elevator rendition of jungle music played softly in the background.

"I'm everywhere," said the concierge. "So's your wife. So are you. That's the problem. You are lost, and so are about a zillion non-convergent versions of you wandering about the inn where they don't belong. Of course, there are a lot of you who didn't get lost either. The worlds aren't parallel. At least your wife had the wit to come back through the same doors she exited."

"She has a pretty good sense of direction." Dorian shook his head. "I didn't come this way. I don't remember this."

"Short cuts. Your clock is ticking. With any luck, another version of me is hustling another version of you, the right one, back to my lobby where that woman you met is waiting. How long has it been since you went through the first transition?"

"I'm sure it hasn't been two hours yet." When had he started looking?

"Good. We should make it without any trouble."

Finally they entered a transition with a western theme, rough textured pine walls and the smell of cactus.

"This is the first zone I entered."

The concierge sighed and smiled for the first time since Dorian talked to him in the lobby. "Fifteen minutes back for me. Piece of cake. From here, all I need is your room key."

Looking at the key, the concierge plucked another phone from a hidden niche. He read a string of numbers into the mouthpiece.

Minutes later, they stood at the transition back to the inn Dorian had come from. The concierge put out his hand. "I'm glad that I could help you, sir. A bellboy on the other side will escor you to the lobby, where I'm sure your wife will be glad to see you." He paused. "We've always said that a guest should lose himself in the experience."

Dorian grimaced. "I didn't think that was funny the first time I heard it."

When he entered the lobby, he spotted Stephanie right away. Her back was to him, but her blonde hair, lightly curled at the end, barely touching her shoulders, caught a ray of sun through the window and practically glowed. He remembered that once he'd told her that he liked looking for her in crowded places. "I just tell myself that I'm looking for the prettiest woman in the building, and when I find you, I'm done."

She turned, but her smile was tentative.

"Dorian? The real Dorian?"

He tried to speak. Nothing came out, and his eyes blurred.

She was in his arms. Dorian held her tightly, afraid to let go. She buried her face in his neck, and he could feel her tears on his skin. He thought about the first time he'd held her, a night when they'd parked on a cliff's edge with the city's lights spread out in the valley below, when he knew that they would be together forever. Her breathing had synchronized with his. Her shoulder fit under his arm as if the two of them had been sculpted at the same time to go together. Dorian shook with sobs, and she held him. Her crying matched his own.

A long time later, it seemed, when they'd dried their faces, made their apologies to the concierge, who just seemed happy that they were where they belonged again, and all thoughts of further repercussions for going through transitions were forgotten, they walked toward their room. Stephanie's arm wrapped around Dorian's waist, and he kept a hand on her shoulder, as if afraid that she might slip away again.

"Where were you at lunch?" Dorian asked. "I waited for an hour."

Stephanie's inhalation still sounded shaky. "I was in the wrong restaurant. When you didn't show up, I went back to the room. But you didn't come, so I started looking for you. That's when I went through the transitions. Dorian, it was all so beautiful. I lost track of time." She frowned. "They brought a man who looked like you, but he wasn't you. I've never been so frightened before."

"I know."

Dorian pulled her even tighter. It didn't matter why they'd been apart, as long as they were no longer lost. He loved the feel of her walking beside him. He loved that he could match strides with her so they wouldn't jar each other. Twenty years of marriage, and he loved that she still surprised him with her laugh.

They reached the room. Dorian slid his plastic key into the lock, but it didn't work.

"Let me," Stephanie said. The door recognized her key and let them in. "I'm so tired, I could sleep for a week." She leaned against the wall, looking at him.

"Me too. I haven't slept since yesterday."

She headed for the bed, and Dorian was glad because she couldn't see the change in expression on his face. He hadn't slept since yesterday, he'd said, but that wasn't true. He'd slept in the moon room, where he'd dreamed of Stephanie. "You're so far away," she'd said in the dream.

How long had he slept?

Stephanie pulled back the sheets. Dorian watched. Was that *ex-*

actly the way Stephanie unmade the bed? Didn't she always wash her face first?

She walked past him into the bathroom. Her fingers touched his as she rounded the corner. "You look like you swallowed something gross."

The sink turned on. Water splashed. Dorian backed up to the edge of the bed, but he didn't sit down. Stephanie had left the door open. She always closed the bathroom door, even to brush her teeth, even to blow her nose. Her shadow moved on the carpet in the light of the open door.

How long had he slept?

Much, much later that night, long after the woman had fallen asleep, Dorian lay with his eyes wide open, listening. Straining. What did his wife sound like when she breathed? Could this possibly be her beside him, and what if it wasn't? How long would it be before she noticed? A year? Ten years? Never?

Or could she wake up right now and know? Would she lever herself up on one elbow and look at him in the dark? "You're not Dorian," she'd say. Her breath wouldn't smell like Stephanie's. Her voice wouldn't be Stephanie's. Not quite. Not exact. Not real.

She stirred slightly. Every muscle in Dorian's body tensed, but she didn't wake up.

Not then.

SEARCH ENGINE

Mary Rosenblum

Aman's eyelids twitched as the tiny skull and crossbones icon flashed across his retinal screen. Uh oh. He blinked away the image and scowled at the office door. The feds. "Sit tight and pay attention," he said to the new kid sitting in the chair beside the desk.

"What's up?" New Kid leaned forward. But the door was already opening, the soft whisper as it slid aside a reassurance that this was a high end operation, that your money was being spent wisely. The real-life, physical office, the expensive woolen carpet and real wood furniture echoed that reassurance. No sleazy, virtual private eye here . . . you were at the top of the ladder in a hard office.

Not that the suit cared. He took off his shades, slipped 'em into the pocket of his very well made business tunic and fixed icy gray eyes on Aman's face. If he didn't like what he saw, he was too well trained to let it show. "Mr. Boutros." The suit didn't offer his hand, sat down immediately in the chair across from the desk. Cast New Kid a single pointed glance . . . Jimi, Aman remembered his name at last. Raul's latest, given to him to babysit and maybe even train.

"My assistant." Aman put fnality in the tone. New Kid stays. He kept his body language relaxed and alpha, waited out the suit's evaluation of his options. Inclined his head at the suit's very slight nod. He had won that round. You won when you could. "How may I help you?"

The suit pulled a small leather case from inside his tunic, slipped a tiny data disk from it. Without a word, Aman extended a port. Clients did not store their files on the net. Not if they were paying Search Engine's fees. The disk clicked into place and Aman's desktop lit up. A man's head and shoulders appeared in the holofield, turning slowly. Medium-dark, about twenty, mixed Euro/African and Hispanic genes, Aman noted. About the same phenotype as New Kid—Jimi—a history of war, rape, and pillage made flesh. The Runner's scalp gleamed naked, implanted with fiberlight gang-sign. Aman read it and sighed, thinking of his fight with Avi over his fiberlights. Tattoo your political incorrectness on your body for the cops, son. Just in case they don't notice you on their own. Stupid move, Avi. That hadn't been the final argument, but it had been damn close. Several data-file icons floated at the bottom of the field. Food preferences, clothing, personal services, sex. Aman nodded because the feds knew what he needed and it would all be here. "Urgency?" he asked.

"High." The suit kept his eyes on the Runner's light-scribed profile.

Aman nodded. Jimi was getting tense. He didn't even have to look at him, the kid was radiating. Aman touched the icon bubbles, opening the various files, hoping Jimi would keep his mouth shut. Frowning, because you never wanted the client to think it was going to be easy, he scanned the rough summary of the Runner's buying habits. Bingo. He put his credit where his politics were. Not a problem, this one. He was going to stand up and wave to get their attention. "Four days," he said. Start high and bargain. "Plus or minus ten percent."

"Twenty-four hours." The suit's lips barely moved.

Interesting. Why this urgency? Aman shook his head. No kinky sex habits, no drugs, so they'd have to depend on clothes and food. Legal-trade data files took longer. "Three point five," he finally said. "With a failure-exemption clause."

They settled on forty-eight hours with no failure-exemption. "Ten percent bonus if you get him in less." The suit stood. For a moment he looked carefully and thoroughly at Jimi. Storing his image in the bioware overlay his kind had been enhanced with? If he ran into Jimi on the street a hundred years from now he'd remember him. Jimi had damn well better hope it didn't matter.

"They really want this guy." Jimi waited for the green light to come on over the door, telling them that the suit hadn't left anything behind that might listen. "The Runner's wearing Gaist sign."

No kidding. Aman knew that scrawl by heart.

"What did he do?"

"How the hell should I know?" Aman touched one of the file icons, closing his eyes as his own bioware downloaded and displayed on his retina. *That* had been the final argument with Avi.

"Oh, so we just do what we're told, I get it." Jimi leaned back, propped a boot up on the corner of the desktop. "Say yessir, no questions asked, huh? Who cares about the reason, as long as there's money?"

"He's government." Aman blinked the display away, ignored Jimi's boot. Why in the name of everyone's gods had Raul hired this wet-from-birth child? Well, he knew *why*. Aman eyed the kid's slender, androgynous build. His boss had a thing for the African/Hispanic phenotype. Once, he'd kept it out of the business. Aman suppressed a sigh, wondering if the kid had figured it out yet. Why Raul had hired him. "How much of the data-dredging that you do is legal?" He watched Jimi think about that. "You think we're that good, huh? That nobody ever busts us? There is always a price, kid, especially for success."

Jimi took his foot off the desktop. "The whole crackdown on the Gaiists is just crap. Bread and circus move because the North American Alliance . . ."

Aman held up a hand. "Good thing you don't write it on *your* head in light," he said mildly. "Just don't talk politics with Raul."

Jimi flushed. "So how come you let him back you down from four days? An Xuyen is already backed up with the Ferrogers search."

"We won't need Xuyen." Aman nodded at the icons. "Our Runner is organic. Vegan. Artisan craft only, in clothes and personal items. You could find him all by yourself in about four hours."

"But if he's buying farm raised and hand made?" Jimi frowned. "No Universal tags on those."

Aman promised himself a talk with Raul, but it probably wouldn't change anything. Not until he got tired of this one, anyway. "Get real." He got up and crossed to the small nondescript desktop at the back of the office, camouflaged by an expensive Japanese shoji screen. This was the real workspace. Everything else was stage-prop, meant to impress clients. "You sell stuff without a U tag and you suddenly find you can't get a license, or your E coli count is too high for an organic permit, or your handspinning operation might possibly be a front for drug smugglers." He laughed. "Everything has a U tag in it." Which wasn't quite true, but knowledge was power. Jimi didn't have any claim on power yet. Not for free.

"Okay." Jimi shrugged. "I'll see if I can beat your four hours. Start with sex?"

"He's not a buyer. I'll do it."

"How come?" Jimi bristled. "Isn't it too easy for you? If even *I* can do it?"

Aman hesitated, because he wasn't really sure himself. "I just am." He sat down at his workdesk as Jimi stomped out. Brought up his secure field and transferred the files to it. The Runner got his sex for free or not at all, so no point in searching that. Food was next on the immediacy list. Aman opened his personal searchware and fed the Runner's ID chipprint into it. He wasn't wearing his ID chip any more, or the suit wouldn't have showed up here. Nobody had figured out yet now to make a birth-implanted ID chip really permanent. Although they kept trying. Aman's AI stretched its thousand thousand fingers into the datasphere and started hitting all the retail data pools. Illegal, of course, and retail purchase data was money in the bank so it was well protected, but if you were willing to pay, you could buy from the people who were better than the people who created the protection. Search Engine, Inc. was willing to pay.

Sure enough, forsale.data had the kid's profile. They were the biggest. Most of the retailers fed directly to them. Aman pulled the Runner's raw consumables data. Forsale profiled, but his AI synthesized a profile to fit the specific operation. Aman waited the thirty seconds while his AI digested the raw dates, amounts, prices of every consumable item the Runner had purchased from the first credit he spent at a store to the day he paid to have a back-alley cutter remove his ID chip. Every orange, every stick of gum, every bottle of beer carried an RNA signature and every purchase went into the file that had opened the day the Runner was born and the personal ID chip implanted.

The AI finished. The Runner was his son's age. Mid-twenties. He looked younger. Testament to the powers of his vegetarian and organic diet? Aman smiled sourly. Avi would appreciate that. That had been an early fight and a continuing excuse when his son needed one. Aman scanned the grocery profile. It had amazed him, when he first got into this field, how much food reflected each person's life and philosophy. As a child, the Runner had eaten a 'typical' North American diet with a short list of personal specifics that Aman skipped. He had become a Gaiist at nineteen. The break was clear in the profile, with the sudden and dramatic shift of purchases from animal proteins to fish and then vegetable proteins only. Alcohol purchases flatlined, although marijuana products tripled as did wild-harvest hallucinogenic mushrooms. As he expected, the illegal drug purchase history revealed little. The random nature of his purchases suggested that he bought the drugs for someone else or a party event rather than for regular personal consumption. No long-term addictive pattern.

A brief, steady purchase rate of an illegal psychotropic, coupled with an increase in food purchase volume suggested a lover or live-in friend with an addiction problem, however. The sudden drop-off suggested a break up. Or a death. The food purchases declined in parallel. On a whim, because he had time to spare, Aman had his AI correlate the drop off of the drug purchases to the newsmedia database for Northwestern North America, the region where the drug purchases were made. Bingo. A twenty year old woman had died within eighteen hours of the last drug purchase. His lover? Dead from an overdose? Aman's eyes narrowed. The cause of death was listed as heart failure, but his AI had flagged it.

"Continue." He waited out the seconds of his AI's contemplation.

Insufficient data, it murmured in its androgynous voice. *Continue?* Aman hesitated because searches like this cost money, and the connection was weak, if there at all. "Continue." No real reason, but he had learned long ago to follow his hunches.

He was the last one out of the office, as usual. The receptionist said good night to him as he crossed the plush reception area, her smile as fresh as it had been just after dawn this morning. As the door locked behind him, she turned off. Real furniture and rugs meant a money and position. Real people meant security risks. The night watchman—another holographic metaphor—wished him good night as he crossed the small lobby. Koi swam in the holographic pond surrounded by blooming orchids. Huge vases of flowers— lilies today—graced small tables against the wall. The display company had even included scent with the holos. The fragrance of lilies followed Aman out onto the street. He took a pedal taxi home, grateful that for once, the small wiry woman on the seat wasn't interested in conversation as she leaned on the handlebars and pumped them through the evening crush in the streets.

He couldn't get the suit out of his head tonight. Jimi was right. The Gaiists were harmless, back to the land types. The feds wanted this kid for something other than his politics, although that might be the media reason. Absently, Aman watched the woman's muscular back as she pumped them past street vendors hawking food, toys, and legal drugs, awash in a river of strolling, eating, buying people. He didn't ask 'why' much any more. Sweat slicked the driver's tawny skin like oil. Maybe it was because the Runner was the same age as Avi and a Gaiist as well. Aman reached over to tap the bell and before the silvery chime had died, the driver had swerved to the curb. She flashed him a grin at the tip as he thumbprinted her reader, then she sped off into the flow of taxis and scooters that clogged the street.

Aman ducked into the little grocery on his block, enjoying the relief of its nearly empty aisles this time of night. He grabbed a plastic basket from the stack by the door and started down the aisles. *You opened the last orange juice today.* The store's major-domo spoke to him in a soft, maternal voice as he strode past the freezer cases. True. The store's major-domo had scanned his ID chip as he entered, then uplinked to smartshopper.net, the inventory control company he subscribed to. It had searched his personal inventory file to see if he needed orange juice and the major-domo had reminded him. He tossed a pouch of frozen juice into his basket. The price displayed on the basket handle, a running total that grew slowly as he added a couple of frozen dinners and a packaged salad. *The Willamette Vineyard's Pinot Gris is on sale this week.* The major-domo here at the wine aisle used a rich, male voice. *Three dollars off.* That was his favorite white. He bought a bottle, and made his way to the checkout gate to thumbprint the total waiting for him on the screen.

"Don't we make it easy?"

Aman looked to up find Jimi lounging at the end of the checkout kiosks.

"You following me?" Aman loaded his groceries into a plastic bag. "Or is this a genuine coincidence?'

'I live about a block from your apartment." Jimi shrugged. 'I always shop here." He hefted his own plastic bag. "Buy you a drink?"

"Sure,' Aman said, to atone for not bothering to know where the newbie lived. They sat down at one of the sidewalk tables next to the grocery, an island of stillness in the flowing river of humanity.

"The usual?" the table asked politely. They both said yes, and Aman wondered what Jimi's usual was. And realized Jimi was already drunk. His eyes glittered and a thin film of sweat gleamed on his face.

Not usual behavior. He'd looked over the intoxicant profiles himself when they were considering applicants. Aman sat back as a petite woman set a glass of stout in front of him and a mango margarita in front of Jimi. Aman sipped creamy foam and bitter beer, watched Jimi down a third of his drink in one long swallow. "What's troubling you?"

"You profile all the time?" Jimi set the glass down a little too hard. Orange slurry sloshed over the side, crystals of salt sliding down the curved bowl of the oversized glass. "Does it ever get to you?"

"Does what get to me?"

"That suit owned you." Jimi stared at him. "That's what you told me."

"They just think they do." Aman kept his expression neutral as he sipped more beer. "Think of it as a trade."

"They're gonna crucify that guy, right? Or whack him. No fuss, no muss."

"The government doesn't assassinate people," Aman said mildly.

"Like hell. Not in public, that's for sure."

Well, the indication had been there in Jimi's profile. He had been reading in the fringe ezines for a long time, and had belonged to a couple of political action groups that were on the 'yellow' list from the government . . . not quite in the red zone but close. But the best profilers came from the fringe. You learned early to evaluate people well, when you had to worry about betrayal.

"I guess I just thought I was working for the good guys, you know? Some asshole crook, a bad dealer, maybe the jerks who dump their kids on the public. But this . . ." He emptied his glass. "Another." He banged the glass down on the table.

You have exceeded the legal limit for operating machinery, the table informed him in a sweet, motherly voice. *I will call you a cab, if you wish. Just let me know.* A moment later, the server set his fresh margarita down in front of him and whisked away his empty.

"Privacy, what a joke." Jimi stared at his drink, words slurring just a bit. "I bet there's a record of my dumps in some data-base or other."

"Maybe how many times you flush."

"Ha ha." Jimi looked at him blearily, the booze hitting him hard and fast now. "When d'you stop asking why? Huh? Or did you ever ask?"

"Come on." Aman stood up. "I'll walk you home. You're going to fall down."

"I'm not that drunk," Jimi said, but he stood up. Aman caught him as he swayed. "Guess I am." Jimi laughed loudly enough to make heads turn. "Guess I should get used to it, huh? Like you."

"Let's go." Aman moved him, not all that gently. "Tell me where we're going."

"We?"

"Just give me your damn address."

Jimi recited the number, sulky and childlike again, stumbling and lurching in spite of Aman's steadying arm. It was one of the cheap and trendy loft towers that had sprouted as the neighborhood got popular. Jimi was only on the sixth floor, not high enough for a pricey view. Not on his salary. The door unlocked and lights glowed as the unit scanned Jimi's chip and let them in. Music came on, a retro-punk nostalgia band that Aman recognized. A cat padded over and eyed them greenly, its golden fur just a bit ratty. It was real, Aman realized with a start. Jimi had paid a hefty fee to keep a flesh and blood animal in the unit.

"I got to throw up," Jimi mumbled, his eyes wide. They made it to the tiny bathroom . . . barely. Afterward, Aman put him to bed on the pull out couch that served as bed in the single loft room. Jimi passed out as soon as he hit the pillow. Aman left a waste basket beside the couch and a big glass of water with a couple of old fashioned aspirin on the low table beside it. The cat stalked him, glaring accusingly, so he rummaged in the cupboards of the tiny kitchenette, found cat food pouches and emptied one onto a plate. Set it on the floor. The cat stalked over, its tail in the air.

It would be in the database . . . that Jimi owned a cat. And to-night's bender would be added to his intoxicant profile, the pur-chase of the margarita's tallied neatly, flagged because this wasn't usual behavior. If his productivity started to fall off, Raul would look at that profile first. He'd find tonight's drunk.

"Hey."

Aman paused at the door, looked back. Jimi had pushed himself up on one elbow, eyes blurry with booze.

"Thanks . . . f'r feeding him. I'm not . . . a drunk. But you know that, right?"

"Yeah," Aman said. "I know that."

"I knew him. Today. Daren. We were friends. Kids together, y'know? Were you ever a kid? Suit's gonna kill him. You c'd tell."

Tears leaked from the corners of his eyes. "How come? You didn't even ask. You didn't even ask me if I knew him."

Damn. He'd never even thought of looking for a connection there. "I'm sorry, Jimi," Aman said gently. But Jimi had passed out again, head hanging over the edge of the sofa. Aman sighed and retraced his steps, settling the kid on the cushions again. Bad break for the kid. He stared down at Jimi's unconscious sprawl on the couch-bed. *Why?* Didn't matter. The suit wouldn't have told them the truth. But Jimi was right. He should have asked. He thought about today's profile of the Runner, that break where he had changed what he ate, what he wore, what he spent his money on. You could see the break. What motivated it . . . that you could only guess at.

What would Avi's profile look like?

No way to know. Avi's break had been a back-cutter.

Aman closed the door and listened to the unit lock it behind him.

He carried his groceries the few scant blocks to his own modest condo tower. No music came on with the lights. No cat, just Danish furniture and an antique Afghani carpet knotted by the childhood fingers of women who were long dead now. He put the food away, stuck a meal in the microwave, and thought about pouring himself another beer. But the stout he'd drunk with Jimi buzzed in his blood like street-grade amphetamine. He smiled crookedly, thinking of his grandfather, a devout man of Islam, and his lectures about the demon' blood, alcohol. It felt like demon's blood tonight. The microwave chimed. Aman set the steaming tray on the counter to cool , sat down crosslegged on the faded wool patterns of crimson and blue, and blinked his bioware open.

His AI had been working on the profile. It presented him with five options. Aman settled down to review the Runner's profile first. It wasn't all a matter of data. You could buy a search AI, and if that was all there was to it, Search Engine Inc wouldn't be in business. Intuition mattered—the ability to look beyond the numbers and sense the person behind them. Aman ran through the purchases, the candy bars, the vid downloads for the lonely times, the gifts that evoked the misty presence of the girlfriend, the hope of love expressed in single, cloned roses, in Belgian chocolate, and tickets in pairs. They came and went, three of them for sure. He worried about his weight, or maybe just his muscles for awhile, buying gym time and special foods.

Someone died. Aman noted the payments for flowers, the crematorium, a spike in alcohol purchases for about three months. And then . . . the break. Curious, Aman opened another file from the download the suit had given him, read the stats. Daren had been a contract birth—the new way for men to have children. Mom had left for a career as an engineer on one of the orbital platforms. Nanny, private school. The flowers had been for Dad, dead at 54 from a brain aneurysm.

He had joined the Gaiists after his father had died.

Unlike Avi, who hadn't waited.

Aman looked again at the five profiles the AI had presented. All featured organic, wild harvest, natural fiber purchasing profiles. Three were still local. One had recently arrived in Montreal, another had arrived in the Confederacy of South America, in the state of Brazil. Aman scanned the data. That one. He selected one of the local trio. The purchases clustered northeast of the city in an area that had been upscale suburb once, was a squalid cash-worker settlement now. He was walking. Couldn't use mass transit without a chip and didn't have access to a vehicle, clearly. Naïve. Aman let his breath out slowly. Frightened. A little kid with his head under the sofa cushions, thinking he was invisible that way. He wondered sometimes if he could find Avi. It would be a challenge. His son knew how he worked. He knew how to really hide.

Aman had never looked.

On a whim, he called up the AI's flag from his earlier search. It had flagged the woman who had died, who had probably been a live in friend or lover. This time, the AI presented him with clustered drug overdose deaths during the past five years. A glowing question mark tagged the data, crimson, which meant a continuation would take him into secure and unauthorized data. Pursue it? He almost said no. "All right, Jimi." He touched the blood-colored question mark. "Continue." It vanished. Searching secure government data files was going to cost. He hoped he could come up with a reason for Raul, if he caught it.

His legs wanted to cramp when Aman finally blinked out of his bioware and got stiffly to his feet. The AI hadn't yet finished its search of the DEA data files. The meal tray on the counter was cold and it was well past midnight. He stuck the tray in the tiny fridge and threw himself down on the low couch. Like Jimi, but not drunk on margaritas.

* * *

In the morning, he messaged Raul that he wasn't feeling well and asked if he should come in. As expected, Raul told him no way, go get a screen before you come back. You could count on Raul with his paranoia about bio-terrorism.

It wasn't entirely a lie. He wasn't feeling well. *Well* covered a lot of turf. The AI had nothing for him on the overdose cluster it had flagged and that bothered him. There wasn't a lot of security that could stop it. He emailed Jimi, telling him to work on the Sauza search on his own and attached a couple of non-secure files that would give him something he could handle in what would surely be a fuzzy and hung over state of mind. He found the clothes he needed at the back of his closet, an old, worn tunic-shirt and a grease-stained pair of jeans. He put on a pair of scuffed and worn out boots he'd found in a city recycle center years ago, then caught a ped-cab to the light rail and took the northeast run. He paid cash to the wary driver and used it to buy a one way entry to the light rail. Not that cash hid his movements. He smiled grimly as he found a seat. His ped-cab and light rail use had been recorded by citizen.net, the data company favored by most transportation systems. It would just take someone a few minutes longer to find out where he had gone today.

City ran out abruptly in the Belt, a no-man's-land of abandoned warehouses and the sagging shells of houses inhabited by squatters, the chipless bilge of society. Small patches of cultivation suggested an order to the squalid chaos. As the train rocketed above the sagging roofs and scrubby brush that had taken over, he caught a brief snapshot glimpse of a round faced girl peering up at him from beneath a towering fountain of rose canes thick with bright pink blossoms. Her shift, surprisingly clean and bright, matched the color of the roses perfectly and she waved suddenly and wildly as the train whisked Aman past. He craned his neck to see her, but the curve of the track hid her instantly.

At his stop, he stepped out with a scant handful passengers, women mostly and a couple of men, returning from a night of cleaning or doing custom hand-work for the upscale clothiers. None of them looked at him as they plodded across the bare and dirty concrete of the platform, but a sense of observation prickled the back of his neck.

Why would anyone be following him? But Aman loitered to examine the melon slices and early apples hawked by a couple of bored boys at the end of the platform. He haggled a bit, then spun around and walked quickly away—which earned him some inventive epithets from the taller of the boys. No sign of a shadow. Aman shrugged and decided on nerves. His AI's lack of follow-up data bothered him more with every passing minute. The rising sun already burned the back of his neck as he stepped off the platform and into the street.

The houses here were old, roofs sagging or covered with cheap plastic siding, textured to look like wood and lapped to shed rain. It was more prosperous than the no-man's-land belt around the city center, but not by much. Vegetables grew in most of the tiny yards, downspouts fed hand-dug cisterns and small, semi-legal stands offered vegetables, home-made fruit drinks, snacks, and various services—much like the street vendors on his block, but out here, the customers came to the vendors and not the other way around.

He paused at a clean-looking stand built in what had been a parking strip, and bought a glass of vegetable juice, made in front of his eyes in an antique blender. The woman washed the vegetables in a bucket of muddy water before she chopped them into the blender, but he smelled chlorine as he leaned casually on the counter. Safe enough. His vaccinations were up to date, so he took the glass without hesitation and drank the spicy, basil flavored stuff. He didn't like basil particularly, but he smiled at her. "Has Daren been by today?" He hazarded the Runner's real name on the wild chance that he was too naïve to have used a fake. "He was supposed to meet me here. Bet he overslept."

Her face relaxed a bit, her smile more genuine. "Of course." She shrugged, relaxing. "Doesn't he always? I usually see him later on. Like noon." And she laughed a familiar and comfortable 'we're all friends' laughter.

He was using his real name. Aman sipped some more of the juice, wanting to shake his head. Little kid with his head under the friendly sofa cushions. A figure emerged from a small, square block of a house nearly invisible beneath a huge tangle of kiwi and kudzu vines and headed their way, walking briskly, his hand-woven, natural-dyed tunic as noticeable as a bright balloon on this street. Loose drawstring pants woven of some tan fiber and the string of carved beads around his neck might as well have been a neon arrow pointing. "Ha, there he is," Aman said, and the woman's glance and smile confirmed his guess. Aman waited until the Runner's eyes were starting to sweep his way, then stepped quickly forward. "Daren, it's been forever." He threw his arms around the kid hugging him like a long lost brother, doing a quick cheek-kiss that allowed him to hiss into the shocked kid's ear, *Act like we're old friends and maybe the feds won't get you. Don't blow this.*

The kid stiffened, panic tensing all his muscles, fear sweat sour in Aman's nostrils. For a few seconds, the kid thought it over. Then his muscles relaxed all at once, so much so that Aman's hands tightened instinctively on his arms. He started to tremble.

"Come on. Let's take a walk," Aman said. "I'm not here to bust you."

"Let me get some juice . . ."

"No." Aman's thumb dug into the nerve plexis in his shoulder and the kid gasped. "Walk." He twisted the kid around and propelled him down the street, away from the little juice kiosk, his body language suggesting two old friends out strolling, his arm companionably over the kid's shoulder, hiding the kid's tension with his own body, thumb exerting just enough pressure on the nerve to remind the kid to behave. "You are leaving a trail a blind infant could follow," he said conversationally, felt the kid's jerk of reaction.

"I'm not chipped." Angry bravado tone.

"You don't need to be chipped. That just slows the search down a few hours. You went straight from the hack-doc to here, walked through the belt because you couldn't take the rail, you buy juice at this stand every day, and you bought those pants two blocks up the street, from the lady who sells clothes out of her living room. Want me to tell you what had for dinner last night, too?"

"Oh, Goddess," he breathed.

"Spare me." Aman sighed. "Why do they want you? You blow something up? Plant a virus?"

"Not us. Not the Gaiists." He jerked free of Aman's grip with surprising strength, fists clenched. "That's all a lie. I don't know why they want me. Yeah, they're claiming bio terrorism, but I didn't do it. There wasn't any virus released where they said it happened. How can they *do* that? Just make something up?" His voice had gone shrill. "They have to have proof and they don't have any proof. Because it didn't happen."

He sounded so much like Avi that Aman had to look away. "They just made it all up, huh?" He made his voice harsh, unbelieving.

"I . . . guess." The kid looked down, his lip trembling. "Yeah, it sounds crazy, huh. I just don't get *why*? Why *me*? I don't even do protests. I just . . . try to save what's left to save."

"Tell me about your girlfriend."

"Who?" He blinked at Aman, his eyes wet with tears.

"The one who died."

"Oh. Reyna." He looked down, his expression instantly sad. "She really wanted to kick 'em. The drugs. I tried to help her. She just . . . she just had so much fear inside. I guess . . . the drugs were the only thing that really helped the fear. I . . . I really tried."

"So she killed herself?"

"Oh, no." Daren looked up at him, shocked. "She didn't want to *die*. She just didn't want to be afraid. She did the usual hit that morning. I guess . . . the guy she bought from, he called himself Skinjack, I guess he didn't cut the stuff right. She ODed. I . . . went looking for him." Daren flushed. "I told myself I was going to beat him up. I guess . . . maybe I wanted to kill him. Because she was getting better. She would have made it." He drew a shaky breath. "He just disappeared. The son of a bitch. I kept looking for him but . . . he was just gone. Maybe he ODed, too," he added bitterly. "I sure hope so."

All of a sudden, it clicked into place. The whole picture.

Why.

They had reached an empty lot. Someone was growing grapes in it and as they reached the end of the rows, sudden movement in the shadows caught Aman's eye. Too late. He was so busy sorting it all out, he'd stopped paying attention. The figure stepped out of the leaf shadows, a small, ugly gun in his hand.

"I was right." Jimi's eyes glittered. "Didn't think I was smart enough to track you, huh? I'm stupid, I know, but not that stupid."

"Actually, I thought you'd be too hung over." Aman spread his hands carefully. "I think we're on the same side, here, and I think we need to get out of here n*ow*."

"Shut up," Jimi said evenly, stepping closer, icy with threat. "Just shut *up*."

"Jimi?" Daren pushed forward, confused. "Goddess, I haven't seen you . . . what are you doing?"

"He found you," Jimi said between his teeth. "For the Feds. You're not hiding very well, Daren, you idiot. Everything you buy has a damn tag on it. He looked up your buying habits and picked you out of the crowd, just like that. He laughed about how easy it was. You were too easy for him to even give the job to a newbie like me." Jimi's eyes burned into the kid's. "You got to . . ."

Aman shifted his weight infinitesimally, made a tiny, quick move with his left hand, just enough to catch Jimi's eye. Jimi swung right, eyes tracking, gun muzzle following his eyes. Aman grabbed Jimi's gun hand with his right hand, twisted, heard a snap. With a cry Jimi let go of the gun and Aman snatched it from the air, just as Daren tackled him, grabbing for the gun. The hissing snap of a gas-powered gunshot ripped the air. Again. Aman tensed, everything happening in slow motion now. No pain. Why no pain? Hot wetness spattered his face and Jimi sprawled backward into the grape leaves, arms and legs jerking. Aman rolled, shrugging Daren off as if he weighed nothing, seeing the suit now, three meters away, aiming at Daren.

Aman fired. It was a wild shot, crazy shot, the kind you did in sim-training sessions and knew you'd never pull off for real.

The suit went down.

Aman tried to scramble to his feet, but things weren't working right. After a while, Daren hauled him the rest of the way up. White ringed his eyes and he looked ready to pass out from shock.

"He's dead. Jimi. And the other guy." He clung to Aman, as if Aman was supporting him and not the other way around. "Goddess, you're bleeding."

"Enough with Goddess already." Aman watched red drops fall from his fingertips. His left arm was numb, but that wouldn't last.

"Why? What in the . . . what the *hell* is going on here?" His fingers dug into Aman's arm.

"Thank you." Hell was about right. "We need to get out of here. Do you know the neighborhood?"

"Yes. Sort of. This way." Daren started through the grapes his arm around Aman. "I'm supposed to meet . . . a ride. This afternoon. A ride to . . ." He gave Aman a sideways, worried look. "Another place."

"You're gonna have to learn some things . . ." Aman had to catch his breath. "Or you're gonna bring the suits right after you." After that he stopped talking. The numbness was wearing off. Once, years and years ago, he had worked as private security, licensed for lethal force, paying his way though school. A burglar shot him one night.

It hurt worse than he remembered, like white hot spears digging into his shoulder and side with every step. He disconnected himself from his body after awhile, let it deal with the pain. He wondered about Jimi's cat. Who would take care of it? Raul would be pissed, he thought dreamily. Not about Jimi. Raul had no trouble finding Jimis in the world. But Aman was a lot better than Raul. Better even than An Xuyen, although Xuyen didn't think so. Raul would be pissed.

He blinked back to the world of hot afternoon and found himself sitting in dim light, his back against something solid.

"Man you were out on your feet." The kid squatted beside him, streaked with sweat, drying blood, and gray dust, his face gaunt with exhaustion and fear. Daren, not Jimi. Jimi was dead.

"I don't have any first aid stuff, but it doesn't look like you're bleeding too much anymore. Water?" He handed Aman a plastic bottle. "It's okay. It's from a clean spring."

Aman didn't really care, would have drunk from a puddle. The ruins of an old house surrounded them. The front had fallen—or been torn—completely off, but a thick curtain of kudzu vine shrouded the space. Old campfire scars blackened the rotting wooden floor. The belt, he figured. Edge of it anyway.

"What happened?" Daren's voice trembled. "Why did he shoot Jimi? Who was he? Who are *you*?"

The water helped. "What sent you to get hacked?" Aman asked.

"Someone searched my apartment." The kid looked away. "I found . . . a bug in my car. I'm . . . good at finding those. I . . . told some of my . . . friends . . . and they said go invisible. It didn't matter if I'd done anything or not. They were right." His voice trembled. "I'd never do what they said I did."

"They know you didn't do anything." Aman closed his eyes and leaned back against the broken plasterboard of the ruined wall. Pain thudded through his shoulder with every beat of his heart. "It's the guy who killed your girlfriend."

"Why? I never hurt him. I never even found him . . ."

"You looked for him," Aman mumbled. "That scared 'em."

The kid's blank silence forced his eyes open.

"I'm guessing the local government is running a little . . . drug eradication program be eliminating the market," he said heavily. Explaining to a child. "They cut a deal with the street connections and probably handed them a shipment of . . . altered . . . stuff to put into the pipeline. Sudden big drop in users."

"Poisoned?" Daren whispered. "On purpose?"

"Nasty, huh? Election coming up. Numbers count. And who

looks twice at an OD in a confirmed user?" Aman kept seeing Jimi's childlike curl on the couch, the cat regarding him patiently. Couldn't make it go away. "Maybe they thought you had proof. Maybe they figured you'd guess and tell your . . . friends. They might make it public." He started to shrug . . . sucked in a quick breath. Mistake. Waited for the world to steady again. "I should have guessed . . . the suit would know about Jimi. Would be tailing him." That was why the long look in the office. Memory impression so the suit could spot him in a crowd. "I figured it out just too late." His fault, Jimi's death. "How soon are your people going to pick you up?"

"Soon. I think." The kid was staring at the ground, looked up suddenly. "How come you came after me? To arrest me?"

"Listen." Aman pushed himself straighter, gritted his teeth until the pain eased a bit. "I told you you're leaving a trail like a neon sign. You listen hard. You got to think about what you buy . . . food, clothes, toothpaste, okay?" He stared into the kid's uncomprehending face, willing him to get it. "It's all tagged, even if they say it's not. Don't doubt it. I'm telling you truth here, okay?"

The kid closed his mouth, nodded.

"You don't buy exactly the opposite—that's a trail we can follow, too—but you buy random. Maybe vegan stuff this time, maybe a pair of synth-leather pants off the rack at a big chain next purchase. Something you'd never spend cash on. Not even before you became a Gaiist, got it? You think about what you really want to buy. The food. The clothes. The snacks, toys, services. And you only buy them every fifth purchase, then every fourth, then every seventh. Got it? Random. You do that, buy stuff you don't want, randomly, and without a chip, you won't make a clear track. You'll be so far down on the profile that the searcher won't take you seriously.

"I've been buying in the belt," the kid protested.

"Doesn't matter." He had explained why to Jimi. Couldn't do it again. Didn't have the strength. Let his eyes droop closed.

"Hey." The kid's voice came to him from a long way away. "I got to know. How come you came after me? To tell me how to hide from you? You really want me to believe that?"

"I don't care if you do or not." Aman struggled to open his eyes, stared into the blurry green light filtering through the kudzu curtain. "I'm . . . not sure how come I followed you." Maybe because he hadn't asked why and Jimi had. Maybe because Avi had been right and the job had changed him after all.

"But why? You a closet Gaiist?"

Aman wanted to laugh at that, but he didn't. It would hurt too much.

Voices filtered through nightmares full of teeth. People talking. No more green light, so it must be almost dark. Or maybe he was dying. Hard to tell. Footsteps scuffed and the kid's face swam into view, Jimi's at first, morphing into the other kid . . . Daren. He tried to say the name but his mouth was too dry.

"We're gonna drop you at an emergency clinic." Daren leaned close, his eyes anxious. "But . . . well, I thought maybe . . . you want to go with us? I mean . . . they're going to find out you killed that Fed guy, right? You'll go to prison."

Yes, they would find out. But he knew how it worked. They'd hold the evidence and the case open. No reason to risk pointing some investigative reporter toward the little dope deal they'd been covering up. They'd have expectations, and he'd meet them, and Jimi's death would turn out to have been another nasty little killing in the belt. He could adopt Jimi's cat. No harm done. Just between us.

"I'll come with you," he croaked. "You could use some help with your invisibility. And I have the track to the proof you need . . . about that drug deal. Make the election interesting." Wasn't pleading. Not that. Trade.

"You can't come chipped." A woman looked over Daren's shoulder, Hispanic, ice cold, with an air that said she was in charge. "And we got to go *now*."

"I know." At least the chip was in his good shoulder.

She did it, using a tiny laser scalpel with a deft sureness that suggested med school or even an MD. And it hurt, but not a lot compared to the glowing coals of pain in his left arm and then they were loading him into the back of a vehicle and it was fully dark outside.

He was invisible. Right now. He no longer existed in the electronic reality of the city. If he made it back to his apartment it wouldn't let him in. The corner store wouldn't take his card or even cash. He felt naked. No, he felt as if he no longer existed. Death wasn't as complete as this. Wondered if Avi had felt like that at first. I probably could have found him, he thought. If I'd had the guts to try.

"I'm glad you're coming with us." Daren sat beside him as the truck or whatever it was rocked and bucked over broken pavement toward the nearest clear street. "Lea says you probably won't die."

"I'm thrilled."

"Maybe we can use the drug stuff to influence the election, get someone honest elected."

He was as bad as Jimi, Aman thought. But . . . why not hope?

"You'll like the head of our order," Daren said thoughtfully. "He's not a whole lot older than me, but he's great. Really brilliant and he cares about every person in the order. *She* really matters to him . . . the Earth I mean. Avi will really welcome you."

Avi.

Aman closed his eyes.

"Hey, you okay?" Daren had him by the shoulders. "Don't die now, not after all this." He sounded panicky.

"I won't," Aman whispered. He managed a tiny laugh that didn't hurt too bad.

Maybe it hadn't been the final fight after all.

Could almost make him believe in Avi's Goddess. Almost.

"Your head of the order sucks at hiding," he whispered. And fainted.

"YOU" BY ANONYMOUS

Stephen Leigh

You wonder about the title, but you start to read.

You also grimace a bit at the use of second person, thinking it both a bit awkward and pretentious, and you wonder if the author is trying to make you think *you* are the protagonist of the story, that this paragraph is referring to you personally.

It is.

Now, you read those words and you grimace again and give a little half-exasperated huff of air. Almost, you start to argue back to the page, denying it, and then you stop. And there's just the faintest, the *tiniest* bit of wonder, of something akin to hope—after all, you think, that would be interesting. That would be unusual. You can almost hear Rod Serling intoning the introduction for *The Twilight Zone*. You've always wanted something like that to happen to you, haven't you?

Well, you're right. These words are directed to *you*. Truly.

You're not quite certain how that could be. After all, there are thousands of copies of this book out there circulating and how could the story know that it's really you and not that overweight, balding programmer with a graying beard in the paper-stuffed apartment in Queens who's also currently reading this at the moment. But it *is* you, not him. Why would it be him? He's a loser. He hasn't had more than one date with a woman for three years, and even those single dates have been rare. He goes out to bars once a month or so hoping to get lucky, but his social skills, never very good, have atrophied even further since his job doesn't require him to actually hold a conversation with anyone, and so he usually ends wandering from circle to circle being ignored until closing time, and then going back to his room and popping one of his pornographic DVDs into the player.

You're not him. In fact, he stopped reading at the porn reference, tossing the book across the room in angry and futile denial.

You think that's a rather harsh and brutal characterization (since you've known a few people who could fit that description) and you're somewhat annoyed at it, but though the description is rather on the cold side it *is* accurate and besides, *you* didn't write it, so you don't need to feel responsible. Even Bob the programmer (hi, Bob—don't you love it when you see your name in print?), in those self-flagellating moments when he's alone in his apartment with only the blue light of his laptop's monitor illuminating the stacks of paperback books on his desk, would admit the truth in what you just read. It may soothe you to know that he'll pick up this story again, an hour from now. This time he'll finish it, wondering if he'll see himself again and perhaps a little envious that the story's for you, not him.

This story is for you.

You pause a moment, confused, because you're not used to a story interfering quite so directly. After all, this is genre fiction. Popular fiction, not some post-modern mainstream story. This is that "crazy sci-fi stuff." You read this type of anthology for escape and for that lovely 'sense of wonder,' not for pretension and experimentation. Over the years, you've slipped a thousand times between covers with sleek spaceships and square-jawed heroes, scantily-clad women and grotesque aliens slithering across a two-mooned landscape. You've lost yourself in a thousand worlds and glimpsed myriad universes painted in words garish or subtle, poetic or plain. You've allowed yourself to *be* the protagonist—any age, gender, or race—and you've bled and loved, triumphed or died everywhere from the medieval past to distant galaxies. You have the gift of imagination yourself—and that's why this story's for you. You can *become*.

You've read the books and watched the movies since you were a kid, and sometimes you've wondered how it would be if lights descended from the sky in front of you one night, whirling down to the lonely county road as you step from your car, drawn by mingled fear and curiosity, and then the side of the ship melts and there, in a rectangle of blinding light, *it* appears, the *Other*. You've wanted it to happen.

It's not going to, though. At least not that way. You know that; you realized long ago that any life that's out there is going to be so profoundly different from you that it may not even be recognizable. Even if it were, the Other's interests and values aren't going to be yours.

That's you, right? The one reading this?

You're still not convinced, though. Fine. *So convince me,* you think, even though at the same time the deeper skeptical part of you insists that it's not possible. And it's not. Not totally. This story could tell you that you lost someone close to you not all that long ago, and that you've kept a memento of them because it brings back the memories. That's the case, of course, and your eyes narrow again because the words have struck too close to home. You also know that it's exactly the kind of vague statement a supposed psychic would use in a cold reading, but . . .

You shiver, as if cold fingers just brushed your spine. You wonder, as you have before, just who's having this one-sided conversation with you, and why. *So tell me*, you think, nearly saying the words aloud.

Fine. Here's why.

Elephants.

You almost laugh at that. But it's true. Remember that old elementary school 'mind trick' where someone says: "Think of anything you want, but just don't think of elephants." And as soon as they say that, you instantly can't think of anything *but* elephants. An entire herd of them go rampaging through your forebrain, trumpeting and ear-flapping, raising the dust from your cerebellum.

Here. Let's try it. Think of anything but parasites.

Ah, your eyebrows lifted at that, and my, the images in your head . . .

Parasites. You shift uncomfortably in your seat.

"What if . . . ?" That's the genesis of so much of the genre that you read, isn't it? "What if . . . ?" the author muses, and erects a plot from there. Here's one for you. What if a parasite wanted to enter the human mind: a sentient parasite, a very intelligent parasite? What would be an interesting reproductive strategy? Reproduction is just engaging in patterns, after all. DNA is an arrangement of simple genetic codes and yet it encompasses all the wild variety and complexity of life. And words . . . words are just an arrangement of simple letters. But my, how powerful they are in your head, in all their various wonderful combinations.

Words are a conduit into your mind. Words are wound so deeply into your thoughts processes that you can't even imagine the world without them. If someone—or something—wanted to control you, they would use words, wouldn't they? Why, with just the right, compelling pattern of words, your mind would open like a raw wound and who knows what could slither in . . .

So don't think of elephants, no matter what.

Too late.

You've heard of all those stories that change your life, that stay with you forever. It just happened.

For you. Just for you.

You deny it, but even though you take the page in your fingers, ready to turn to the next story, you wonder. You think to yourself that once the page turns you'll forget all this; that a week, a month, a year from now you won't even recall having ever read this.

Oh, you'll remember. At this point you don't have a choice. It's already started, inside. You squint and you deny, but you'll remember because everything from here on has changed for you. You have the words inside you now, and you won't like where they take you. Where *I* take you. But you'll remember.

Won't you?

THE JENNA SET

Daniel Kaysen

He told me he'd ring me. He didn't.

"This is my surprised voice," said Kelly.

Kelly works in software and spends her life sniffing round the tricky bits in manuals. And sniffing round the tricky bits of my dating life, too. She's my sister. It's her job.

"Maybe my answerphone's broken?"

"Yeah, right," she said.

I sighed. "Maybe I should get a telesales script for dating."

When you work in telephone sales they give you a script. You ask each person question 1 and then, depending on whether they say yes or no, you ask question 2a or question 2b, and so on. If they say no, you keep asking questions until they say yes to something. Then you've got them, like a fish on a hook.

"A dating script?" said Kelly, sounding dubious.

"Yeah, you know. 'This special date offer includes dinner at my apartment and the potential for oral sex on my couch afterwards. Would that be something you are interested in?' And then if they say no you flip to page two and you ask them if it's the dinner or the oral sex that they have the problem with."

"Yeah, Jenna, that might help," Kelly said, like it wasn't a joke.

I hung up and went back to making my telesales calls.

My 34th call was answered by a teenage girl.

"Could I speak to a parent or guardian?" I said.

"Why?"

"Because if you take up the offer there's a contract to sign, and persons under eighteen—"

"I'm under eighteen but I've signed contracts before."

"Who with?"

"This new phone company. All my calls are free now. And there's tons of cool features."

"Really? Is the answerphone any good?"

"It's the best."

"So what do you have to do to get this deal?" I was a little worried it might involve something seedy.

"I'm a pilot customer. I just have to give them feedback on their system. They're looking for other pilot customers, you know. And it's all free. Would that be something you are interested in?"

"I guess so. Yes."

Damn, she was good.

I rang the number she gave me.

The company was called Palavatar.

The woman who answered my call confirmed that all my phone usage would be absolutely free. She added that Palavatar also offered additional free features such as the very latest in neural network and genetic algorithm communications technology and—

"What's the answerphone like?"

"It's the best."

"Done deal," I said.

"It will take a few hours before your new Palavatar features take effect," she said.

She wished me a nice day and said the contract would be in the post.

As an afterthought I asked her if she would be interested in a subscription to one of our fine range of magazine titles including—

But she'd hung up.

My mother rang then and we continued our argument about whether or not I would be going down to Cornwall for Cousin Steven's wedding. My answer was a definite no, I wouldn't be, as I couldn't stand Cousin Steven, and my mother's answer was a definite yes, I would be, and who was I to be all high and mighty?

We haggled each other down to a we'll see.

I hung up, and phoned Kelly, who had also had the Mother Treatment, so we had a postmortem and tried to encourage each other not to cave in.

When I hung up from talking to Kelly the phone made a weird brring sound that I hadn't heard before.

"This is Palavatar Message Minder," said the voice when I picked up. "You have one new message. Press One to hear your message."

It was mother. Another reason I should go to Cousin Steven's wedding was because his wife might be able to get me a job with her firm.

And then Palavatar again: "Press One to repeat the message. Press Two to return the call. Or why not try our exclusive feature: press Three to generate a fully automated real-time reply, using the very latest in neural network and genetic algorithm technology."

I couldn't resist. I pressed Three.

"Please note," the synthesised voice told me, "that during the automatically generated call anything you say in person will not be audible to the other caller. To cancel the automated reply at any time, press Zero. The call will now commence."

I listened to the staccato beeps as Palavatar dialled my mother's number. After a short pause, my mother picked up.

"Hello?" she said.

Palavatar did their techno-magic and I heard a very uncanny impression of my voice saying "Mother, give it a rest, okay? If I go to Steven's wedding it will be because the scenery will be great, not because I'm crawling on my knees for a job."

The Palavatar version of me certainly didn't back down too easily.

"Did I say anything about crawling?" said my mother. "Did I?"

"Look, I've got to go," said Palavatar-me. "I've got a dinner and oral sex date."

There was a very long pause on the other end, during which I nearly swallowed my tongue in embarrassment.

"Jenna, are you high?" said my mother, eventually.

I pressed buttons wildly because I'd forgotten which one terminated the automatically generated call. It was Zero, I finally discovered.

But by then Mother had hung up.

Oh God.

The phone rang. It was Palavatar again, wanting feedback on the auto-call service. There were options, lots of options, to choose from: did I think the call content was too stilted, too humorous, too weather-based, not weather-based enough? I pressed Nine for further category options, and settled on Seven: "the content of the call was too informal." That produced nine more options, and I pressed

Four to agree that "the sexual or profane content of the automatic call was inappropriate."

The Palavatar system thanked me for my feedback.

I hung up and glared at the phone.

Kelly rang five minutes later. "Mother said you said were going to have oral pleasure—her words—after dinner. Do you think she's getting Alzheimer's?"

"No, it's . . . well, it's a long story."

"Believe me, for this one I've got as long as it takes."

Then a beep and the Palavatar-lady asked me if I wished to go to automatic. I pressed Two for no.

"Your manually controlled call is being continued," she said.

So I started telling Kelly the story. "See, I got this offer from a phone company and—"

The line buzzed static for a few seconds. Then the lady from Palavatar came back on. "Warning, your Palavatar pilot customer status is commercially confidential. Any communication about Palavatar via speech, text, or other symbolic medium is a breach of contract and may result in prosecution. Your call has been terminated."

Well, that told me.

Kelly rang me back, and this time I decided what the hell, let Palavatar sort it out, so I went to auto-reply when they offered me the option.

"You were just telling me about oral pleasure," said Kelly.

"Right," said Palavatar-me. "Except I was talking about ice cream, not, you know, anything amorous."

Hey, nice lie!

"Amorous?!" said Kelly. "Since when do you use that word?"

Oops.

Palavatar-me ignored her: "Look, I better give mother a call to explain."

So I did—or Palavatar did, after a little prologue in which the synthesised lady told me that as I had been unhappy with my previous auto-call to this number I could select a special tone-and-content setting. They gave me a list of possibles. I pressed Six, for respectful.

"Jenna, you're being nice to me," said my mother doubtfully, a few minutes into the call.

"I just wanted to say I loved you," said Palavatar-me.

"How lovely," said my mother.

And this time when the line went dead I pressed One to say I was "happy or very happy" with the outcome of the call.

So.

Welcome to the cool new future.

Of course, I still talked to Kelly manually. Sometimes. But sometimes it was easier just to let Palavatar do the talking. Palavatar-me was so much more patient. When Kelly said that I didn't get out enough, Palavatar-me didn't rise to the bait. Instead, Palavatar asked her if she happened to know where all the nice straight men were.

"Um. Try the telephone dating lines," said Kelly.

"Really?"

"No, of course not. They're sleaze central."

But what did Kelly know? She'd been single for a million years.

So I set Palavatar-me loose on the dating lines.

In two hours it had garnered the home telephone numbers of a surprisingly large number of enchanted and hopefully highly eligible male callers. I sat and real-me talked to my prospective dates.

Oh my. It was a treasure trove of horror men.

Apart from one.

His name was Ray, and he had it all. Warm voice, good sense of humour. No ties.

I went for dinner with him, and had a very nice time. Okay, so he didn't look like a movie star, but then again, neither do I.

Anyway, after the dinner with Ray I took a cab home alone, in the spirit of not hurrying things. Of course, when I got back to my apartment I wished that I had hurried things, so I real-me phoned him at midnight, from my cell phone, from bed.

"What are you thinking?" I said, huskily.

"What are you wearing?" Ray said, suddenly somewhat husky himself.

So I described what I was wearing, and what I was thinking, and what I was doing, and what I was thinking of doing.

And then Palavatar interrupted.

"This conversation violates your custom-set parameters on sexual frankness or profanity. Press One to retain those custom-set parameters. Press Two to relax those parameters temporarily. Press Three to allow full sexual and profane content."

I pressed Three, which whisked me into accepting lots of options about tone frankness and all-call permanence of settings and other stuff that I didn't pay attention to, what with Ray waiting.

"I'm back," I said, when I'd pressed Three enough times to be allowed back to manual.

"Mmmmm," he said.

And that was the start of a very nice conversation.

It was so nice that I asked him whether he'd like to come to my apartment, like, now. I wanted to see what sex was like with Ray in real-land, not telephone-land.

He came round.

Sex, sadly, wasn't nearly as good in real-land. It was so much better when I was calling him on manual.

But I didn't get a chance to tell him that. When he'd finished—which, incidentally, was well before I had—he fell straight asleep.

On waking the next morning it took me five seconds to work out who the man beside me was, one second to remember why I didn't want to see him again, and a depressing few minutes while I gathered he wasn't going to wake up any time soon. So I lay there, idly thinking about love and life and the Palavatar system, and how last night I'd changed—

"—the parameters!!!" I screamed, as I realised all at once what I'd done by pressing option Three too many times the night before.

"Where!?!" shouted Ray, sitting bolt upright.

I ignored him and ran to the other room. I picked up the phone and listened to a few seconds of Palavatar-me talking to a telephone sales person who was trying to sell me life insurance.

Oh. God.

Palavatar-me was making these breathy little moan-of-appreciation things that I thought I recognised from my call with Ray the night before.

Oh God.

I got through to my Palavatar options and changed them all to super-respectful, without even a hint of anything indecorous.

That took care of the future.

But what about the recent past? I dreaded finding out how many messages I had.

I imagined horrified messages from my mother, my sister, and one from the people in white coats telling me they were coming to take me away.

I dialled my answerphone.

"You have no new messages," said Palavatar.

I swore a lot in gratitude at the synthesised tidings, and then I caught sight of myself in the mirror. Stark naked, raving at the phone.

Ray stuck his head round the door, took one look, and didn't have to be told that this was not the moment for a glowing debriefing on his performance last night. He left in a hurry, with a Michael-Douglas-begins-to-see-Glenn-Close-in-a-new-light sort of expression.

He left in such a hurry that he forgot his cell phone.

Which was handy, as there was still the problem of incoming calls that might have been answered by Palavatar-me.

I rang mother. Luckily, she hadn't called.

Unluckily, Kelly had.

"Jenna, what you suggested earlier was illegal," she said, when I got through to her. "I'm your sister."

"Listen, I need to tell you a bunch of stuff. My phone's been, er, hacked. Yes, hacked. It wasn't me that you spoke to."

And then I told her the whole story, from the beginning. I was using Ray's cell phone, so the synthesised lady couldn't touch me.

I told Kelly about Palavatar-me and all those dreaded option Threes I'd pressed. I told her about phone sex and auto-call. I told her everything.

"But that's terrible!" she said, at the end of the story.

"I know, think of it—if mother had phoned and I'd done all that moaning to her! She'd have had me committed!"

"No, not the sex stuff. It's the other stuff," she said. "It's the you stuff! You used the auto-call on me and I didn't notice that I wasn't talking to you! You realise what this means?"

"What?"

"It means you're not a very complex system. That's horrible!"

"I am complex too," I said.

"If I can't tell the real-you from the Palavatar-you then that means you're no more complicated than the Palavatar programming code. It's called the Turing Test. It's sort of backwards, in this case, but—look, the point is that the algorithms of some shady telecoms company captured you! They captured your whole being, and it even fooled me, your sister. What does that say about your personality, huh?"

"What does that say about your listening skills? Huh?" I said.

"Hang on, let me think for a minute."

I sat and listened to the cogs whirr.

When she came back she was breathless with excitement. "Oh my God, listen! We're all basically digital systems, at the neuronal level. But just because the neuronal permutations are supermassive doesn't mean that there aren't stereotyped behaviours, which are equivalent to attractors in phase space!"

I tried to sound enthusiastic, but Kelly always gets too technical too fast.

"God, it's beautiful. You could draw a map in a zillion dimensions and we'd all cluster in this sort of hyperdimensional—"

"Kelly, focus! What do I do from now on? I want to be a complex system!"

"Oh," she said, reluctantly coming back to earth. She always preferred theory to practice. "Well, I guess you have to start living on your terms, not theirs. When offered a list of options, press Ten on your telephone keypad," she said.

"There is no Ten on the telephone keypad," I said.

"Exactly! Get out of the option tree! Think blue sky!"

"I hate flying, you know that."

"Do anything!" she said. "Do everything you've never wanted to do and see if you like it."

"Such as?"

"Don't ask me, think for yourself. That's the whole point. Look, do you mind if I write up the hyperdimensional thing? God, it's beautiful."

My sister always had the strangest taste.

But I took her advice.

I severed my Palavatar contract and for the next few weeks I tried to metaphorically press Ten a lot. I tried kickboxing, which was fun, and pottery, which wasn't. I tried to listen to jazz, but it reminded me of cats fighting so I turned it off. I have a cat allergy you wouldn't believe.

I went a whole day without television. Boy did the time pass slowly.

And I even went to Cousin Steven's wedding. The scenery was great.

But as for the rest . . . well, it was the final straw.

So I phoned Kelly, when I came back from Cornwall.

"Look," I said. "It's not working. I still want to watch old episodes of Friends. I still want to—"

"Jenna, listen!" she said. "It's okay! I've realised you can't get out of the option tree—no one can. If you try to be really really different, like say you get the faces of astronauts tattooed on your butt, then you just end up in the 'really really different' category of people, along with golf-cart enthusiasts and Klingon translators. So whatever you do, you're doomed to be in one herd or another."

"Aw," I said. "Cheer me up why don't you."

"But this is the great thing," she said. "You will always be a bit different!"

"How so?"

"Because now you're a psycho-socio-mathematical Thing!"

I told her that didn't sound so good.

"But it is! It's the Jenna Set! I wrote an article on all this and named a hyperdimensional point-set after you. I'll send you a copy of the journal article if you want."

"Yeah?" I said, wondering if I should feel honoured or cheapened.

"Jenna, it's a great honour. Your name will live forever!"

"Aw," I said, trying to sound humble.

But though Kelly had described a hyperdimensional point-set— and named it after me—she didn't have any luck tracking down the people behind Palavatar.

She wanted to credit them in her article, but they had disappeared. All the customer service numbers were disconnected, and Google drew a blank on Palavatar apart from a part-word match in some Finnish pdf files. But Kelly said every word ever gets a partial match in Finnish pdf files. It's that kind of language.

So she asked around among her hacker friends, to see if they'd heard any rumours.

The rumour with the most substance was that Palavatar was all a school-science-project-slash-hacker-joke, created by this girl genius called Abbie. According to the rumour, there was only ever one pilot customer.

Abbie was no longer to be found, and everything had been shut down.

But then I got an email, from Palavatar.

> Hey Jenna!
> Hope I didn't mess up your life.
> Want to do coffee?
> Abbie

I hit Reply. We fixed a time and place.

When I got to the coffee shop there was a teenage girl sitting by the window, looking like she was waiting for someone.

Such youth, such genius.

"Abbie?" I said.

"Uh, no," she said.

I waited for her to explain that Abbie was her hacker name and that her real name was Helen or something, but she didn't. She just stared at me. "Uh, get out of my face," she said.

"You're nothing to do with Palavatar?"

"My Dad's a policeman," she said. "Want me to call him?"

Then there was a cough behind me. I turned round. A super skinny guy with a programmer's tan was standing there.

"Jenna, I'm Abbie," he said.

"You sure?" I said. "The grapevine said you were a—"

"That was my cover. Can I buy you a coffee?"

I thought about it.

What if he spiked my drink and I woke up in a room with wall-to-wall UNIX manuals?

Well, it would remind me of my sister's place, that's what.

So I said yes.

"Great!" he said, too enthusiastically.

And then I had a nasty thought: was I on an inadvertent date?

"Look, Abbie, I should tell you I'm taken," I lied.

He looked horrified. "Not you. I'm not interested in you."

Then he tried to dig himself out of the hole. "I mean, I did want to meet you, sure. But I was hoping you would put in a word for me. With, you know . . ."

"With who?"

He gave me the look that Kelly gives me when I'm missing something obvious.

And then I got it. "My sister?"

Well, it made sense. Kelly was a techie too. And kind of blunt. In fact, I could almost hear the wedding bells.

"You must have her number already, from the system," I said.

"Yeah, but all my exes say I'm really bad on the phone. It's why I invented Palavatar. It was only intended for me, but you rang our number when I was trying to see if it would generate calls from my sister."

"Your sister recommended Palavatar to me?"

"No, it was on auto-reply when you rang. Palavatar recommended itself."

I was getting travel sick. I needed solid ground.

"So who was the woman I spoke to about setting up the system?"

"That's my mother. I mean, that's her voice. But it was Palavatar really. See, the really beautiful thing about it is—"

"Okay! Okay! I'll phone Kelly," I said. I could sense that he was going to get technical really fast.

So I dialled my sister there and then. I told her the situation. Then I put her on with him.

All his exes were right. He was terrible on the phone: ten minutes later he was still gabbling on to her about the potential for auto-call generation in the age of the videophone. And she was gabbling back.

When they got on to talking about fuzzy databases for MPEG webcam-grabs I decided enough was enough. Plus I could hear moans of appreciation from Kelly's side of the conversation.

Third-party phone sex has never been my thing.

But talking of phone sex . . .

Just as I got back to my apartment my cell phone rang.

I looked at the screen to see who was ringing me.

The screen said JENNA CALLING.

Good old me, always good to hear from her.

My stomach did that thing it had taken to doing, each time her name came up on my phone.

"Hi," I said.

"Hi," said a warm voice, with a good sense of humour. And no ties to speak of, apart from with me. "Are you in the mood for—"

See, when Ray scooted out of my apartment that morning after our first date and left his cell phone, it was because he'd picked up my cell phone by mistake. So when he realised his mistake he rang his cell phone from mine and apologised for his less-than-stellar performance the night before.

"Yeah, I noticed that," I said, still cross he'd gone to sleep. But sort of admiring his bravery for bringing it up. And, to be honest, rather liking his shrewdness in noticing that I hadn't been swinging from the chandelier with joy.

"Will you let me buy you dinner again?" he said.

I told him I was a modern woman, not a pet. I could buy my own dinner, thank you very much.

"In that case," he said, persisting in a likeable way, "will you let me let you buy me dinner?"

I spent twenty seconds sorting out the grammar of that offer.

"Would that be something you'd be interested in?" he said, tentatively.

The last time I'd answered yes to that question I'd got in all sorts of trouble.

On the other hand, he had a warm voice, a good sense of humour, we'd had a good time on the phone and at dinner, and he'd noticed that I hadn't even come close to orgasm the night before and that is a rare gift, I'm telling you, so . . .

"Yes," I said.

And yes, we had oral pleasure on my couch afterwards.

And yes, Ray knew the merits of not getting too technical too quickly.

Moving swiftly on.

We dated for a few months.

I finally bit the bullet and introduced Ray and Abbie, who after several hours of awkward conversational false starts found they shared a passion for cricket, of all godforsaken things. But it keeps them happy at social occasions.

And at least cricket was a step up on Ray and Kelly, who were still having hours of awkward false starts trying to find the faintest interest they had in common.

In the end it got too painful.

"Hey," I said to them. "You have me in common."

Kelly's eyes went wide.

"God, that's beautiful!" she said. Then she went and found Abbie and told him what I'd said.

"God, that's beautiful!" he said, understanding instantly.

I didn't, of course.

The joint paper they published on the new discovery wasn't any help, to be honest, but after several evenings of explanation with diagrams on crumpled-up napkins, and stacked-up chess boards representing N-dimensional something or other, they said that—

Or we could just cut to the chase.

In their joint paper they noted that people, as well having interests in common, can also have friends and family in common, who aren't represented in Jenna Space, as they call it.

I'm not just a Set, I'm also a Space.

I try to stay humble.

But—funnily enough—my boyfriend is one of the few men in the world who can keep me humble.

Because, wouldn't you know it, there's such a thing as Ray Space now, where people are defined not by their interests but by people they know.

"Of course," said Kelly, "if you're a Kevin Bacon fan you might know some of this stuff already." As if that explained everything.

But, apparently, Kelly and Abbie have added some new twists, because there's also such a thing as Negative Jenna Space, in which you're defined by all the things you find horrifically boring or obnoxious—like motor racing, in my case—and there's also Negative Ray Space which is pretty much the same, but with cousins instead of cars.

The Negative Spaces are all terribly exciting, and it all makes perfect sense if you think of the set of actors who Kevin Bacon refuses to work with.

Or I'm told that it all makes sense, if you think of that.

I smile nicely and try not to let on that I don't quite understand where Kevin Bacon comes into things, although he was very fine in *Stir of Echoes* which is highly recommended if you like very spooky horror films in which cute boy actors go around with their shirts off.

Ray, on the other hand, likes spooky horror films in which cute girl actors go around with their shirts off.

He's rather mannish, in that respect.

And that, finally, is our secret.

We have similar interests, but not identical.

And yes, I mentioned that idly to Kelly and Abbie, who got all excited and started measuring frequencies of average Jenna Space interest-distances in all the couples they knew. There's an optimum range of values, apparently, which Abbie and Kelly call the Hot Spot, and—wouldn't you know—Ray and I fall bang smack in the middle with a score of 1.772, which is now the JennaRay Number and means that our relationship is enshrined forever in psycho-socio-mathematical law.

"Is that better than being married?" I said to Kelly and Abbie. "I mean, it sounds very pleasing and solid, but is that bond stronger or weaker than—"

Their eyes went wide.

"God, that's beauti—"

I covered my ears and started singing to myself so I couldn't hear them.

A girl can spark off too many mathematical papers, you know. It can get kind of wearing.

But when Kelly wrestled my hands from my ears and stopped me singing she was breathless and excited but not about maths at all.

"Let's all get married!" she said. "The four of us! A double wedding!"

"But no maths," I said, wanting to take a stand before I said yes. After all, I didn't want to find I was vowing to uphold the value of pi or anything.

"No maths at all," she said. "Although of course we'll seat the guests by minimising the distance between neighbours in Ray Space and Jenna Space, while maximising their Negative Ray Space and Negative Jenna Space distances."

"What does that mean?" I said.

"That means Cousin Steven sits with the caterers," said Abbie. And that decided it.

Though of course I hadn't, technically, asked Ray to marry me yet.

So I waited for an opportune moment. A trip to Paris, say, or a walk along a starlit beach. But as we showed no sign of doing either of those things in the next few hours—and as I'm impatient—I chomped down on the bullet and selected the next most opportune moment.

That evening we were sitting on my couch, after oral pleasure. Of the ice-cream variety.

I idly brought up the subject of marriage and watched him closely for signs of falling off the couch in shock and fear.

He remained admirably vertical.

"Marriage?" he said.

"Would . . . would that be something you are interested in?" I said.

"Yes," he said, with a big soppy smile. He kissed me. I kissed him back.

Then I looked round for orchestras and fireworks and happy couples on gondolas, applauding, like they always do in movies when the leads get engaged, but as we were alone in my apartment there was a shortage of those sorts of things.

So instead we clinked our spoons in a celebratory manner, and finished off the rest of the ice cream.

Then we switched off every phone in the house and went to bed.

And then we tried to reduce to zero the distance between Jenna Space and Ray Space.

Which, according to a forthcoming joint paper by a certain couple, is mathematically impossible.

But, what do you know, we just did great.

UNDERSTANDING SPACE AND TIME

Alastair Reynolds

"Mars ain't the kind of place to raise your kids"

Part One

Something very strange appeared in the outer recreation bubble on the day that Katrina Solovyova died. When he saw it, John Renfrew rushed back to the infirmary where he had left her. Solovyova had been slipping in and out of lucidity for days, but when he arrived he was glad to find her still conscious. She seldom turned her face away from the picture window, transfixed by the silent and vast twilight landscape beyond the armoured glass. Hovering against the foothills of Pavonis Mons, her reflection was all highlights, as if sketched in bold strokes of chalk.

Renfrew caught his breath before speaking.

"I've seen a piano."

At first he did not think she had heard him. Then the reflection of Solovyova's mouth formed words.

"You've seen a *what*?"

"A piano," Renfrew said, laughing. "A big, white, Bösendorfer grand."

"You're crazier than me."

"It was in the recreation bubble," Renfrew said. "The one that took a lightning hit last week. I think it fried something. Or unfried something, maybe. Brought something back to life."

"A piano?"

"It's a start. It means things aren't totally dead. That there's a glimmer of . . . something."

"Well, isn't that the nicest timing," Solovyova said.

With a creak of his knees Renfrew knelt by her bedside. He'd connected Solovyova to a dozen or so medical monitors, only three of which were working properly. They hummed, hissed and bleeped with deadening regularity. When it began to seem like music—when he started hearing hidden harmonies and tonal shifts—Renfrew knew it was time to get out of the infirmary. That was why he had gone to the recreation bubble: there was no music there, but at least he could sit in silence.

"Nicest timing?" he said.

"I'm dying. Nothing that happens now will make any difference to me."

"But maybe it would," Renfrew said. "If the rec systems are capable of coming back on line, what else might be? Maybe I could get the infirmary back up and running . . . the diagnostic suite . . . the drug synth . . ." He gestured at the banks of dead grey monitors and cowled machines parked against the wall. They were covered in scuffed decals and months of dust.

"Pray for another lightning strike, you mean?"

"No . . . not necessarily." Renfrew chose his words with care. He did not want to offer Solovyova false optimism, but the apparition had made him feel more positive than at any time he could remember since the Catastrophe. They could not unmake the deaths of all the other colonists, or unmake the vastly larger death that even now it was difficult mention. But if some of the base systems they had assumed broken could be brought back, he might at least find a way to keep Solovyova alive.

"What, then?"

"I don't know. But now that I know that things aren't as bad as we feared . . ." He trailed off. "There are lots of things I could try again. Just because they didn't work first time . . ."

"You probably imagined the piano."

"I know I didn't. It was a genuine projection, not a hallucination."

"And this piano . . ." The reflection froze momentarily. "How long did it last, Renfrew? I mean, just out of curiosity?"

"Last?"

"That's what I asked."

"It's still there," he said. "It was still there when I left. Like it was waiting for someone to come and play it."

The figure in the bed moved slightly.

"I don't believe you."

"I can't show you, Solovyova. I wish I could, but . . ."

"I'll die? I'm going to die anyway, so what difference does it make?" She paused, allowing the melancholic chorus of the machines to swell and fill the room. "Probably by the end of the week. And all I've got to look forward to is the inside of this room or the view out this window. At least let me see something different."

"Is this what you really want?"

Solovyova's reflection tipped in acknowledgement. "Show me the piano, Renfrew. Show me you aren't making this shit up."

He thought about it for a minute, perhaps two, and then dashed back to the recreation bubble to check that the piano was still there. The journey took several minutes even at a sprint, through sunken tunnels and window-lined connecting bridges, up and down grilled ramps, through ponderous internal airlocks and sweltering aeroponics labs, taking this detour or that to avoid a blown bubble or failed airlock.

Parts of the infrastructure creaked ominously as he passed through. Here and there his feet crunched through the sterile red dust that was always finding ways to seep through seals and cracks. Everything was decaying, falling apart. Even if the dead had been brought back to life the base would not have been able to support more than a quarter of their number. But the piano represented something other than the slow grind of entropy. If one system had survived apparent failure, the same might be true of others.

He reached the bubble, his eyes closed as he crossed the threshold. He half expected the piano to be gone, never more than a trick of the mind. Yet there it was: still manifesting, still hovering a few inches from the floor. Save for that one suggestion of ghostliness, it appeared utterly solid, as real as anything else in the room. It was a striking pure white, polished to a lambent gloss. Renfrew strode around it, luxuriating in the conjunction of flat planes and luscious curves. He had not noticed this detail before, but the keys were still hidden under the folding cover.

He admired the piano for several more minutes, forgetting his earlier haste. It was as beautiful as it was chilling.

Remembering Solovyova, he returned to the infirmary.

"You took your time," she said.

"It's still there, but I had to be sure. You certain you want to see it?"

"I haven't changed my mind. Show me the damned thing."

With great gentleness he unplugged the vigilant machines and wheeled them aside. He could not move the bed, so he took Solov-yova from it and placed her in a wheelchair. He had long grown ac-customed to how frail human bodies felt in Martian gravity, but the ease with which he lifted her was shocking, and a reminder of how close to death she was.

He'd hardly known her before the Catastrophe. Even in the days that followed—as the sense of isolation closed in on the base, and the first suicides began—it had taken a long time for them to drift together. It had happened at a party, the one that the colonists had organised to celebrate the detection of a radio signal from Earth; originating from an organised band of survivors in New Zealand. In New Zealand they had still had something like a government, some-thing like society, with detailed plans for long-term endurance and reconstruction. And for a little while it had seemed that the survi-vors might—by some unexplained means—have acquired immunity to the weaponised virus that had started scything its way through the rest of humanity in June 2038.

They hadn't. It just took a little longer than average to wipe them out.

Renfrew pushed her along the tortuous route that led back to the bubble.

"Why a . . . what did you call it?"

"A Bösendorfer. A Bösendorfer grand piano. I don't know. That's just what it said."

"Something it dragged up from its memory? Was it making any music?"

"No. Not a squeak. The keyboard was hidden under a cover."

"There must be someone to play it," Solovyova said.

"That's what I thought." He pushed her onward. "Music would make a difference, at least. Wouldn't it?"

"Anything would make a difference."

Except not for Solovyova, he thought. Very little was going to make a difference for Solovyova from this point on.

"Renfrew . . ." Solovyova said, her tone softer than before. "Renfrew, when I'm gone . . . you'll be all right, won't you?"

"You shouldn't worry about me."

"It wouldn't be human not to. I'd change places if I could."

"Don't be daft."

"You were a good man. You didn't deserve to be the last of us."

Renfrew tried to sound dignified. "Some might say being the

last survivor is a sort of privilege."

"But not me. I don't envy you. I know for a fact I couldn't handle it."

"Well, I can. I looked at my psychological evaluation. Practical, survivor mentality, they said."

"I believe it," Solovyova said. "But don't let it get to you. Understand? Keep some self respect. For all of us. For me."

He knew exactly what she meant by that.

The recreation bubble loomed around the curve in the corridor. There was a moment of trepidation as they neared, but then he saw the white corner of the floating piano, still suspended in the middle of the room, and sighed with relief.

"Thank God," he said. "I didn't imagine it."

He pushed Solovyova into the bubble, halting the wheelchair before the hovering apparition. Its immense mass reminded him of a chiselled cloud. The polished white gleam was convincing, but there was no sign of their own reflections within it. Solovyova said nothing, merely staring into the middle of the room.

"It's changed," he said. "Look. The cover's gone up. You can see the keys. They look so real . . . I could almost reach out and touch them. Except I can't play the piano." He grinned back at the woman in the wheelchair. "Never could. Never had a musical bone in my body."

"There is no piano, Renfrew."

"Solovyova?"

"I said, there is no piano. The room is empty." Her voice was dead, utterly drained of emotion. She did not even sound disappointed or annoyed. "There is no piano. No grand piano. No Bösendorfer grand piano. No keyboard. No nothing. You're hallucinating, Renfrew. You're imagining the piano."

He looked at her in horror. "I can still see it. It's here." He reached out to the abstract white mass. His fingers punched through its skin, into thin air. But he had expected that.

He could still see the piano.

It was real.

"Take me back to the infirmary, Renfrew. Please." Solovyova paused. "I think I'm ready to die now."

He put on a suit and buried Solovyova beyond the outer perimeter, close to the mass grave where he had buried the last survivors when

Solovyova had been too weak to help. The routine felt familiar enough, but when Renfrew turned back to the base he felt a wrenching sense of difference. The low-lying huddle of soil-covered domes, tubes and cylinders hadn't changed in any tangible way, except that it was now truly uninhabited. He was walking back toward an empty house, and even when Solovyova had been ill—even when Solovyova had been only half present—that had never been the case.

The moment reached a kind of crescendo. He considered his options. He could return to the base, alone, and survive months or years on the dwindling resources at his disposal. Tharsis Base would keep him alive indefinitely provided he did not fall ill: food and water were not a problem, and the climate recycling systems were deliberately rugged. But there would be no companionship. No network, no music or film, no television or VR. Nothing to look forward to except endless bleak days until something killed him.

Or he could do it here, *now*. All it would take was a twist of his faceplate release control. He had already worked out how to override the safety lock. A few roaring seconds of pain and it would all be over. And if he lacked the courage to do it that way—and he thought he probably did—then he could sit down and wait until his air-supply ran low.

There were a hundred ways he could do it, if he had the will.

He looked at the base, stark under the pale butterscotch of the sky. The choice was laughably simple. Die here now, or die in there, much later. Either way, his choice would be unrecorded. There would be no eulogies to his bravery, for there was no one left to write eulogies.

"Why me?" he asked, aloud. "Why is it me who has to go through with this?"

He'd felt no real anger until that moment. Now he felt like shouting, but all he could do was fall to his knees and whimper. The question circled in his head, chasing its own tail.

"Why me," he said. "Why is it me? Why the fuck is it *me* who has to ask this question?"

Finally he fell silent. He remained frozen in that position, staring down through the scuffed glass of his faceplate at the radiation-blasted soil between his knees. For five or six minutes he listened to the sound of his own sobbing. Then a small, polite voice advised him that he needed to return to the base to replenish his air supply. He listened to that voice as it shifted from polite to stern, then from stern to strident, until it was screaming into his skull, the boundary of his faceplate flashing brilliant red.

Then he stood up, already light-headed, already feeling the weird euphoric intoxication of asphyxia, and made his ambling way back toward the base.

He had made a choice. Like it said in the psych report, he was a practical-minded, survivor type. He would not give in.

Not until it got a lot harder.

Renfrew made it through his first night alone.

It was easier than he had expected, although he was careful not to draw any comfort from that. He knew that there would be much harder days and nights ahead. It might happen a day or a week or even a year from now, but when it did he was sure that his little breakdown outside would shrink to insignificance. For now he was stumbling through fog, fully aware that a precipice lay before him, and also that he would have to step over that precipice if he hoped to find anything resembling mental equilibrium and true acceptance.

He wandered the corridors and bubbles of the base. Everything looked shockingly familiar. Books were where he had left them; the coffee cups and dishes still waiting to be washed. The views through the windows hadn't become mysteriously more threatening overnight, and he had no sense that the interior of the base had become less hospitable. There were no strange new sounds to make the back of his neck tingle; no shadows flitting at the corner of his eye, no blood freezing sense of scrutiny by an unseen watcher.

And yet . . . and yet. He knew something was not quite right. After he had attended to his usual chores—cleaning this or that air filter, lubricating this or that seal, scrutinising the radio logs to make sure no one had attempted contact from home—he again made his way to the recreation bubble.

The piano was still there, but something was different about it today. Now there was a single gold candelabra sitting above the keyboard. The candles burned, wavering slightly.

It was as if the piano was readying itself.

Renfrew leaned through the piano and passed his fingers through the candle flames. They were as insubstantial as the instrument itself. Even so, he could not help but sniff the tips of his fingers.

His brain refused to accept that the flames were unreal, and expected a whiff of carbon or charred skin.

Renfrew remembered something.

He had spent so long in the base, so long inside its electronic cocoon, that until this moment he had forgotten precisely how the bubble worked. The things that appeared inside it were not true holograms, but projections mapped into his visual field. They were woven by tiny implants buried in the eye, permitting the images to have a sense of solidity that would have been impossible with any kind of projected hologram. The surgical procedure to embed the implants had taken about thirty seconds, and from that moment on he had never really needed to think about it. The implants allowed the base staff to digest information in vastly richer form than allowed by flat screens and clumsy holographics. When Renfrew examined a mineral sample, for instance, the implant would overlay his visual impression of the rock with an X-ray tomographic view of the rock's interior. The implants had also permitted access to recreational recordings . . . but Renfrew had always been too busy for that kind of thing. When the implants began to fail—they'd never been designed to last more than a year or two in vivo, before replacement—Renfrew had thought no more of the matter.

But what if his had started working again? In that case it was no wonder Solovyova had not been able to see the piano. Some projection system had decided to switch on again, accessing some random fragment from the entertainment archives, and his reactivated implant had chosen to allow him to see it.

It meant there was still a kind of hope.

"Hello."

Renfrew flinched at the voice. The source of it was immediately obvious: a small man had appeared out of nowhere at the end of the piano. The small man stood for a moment, pivoting around as if to acknowledge a vast and distant invisible audience, his eyes—largely hidden behind ostentatious pink glasses—only meeting Renfrew's for the briefest of instants. The man settled into a stool that had also appeared at the end of the piano, tugged up the sleeves of the plum paisley suit jacket he wore, and began to play the piano. The man's fingers were curiously stubby, but they moved up and down the keyboard with a beguiling ease.

Transfixed, Renfrew listened to the man play. It was the first real music he had heard in two years. The man could have played the most uncompromisingly difficult exercise in atonality and it would still have sounded agreeable to Renfrew's ears. But it was much easier than that. The man played the piano and sang a song; one that Renfrew recognised—albeit barely—from his childhood. It had been an old song even then, but one that was still played on the radio with some regularity. The man sang about a trip to Mars: a song about a man who did not expect to see home again.

The song concerned a rocket man.

Renfrew maintained the ritual that he and Solovyova had established before her death. Once a week, without fail, he cocked an ear to Earth to see if anyone was sending.

The ritual had become less easy in recent weeks. The linkage between the antenna and the inside of the base was broken, so he had to go outside to perform the chore. It meant pre-breathing; it meant suiting up; it meant a desolate trudge from the airlock to the ladder on the side of the comms module, and then a careful ascent to the module's roof, where the antenna was mounted on a turret-like plinth. He'd spend at least half an hour scooping handfuls of storm dust from the steering mechanism, before flipping open the cover on the manual control panel, powering up the system and tapping a familiar string of commands into the keyboard.

After a few moments the antenna would begin to move, grinding as it overcame the resistance of the dust that had already seeped into its innards. It swung and tilted on multiple axes, until the openwork mesh of the dish was locked onto the Earth. Then the system waited and listened, LEDs blinking on the status board, but none of them brightening to the hard, steady green that would mean the antenna had locked onto the expected carrier signal. Occasionally the lights would flicker green, as if the antenna was picking up ghost echoes from *something* out there, but they never lasted.

Renfrew had to keep trying. He wasn't expecting rescue, not any more. He'd resigned himself to the idea that he was going to die on Mars, alone. But it would still be some comfort to know that there were survivors back on Earth; that there were still people who could begin to rebuild civilisation. Better still if they had the kindness to signal him, to let him know what was happening. Even if only a few thousand people had survived, it wouldn't take much for one of them to remember the Mars colony, and wonder what was happening up there.

But Earth remained silent. Some part of Renfrew knew that there would never be a signal, no matter how many times he swung the dish around and listened. And one day soon the dish was simply not going to work, and he was not going to be able to repair it. Dutifully, when he had powered down the antenna and returned to the inside of the base, he made a neat entry in the communications log, signing his name at the top of the page.

On his rounds of the base, Renfrew made similar entries in many other logs. He noted breakdowns and his own ramshackle repair efforts. He took stock of spare parts and tools, entering the broken or life-expired items into the resupply request form. He noted the health of the plants in the aeroponics lab, sketching their leaves and marking the ebb and flow of various diseases. He kept a record of the Martian weather, as it tested the base's integrity, and at the back of his mind he always imagined Solovyova nodding in approval, pleased with his stoic refusal to slide into barbarism.

But in all his bookkeeping, Renfrew never once referred to the man at the piano. He couldn't quite explain this omission, but something held him back from mentioning the apparition. He felt he could rationalise the appearance of the piano, even of the personality that was programmed to play it, but he still wasn't sure that any of it was real.

Not that that stopped the piano man from appearing.

Once or twice a day, most days, he assumed existence at the piano and played a song or two. Sometimes Renfrew was there when it happened; sometimes he was elsewhere in the base and he heard the music starting up. Always he dropped whatever he was doing and raced to the recreation bubble, and listened.

The tunes were seldom the same from day to day, and the small man himself never looked quite the same. His clothes were always different, but there was more to it than that. Sometimes he had a shapeless mop of auburn hair. At other times he was balding or concealed his crown beneath a variety of ostentatious hats. He frequently wore glasses of elaborate, ludicrous design.

The man had never introduced himself, but once or twice Renfrew felt that he was close to remembering his name. He racked his memory for the names of twentieth century musicians, feeling sure it would come to him eventually.

In the meantime he found that it helped to have someone to talk to. Between songs the man would sometimes sit silently, hands folded in his lap, as if waiting for some instruction or request from Renfrew. That was when Renfrew talked aloud, unburdening himself of whatever thoughts had been spinning around in his skull since the last visitation. He told the man about the problems with the base, about his loneliness, about the despair he felt every time the antenna failed to pick up anything from Earth. And the man simply sat and listened, and when Renfrew was done—when he had said his piece- the man would unlace his fingers and start playing something.

Now and then the man *did* speak, but he never seemed to be addressing Renfrew so much as a larger unseen audience. He'd introduce the songs, tell a few jokes between numbers, throw out an offer to take requests. Renfrew sometimes answered, sometimes tried to persuade the pianist to play one of the songs he'd already performed, but nothing he said seemed to reach through to the man.

But still: it was better than nothing. Although the style of the music never varied greatly, and one or two of the songs began occasionally to chafe at Renfrew's nerves, he was generally happiest when the music was playing. He liked *A Song For Guy, I Guess That's Why They Call It The Blues, Tiny Dancer*. When the piano man was playing, he did not feel truly alone.

Renfrew made a point of tending to Solovyova's grave. He cared about the other dead, but Solovyova mattered more: she'd been the last to go, the last human being Renfrew would ever know in his life. It would be too much work to keep the dust from covering the mass burial site, but he could at least do something for Solovyova. Sometimes he detoured to clean her grave when he was outside on the antenna duty; other times he pre-breathed and suited up just for Solovyova, and always when he returned to the base he felt cleansed, renewed of purpose, determined that he could get through the days ahead.

That feeling didn't last long. But at least tending the grave kept the darkness at bay for a while.

There were moments when his stratagems failed, when the reality of his situation came crashing back in its full existential horror, but when that happened he was able to slam a mental door almost as soon as the scream had begun. As time had passed he had found that he became more adept at it, so that the moments of horror became only instants, like blank white frames spliced into the movie of his life.

When he was outside, he often found himself watching the sky, especially when the cold sun was low and twilight stars began to stud the butterscotch sky. A thought occurred to him, clean and bright and diamond hard: humanity might be gone, but did that necessarily mean he was the last intelligent creature in the universe? What if there was someone *else* out there?

How did that change the way he felt?

And what if there was in fact no one else out there at all: just empty light years, empty parsecs, empty megaparsecs, all the way out to furthest, faintest galaxies, teetering on the very edge of the visible universe?

How did *that* make him feel?

Cold. Alone. Fragile.

Curiously precious.

Part Two

Weeks slipped into months, months slipped into a long Martian year. The base kept functioning, despite Renfrew's grimmest expectations. Certain systems actually seemed to be more stable than at any time since Solovyova's death, as if they'd grudgingly decided to cooperate in keeping him alive. For the most part, Renfrew was glad that he did not have to worry about the base failing him. It was only in his darkest moments that he wished for the base to kill him, swiftly, painlessly, perhaps when he was already asleep and dreaming of better times. There'd be nothing undignified about going out that way; nothing that violated the terms of his vow with Solovyova. She wouldn't think badly of him for wishing death on those terms.

But the fatal failure never came, and for many days in a given month Renfrew managed not to think about suicide. He supposed that he had passed through the anger and denial phases of his predicament, into something like acceptance.

It helped to have someone to talk to.

He spoke to the piano man a lot now, quite unselfconsciously. The odd thing was that the piano man spoke back, too. On one level, Renfrew was well aware that the responses were entirely in his imagination; that his brain had started filling in the other half of the one-sided conversation, based around the speech patterns that the piano man used between songs. On another level the responses seemed completely real and completely outside his own control, as if he no longer had access to the part of his brain that was generating them. A form of psychosis, perhaps: but even if that were the case, it was benign, even comforting, in its effects. If the thing that kept him sane was a little self-administered madness, confined solely to the piano man, then that seemed a small price to pay.

He still didn't know the man's real name. It was nearly there, but Renfrew could never quite bring it to mind. The piano man offered no clues. He introduced his songs by name, often spinning elaborate stories around them, but never had cause to say who he was. Renfrew had tried to access the rec system's software files, but he'd given up as soon as he was confronted by screen after screen of scrolling possibilities. He could have delved deeper, but he was wary of breaking the fragile spell that had brought the piano man into existence in the first place. Renfrew reckoned it was better not to know, than lose that one flicker of companionship.

"It's not exactly a rich human life," Renfrew said.

"Probably not." Piano Man glanced at the window, out towards the point where the others had been buried. "But you have to admit. It's a hell of a lot better than the alternative."

"I suppose so," Renfrew said doubtfully. "But what am I meant to do with the rest of my life? I can't just mope around here until I drop dead."

"Well, that's always one possibility. But what about doing something a little bit more constructive?"

Piano Man fingered the keys, sketching a tune.

"Learn to play the piano? No point, is there? Not while you're around."

"Don't count on me always being here, luv. But I was thinking more along the lines of a bit of reading. There are books, aren't there? I mean real ones."

Renfrew imagined Piano Man miming the opening of a book. He nodded in return, without much enthusiasm. "Nearly a thousand."

"Must have cost a bomb to bring them here."

"They didn't—not most of them, anyway. They were printed locally, using recycled organic matter. The printing and binding was totally automatic, and you could ask for a copy of just about any book that had ever been printed. Of course it doesn't work now . . . the thousand is all we've got left."

"You already know this, Renfrew. Why are you telling me?"

290 | UNDERSTANDING SPACE AND TIME

"Because you asked."

"OK. Fair enough." Piano Man pushed his glasses back onto the bridge of his little nub of a nose. "A thousand books, though: that should keep you going for a while."

Renfrew shook his head. He had already glanced through the books and he knew that there were a lot less than a thousand that were of any interest to him. Most of the books had been produced purely for recreational value, since the technical journals and documentation had always been available for consultation via the optic implants or handhelds. At least two hundred volumes were children's books or juvenile material. Another three hundred were in Russian, French, Japanese or some other language he did not understand. He had time, but not *that* much time.

"So there are how many left—what? Five hundred or so that you might want to read?"

"It isn't that easy either," Renfrew said. "I tried reading fiction. Bad mistake. It was too depressing, reading about other people going about their lives before the accident."

Piano Man peered at him over the rims of his glasses. "Fussy bugger aren't you. So what's left if we throw out the fiction?"

"It doesn't get much better. Travelogues . . . historical biographies . . . atlases and books on natural history . . . all any of it does is remind me of what I'm never going to see again. Never another rainstorm. Never another bird, never another ocean, never another . . ."

"OK, point made. Fine: throw out the coffee table books— guests are going to be a bit thin on the ground anyway. What does that leave us with?"

Renfrew had done exactly that, his pile of books becoming smaller. There were philosophical texts: Wittgenstein's Philosophical Investigations; Sartre's Being and Nothingness; Foucault's The Order of Things; a dozen others.

"Who had those printed?"

"I don't know."

"Must have been a right lonely sod, whoever he was. Still; did you make any progress with them?"

"I gave them my best shot."

Renfrew had flicked through them, allured and at the same time appalled at the density of the philosophical speculation within them. On one level, they dealt with the most fundamental of human questions. But the books were so detached from anything that

Renfrew considered mundane reality that he could consult them without triggering the episodes of loss and horror that came with the other books. That was not to say that he dismissed the arguments in the books as irrelevant, but because the books dealt with human experience in the mass there was far less than pain than when Renfrew was forced to consider a specific individual other than himself. He could deal with the thought of losing the rest of humanity.

It was the idea of losing anyone specific that cut him open.

"So the heavy German guys weren't a total waste of time. All right. What else?"

"Well, there was a Bible," Renfrew said.

"Read it much?"

"Religiously." Renfrew shrugged. "Sorry. Bad joke."

"And now . . . after the accident?"

"I must admit I've started thinking about some things I never thought about before. Why we're here. Why I'm here. What it all means. What it'll all mean when I'm gone. That doesn't mean I expect to find any useful answers."

"Maybe you're not looking in quite the right place. What else was left in your pile?"

"Scientific stuff," Renfrew said. "Mathematics, quantum theory, relativity, cosmology . . ."

"I thought you told me all that stuff was available on the handhelds?"

"These are more like textbooks. Not bang up to date, but not horribly out of date either. Someone's idea of light reading."

"Looks like you're stuck with them, in that case. They shouldn't be too daunting, should they? I thought you were a scientist as well."

"A geologist," Renfrew told him. "And you don't need much tensor algebra to study rocks."

"You can always learn. You've got plenty of time. And—let's face it—it has to be easier than Japanese, doesn't it?"

"I suppose so. You still haven't told me why I should bother."

Piano Man looked at him with sudden seriousness, the mirrored facets of his glasses like holes punched through to some burnished silver realm. "Because of what you just said. Because of the questions you want answered."

"You think a load of physics books is going to make a difference?"

"That's up to you. It's all a question of how much you want to understand. How deep you want to go."

Piano Man turned back to the keyboard and started playing *Saturday Night's All Right for Fighting.*

Piano Man was right. It was a question of how deep he wanted to go.

But surely there was more to it than that. Something else was spurring him on. It felt like a weird sense of obligation, an onus that weighed upon him with pressing, judicial force. He was certain now that he was the last man alive, having long since abandoned hope that anyone was left on Earth. Was it not therefore almost required of him to come to some final understanding of what it meant to be human, achieving some final synthesis of all the disparate threads in the books before him? There could only be one witness to his success, he knew, but it seemed that if he were to fail he would be letting down the billions who had come before him. He could almost feel the weight of their expectation reaching to him from the past, urging him to come to that difficult understanding that had always eluded them. They were dead but he was still alive, and now they were looking over his shoulder, anxiously waiting to see how he solved the puzzle that had bettered them.

"Hey, genius?" Piano Man asked, a week into his study. "Solved the mysteries of the universe yet?"

"Don't be silly. I've only just begun."

"OK. But I take it you've made at least a smidgeon of progress." Piano Man wore a sparkling white suit and enormous star-shaped spectacles. He was grinning a lot and playing some of his weaker material.

"Depends what you mean by progress," Renfrew said. "If you mean absorbing what I've read, and not being thrown by anything so far . . ." He shrugged. "In that case, so far it's been a piece of piss."

"Ah-ha."

"But I'm under no illusions that it's going to stay that way. In fact I'm well aware that it's going to get a lot harder. So far all I'm doing is catching up. I haven't even begun to think about moving beyond the existing theories."

"All right. No point trying to run before you can crawl."

"Precisely."

Piano Man swept his fingers down the keys in an exuberant glissando. "But you can still tell me what you've learned, can't you?"

"Are you sure you're interested?"

"Of course I'm interested, luv. Why else would I ask?"

He told Piano Man what he had learned so far.

He had read about the dual histories of cosmology and quantum mechanics, two braids of thought that had their origins in the early twentieth century. The one dealt with the vast and ancient, the other with the microscopic and ephemeral. Cosmology encompassed galaxies and superclusters of galaxies, Hubble flows and the expansion of the universe. Quantum mechanics dealt with the fizzing, indeterminate cauldron of subatomic reality, where things could be in more than one place at once and where apparently rock-solid concepts like distance and the one-way flow of time became almost obscenely pliant.

Handling the concepts of classical cosmology required an imaginative leap, and the ability to think of space and time as facets of the same thing. But once he had made that mental adjustment, which became slightly easier with practise, Renfrew found that the rest was merely a question of elaboration of scale and complexity. It was like holding the architecture of a vast, dark cathedral in his skull. At first it required a supreme effort of will to imagine the basic components of the building: the choir, the nave, the transepts, the spire. Gradually, however, these major architectural elements became fixed in his mind and he was able to start concentrating on the embellishments, the buttresses and gargoyles. Once he was comfortable with the classical cosmological model he found it easy enough to revise his mental floor plan to accommodate inflationary cosmology and the various models that had succeeded it. The scales became vaster, the leaps of perspective all the more audacious, but he was able to envisage things within some kind of metaphoric framework, whether it was the idea of galaxies painted on the skin of an expanding balloon, or the 'phase transition' of water thawing in a frozen swimming pool.

This was not the case with quantum mechanics. Very quickly, Renfrew realised that the only tool for understanding the quantum realm was mathematics; all else failed. There were no convenient metaphors from everyday human experience to assist with the visualisation of wave-particle duality, the Heisenberg principle, quantum non-locality, or any of the other paradoxical properties of the microscopic world. The human mind had simply not evolved the appropriate mental machinery to deal with quantum concepts in the abstract. Trying to 'understand' any of it in workaday terms was futile.

Renfrew would have found this hard to accept had he not been in good company. Almost all of the great thinkers who had worked on quantum mechanics had been troubled by this to one degree or another. Some had accepted it, while others had gone to the grave with the nagging suspicion that a layer of familiar, Newtonian order lay beneath the shifting uncertainties of QM.

Even if quantum physics was 'correct', how did that fuzzy view of reality join up with the hard-edged concepts of General Relativity? The two theories were astoundingly successful at predicting the behaviour of the universe within their own specified areas of application, but all attempts to unify them had collapsed in failure. QM produced absurd results when applied to the kinds of macroscopic objects encountered in the real world: cats, boxes, Bösendorfer grand pianos, galactic superclusters. GR collapsed when it was used to probe the very small, whether it was the universe an instant after the Big Bang, or the infinitely dense, infinitely compact kernel of a black hole.

Thinkers had spent three quarters of a century chasing that fabled unification, without success. But what if all the pieces had been in place at the time of the Catastrophe, and all that was needed was someone to view them with a fresh eye?

Some chance, Renfrew thought to himself. But again he smiled. Was it arrogant to think that he could achieve what no one had managed before? Perhaps: but given the uniqueness of his situation, nothing seemed improbable. And even if he did not succeed in that task, who was to say that he would not pick up one or two useful insights along the way?

At the very least it would give him something to do.

Still, he was getting ahead of himself. He had to understand QM before he could demolish it and replace it with something even more shiny and elegant, something which at the same time would be utterly consistent with every verified prediction of GR and at the same time nicely resolve all the niggling little details of observational mismatch . . . while at the same time making testable predictions of its own.

"Are you sure you still want to go through with this?" Piano Man asked.

"Yes," Renfrew told him. "More than ever."

His companion looked out toward the burial zone. "Well, it's your funeral."

And then started playing *Candle in the Wind*.

Renfrew powered up the antenna again. Once more it laboured into life, gears crunching against the resistance of infiltrated dust as it steered onto target. It was twilight and Earth was a bright star a few degrees above the horizon. The antenna locked on, Renfrew sighting along the main axis to confirm that the device really was pointed at the planet, and wasn't misaligned due to some mechanical or software fault. As always, as near as he could judge, the dish was aimed at Earth.

He waited to see the lights on the status board, never quite able to kill the hope that the flickering signal LED would harden into a steady, insistent green, indicating that the antenna had picked up the expected carrier transmission.

Never quite able to kill the hope that someone was still sending.

But the board told him the same thing it always did. No dice: it wasn't hearing anything beyond the random snap and crackle of interplanetary static.

Renfrew tapped the buttons to tell the dish to stow itself until his next visit. He stood back from the operating panel as the machinery moved, waiting to see it stow itself safely in readiness for his next dutiful visit.

Something shone on the panel: a momentary brightening of the LED. It only lasted an instant, but it caught Renfrew's attention like a glint of gold in a prospector's stream. He'd seen the antenna slew back countless times before, and he'd never seen more than a glimmer from the LED. It had been too hard, too clear, to be caused by random contamination, and he certainly hadn't imagined it.

He told himself to be calm. If the LED had brightened when the antenna was locked onto Earth—well, that might be worth getting excited about. Might. But as it slewed back to stow, the antenna was just sweeping over empty sky.

All the same: plenty of cosmic radio signals out there, but none of them should be outputting in the narrow frequency range that the antenna was built to sniff. So maybe it had picked up something, unless the electronics were finally going south.

One way to tell.

Renfrew told the dish to track back onto Earth. He watched the board carefully this time, for he hadn't been paying attention the first time the antenna had moved.

But there it was again: that same brightening. And now that he'd seen it twice, he saw that the LED brightened and dimmed in a systematic fashion.

Exactly as if the dish was tracking across a concentrated radio source.

Exactly as if something was out there.

Renfrew backed up and repeated the cycle, using manual override to guide the antenna onto the signal. He waggled the dish until he judged that the LED was at its brightest, then watched the steady green light with a growing and cautious amazement.

He noted the coordinates of the source, remembering that he had only chanced upon it by accident, and that the same slew operation wouldn't necessarily pick up the mystery signal a day or a week from now. But if he recorded the position of the source now, and kept an eye on it from hour to hour and then day to day, he should at least be able to tell if it was an object moving inside the solar system, rather than some distant extragalactic radio source that just happened to look artificial.

Renfrew dared not invest too much hope in the detection. But if it was local, if it was coming from something within the system . . . then it might have serious implications.

Especially for him.

Renfrew's excitement was tempered with caution. He vowed not to speak of the matter to Piano Man until he could be certain that the object was all that he hoped it might be: some tangible sign that someone had survived.

He'd expected that the discovery might make it hard for him to keep his mind on his studies, like a student distracted by something more interesting out the window. But to his surprise exactly the reverse was the case. Spurred on by the possibility that his future might hold surprises, that it was not necessarily pre-ordained that he would die alone and on Mars, Renfrew found that his intellectual curiosity was actually heightened. He redoubled his efforts to understand his predicament, gulping down pages of text that had seemed opaque and impenetrable only days before, but which now seemed lucid, transparent, even childlike in their simplicity. He found himself laughing, delighted with each tangible instance of progress towards his goal. He barely ate, and neglected some of the less pressing matters of base maintenance. And as the radio source refused to away—as it looked more and more like something approaching Mars—Renfrew was gripped by the sense that he was engaged in a race; that he was in some way obliged to complete his task before the source arrived, that they would be waiting to hear what he had to say.

By night he dreamed cosmology, his dreams becoming ever more epic and ambitious as his knowledge of the science improved. With a fever-like sense of repetition he recapitulated the entire history of the universe, from its first moment of existence to the grand and symphonic flourishing of intelligence.

At the beginning there was always nothingness, an absence not only of space and time but of existence itself, and yet at the same time he was aware of a trembling pre-potential, a feeling that the nothingness was poised on the cusp of an awesome instability, as if the unborn universe was itching to bring itself into being. With nightly inevitability it came: less an explosion than a kind of delicate clockwork unravelling, as cunningly-packed structures unwound with inflationary speed, crystallising out into brand new superluminally expanding vacuum. He dreamed of symmetries snapping apart, mass and energy becoming distinct, force and matter bootstrapping into complex structures. He dreamed of atoms stabilising, linking to form molecules and crystals, and from those building blocks he dreamed the simple beginnings of chemistry. He dreamed of galaxies condensing out of gas, of supermassive young suns flaring brilliantly and briefly within those galaxies. Each subsequent generation of stars was more stable than the last, and as they evolved and died they brewed metals and then coughed them into interstellar space. Out of those metals condensed worlds—hot and scalding at first, until comets rained onto their crusts, quenching them and given them oceans and atmospheres.

He dreamed of the worlds ageing. On some the conditions were right for the genesis of microbial life. But the universe had to get very much older and larger before he saw anything more interesting than that. Even then it was scarce, and the worlds where animals stalked ocean beds before flopping and oozing ashore had a precious, gem-like rarity.

Rarer still were the worlds where those animals staggered toward self-awareness. But once or twice in every billion years it did happen. Occasionally life even learned to use tools and language, and look towards the stars.

Toward the end of one particularly vivid cosmological dream Renfrew found himself focussing on the rarity of intelligence in the universe. He saw the galaxy spread out before him, spiral arms of creamy white flecked here and there by the ruby reds of cool supergiants or the dazzling kingfisher blues of the hottest stars. Dotted across the galaxy's swirl were candles, the kind he remembered from birthday cakes. There were a dozen or so to start with, placed randomly in a rough band that was not too near the galactic core nor too close to the outer edges. The candles wavered slightly, and then— one by one—they began to go out.

Until only one was left. It was not even the brightest of those that had been there to begin with.

Renfrew felt a dreadful sense of that solitary candle's vulnerability. He looked up and below the plane of the galaxy, out toward its neighbours, but he saw no signs of candles elsewhere.

He desperately wanted to cradle that remaining candle, shelter it from the wind and keep it burning. He heard Piano Man singing: *And it seems to me you've lived your life . . .*

It went out.

All was void. Renfrew woke up shivering, and then raced to the suiting room and the airlock, and the waiting antenna, seeking contact with that radio signal.

"I think I understand," he told Piano Man. "Life has to be here to observe the universe, or it doesn't have any meaning. It's like the idea of the observer in quantum mechanics, collapsing an indeterminate system down to one possibility, opening the box and forcing the cat to chose between being dead or alive . . ."

Piano Man took off his glasses and polished them on his sleeve. He said nothing for at least a minute, satisfying himself that the glasses were clean before carefully replacing them on his nose. "That's what you think, is it? That's your big insight? That the universe needs its own observer? Well, break out the bubbly. Houston, I think we have a result."

"It's better than nothing."

"Right. And do how did this universe manage for fifteen billion years before we dropped by and provided an intelligent observer?

Are you seriously telling me it was all fuzzy and indeterminate until the instant some anonymous caveman had a moment of cosmic epiphany? That suddenly the entire quantum history of every particle in the visible universe—right out to the furthest quasar—suddenly jumped to one state, and all because some thicko in a bearskin had his brain wired up slightly differently to his ancestor?"

Renfrew thought back to his dream of the galactic disk studded with candle light. "No . . . I'm not saying that. There were other observers before us. We're just the latest."

"And these other observers—they were there all along, were they? An unbroken chain right back to the first instant of creation?"

"Well, no. Obviously the universe had to reach a certain minimum age before the preconditions for life—intelligent life—became established. But once that happened . . ."

"It's *bollocks*, though, isn't it, luv? What difference does it make if there's a gap of one second where the universe is unobserved, or ten billion years? None at all, as far as I'm concerned."

"Look, I'm trying, all right? I'm doing my best. And anyway . . ." Renfrew felt a sudden lurch of intuitive breakthrough. "We don't need all those other observers, do we? We *have* observed the entire history of the universe, just by looking out at higher and higher redshifts, with increasing look-back times. It's because the speed of light is finite. If it wasn't, information from the very further parts of the universe would reach us immediately, and we'd have no way of viewing earlier epochs."

"Fuck me man, you almost sound like a cosmologist."

"I think I might have become one."

"Just don't make a career of it," Piano Man said. He shook his head exasperatedly, then started playing *Benny and the Jets*.

A week later he told him the news. Renfrew's companion played the tentative ghost of a melody on the keyboard, something that hadn't yet crystallised into true music.

"You waited until now to tell me?" Piano Man asked, with a pained, disappointed look.

"I had to be certain. I had to keep tracking the thing, making sure it was really out there, and then making sure it was something worth getting excited about."

"And?"

Renfrew offered a smile. "I think it's worth getting excited about."

Piano Man played an icy line, dripping sarcastic bonhomie. "Really."

"I'm serious. It's a navigation signal, a spacecraft beacon. It keeps repeating the same code, over and over again." Renfrew leaned in closer: if he'd been able to lean on the phantom piano, he would have. "It's getting stronger. Whatever's putting out that signal is getting closer to Mars."

"You don't know that."

"OK, I don't. But there's the Doppler to consider as well. The signal's changing frequency a little from day to day. Put the two things together and you've got a ship making some kind of course correction, coming in for orbital insertion."

"Good for you."

Renfrew stepped back from the piano, surprised at his companion's dismissive reaction.

"There's a ship coming. Aren't you happy for me?"

"Tickled pink, luv."

"I don't understand. This is what I've been waiting for all this time: news that someone's survived, that it doesn't all end here." For the first time in their acquaintance, Renfrew raised his voice with Piano Man. "What the hell's wrong with you? Are you jealous that you won't be all the company I'm ever going to have?"

"Jealous? I don't think so."

Renfrew plunged his fist through the white nothingness of the piano. "Then show some reaction!"

Piano Man lifted his hands from the keyboard. He closed the keyboard cover very gently and then sat with his hands in his lap, demurely, just the way he'd been when Renfrew had first witnessed him. He looked at Renfrew, his expression blank, whatever message his eyes might have conveyed lost behind the star-shaped mirrors of his glasses.

"You want a reaction? Fine, I'll give you one. You're making a very, very serious mistake."

"It's no mistake. I know. I've double-checked checked everything . . ."

"It's still a mistake."

"The ship's coming."

"Something's coming. It may not be all that you expect."

Renfrew's fury boiled over. "Since when have you the faintest fucking idea what I expect or don't expect? You're just a piece of software."

"Whatever you say, luv. But remind me: when was the last time software encouraged you to take a deep interest in the fundamental workings of the universe?"

Renfrew had no answer for that. But he had to say something. "They're coming. I know they're coming. Things are going to get better. You'll see when the ship comes."

"You're going to do yourself a lot of harm."

"As if you cared. As if you were capable of caring."

"You've found a way to stay sane, Renfrew—even if that means admitting a tiny piece of piano-playing madness into your world. But there's a cost to that sanity, and it isn't *moi*. The cost is you can't ever allow yourself an instant of hope, because hope is something that will always be crushed, crushed utterly, and in the crushing of hope you will be weakened forever, just as surely as if you'd mainlined some slow-acting poison." Piano Man looked at Renfrew with a sudden, scholarly interest. "How many instants of defeat do you think you can take, big guy? One, two, three? From where I'm sitting I wouldn't bet on three. I think three might easily kill you. I think two might get you on a shitty day."

"Something's coming," Renfrew said, plaintively.

"I thought for a while you had the balls to get through this. I thought you'd banished hope, learned to keep it outside in the cold. I was wrong: you've let it in again. Now it's going to stalk you, like a starved, half-crazed wolf."

"It's my wolf."

"There's still time to chase it away. Don't let me down now, Renfrew. I've counting on you not to screw things up."

That night Renfrew dreamed not of cosmology, but of something stranger and more upsetting. It was not one of the dreams he used to have about the past, for he had trained himself not to have those any more; the sense of sadness and loss upon waking almost too much to bear. Nor was it one of the equally troubling ones about visitors, people coming down out of cold blue skies and landing near the base. When then came through the airlock they arrived with flowers—Hawaiian luas—and utterly pointless but lovingly gift-wrapped presents. Their faces were never familiar at first, but by the end of each visitation, just before he woke, they would always start to transmute into old friends and loved ones. Renfrew hadn't yet trained himself not to have that kind of dream, and given the news about the radio signal he was sure at least one of them would haunt his sleep in the days ahead.

It was not that kind of dream. What happened in the dream was that Renfrew rose like a sleepwalker from his bed in the middle of the night and crept through the base to the same medical lab where Solovyova had died, and placed his head into one of the functioning scanners, conjuring a glowing lilac image of his skull on the main screen, and then emerged from the scanner and examined the read-out to learn that his optic implants had been dead for years; that there was no possible way it was picking up the Bösendorfer, let alone the talking ghost that played it.

In the morning, when he woke from the dream, Renfrew couldn't bring himself to visit the medical lab, in case he had already been there in the night.

By day he kept a weather eye on the radio signal. It strengthened and Dopplered, moving quickly against the stars as it fell into the grasp of Mars. Then the signal altered, switching to a different, equally meaningless burst of repeating binary gibberish. Renfrew knew that it meant something, and intensified his vigil.

A day later, a meteor flared across the twilight sky, etching a fire trail, and dropped behind the closest range of hills under a dark umbrella of parachutes.

"I'm going out to find where they came down," Renfrew said.

"How far?"

"I don't know how far. Can't be all that far beyond the western marker."

"That's still twenty kilometres away."

"I'll take the car. It still works."

"You've never driven it alone. It's a long walk home if something goes wrong."

"Nothing's going wrong. I won't be alone."

Piano Man started to say something, but Renfrew wasn't listening.

He pre-breathed, suited up, climbed onto the skeletal chassis of the buggy, then went out to meet the newcomers. As the mesh-wheeled vehicle bounced and gyred its way to the horizon, Renfrew felt a thrilled elation, as if he were on his way to a date with a beauti-

ALASTAIR REYNOLDS | 303

ful and mysterious woman who might be his lover by the end of the evening.

But when he crested the hills and saw the fallen ship, he knew that nobody had ridden it to Mars. It was too small for that, even if this was just the re-entry component of a larger ship still circling the planet. What had come down was just a cargo pod, a blunt cylinder the size of a small minibus. It was tangled up with its own parachutes and the deflated gasbags it had deployed just before impact.

Renfrew parked the buggy, then spent ten minutes clearing fabric away from the cargo pod's door. The re-entry had scorched the decals, flags and data panels on the pod's skin to near-illegibility, but Renfrew knew the drill. Back when the base was inhabited, he'd occasionally drawn the short straw to drive out to recover a pod that had fallen away from the usual touchdown beacon.

He was sorry it wasn't a crewed ship, but the pod was the next best thing. Maybe they were still getting the infrastructure back up to speed. Sending out a manned vehicle was obviously too much of a stretch right now, and that was understandable. But they'd still had the presence of mind not to forget about Mars, even if all they could muster was a one-shot cargo pod. He would not be ungrateful. The pod could easily contain valuable medicines and machine parts, enough to relieve him of several ever-present worries. They might even have sent some luxuries, as a token of goodwill: things that the synths had never been very good at.

Renfrew touched a hand against the armoured panel next to the door, ready to flip it open and expose the pyrotechnic release mechanism. That was when one of the scorches caught his eye. It was a data panel, printed in spray-stencilled letters.

HTCV-554
Hohmann Transfer Cargo Vehicle
Scheduled launch: Kagoshima 05/38
Destination: Tharsis Base, Mars
Payload: replacement laser optics
Property: Mars Development Corporation

According to the data panel, the cargo pod had been scheduled to lift from Kagoshima spaceport one month before the virus hit. Maybe the panel was wrong; maybe this pod had been prepared and sprayed and then held on the pad until the virus had passed and the reconstruction had begun . . .

But why send him glass?

Renfrew knew, with an appalling certainty, that the vehicle had not been delayed on the pad. It had launched just as its owners had intended, *on time*, with a consignment of precision glassware that might just have been useful back when the base was fully inhabited and they'd needed a steady supply of laser optics for the surveying work.

But somewhere between Earth and Mars, the cargo pod had lost its way. When the virus hit, the pod would have lost contact with the Earth-based tracking system that was supposed to guide it on its way. But the pod hadn't simply drifted into interplanetary space, lost forever. Instead, its dumb-as-fuck navigation system had caused it to make an extra fuel-conserving loop around the sun, until it finally locked onto the Mars transponder.

Renfrew must have picked it up shortly afterwards.

He stumbled back to the buggy. He climbed into the openwork frame, settled into the driver's seat and didn't bother with the harness. He kept his breathing in check. The disappointment hadn't hit yet, but he could feel it coming, sliding toward him with the oiled glide of a piston. It was going to hurt like hell when it arrived. It was going to feel like the weight of creation pushing down onto his chest. It was going to squeeze the life out of him; it was going to make him open that helmet visor, if he didn't make it home first.

Piano Man had been right. He'd allowed hope back into his world, and now hope was going to make him pay.

He gunned the buggy to maximum power, flinging dust from its wheels, skidding until it found traction. He steered away from the cargo pod, not wanting to look at it, not even wanting to catch a glimpse of it in the buggy's rear view mirrors.

He'd made it to within five kilometres of the base when he hit a boulder, tipping the buggy over. Renfrew tumbled from the driver's seat, and the last thing he saw—the last thing he was aware of—was an edge of sharp rock rising to shatter his visor.

Part Three

And yet Renfrew woke.

Consciousness came back to him in a crystal rush. He remembered everything, up to and including the last instant of his accident. It seemed to have happened only minutes earlier: he could almost taste blood in his mouth. Yet by the same token the memory seemed inhumanly ancient, calcified into hardness, brittle as coral.

He was back in the base, not out by the crashed buggy. Through narrow, sleep-gummed eyes he picked out familiar décor. He'd come around on the same medical couch where he had seen Solov-yova die. He moved his arm and touched his brow, flinching as he remembered the stone smashing through the visor, flinching again as he recalled the momentary contact of stone against skin, the hard-ening pressure of skin on bone, the yielding of that pressure as the edge of the stone rammed its way into his skull like a nuclear-pow-ered icebreaker cracking hard arctic pack-ice.

The skin under his fingers was smooth, unscarred. He touched his chin and felt the same day's growth of stubble he'd been wearing when he went out to meet the pod. There was stiffness in his mus-cles, but nothing he wouldn't have expected after a hard day's work. He eased himself from the couch, touched bare feet to cold ceramic flooring. He was wearing the one-piece inner-layer that he'd put on under the spacesuit before he went outside. But the inner-layer was crisper and cleaner than he remembered, and when he looked at the sleeve the tears and frays he recalled were absent.

Gaining steadiness with each step, Renfrew padded across the medical lab to the window. He remembered seeing Solovyova's face reflected in the glass, the first time he'd seen the piano. It had been twilight then; it was full daylight now, and as his eyes adjusted to wakefulness, they picked out details and textures in the scenery with a clarity he'd never known before.

There were things out there that didn't belong.

They stood between the base and the foothills, set into the dust like haphazardly placed chess pieces. It was hard to say how tall they were—metres or tens of metres—for there was something slippery and elusive about the space between the forms and the base, con-founding Renfrew's sense of perspective. Nor could he have re-ported with any certainty on the shapes of the objects. One moment he saw blocky, unchanging chunks of crystalline growth—some-thing like tourmaline, tinted with bright reds and greens—the next he was looking at stained-glass apertures drilled through the very skein of reality, or skeletal, prismatic things that existed only in the sense that they had edges and corners, rather than surfaces and interiors. And yet there was never any sense of transition between the opposed states.

He knew, instantly and without fear, that they were alive, and that they were aware of him.

Renfrew made his way to the suiting room, counted the intact suits that were hanging there, and came up with the same number he remembered before the buggy accident. No sign of any damage to the racked helmets.

He suited up and stepped out into Martian daylight. The forms were still there, surrounding the base like the weathered stones of some grand Neolithic circle. Yet they seemed closer now, and larger, and their transformations had an accelerated, heightened quality. They had detected his emergence; they were glad of it; it was what they had been waiting for.

Still there was no fear.

One of the shapes seemed larger than the others. It beckoned Renfrew nearer, and the ground he walked upon melted and surged under him, encouraging him to close the distance. The transformations became more feverish. His suit monitor informed him that the air outside was as cold and thin as ever, but a sound was reaching him through the helmet that he'd never heard in all his time on Mars. It was a chorus of shrill, quavering notes, like the sound from a glass organ, and it was coming from the aliens. In that chorus was ecstasy and expectation. It should have terrified him; should have sent him scurrying back inside, should have sent him into gibbering catatonia, but it only made him stronger.

Renfrew dared to look up.

If the aliens gathered around the base were the crew, then the thing suspended over the base—the thing that swallowed three fifths of the sky, more like a weather system than a machine—had to be their ship. It was a vast frozen explosion of colours and shapes, and it made him want to shrivel back into his skull. The mere existence of the aliens and their ship told him that all he had learned, all the wisdom he had worked so hard to accrue, was at best a scratch against the rock face of reality.

He still had a long, long way to go.

He looked down, and walked to the base of the largest alien. The keening reached a shrill, exultant climax. Now that he was close, the alien's shape-and-size shifting had subsided. The form looming over him was stable and crystalline, with the landscape behind it faintly visible through the refracted translucence of the alien's body.

The alien's voice, when it came, felt like the universe whispering secrets into his head.

"Are you feeling better now?"

Renfrew almost laughed at the banality of the question. "I'm feeling . . . better, yes."

"That's good. We were concerned. Very, very concerned. It pleases us that you have made this recovery."

The keening quietened. Renfrew sensed that the other aliens were witnesses to a one-on-one conversation between him and this largest entity, and that there was something utterly respectful, even subservient, in their silence.

"When you talk about my recovery . . . are you saying . . ." Renfrew paused, choosing his words with care. "Did you make me better?"

"We healed you, yes. We healed you and learned your language from the internal wiring of your mind."

"I should have died out there. When I tipped the buggy . . . I thought I was dead. I *knew* I was dead."

"There were enough recoverable patterns. It was in our gift to remake you. Only you, however, can say whether we did a good enough job."

"I feel the same way I always did. Except better: like I've been turned inside out and flushed clean."

"That is what we hoped."

"You mind if I ask . . ."

The alien pulsed an inviting shade of pink.

"You may ask anything you like."

"Who are you? What are you doing here? Why have you come *now?*"

"We are the Kind. We have arrived to preserve and resurrect what we may. We have arrived now because we could not arrive sooner."

"But the coincidence . . . to come now, after we've been waiting so long . . . to come *now*, just after we've wiped ourselves out. Why couldn't you come sooner, and stop us fucking things up so badly?"

"We came as fast as we could. As soon as we detected the electromagnetic emanations of your culture . . . we commenced our journey."

"How far have you come?"

"More than two hundred of your light years. Our vehicle moves very quickly, but not faster than light. More than four hundred years have passed since the transmission of the radio signals that alerted us."

"No," Renfrew said, shaking his head, wondering how the aliens could have made such a basic mistake. "That isn't possible. Radio hasn't been around that long. We've had television for maybe a hundred years, radio for twenty or thirty years longer . . . but not four hundred years. No way was it *our* signals you picked up."

The alien shifted to a soothing turquoise.

"You are mistaken, but understandably so. You were dead longer than you realise."

"No," he said flatly.

"That is the way it is. Of course you have no memory of the intervening time."

"But the base looks exactly the way it did before I left."

"We repaired your home, as well. If you would like it changed again, that is also possible."

Renfrew felt the first stirrings of acceptance; the knowledge that what the alien was telling him was correct.

"If you've brought me back . . ."

"Yes," the alien encouraged.

"What about the others? What about all the other people who died here—Solovyova and the ones before her? What about all the people who died on Earth?"

"There were no recoverable forms on the Earth. We can show you if you would like . . . but we think you would find it distressing."

"Why?"

"We did. A lifecrash is always distressing, even to machine-based entities such as us. Especially after such a long and uninterrupted evolutionary history."

"A lifecrash?"

"It did not just end with the extinction of humanity. The agent that wiped out your species had the capacity to change. Eventually it assimilated every biological form on the planet, leaving only itself: endlessly cannibalising, endlessly replicating."

Renfrew dealt with that. He'd already adjusted to the fact that humanity was gone and that he was never going to see Earth again. It did not require a great adjustment to accept that Earth itself had been lost, along with the entire web of life it had once supported.

Not that he was exactly thrilled, either.

"OK," he said falteringly. "But what about the people I buried here?"

Renfrew sensed the alien's regret. Its facets shone a sombre amber.

"Their patterns were not recoverable. They were buried in caskets, along with moisture and microorganisms. Time did the rest. We did try, yes . . . but there was nothing left to work with."

"I died out there as well. Why was it any different for me?"

"You were kept cold and dry. That made all the difference, as far as we were concerned."

So he'd mummified out there, baked dry under that merciless sterilising sky, instead of rotting in the ground like his friends. Out there under that Martian sun, for the better part of three hundred years . . . what must he have looked like when they pulled him out of the remains of his suit, he wondered? Maybe a bleached and twisted thing, corded with the knotted remains of musculature and tissue: something that could easily have been mistaken for driftwood, had there been driftwood on Mars.

The wonder and horror of it all was almost too much. He'd been the last human being alive, and then he had died, and now he was the first human being to be resurrected by aliens.

The first and perhaps the last: he sensed even then that, as Godlike as the Kind appeared, they were bound by limits. They were as much prisoners of what the universe chose to allow, and what it chose not to allow, as humanity, or dust, or atoms.

"Why?" he asked.

A pulse of ochre signified the alien's confusion.

"Why what?"

"Why did you bring me back? What possible interest am I to you?"

The alien considered his remark, warming through shades of orange to a bright venous red. Like an echo, the shade spread to the other members of the gathering.

"We help," the leader told Renfrew. "That is what we do. That is what we have always done. We are the Kind."

*　　　　*　　　　*

He returned to the base and tried to continue his affairs, just as if the Kind had never arrived. Yet they were always out there whenever he passed a window: brighter and closer now as evening stole in, as if they had gathered the day's light and were now re-radiating it in subtly altered shades. He closed the storm shutters but that didn't help much. He did not doubt that the ship was still poised above, suspended over the base as if guarding the infinitely precious thing that he had become.

Renfrew's old routines had little meaning now. The aliens hadn't just brought the base back to the way it had been before he crashed the buggy. They had repaired all the damage that had accrued since the collapse of Earthside society, and the base systems now functioned better than at any point since the base's construction. As mindless as his maintenance tours had been, they had imposed structure on his life that was now absent. Renfrew felt like a rat that'd had his exercise wheel taken away.

He went to the recreation room and brought the system back online. Everything functioned as the designers had intended. The aliens must have repaired, or at least not removed, his implant. But when he cycled through the myriad options, he found that something had happened to Piano Man.

The figure was still there—Renfrew even knew his name, now—but the companion he remembered was gone. Now Piano Man behaved just like all the other generated personalities. Renfrew could still talk to him, and Piano Man could still answer him back, but nothing like their old conversations was now possible. Piano Man would take requests, and banter, but that was the limit of his abilities. If Renfrew tried to steer the conversation away from the strictly musical, if he tried to engage Piano Man in a discussion about cosmology or quantum mechanics, all he got back was a polite but puzzled stare. And the more Renfrew persisted, the less it seemed to him that there was any consciousness behind that implant-generated face. All he was dealing with was a paper-thin figment of the entertainment system.

Renfrew knew that the Kind hadn't 'fixed' Piano Man in the sense that they had fixed the rest of the base. But—deliberately or otherwise—their arrival had destroyed the illusion of companionship. Perhaps they had straightened some neurological kink in Renfrew's brain when they put him back together. Or perhaps the mere fact of their arrival had caused his subconsciousness to discard that earlier mental crutch.

He knew it shouldn't have meant anything. Piano Man hadn't existed in any real sense. Feeling sorrow for his absence was as ridiculous as mourning the death of a character in a dream. He'd made Piano Man up; his companion had never had any objective existence.

But he still felt that he had lost a friend.

"I'm sorry," he said, to that polite but puzzled face. "You were right, and I was wrong. I was doing fine just the way things were. I should have listened to you."

There was an uncomfortable pause, before Piano Man smiled and spread his fingers above the keyboard.

"Would you like me to play something?"

"Yes," Renfrew said. "Play Rocket Man. For old time's sake."

He allowed the Kind into Tharsis Base. Their crystalline forms were soon everywhere, spreading and multiplying in a mad orgy of prismatic colour, transforming the drab architecture into a magical lantern-lit grotto. The beauty of it was so startling, so intoxicating, that it moved Renfrew to tears with the knowledge that no one else would ever see it.

"But it could be different," the leader told him. "We did not broach this earlier, but there are possibilities you may wish to consider."

"Such as?"

"We have repaired you, and made you somewhat younger than you were before your accident. In doing so we have learned a great deal about your biology. We cannot resurrect the dead of Earth, or your companions here on Mars, but we can give you other people."

"I don't follow."

"It would cost us nothing to weave new companions. They could be grown to adulthood at accelerated speed, or your own ageing could be arrested while you give the children time to grow."

"And then what?"

"You could breed with them, if you chose. We'd intervene to correct any genetic anomalies."

Renfrew smiled. "Mars ain't the kind of place to raise your kids. At least, that's what a friend of mine told me that once."

"Now there is nowhere *but* Mars. Doesn't that make a difference? Or would you rather we established a habitable zone on Earth and transplanted you there?"

They made him feel like a plant: like some incredibly rare and delicate orchid.

"Would I notice the difference?"

"We could adjust your faculties so that Earth appeared the way you remembered. Or we could edit your memories to match the present conditions."

"Why can't you just put things back the way they were? Surely one runaway virus isn't going to defeat you."

The alien turned a shade of chrome blue that Renfrew had learned to recognise as indicative of gentle chiding. "That's not our way. The runaway agent now constitutes its own form of life, brimming with future potential. To wipe it out now would be akin to sterilising your planet just as your own single-celled ancestors were gaining a foothold."

"You care about life that much?"

"Life is precious. Infinitely so. Perhaps it takes a machine intelligence to appreciate that." The chrome blue faded, replaced by a placatory olive green. "Given that Earth cannot be made the way it was, will you reconsider our offer to give you companionship?"

"Not now," he said.

"But later, perhaps?"

"I don't know. I've been on my own a long time. I'm not sure it isn't better this way."

"You've craved companionship for years. Why reject it now?"

"Because . . ." And here Renfrew faltered, conscious of his own inarticulacy before the alien. "When I was alone, I spent a lot of time thinking things through. I got set on that course, and I'm not sure I'm done yet. There's still some stuff I need to get straight in my head. Maybe when I'm finished . . ."

"Perhaps we can help you with that."

"Help me understand the universe? Help me understand what it means to be the last living man? Maybe even the last intelligent organism, in the universe?"

"It wouldn't be the first time. We are a very old culture. In our travels we have encountered myriad other species. Some of them are extinct by now, or changed beyond recognition. But many of them were engaged on quests similar to your own. We have watched, and occasionally interceded to better aid that comprehension. Nothing would please us more than to offer you similar assistance. If we cannot give you companionship, at least let us give you wisdom."

"I want to understand space and time, and my own place in it."

"The path to deep comprehension is risky."

"I'm ready for it. I've already come a long way."

"Then we shall help. But the road is long, Renfrew. The road is long and you have barely started your journey."

"I'm willing to go all the way."

"You will be long past human before you near the end of it. That is the cost of understanding space and time."

Renfrew felt a chill on the back of his neck, a premonitionary shiver. The alien was not warning him for nothing. In its travels it must have witnessed things that caused it distress.

Still he said: "Whatever it takes. Bring it on. I'm ready."

"Now?"

"Now. But before we begin . . . you don't call me Renfrew any more."

"You wish a new name, to signify this new stage in your quest?"

"From now on, I'm John. That's what I want you to call me."

"Just John?"

He nodded solemnly. "Just John."

Part Four

The Kind did things to John.

While he slept, they altered his mind: infiltrating it with tiny crystal avatars of themselves, performing prestigious feats of neural rewiring. When he woke he still felt like himself: still carried the same freight of memories and emotions that he'd taken with him to sleep. But suddenly he had the ability to grasp things that had been impenetrably difficult only hours earlier. Before the accident, he had explored the inlets of superstring theory, like an explorer searching for a navigable route through a treacherous mountain range. He had never found that easy path, never dreamed of conquering the dizzying summits before him, but now, miraculously, he was on the other side, and the route through the obstacle looked insultingly easy. Beyond superstring theory lay the unified territory of M-theory, but that, too, was soon his. John revelled in his new understanding.

More and more, he began to think in terms of a room whose

floor was the absolute truth about the universe: where it had come from, how it worked, what it meant to be a thinking being in that universe. But that floor looked very much like a carpet, and it was in turn concealed by other carpets, one on top of the other, each of which represented some imperfect approximation to the final layer. Each layer might look convincing; might endure decades or centuries of enquiry without hinting that it contained a flaw, but sooner or later one would inevitably reveal itself. A tiny loose thread—perhaps a discrepancy between observation and theory—and with a tug the entire fabric of that layer would come apart. It was in the nature of such revolutions that the next layer down would already have been glimpsed by then. Only the final carpet, the floor, would contain no logical inconsistencies, no threads waiting to be unravelled.

Could you ever know when you'd reached it, John wondered? Some thinkers considered it impossible to ever know with certainty. All you could do was keep testing, tugging at every strand to see how firmly it was woven into the whole. If after tens of thousands of years, the pattern was still intact, then it might begin to seem likely that you had arrived at final wisdom. But you could never know for sure. The ten thousand and first year might bring forth some trifling observation that, as innocent as it first seemed, would eventually prove that there was yet another layer lurking underneath.

You could go on like that forever, never knowing for sure.

Or—as some other thinkers speculated—the final theory might come with its own guarantee of authenticity, a golden strand of logical validation threaded into the very mathematical language in which it was couched. It might be in the nature of the theory to state that there could be no deeper description of the universe.

But even then: it wouldn't stop you making observations. It wouldn't stop you testing.

John kept learning. M-theory became a distant and trifling obstacle, dwarfed by the daunting unified theories that had superseded it. These theories probed the interface not just of matter and space-time, but also of consciousness and entropy, information, complexity and the growth of replicating structures. On the face of it, they seemed to describe everything that conceivably mattered about the universe.

But each in turn was revealed as flawed, incomplete, at odds with observation. An error in the predicted mass of the electron, in the twenty-second decimal place. A one-in-ten-thousandth part discrepancy in the predicted bending of starlight around a certain class of rotating black hole. A niggling mismatch between the predicted and observed properties of inertia, in highly charged spacetime.

The room contained many carpets, and John had the dizzying sense that there were still many layers between him and the floor. He'd made progress, certainly, but it had only sharpened his sense of how far he had to go.

The Kind remade him time and again, resetting his body clock to give him the time he needed for his studies. But each leap of understanding pushed him closer to the fundamental limits of a wet human brain wired together from a few hundred billion neurons, crammed into a tiny cage of bone.

"You can stop now, if you like," the Kind said, in the hundredth year of his quest.

"Or what?" John asked mildly.

"Or we continue, with certain modifications."

John gave them his consent. It would mean not being human for a little while, but given the distance he had come, the price did not strike him as unreasonable.

The Kind encoded the existing patterns of his mind into a body much like one of their own. For John the transition to a machine-based substrate of thinking crystal was in no way traumatic, especially as the Kind assured him that the process was completely reversible. Freed of the constraints of flesh and scale, his progress accelerated even more. From this new perspective, his old human mind looked like something seen through the wrong end of a telescope. Compared to the mental mansion he now inhabited, his former residence looked as squalid and limiting as a rabbit hutch. It was a wonder he'd understood *anything*.

But John wasn't finished.

A thousand years passed. Always adding new capacity to himself, he had become a kilometre-high crystalline mound on the summit of Pavonis Mons. He was larger by far than any of the Kind, but that was only to be expected: he was probing layers of reality that they had long since mapped to their own satisfaction, and from which they had dutifully retreated. Having attained that understanding once, the Kind had no further need for it.

There were other people on Mars now. John had finally acquiesced to the Kind's offer to bring him companions, and they had created children who had now grown to become parents and grand-parents. But when John agreed to the coming of other humans, it had little do with his own need for companionship. He felt too remote from other humans now, and it was only because he sensed that the Kind wished to perform this exercise—that it would please the aliens to have something else to do—that he had relented. But even if he could not relate to the teeming newcomers, he found it pleasing to divert a small portion of his energies to their amusement. He rearranged his outer architecture—dedicated to only the most trivial data-handling tasks—so that he resembled an ornate crystal-line fairy palace, with spires and domes and battlements, and at dusk he twinkled with refracted sunlight, throwing coloured glories across the great plains of the Tharsis Montes. A yellow road spi-ralled around his foot slopes. He became a site of pilgrimage, and he sang to the pilgrims as they toiled up and down the spiral road.

Millennia passed. Still John's mind burrowed deeper.

He reported to the Kind that he had passed through eighteen paradigmatic layers of reality, each of which had demanded a con-comitant upgrade in his neural wiring before he could be said to have understood the theory in all its implications, and therefore re-cognised the flaw that led to the next layer down.

The Kind informed him that—in all the history that was known to them—fewer than five hundred other sentient beings had at-tained John's present level understanding.

Still John kept going, aware that in all significant respects he had now exceeded the intellectual capacity of the Kind. They were there to assist him, to guide him through his transformations, but they had only a dim conception of what it now felt to be John. According to their data less than a hundred individuals, from a hundred different cultures, all of them now extinct, had reached this point.

Ahead, the Kind warned, were treacherous waters.

John's architectural transformations soon began to place an in-tolerable strain on the fragile geology of Pavonis Mons. Rather than reinforce the ancient volcano to support his increasing size and mass, John chose to detach himself from the surface entirely. For twenty six thousand years he floated in the thickening Martian atmosphere, supported by batteries of antigravity generators. For much of that time it pleased him to manifest in the form of a Bösendorfer grand piano, a shape reconstructed from his oldest human memories. He drifted over the landscape, solitary as a cloud, and occasionally he played slow tunes that fell from the sky like thunder.

Yet soon there came a time when he was too large even for the atmosphere. The heat dissipation from his mental processes was starting to have an adverse effect on the global climate.

It was time to leave.

In space he grew prolifically for fifteen million years. Hot blue stars formed, lived and died while he gnawed away at the edges of certain intractables. Human civilisations buzzed around him like flies. Among them, he knew, were individuals who were engaged in something like the same quest for understanding. He wished them well, but he had a head start none of them had a hope of ever over-taking. Over the years his density had increased, until he was now composed mostly of solid nuclear matter. Then he had evolved to substrates of pure quark matter. By then, his own gravity had become immense, and the Kind reinforced him with mighty spars of exotic matter, pilfered from the disused wormhole transit system of some long-vanished culture. A binary pulsar was harnessed to power him; titanic clockwork enslaved for the purposes of pure mentation.

And still deeper John tunnelled.

"I . . . sense something," he told the Kind one day.

They asked him what, fearing his answer.

"Something ahead of me," he said. "A few layers down. I can't quite see it yet, but I'm pretty sure I can sense it."

They asked him what it was like.

"An ending," John told them.

"This is what we always knew would come to pass," the Kind told him.

They informed him that only seven other sentient beings had reached John's current state of enlightenment; none in the last three billion years. They also told him that to achieve enlightenment he would have to change again; become denser still, squeezed down into a thinking core that was only just capable of supporting itself against its own ferocious gravity.

"You'll be unstable," they told him. "Your very thought pro-cesses will tend to push you into your own critical radius."

He knew what they meant, but he wanted to hear them spell it out. "And when that happens?"

"You become a black hole. No force in the universe will be able

to prevent your collapse. These are the treacherous waters we mentioned earlier."

They said 'earlier' as if they meant 'earlier this afternoon,'
rather than 'earlier in the history of this universe.' But John had long
since accustomed himself to the awesome timescales of the Kind.

"I still want you to do it. I've come too far to give up now."

"As you wish."

So they made him into a vast ring of hyperdense matter, poised
on the edge of collapse. In his immense gravitational field, John's
lightning thought processes grew sluggish. But his computational
resources were now vast.

Many times he orbited the galaxy.

With each layer that he passed, he sensed the increasing presence of the *ending*; the final, rock-hard substrate of reality. He knew
it was the floor, not another mirage-like illusion of finality. He was
almost there now: his great quest was nearing its completion, and in
a few thoughts—a few hours in the long afternoon of the universe—he would have arrived.

Yet John called a halt to his thinking.

"Is there a problem?" the Kind asked, solicitously.

"I don't know. Maybe. I've been thinking about what you said
before: about how my own thought processes might push me over
the edge."

"Yes," the Kind said.

"I'm wondering: what would that really mean?"

"It would mean death. There has been much debate on the
matter, but the present state of understanding is that no useful information can ever emerge from a black hole."

"You're right. That sounds an awfully lot like death to me."

"Then perhaps you will consider stopping now, while there is
still time. You have at least glimpsed the final layer. Is that not
enough for you? You've come further than you could ever have
dreamed when you embarked on this quest."

"That's true."

"Well, then. Let this be an end to it. Dwell not on what is left to
be done, but, yes, on what you have already achieved."

"I'd like to. But there's this nagging little thing I can't stop
thinking about."

"Please. To think about *anything* in your present state is not
without risk."

"I know. But I think this might be important. Do you think it's coincidence that I've reached this point in my quest, at the same time that I'm teetering on the edge of collapsing into myself?"

"We confess we hadn't given the matter a great deal of thought, beyond the immediate practicalities."

"Well, I have. And I've been thinking. Way back when, I read a theory about baby universes."

"Continue . . ." the Kind said warily.

"How they might be born inside black holes, where the ordinary rules of space and time break down. The idea being that when the singularity inside a black hole forms, it actually buds off a whole new universe, with its own subtly altered laws of physics. That's where the information goes: down the pipe, into the baby universe. We see no evidence of this on the outside—the expansion's in a direction we can't point; it isn't as if the new universe is expanding into our own like an explosion—but that doesn't mean it isn't happening every time a black hole forms somewhere in our universe. In fact, it's entirely possible that *our* universe might well have been budded off from someone else's black hole."

"We are aware of this speculation. And your point being?"

"Perhaps it isn't coincidence. Perhaps this is just the way it has to be. You cannot attain ultimate wisdom about the universe without reaching this point of gravitational collapse. And at the moment you do attain final understanding—when the last piece falls into place, when you finally glimpse that ultimate layer of reality—you slip over the edge, into irreversible collapse."

"In other words, you die. As we warned."

"But maybe not. After all, by that point you've become little more than pure information. What if you survive the transition through your own singularity, and slip through into the baby universe?"

"To become smeared out and re-radiated as random noise, you mean?"

"Actually, I had something else in mind. Who's to say that you don't end up encoding yourself into the very structure of that new universe?"

"Who's to say that you do?"

"I admit it's speculative. But there is something rather beautiful and symmetric about it, don't you think? In the universes where there is intelligent life, one or more sentient individuals will eventually ask the same questions I asked myself, and follow them through to this point of penultimate understanding. When they achieve enlightenment, they exceed the critical density and become baby universes in their own right. They become what they sought to understand."

"You have no proof of this."

"No, but I have one hell of a gut feeling. There is, of course, only one way to know for sure. At the moment of understanding, I'll know whether this happens or not."

"And if it doesn't . . ."

"I'll still have achieved my goal. I'll know that, even as I'm crushed out of existence. If, on the other hand, it does happen . . . then I won't be crushed at all. My consciousness will continue, on the other side, embedded in the fabric of space and time itself." John paused, for something had occurred to him. "I'll have become something very close to . . ."

"Don't say it, please," the Kind interjected.

"All right, I won't. But you see now why I hesitate. This final step will take me as far from humanity as all the steps that have preceded it. It's not something I'm about to take lightly."

"You shouldn't."

"The others . . ." John began, before trailing off, aware of the fear and doubt in his voice. "What did they do, when they got this far? Did they hesitate? Did they just storm on through?"

"Only three have preceded you, in all of recorded history. Two underwent gravitational collapse: we can show you the black holes they became, if you wish."

"I'll pass. Tell me about the third."

"The third chose a different path. He elected to split his consciousness into two streams, by dividing and reallocating portions of his architecture. One component continued with the quest for ultimate understanding, while the other retreated, assuming a less-dense embodiment that carried no risk of collapse."

"What happened to the component that continued?"

"Again," the Kind said, with the merest flicker of amusement at John's expense, "we'd be delighted to show you the results."

"And the other half? How could he have preserved the understanding he'd achieved, if he backtracked to a simpler architecture?"

"He couldn't. That's exactly the point."

"I don't follow. Understanding required a certain level of complexity. He couldn't have retained that understanding, if he stripped himself back."

"He didn't. He did, however, retain the memory of having understood. That, for him, was sufficient."

"Just the memory?"

"Precisely that. He'd glimpsed enlightenment. He didn't need to retain every detail of that glimpse to know he'd seen it."

"But that's not understanding," John said exasperatedly. "It's a crude approximation, like the postcard instead of the view."

"Better than being crushed out of existence, though. The being under discussion seemed adequately content with the compromise."

"And you think I will be, too?"

"We think you should at least consider the possibility."

"I will. But I'll need time to think about it."

"How long?"

"Just a bit."

"All right," the Kind said. "But just don't think *too* hard about it."

It passed that, much less than a million years later, John announced to the Kind that he wished to follow the example of the third sentient being they had mentioned. He would partition his consciousness into two streams, one of which would continue towards final enlightenment, the other of which would assume a simpler and safer architecture, necessarily incapable of emulating his present degree of understanding. For John the process of dividing himself was as fraught and delicate as any of the transformations he had hitherto undergone. It required all of the skill of the Kind to affect the change in such a way as to allow the preservation of memories, even as his mind was whittled back to a mere sketch of itself. But by turns it was done, and the two Johns were both physically and mentally distinct: the one still poised on the edge of gravitational annihilation, only a thought away from transcendence, the other observing matters from a safe distance.

So it was that Simple John witnessed the collapse and infall of his more complex self: an event as sudden and violent as any natural stellar catastrophe in recent galactic times. In that moment of understanding, he had pushed his own architecture to the limit. Somewhere in him, matter and energy collapsed to open a howling aperture to a new creation. He had reached the conclusion of his quest.

In the last nanoseconds of his physical existence however—before he was sucked under the event horizon, beyond which no information could ever emerge—Complex John did at least manage to encode and transmit a parting wave of gravitational energy, a message to his other half.

The content was very brief.

It said only: "Now I get it."

That might have been the end of it, but shortly afterwards Simple John took a decision that was to return him to his starting point. He carried now the memory of near-enlightenment, and the memory was—as the Kind had promised, despite John's natural scepticism—very nearly as illuminating as the thing itself. In some ways, perhaps, *more so*—it was small and polished and gemlike, and he could examine it from different angles; quite unlike the unwieldy immersiveness of the experience itself, from which the memory had been expertly distilled.

But why, he wondered, stop there? If he could revert back to this simplified architecture and still retain the memory of what he had been before, why not take things further?

Why not go all the way back?

The descent from near-enlightenment was not a thing to be rushed, for at every stage—as his evolved faculties were stripped back and discarded—he had to be assured that the chain of memory remained unbroken. As he approached being human again, he knew on an intellectual level that what he now carried was not the memory of understanding, but the memory of a memory of a memory . . . a pale, diminished, reflected thing, but no less authentic for that. It still felt genuine to John, and now—as they packed his wet, cellular mind back into the stifling cage of a *Homo sapiens* skull—that was all that truly mattered.

And so it came time for him to return to Mars.

Mars by then was a green and blue marble of a world much like old Earth. Despite the passage of time the rekindled human civilisation had spread no further than the solar system, and—since Earth was out of bounds—Mars remained its capital. Sixteen million people lived there now, many of them gathered into small communities scattered around the gentle foot slopes of Pavonis Mons. Deep inside Mars, a lattice of artificial black holes created a surface gravity

indistinguishable from that of old Earth. Mammoth sunken buttresses kept the ancient landscape from falling in on itself. The seas
were soupy with life; the atmosphere thick and warm, brimming
with insects and birds.

Certain things had been preserved since John's departure.
The spiralling yellow road, for instance, still wormed its way to
the summit of Pavonis Mons, and pilgrims made the long but
hardly arduous ascent, pausing here and there at the many
pennanted tea houses and hostels that lined the route. Though
they belonged to different creeds, all remembered John in some
form or another, and many of their creeds spoke of the day when
he would come back to Mars. To this end, the smooth circular plateau at the top of the volcano had been kept clear, awaiting the day
of John's return. Monks brushed the dust from it with great
brooms. Pilgrims circled the plateau, but none ventured very far
inwards from the edge.

John, human again, dropped from the sky in a cradle of alien
force. It was day, but no one witnessed his arrival. The Kind had arranged an invisibility barrier around him, so that from a distance he
resembled only a pillar of warm air, causing the scene behind him to
tremble slightly as in a mirage.

"Are you sure you're ready for this?" the Kind asked. "You've
been gone a long time. They may have some trouble dealing with
your return."

John adjusted the star-shaped spectacles he had selected for his
return to Mars, settling them onto the small nub of his nose.

"They'll get used to me sooner or later."

"They'll expect words of wisdom. When they don't get any,
they're likely to be disappointed. 'I get it now' isn't likely to pass
muster."

"They'll get over it."

"You may wish to dispense some harmless platitudes: just
enough to keep them guessing. We can suggest some, if you'd like:
we've had considerable practise at this sort of thing."

"I'll be fine. I'm just going to be straight with them. I came, I
saw, I backed off. But I did see it, and I do remember seeing it. I think
it all makes sense."

"'I think it all makes sense'," the Kind repeated. "That's the best
you're going to give them?"

"It was my quest. I never said it had to measure up to anyone else's expectations." John ran a hand over his scalp, flattening down his thin auburn thatch against the air currents in the invisibility field. He took a step forward, teetering on the huge red boots he had selected for his return. "How do I look, anyway?"

"Not quite the way you started out. Is there any particular reason for the physiological changes, the costume?"

John shrugged. "None in particular."

"Fine, then. You'll knock them out. That *is* the appropriate turn of phrase, isn't it?"

"It'll do. I guess this is it, then . . . I step through here, and I'm back with people. Right?"

"Right. You have plans, we take it?"

"Nothing set in stone. See how things go, I thought. Maybe I'll settle down, maybe I won't. I've been on my own for a long time now: fitting back into human society isn't going to be a breeze. Especially some weird, futuristic human society that half thinks I'm some kind of god."

"You'll manage."

John hesitated, ready to step through into daylight, into full visibility. "Thanks, anyway. For everything."

"It was our pleasure."

"What about you, now?"

"We'll move on," the Kind said. "Find someone else in need of help. Perhaps we'll swing by again, further down the line, see how you're all doing."

"That would be nice."

There was an awkward lull in the conversation.

"John, there is one thing we need to tell you, before you go."

He heard something in the Kind's tone that, in all their time together, was new to him.

"What is it?"

"We lied to you."

He let out small, involuntary laugh: it was the last thing he had been expecting. He did not think the Kind had ever once spoken an untruth to him.

"Tell me," he said.

"The third sentient being we spoke about . . . the one that split itself into two consciousness streams?"

John nodded. "What about it?"

"It didn't exist. It was a story we made up, to persuade you to follow that course of action. In truth, you were the first to do such thing. No other entity had reached such a final stage of - enlightenment without continuing on to final collapse."

John absorbed that, then nodded slowly. "I see."

"We hope you are not too angry with us."

"Why did you lie?"

"Because we had grown to like you. It was wrong . . . the choice should have been yours, uncontaminated by our lies . . . but without that example, we did not think you would have chosen the route you did. And then we would have lost you, and you would not be standing here, with the memories that you have."

"I see," he said again, softer this time.

"Are you cross with us?"

John waited a little while before answering. "I should be, I suppose. But really, I'm not. You're probably right: I would have carried on. And given what I know now—given the memories I have—I'm glad this part of me didn't."

"Then it was the right thing to do?"

"It was a white lie. There are worse things."

"Thank you, John."

"I guess the next time you meet someone like me—some other sentient being engaged on that quest—you won't have to lie, will you?"

"Not now, no."

"Then we'll let it be. I'm cool with the way things turned out." John was about to step outside, but then something occurred to him. He fought to keep the playful expression from his face. "But I can't let you get away without at least doing one final favour for me. I know it's a lot to ask after you've done so much . . ."

"Whatever it is, we will strive to do our best."

John pointed across the mirror-smooth surface of the plateau, to the circling line of distant pilgrims. "I'm going to step outside in a moment, onto Pavonis Mons. But I don't want to scare the living daylights out of them by just walking out of thin air with no warning."

"What did you have in mind?"

John was still pointing. "You're going to make something appear before I do. Given your abilities, I don't think it will tax you very much."

"What is it that you would like?"

"A white piano," John said. "But not just any old piano. It has to be a Bösendorfer grand. I was one once, remember?"

"But this one would be smaller, we take it?"

"Yes," John said, nodding agreeably. "A lot smaller. Small enough that I can sit at the keyboard. So you'd better put a stool by it as well."

Swift machinery darted through the air, quick as lightning. A piano assumed startling solidity, and then a red-cushioned stool. Across the plateau, one or two pilgrims had already observed its arrival. They were gesticulating excitedly, and the news was spreading fast.

"Is that all?"

John tapped the glasses back onto the bridge of his nose. "There's one final thing. By the time I reach that stool, I need to be able to play the piano. I made music before, but that was different. Now I need to do it with my fingers, the old way. Think you can oblige?"

"We have much knowledge of music. The necessary neural scripting can be implemented by the time you arrive at the Bösendorfer. There may be a slight headache . . ."

"I'll deal with it."

"It only remains to ask . . . is there anything in particular you want to play?"

"Actually," John said, stretching his fingers in readiness for the performance, "there is one song I had in mind. It's about Mars, as it happens."

CONTRIBUTORS

MICHAEL SWANWICK is one of the most acclaimed science fiction and fantasy writers of his generation. He has received a Hugo Award for short fiction five times in six years—an unprecedented accomplishment. He has also received the Nebula, Theodore Sturgeon, and World Fantasy Awards, and his work has been translated and published throughout the world. His most recent novel is *Bones of the Earth*. Swanwick lives in Philadelphia with his wife, Marianne Porter.

TOM PURDOM started reading science fiction in 1950, when the big science fiction boom of the 1950s was just getting started, and sold his first story in 1957, just before he turned twenty-one. His bibliography includes sales to Don Wollheim's Ace Double series, John W. Campbell's *Analog*, and H.L. Gold's *Galaxy*. In recent years he has been writing short stories and novelettes which have mostly appeared in *Asimov's*. He and his wife Sara live in downtown Philadelphia, the city he happened to land in over fifty years ago, after a nomadic childhood as a Navy brat.

On "Bank Run" he noted that the sources for the background include "an interest in economics that goes back to the early sixties, twenty-five years of reading *The Economist* and *Barron's*, my experiences as a small investor, my experiences rehabbing two city houses and owning a rental property, my work as a freelance writer with a friend who started his own company, and all the opportunities to observe people interacting with money that you encounter in a big city."

DOUGLAS LAIN is a fiction writer living in Portland, Oregon. His first book, a collection entitled *Last Week's Apocalypse*, was published by Night Shade Books in early 2006.

On the "Coffee Cup" story he says, "It's obviously a meditation on September 11th, but it also ended up having a sort of spiritual or transcendental message. I can't decide if that makes the story escapist crap or not."

JAMES PATRICK KELLY has had an eclectic writing career. He has written novels, short stories, essays, reviews, poetry, plays and planetarium shows. His books include *Burn*, *Strange But Not a Stranger*, *Think Like A Dinosaur and other stories*, *Wildlife*, *Heroines*, *Look Into The Sun*, *Freedom Beach* and *Planet of Whispers*. He won the World Science Fiction Society's Hugo Award twice: in 1996, for his novelette "Think Like a Dinosaur," and in 2000, for his novelette, "Ten to the Sixteenth to One."

In 2004 Jim brought an unfinished draft of "The Edge of Nowhere" to the Rio Hondo Writers' Workshop in Taos, New Mexico and finished the story while at the workshop. He is grateful to his colleagues for pointing out the flaws in the story that arose due to its hasty composition. Several rewrites later, he submitted it to *Asimov's* where it was published in 2005, marking his twenty-first consecutive appearance in the June issue of that magazine.

JOE HALDEMAN first won the Hugo Award for his novel *The Forever War*. His work includes the Hugo and Nebula Award-winning novel *The Hemingway Hoax* and the acclaimed Worlds Trilogy. He has won a total of three Nebula Awards and four Hugo Awards. A Vietnam veteran who was wounded, Joe Hadleman teaches writing at M.I.T. and lives part-time in Florida with his wife, Gay.

SUSAN PALWICK is an Associate Professor of English at the University of Nevada, Reno. She has published two novels with Tor, *Flying in Place* and *The Necessary Beggar*. A third novel, *Shelter*, is forthcoming in 2007. "The Fate of Mice" is the title story of a short-story collection which will also appear in 2007, from Tachyon Publications.

HOWARD WALDROP, who was born in Mississippi and now lives in Austin, Texas, is one of the most iconoclastic writers working today. His highly original books include the novels *Them Bones* and *A Dozen Tough Jobs*, and the collections *Howard Who?*, *All About Strange Monsters of the Recent Past*, *Night of the Cooters*, and *Going Home Again*. He won the Nebula and World Fantasy Awards for his novelette "The Ugly Chickens."

LEAH BOBET was born and lives in Toronto, Canada with a garden, a computer, and many books. She studies Linguistics part-time at the University of Toronto, edits at *Ideomancer Speculative Fiction*, and works at Bakka-Phoenix Books, Canada's oldest science fiction bookstore.

During the last two decades, **ROBERT REED** has produced more than a dozen novels and approximately 150 published works of short fiction. He has become a fixture both in *The Magazine of*

Fantasy & Science Fiction and *Asimov's Science Fiction*, and he was a frequent contributor to the wonderful and much-missed *Sci Fiction*. Reed has been nominated for five Hugos, as well as one Nebula and one World Fantasy Award. His most recent novel is *The Well of Stars*.

Reed lives in Lincoln, Nebraska with his wife and young daughter. His typical day is built from long stretches of laziness punctuated with moments of furious motion and the occasional workable page.

As far as Reed can remember, "Finished" began more as a mood piece than a plot line. Working on the opening scene, he knew absolutely nothing about the characters or their motivations. By the end, he felt slightly more informed. Certain elements of what happen in the story were a surprise to him, and hopefully they will be to new readers as well.

JAMES VAN PELT teaches high school and college English in western Colorado. He has been publishing fiction since 1990, with numerous appearances in most of the major science fiction and fantasy magazines, including *Talebones, Realms of Fantasy, Analog, Asimov's Science Fiction, Weird Tales, Sci Fiction,* and many anthologies, including several "year's best" collections. His first collection of stories, *Strangers and Beggars* was released in 2002 and was recognized as a Best Book for Young Adults by the American Library Association. His second collection, *The Last of the O-Forms and Other Stories*, was a finalist for the Colorado Blue Spruce Young Adult Book Award.

In his own words: "The Inn at Mount Either" really came about because I realized I'd never written a story about how much I love my wife. I asked my wife if her parents had considered a name for her other than the one they gave her (Tammy), and it turned out that "Stephanie" was a strong contender. So, Stephanie appeared in the story, and I knew exactly how Dorian felt about her. Once I know my character's motivation, the rest of the writing becomes so much easier."

MARY ROSENBLUM, a graduate of the 1988 Clarion West writers workshop, first published in *Asimov's Science Fiction* in 1990 with "For a Price," one of her Clarion stories. Since then, she has published more than sixty stories, as well as three novels: *The Drylands, Chimera,* and *Stone Garden.* Her new novel, *Horizon,* will be out shortly. She won the Compton Crook award for Best First Novel, The Asimov's Readers Award, and has been a Hugo Award finalist. She also publishes mysteries as Mary Freeman.

When she is not writing, she trains dogs in tracking, sheep herding, and obedience work and grows all her fruits and vegetables on country acreage in the Pacific Northwest. You can find more information at her website: www.maryrosenblum.com

About her story, she writes: "'Search Engine' is meant to be a scary story. It's barely Science Fiction in that most of the tracking and labeling technology that I described in the story already exists, at least in prototype form. What will we give up in the name of convenience?"

STEPHEN LEIGH, who also writes fantasy as "S.L. Farrell," is a Cincinnati author who has published twenty novels and well over thirty short stories. His most recent book is *Heir of Stone* from DAW Books.

He maintains a web site at: http://www.farrellworlds.com.

Of "You, by Anonymous," Steve writes: "Mike Resnick had asked me to contribute a story for his anthology *I, Alien*, the theme of which was stories told from the first person viewpoint of the alien. With theme anthologies, I always like to push the envelope of the theme a bit. I'd been cogitating on what an unusual alien intelligence might be, and this story emerged after reading an article in *Science News*. It also seemed best told from a second person viewpoint, not first person. I finished the story and sent it off to Mike, telling him that, hey, second person is just first person once removed. Mike insisted there had to be at least one "I" in the story . . . and so there is. See if you can find it. It's the first story I've ever sold in second person; honestly, it may be the first thing other than a few experimental pieces I've *ever* written in second person. It's also the *shortest* story I've ever sold in my entire career . . . and it's become my favorite piece to use for readings."

DANIEL KAYSEN made his fiction debut in *Interzone* in 2002. Since then his short stories—ranging from horror to romantic comedy and back again—have appeared in *The Third Alternative*, *Strange Horizons*, *ChiZine*, *Ideomancer*, and *The Mammoth Book of Tales from the Road*, among others. He has also written satirical journalism and has a screenplay stuck in Development Hell. His resumé includes a Research Fellowship in psychophysics, a strange couple of years editing train timetables, and managing a second-hand bookshop. He lives in England, two roads from the sea, and can be found online at www.angelfire.com/d20/danielkaysen

"The Jenna Set" came out of his continuing love/hate relationship with both computers and the telephone, as well as a happy acceptance of the limits of human individuality. The final version of the story owes a great deal to the editorial nurture of Jed Hartman at *Strange Horizons*, where it first appeared.

ALASTAIR REYNOLDS was born in Barry, South Wales in 1966. After studying astronomy, he worked for twelve years as a scientist within the European Space Agency in the Netherlands. Although he turned full-time writer a couple of years ago, he still lives in Holland, where he is married to his wife Josette (who's French, just to confuse matters). His first published short story was in *Interzone* in 1990, since when he's published around thirty more pieces in various markets. His first novel, *Revelation Space*, appeared in the UK in 2000 and was shortlisted for the BSFA and Clarke awards. His second novel, *Chasm City*, won the BSFA award in 2002. He is now at work on his seventh novel. This year will see the publication of two short story collections: *Galactic North* and *Zima Blue and Other Stories*.

In his words: "Understanding Space and Time" was inspired by the title of a physics lecture series shown on BBC2 in the nineteen-seventies, as part of the Open University home education scheme. I read an early version of this story (a mere 1,500 words!) at the UK's Eastercon in 2001, but I didn't finish it until 2005. I had to take my laptop with me on our honeymoon to finish it, but I think my wife's forgiven me now . . . "

RICH HORTON is a software engineer in St. Louis. He is a contributing editor to *Locus*, for which he does short fiction reviews and occasional book reviews; and to *Black Gate*, for which he does a continuing series of essays about SF history. He also contributes book reviews to *Fantasy Magazine*, and to many other publications.

ACKNOWLEDGMENTS

"Triceratops Summer" by Michael Swanwick. Copyright © 2005 by Michael Swanwick. First published in *Amazon Shorts*. Reprinted by permission of the author.

"Bank Run" by Tom Purdom. Copyright © 2005 by Tom Purdom. First published in *Asimov's*, October-November 2005. Reprinted by permission of the author.

"A Coffee Cup/Alien Invasion Story" by Douglas Lain. Copyright © 2005 by Douglas Lain. First published in *Strange Horizons*, February 7, 2005. Reprinted by permission of the author.

"The Edge of Nowhere" by James Patrick Kelly. Copyright © 2005 by James Patrick Kelly. First published in *Asimov's*, June 2005. Reprinted by permission of the author.

"Heartwired" by Joe Haldeman. Copyright © 2005 by Joe Haldeman. First published in *Nature*, March 24, 2005. Reprinted by permission of the author.

"The Fate of Mice" by Susan Palwick. Copyright © 2005 by Susan Palwick. First published in *Asimov's*, January 2005. Reprinted by permission of the author.

"The King of Where-I-Go" by Howard Waldrop. Copyright © 2005 by Howard Waldrop. First published in *Sci Fiction*, December 7, 2005. Reprinted by permission of the author.

"The Policeman's Daughter" by Wil McCarthy. Copyright © 2005 by Wil McCarthy. First published in *Analog*, June 2005. Reprinted by permission of the author.

"Bliss" by Leah Bobet. Copyright © 2005 by Leah Bobet. First published in *On Spec*, Winter 2005. Reprinted by permission of the author.

"Finished" by Robert Reed. Copyright © 2005 by Robert Reed. First published in *Asimov's*, September 2005. Reprinted by permission of the author.

"The Inn at Mount Either" by James Van Pelt. Copyright © 2005 by James van Pelt. First published in *Analog*, May 2005. Reprinted by permission of the author.

"Search Engine" by Mary Rosenblum. Copyright © Mary

Rosenblum. First published in *Analog*, September 2005. Reprinted by permission of the author.

"You, by Anonymous" by Stephen Leigh. Copyright © Stephen Leigh. First published in *I, Alien*. Reprinted by permission of the author.

"The Jenna Set" by Daniel Kaysen. Copyright © Daniel Kaysen. First published in *Strange Horizons*, March 14, 2005. Reprinted by permission of the author.

"Understanding Space and Time" by Alastair Reynolds. Copyright © Alastair Reynolds. First published in *Novacon 2005 Program Book*. Reprinted by permission of the author.